Loonymoon

An FFSG novel

Bill Dughaille

Contents

Normandy. Sunday. Evening.

The Perfect Honeymoon

'You know, in these days of lists for anything and everything, I'm sure there's a list of the top ten worst things that can go wrong on a honeymoon. Honeymoon nightmares, as it were.'

'The couple turning up at the seaside holiday resort to find out that the brand new hotel they chose has been built next to an ancient and still active but leaking and pungent sewerage works would be close to the top. I'm sure I've read about that happening somewhere.'

'Ye-es, you could be right. I was thinking about another possibility. A bit closer to home, you might say.'

'Finding out that your mother in law – or even both mothers – have come with you. Tucked into your luggage somewhere. By accident, of course.'

'That doesn't even bear thinking about. But what I -'

'Though, thinking about it, I'm sure there wouldn't be a problem if mum did turn up. Apart from her treating me like a five-year-old, asking me if I'm wearing a vest, popping in to tuck me in to bed at night – yes, I suppose that could be a bit tricky.'

'I think I might also find your mother turning up to tuck you into bed while we're on honeymoon somewhat disturbing, darling. I rather think that's supposed to be my job now. Though, getting back to honeymoon disasters, what I was thinking about –'

'One of the honeymoon couple might run off with the hotel porter. Of course it wouldn't have to be the porter, it could be the tennis coach or swimming instructor or something, but the porter would be better. Especially if he was about sixty, grey-haired and had a limp. With only one tooth left and a dirty old eye patch over his right eye.'

'Quite possibly. But –'

'Or they could spend the entire honeymoon in the departure lounge at the airport with their baggage missing. Surviving on fast food and bottled water, sleeping on the floor. Very uncomfortable. And they wake you up and move you on every few hours.'

'That probably happens so often it wouldn't make the top ten. On the other hand –'

'Or, what about this: the husband turns out to be a she. Or the wife turns out to be a he. That would certainly come as a surprise.'

'Somehow I doubt that that would happen. I would imagine they would have made that discovery long before. But, if it's the top ten of honeymoon disasters we're talking about –'

'Oedipus. He has to be at number one, surely. Killed his father, married his mother, ended up blinding himself.'

'As far as I recall that did not all happen on his honeymoon. If the ancient Greeks had honeymoons. Now –'

'The wife discovers that her husband has an obsession with Country and Western songs, and he's brought his whole collection along. Or the husband finds out the wife has brought three hundred different versions of Tom Jones singing My, My Delilah and intends playing them non-stop.'

'Speaking of non-stop – are you going to shut up and let me get a word in edgeways, darling?'

'Sorry, my sweet.'

'What I was going to say,' Detective Inspector Frieda Summers (née Garold) said to Detective Inspector Frank Summers (now ex bachelor), 'was that two newly married detective inspectors finding a body in the bath of their hotel suite in a foreign country on the first night of their honeymoon might just be considered for inclusion in the top ten. Especially when it's a small, family-run hotel which the husband picked out as an especially quiet and comfortable looking place for the couple to enjoy the beginning of the rest of their married life. And especially when the inspectors in question are English and the hotel in question is in France, and the local police appear not to have forgiven us for Agincourt.'

'Well, technically speaking, it's really the second night of our honeymoon, Free, and –'

'You know what I mean Frank.'

Frank rubbed his nose and looked up from the small English-French dictionary he had been browsing.

'Should that be detectives inspector? Rather than detective inspectors?'

'Do shut up, darling.'

'Hokay.' He returned his attention to his dictionary.

They were sitting next to each other in the small bar-cum-reception of the hotel, sipping coffee, while waiting for the local police to finish carrying out their investigations. When they had first arrived and signed in, before they discovered the presence of the body in the bath, there had been a number of locals enjoying an early-evening drink in the bar. The lights had been dimmed, soft accordion music played in the background, the air was full of warm Autumn mellowness. As soon as word got out that the flics were on their way the locals had immediately got on their way too. Now Frank and Frieda sat on their own in an area of wooden tables and chairs, a wooden floor, with the only hint of previous customers being their abandoned glasses. The music had been switched off. All the lights were turned up. The air was becoming sultry. A uniformed woman police officer wearing a peaked cap stood close to the entrance doors, watching them, her eyes and body language leaving them in no doubt that she had already judged them to be guilty of something.

Frieda sat with her arms folded. She was trying to stay positive, to see any of what might be found of the funny side of things, but the truth was that they had had a long day travelling and she was tired, and when she became tired she became irritable. "Or more irritable than usual, some might say", a particularly foolhardy voice at the back of her mind suggested.

She brushed the thought away. She had more pressing worries, worries that concerned the rest of her life. Their wedding had been, some people had obviously thought, somewhat rushed. They had married less than three months after becoming engaged. She would have agreed to do so three hours after Frank had proposed, had he so wished, not the mark of a woman who prided herself on her objective, professional, analytical, efficient and rational approach to life. The three months had been a blur of preparations and work. The constant activity had kept the rational doubts quiet, quiet but simmering, waiting, popping up late at night to ask if she was doing the right thing. To the ghost in her mind who moaned the adage about "marry in haste and repent at leisure" she had replied that she had known her first husband for six years before they married, and that marriage hadn't lasted long. Only long enough for her to realise that his "laddish drinking" was one step short of alcoholism, and that he had the opinion that she was a perfectly acceptable substitute punch bag for all the people he had really wanted to hit during the day. After the second time it had happened she had kicked him out of their house, refused to listen to his tearful promises that he would reform, and buried the hurt in her career. Nobody, she had decided, would ever call her as hard as nails. There were no nails in the world hard enough to suggest the comparison.

Then Frank had turned up in her life, in Wellbury, and why they had both ended up there was something else that grated. It was one of the things she intended to discuss with him during the honeymoon. If she ever got a chance to discuss anything with him during their honeymoon. At that moment the only obvious topic for discussion was along the lines of "So what do you think that attractive young woman was doing in our bath?", and the last thing she wanted in their honeymoon was any other women, especially not the type to be found in a bath they had no right to be in.

At least the girl had had the good taste to be fully clothed. And dry. It had raised questions as to why, but the possible alternatives were best left unmentioned. Frank, naturally, had immediately raised them: "I wonder why she is in an empty bath with all her clothes on? As opposed to – well, you know?" he had asked earlier as they viewed the scene. Which just added to Frieda's multiplying dilemmas, an arithmetic puzzle tending towards infinity: she too now wanted to know.

It was the sort of question a detective automatically asked, no matter how personally romantic the situation should otherwise have been.

No, she told herself, ignore it. It is not relevant. Concentrate on what matters.

Concentrate on a previously failed marriage and now a second, rushed one? To fail in one could be construed as unfortunate, to fail in two ... what was that saying?

Frieda, being Frieda, had passed her driving test first time, with absolutely no mistakes. She had never doubted that she would. Now she was beginning to understand how others felt in taking a second test having previously failed. She found herself traveling in a country she had never visited before. It was called the Land Of Uncertainty and Self-doubt. So far she had established two things: firstly she could not speak the language; and secondly, there was something distinctly odd about the taste of the water.

Without realising it, she sighed and closed her eyes. Frank glanced up, noted her frown, and returned to his dictionary. She opened her eyes and looked at him.

No, she was determined that it would work this time. This honeymoon was going to be the foundation of their married life, and it was going to be a solid foundation. Although if something did go wrong it obviously wasn't going to be the end of the world, or anything similarly melodramatic. It was just that nothing was going to go wrong. She was quite determined.

There was one undeniable fact in the whole whirlwind. She knew that she really loved him. She knew because whenever he smiled at her her heart ached and she had an urge to throw her arms around him and hug him close. She also knew because whenever his mischievous eyes looked into hers with a twinkle that suggested he was about to cause trouble she had an urge to give him a clip around the ear and tell him not to even think of it, whatever "it" might be. "It" would certainly be some boyish prank which would deserve a good clip around the ear.

The question she had managed to avoid so far was: was Frank really in love with her?

There were occasions when she wondered if his proposal to her was related to the time he had been shot and almost killed. The quiff of white hair which she could see above his forehead as he made faces at the dictionary, his mouth silently moving, was a memory of the bullet. She had never been sure that his decision to propose to her wasn't some form of seeking some unattainable "happy ever afterwards" dream to counter the nightmares he had developed. The ones she knew he had had, but which he avoided discussing.

However, if Frank wasn't absolutely in love with her then, she had decided, he would be so by the end of the honeymoon. It wasn't in her nature to be a doormat, but, she had told herself, if she had the strength of character to run a police station, giving orders to both men and women, then she had the strength of character to control herself and let her husband take the lead if he felt he needed to. Their marriage was going to work. And that marriage was going to start with a honeymoon in which she taught Frank just what it meant to have a wife, a woman who loved him and was his for eternity.

That had been her plan. Unfortunately, with Frank, you might as well take any plan you might come up with and throw it straight into the bin. Instead of preparing the negligée she had carefully chosen for their later delights, she was now sitting in the bar in their honeymoon hotel, sipping coffee, waiting for the local police to finish their investigations.

Frieda was holding on to two thoughts. The first was that she loved Frank. The second was that she would never use the phrase, "Darling, do you mind if I ask you a question?" It might seem a strange pre-occupation, but logical, when you thought about it. Firstly it was in itself a question, thus making the request nonsensical. Secondly, happily married people, trusting their spouses, do not need to request permission to ask a question – that was ludicrous. Thirdly … She wasn't quite sure what the thirdly was, unless it was a desperate attempt to cling on to something while everything she had planned vanished as if it had been a chimera.

In fact she knew what the thirdly was. The thirdly was that her mother had told her that that was a question she should never ask her husband. Her mother had been full of advice, advice still ringing in her ears. Possibly her mother had felt that her failure to supply the same for her daughter's first marriage had been partly responsible for that marriage breaking up, and had been determined to make up for the deficit of the first with a surfeit for the second. It wasn't quite the last thing Frieda had needed at the time, but it definitely ranked in the bottom three. It had also given Frieda something extra to worry about: mother knows best, of course. Frieda just wasn't convinced that that saying was meant to refer to her own mother. She had yet to decide whether to follow the advice, or to treat it as exactly what she should not do.

For the moment, she would smile at her darling husband, and not let anything show that she was in the slightest worried.

Because she loved Frank, not because she had never failed at anything, apart from her first marriage. Marrying Frank had not been an opportunity purely to prove that she could succeed at marriage. The thought was ridiculous.

'Rubbermats,' she said softly. It was a word she had come up with when she wanted to swear. 'One dead body in the bath does not a honeymoon break.'

'But she wasn't actually dead,' Frank pointed out, looking up. It was yet another sore point. Frieda had initially thought the girl dead, but it had transpired that although she was unconscious, and with hardly a heart beat a minute, she was still alive. Frieda did not like making mistakes. Making mistakes was something other people did.

'That is something to be grateful for, I suppose,' she said, gritting her teeth and trying to smile at her husband.

'Ah, well, it will give us something to tell our grandchildren,' Frank noted with a wry grin.

'Only you could manage it, Frank,' she snapped. 'Normal people would bring back photographs and happy memories from their honeymoon, you have to have a nearly dead body in the bath. Our bath. Our honeymoon bath.'

'Oh, come on, Free, it's hardly my fault. Anyway, you were the one who found her, which makes it your nearly dead body, not mine.'

Since there was no way of denying this Frieda simply sipped her coffee in a loud, injured silence.

'Look, Free,' Frank said, his knee on the other side of Frieda making little up-and-down jerks as his heel drummed silently and unconsciously on the floor, 'it's probably one of the maids who fell and hit her head on something. Maybe had a minor heart attack, something like that. I'm sure their coppers will sort it out pretty quickly, and then we can enjoy our honeymoon.'

Frieda wrinkled her nose. She was tempted to point out that, being detectives, they had both automatically checked for such things, and there were no signs of the girl hitting her head against the bath, sink or any other item of bathroom furniture, but that would be far too close to getting involved in work. Bringing your work home was bad enough, getting involved in it on honeymoon would be ridiculous.

He was quite right. He was looking at things sensibly. Which added to her irritation. She was supposed to be the sensible one. Frank's duty was to rile her with his boyish sense of humour and easy-going approach to life. She hoped that marriage hadn't made him suddenly sensible. She wasn't sure she could cope with a sensible Frank.

'She looked a bit young to have a heart attack,' she noted.

'I read somewhere of a bloke of twenty-two dying of a heart attack. Anyway, not our problem, is it?'

She pursed her lips.

'Well,' she said, taking another unwanted sip of coffee, 'since we're currently sitting here instead on being in our honeymoon suite, you could argue that it does affect us slightly.'

Frank rubbed the side of his face and yawned.

'Yes,' he said, stifling the yawn, 'let's have a word with the landlady as soon as she turns up. Spending your honeymoon in the same room where someone nearly died a few hours ago … That's a bit much, even for my taste in the macabre. But what I meant is that it isn't our jurisdiction. Right at the moment we aren't police officers, we're a couple on holiday in a strange land. Plain Mr and Mrs Summers, Frieda and Frank, bon jour, monsieur, which way to the entertainments, s'il vous plaît? However much we might sympathise with the girl, with the French coppers, with the landlady, etc, etc, we are not going to get involved. No way, Hose. N'est-ce pas?'

Frieda wrinkled her nose again. She knew from experience what Frank's "I'm not getting involved" declarations normally resulted in. A trail of carnage followed by Frank being injured. She knew that he meant what he said, just that he had a bad habit of letting his curiosity override his intentions. If he managed to keep out of this one it would be as if nature had been inverted.

'And the sooner they allez and get it sorted the happier I'll be,' he continued, nodding towards the French police woman. 'Our jailor doesn't seem to think much of us. Maybe that's the French way. You wouldn't get a British copper looking at us like that. A look of contempt and condescension with more than a soupçon of a sneer.'

'What about Pete Phillips?' Frieda suggested.

'Well, apart from Pete Phillips. Anyway, he wouldn't have a sneer. He might look like he was thinking of murder, but he wouldn't sneer.'

Frieda had to smile at this image. Detective Sergeant Pete Phillips was a stolid sort of copper. Had Pete Phillips attempted a sneer he would have had pulled a muscle.

'So, ma cherie,' Frank said, putting a hand on the back of Frieda's neck and massaging gently, 'we get the landlady to arrange another room, smile at the local plods, say oui sir, non sir, trois bags full sir, then dinner and an early night. What say, oh gorgeous one?'

Frieda stretched her neck under his caress and smiled again.

'I'd say yes, please, very much, darling. I just hope they hurry up.' She looked at him and put her arms around him. 'Sorry about being snappish, Frank. It's just been a tiring day.'

Frank grinned and kissed her. The French police woman stiffened and found something on the opposite wall to concentrate on.

'I know, my darling, I'm knackered myself,' he said. 'Tell you what, why don't we take over the case for the evening? Explain that we're both senior police detectives and we'll carry out the initial investigation. That way we could probably sort everything out in a couple of hours and then send them on their way.'

For a few seconds there was an eager look in Frieda's eyes which suggested that she was seriously considering the option. Then she dusted some non-existent fluff from Frank's shoulder.

'We could do it,' she said. 'I'm sure we could. Pity.'

'I'm lucky in a way. You're too used to being in charge, giving orders, having all the facts at your fingertips. I'm more used to being in the dark, so it doesn't worry me as much.'

Frieda looked at him. "Having all the facts at her fingertips"? Her recollection of certain events at work was mainly in finding out from some other officer that "Frank's out. He didn't say where he was going. No, he didn't say why either." Admittedly he did normally have the grace to return eventually and explain things to her. But this was perhaps not the best time to bring such things up. Later would do.

Just then there was the deafening screech of an alarm bell

going off, filling the room, crashing off the walls. All three jumped. The alarm rang for a few seconds and ended as suddenly as it had begun. Frieda looked at Frank.

'Oh, no, Free, that wasn't me,' he said. 'They're probably just testing the fire alarm. Nothing to do with me. I didn't touch anything.'

'Testing the fire alarm,' she said slowly, making it quite clear that she doubted whether anyone in their right mind would take to testing fire alarms in the middle of a police investigation.

'Gave me a bit of a start,' Frank said softly, his eyes back in the dictionary, 'but it was worth it. Our unfriendly gendarme over there almost jumped out of her bootees.'

Frieda glanced at the woman police officer, who was trying to pretend that nothing had happened, and that there was nothing unusual in having to adjust her cap so that it again sat squarely on her head.

'I can't say I think much of their professionalism,' Frieda said. 'We've been here over an hour and nothing's happened.'

Frank grinned.

'Funnily enough, that's what quite a few of my suspects say when I get around to interviewing them. I wonder how you pronounce this – *heureux*.'

'We do make a good team, though, don't we, darling? Me in control of an operation, you getting out and getting results. You always seem to know who and where to target to get results.'

'It's called the rubbish theory. Kick over enough dustbins, wake up enough people, and eventually you'll find something. I wonder what the French for dustbin is.'

'It's more than that. It's instinct.'

'Now, Free, you know what I think of that word. Small children and animals might have instinct. For anyone else it's mainly just another way of justifying prejudice. Not a good idea in a copper. Gut feeling is usually just an excuse to kick a suspect in the guts to get a result.'

For a moment Frieda's eyes twinkled. She was not known for her sense of humour. On the other hand Frank was not known for having any weak spots – apart from his dislike of words such as "instinct" or anything which suggested some non-logical or mystical capability.

She looked at him. She was about to tease: "What you mean is that you use your instinct all the time and call it something else?" Then she thought better about it. Frieda Garold, she said to herself – Frieda Summers – you are a very lucky woman. You have been given a second chance with a very lovely man. Don't mess it up.

She ran her hand through her hair, watching him.

'Darling,' she said, 'do you mind if I ask you something?'

Ma wife, l'Inspector

Before Frank could answer there was a muted sound of banging from somewhere up the carpeted stairs leading to the rooms above, beyond the first section which they could see. It sounded almost as if someone were jumping up and down on them. Then a man appeared, coming down the stairs. He wore a grubby, tan-coloured raincoat, rumpled brown suit, and a tie which appeared to have reached stalemate in an argument with his shirt collar. He was about mid-fifties, a pork-pie hat covering greying hair, a greying moustache dividing a fleshy face, lugubrious eyes conveying distaste, suspicion and tiredness. He raised his eyes to the uniformed police woman, who immediately joined him. He spoke to her in a low voice. She nodded and broke into a low speech, indicating Frank and Frieda with a jerk of her thumb. The phrase "Les Anglais" was repeated a number of times. It did not come across as a recommendation.

'I hope the natives are friendly,' Frank said loudly. 'Can't say I think much of their manners, mind.'

'Frank! Keep your voice down!'

'Sod it, Free, I've had enough of this. They can have their investigation, I want us to have our honeymoon.'

'Now, Frank, what happened to oui sir, non sir, trois bags full sir?'

Frank sighed.

'I think it's rapidly leaving the longer we sit here. I think I've only got another half hour's politeness and charm left in me.' He gave her a tired grin. 'And that, madame, is reserved for my wife.'

The man in the grubby raincoat finished his conversation with the uniformed police officer and came towards them, with the air of a tired bloodhound which had seen something it did not like and intended, however reluctantly, to fix it to its own satisfaction.

'Monsieur Summers?' he asked.

'Oui, monsieur, bon jour. Or bon soir, rather. How do you do?' said Frank, standing up. 'I'm Inspector Summers of Wellbury police force. And this is my wife, Inspector Summers of Wellbury police force.'

The Frenchman returned a dispassionate gaze. His bloodshot

eyes appeared to sink fractionally deeper into his lined face.

'And I am Inspector Clouseau of the French Sûreté,' he said in a heavy French accent.

'How do you do, Inspector Clouseau?' asked Frank, holding out his hand.

'Darling,' said Frieda, standing up next to him, 'I think he might be being just a tad sarcastic.'

'Can't be, sweetness,' Frank said, turning to her and whispering in a voice that could be heard in the street outside, 'the French don't do sarcasm. They wouldn't know how. Sneering, yes, sarcasm, no.'

'He probably took a course just for us, mon amour.'

'Have I told you how sexy you are when you speak a foreign language, ma cherie?'

'You aren't too bad yourself, mon Francois,' Frieda said, kissing him on his ear. 'Whenever you say the word cherie I think of bed.'

'Are you sure that's not just because you're tired?'

'Sleep is so much better after a little healthy exercise, mon cheri.'

The Frenchman coughed as politely as he could. It seemed somewhat forced, as if a polite cough was something he could do once but had forgotten how.

'Look,' said Frank, turning back to him, 'je suis Frank Summers, et ici sont ma femme, Madame Frieda Summers. Nous sont les officers de la polizei de Grande Bretagne. Mais nous sont ici pas de business official, vous comprehend? Nous sont sur notre l'honeymoon. Pas de work, n'est-ce pas, pas de – travail. We are here travailless. Vous comprehends?'

The man regarded him with one raised and one lowered eyebrow.

'You are upon your loonymoon,' he commented, nodding slowly, half a question, half a declaration that he knew he should not have got out of bed that morning.

'Mais oui, monsieur l'inspecteur, nous sont sur notre l'honeymoon.'

The Frenchman sighed.

'You have identity to prove this?' he asked. 'That you are police officers, not that you are on your loonymoon. However, proof of that would be most – interesting.'

'Mais oui, certainment,' Frank replied, taking out his wallet and extracting his warrant card. Frieda took hers from her handbag and handed it to Frank to pass on. Frank's eyes widened.

'You brought your warrant card on our honeymoon?' he asked.

'You brought yours.'

'It was in my wallet. It's always there.'

'And mine is always in my handbag. You find that surprising?'

'Calm down, Free, yes I was surprised, I don't know why.'

'You're trying to tell me something, aren't you, Frank?'

'Free, I'm not trying to tell you anything. I just never expected to see your warrant card come out during our honeymoon.'

'Funny, that, I never expected to see yours, but, considering the circumstances, I wasn't really surprised. What puzzles me is why you should be surprised to see mine.'

Frank's mouth twisted as he obviously saw a double-entendre. Frieda lifted a warning finger.

'Don't even think about it, Frank.'

'Oh, come on, Free, we're on our honeymoon.'

'That doesn't mean you can act like a ten-year-old-schoolboy with a dirty mind,' she snapped.

The words were out before Frieda had a chance to regret them. She turned away and looked at the table, trying to conceal what she suspected might be tears about to start. The Frenchman looked from one to the other.

'When you have quite finished?' he said with another cough.

'Ah, oui, monsieur, je regrette,' Frank said, turning to him, a forced smile on his face. 'Pardonnez moi, mais vous etre?'

The Frenchman closed his eyes and shook his head slowly.

'Please to speak English. It is painful to hear my language castrated so. Un moment.' He called to the uniformed women police officer, handed her the two warrant cards and gave her orders in a soft voice. She nodded and left the room. He turned back to Frank and Frieda. 'She will arrange to have your identities confirmed, or not.'

'Well, while she's doing that, why don't we sit down and have a cup of coffee,' Frank suggested, holding out Frieda's chair for her. She sat down. Frank squeezed her shoulders and kissed her on the forehead before taking his own seat. Frieda stroked his cheek in acknowledgement. The Frenchman watched this, one side of his mouth curved sardonically, before reluctantly sitting down, hands in his raincoat pockets, body hunched forward. He looked at them in silence for a few seconds, as if debating whether to make a comment.

'I am Inspector Georges Simenon,' he said finally in an official voice. 'I am in charge of this case.' His eyebrows rose as Frank's face broke into a grin. 'You find something amusing, monsieur Summers?'

'Mind if I see your identity card, Inspector?' Frank asked. 'After all, we do need to be sure that you are an inspector, don't we?'

Simenon gave him a baleful and irritated look before reaching into his breast pocket and handing over an identity card.

'Capitaine Georges Simenon,' Frank quoted, reading the card and handing it to Frieda. 'I presume capitaine equals inspector. Looks kosher.'

'Kosher?' asked Georges Simenon.

'Real. Not a fake,' Frank said as Frieda returned the card to the French inspector. 'For a moment I wasn't sure whether you weren't having us on. After all, Georges Simenon wrote the Maigret series.'

'Maigret?' asked Frieda.

'Famous detective in French fiction,' replied Frank. 'Georges Simenon was an incredibly prolific author, wrote something like 400 books in his time.'

Georges Simenon nodded.

'I am surprised,' he said. 'I would not have expected an English policeman to have heard of the name. Many young French people do not know of him.'

'I picked up one of his novels in a second-hand bookshop many years ago. Since then I've been collecting them when I get a chance. Are you related to him?'

'No. I am not sure whether that is a good thing or a bad thing.'

Georges Simenon had relaxed and was sitting back in his chair, one hand placed idly on the table. It was not an approach Frieda approved of. Had it been her interviewing the French officer back in their home town of Wellbury, she would have maintained a strict, official distance. But one of Frank's strengths was an ability to put people at their ease when he wanted to, to have them chatting sociably within minutes. If Georges Simenon were not careful he would find himself enjoying a pint with Frank before long.

With Frieda sitting on the other side to make sure he did not get too comfortable.

Simenon not getting too comfortable, not Frank. Of course not Frank.

'Say, what about a drink,' suggested Frank, on cue. 'We've had a long day, you look knackered – tired that is. A beer or something. A Remy Martin, perhaps?'

Before Georges Simenon could reply the door opened and the uniformed woman police officer returned. She spoke to Simenon, handing over the two warrant cards and a piece of paper. For the first time she glanced approvingly at Frank.

Simenon listened gravely, and then a sudden smile lit his face. He said something to her and she left. As she left she shot a smile back at Frank, which he missed, but Frieda didn't.

'Your identities have been confirmed,' Simenon said, giving the cards back to them. 'I have told the officer to find the man of the bar and bring something to drink.' He chuckled. 'I have a message for you from someone called Sergeant Peter Phillips.' He read from the piece of paper. '"Typical of the silly sod. Not in France five minutes and he's in trouble. Tell him all the best and to behave himself if he can." I presume this "sod" means something not polite.'

'Cheeky bugger,' Frank said, taking the paper and reading the message. 'I'll give him silly sod when we get back.'

'Could you arrange to have a message sent back?' asked Frieda. 'Tell him Inspector Frieda Summers enjoyed his message and will return the compliment when she gets back.'

Simenon winced and Frank chuckled.

'That'll keep him going,' Frank said.

'In what way, darling?' Frieda asked innocently, as if unaware that her nickname back in Wellbury police station was Fabulous when she was happy with your work, Frigid the rest of the time. Frank was spared a reply by the entrance of a stocky young woman carrying a tray holding three glasses and a bottle of wine.

'A local wine,' Simenon said, nodding thanks to the waitress as she almost dropped the tray on the table with a force of someone who believes that life should be lived with a clatter. She nodded back briefly and strode out as if she had work needing doing elsewhere, and this serving of drinks to policemen was getting in the way of that important work. Simenon poured the wine. 'One the locals claim to be the best in all Europe,' he said, 'though I expect all locals claim that. A good wine, however. Despite the fact that it is not actually local.'

'Tastes good,' Frank said, taking a sip. 'Full bodied, with just a bit of a bite.'

'Very nice,' Frieda agreed. 'Inspector Simenon, I don't want to sound rude but you obviously have work to do, and I'm sure you understand that we would like to get this over as soon as possible.'

'Ah, yes,' Frank said, rubbing his hands. 'The girl in the bath. Do we know who she is? Name, age, that sort of thing?'

'Frank!' exclaimed Frieda. 'We're on honeymoon. And it's not our case. Do you mind?'

'Ah, yes. Um, sorry about that.'

'Well, Inspector?' Frieda demanded as politely as possible without making it an order. Which with Frieda meant that was exactly how it came out. Simenon looked from her to Frank and shook his head sadly.

'Please, not to argue on your loonymoon,' he said, sadly grim. 'Now, you arrived late this afternoon, yes?'

'That is correct, Inspector,' replied Frieda.

'Tell me, monsieur, madame, why did you choose this hotel? They renew the kitchen and enlarge the restaurant. These are now closed. There are other similar hotels with kitchen and restaurant open. So why this one?'

'We noticed that the rates seemed quite low, so we telephoned Madame Arneaux, the landlady, to enquire why,' Frank explained, smiling at the change in questioning. Simenon was playing it just as he would. 'She explained that the rates had been dropped while the restaurant was closed. She sounded very pleasant, the hotel sounded ideal, and we were planning on eating out at local restaurants and cafes – I never understand why people want to be stuck in a hotel all the time. So, that's why we chose it.'

Simenon nodded.

'I see. What you call the practimatic?'

'Pragmatic,' said Frieda.

'Just so, the practimatic.' He paused. 'And you plan to see the sights. The Bayeux Tapestry, Rouen Cathedral, this sort of thing, this is correct?'

'Omaha Beach and a couple of D-Day museums tomorrow morning,' said Frank. 'Bayeux Tapestry in the afternoon. Caen on Tuesday. Rouen Wednesday. Either Mont-St-Michel or Giverny – Monet's place – on Thursday. Friday's more or less open, we're planning on visiting a market or two, get some presents to take back. After all, we can't buy cheese too early, it would start to pong a bit. Then Saturday we head towards Calais and back home.' He took a sip of wine. 'The plan is to spend as little time as possible driving. It's a flexible plan, but not to the extent of allowing much time to getting involved in police matters. Actually, the budget for that is nil.'

Simenon nodded.

'You had not met the woman in the bath before?' he asked.

'No,' Frieda replied.

'Not seen her ever, anywhere?'

'No.'

'So the first time was when you found her?'

'That would seem the most logical conclusion, wouldn't you say so, Inspector Simenon?'

'Inspector,' said Frank, deciding to interrupt before Frieda became really angry and bit the Frenchman's head off, in English, though he wouldn't need a translator, 'much as we'd like to help you I'm afraid we really know nothing apart from finding the woman lying in the bath. We didn't touch her apart from checking to see whether she was still alive. After that we called the landlady and asked her to phone for an ambulance and yourselves. You'll find two glasses with remains of whiskey and our fingerprints on in the room, but other than that we tried not to interfere with the scene of crime – if it was a crime. Otherwise – well, I can't see that we can be of any help. With all due respect, we're here on our honeymoon. Nothing else really matters much. Actually, nothing else matters at all. Not to us.'

'You did nothing else?' Simenon asked, taking a disinterested sip of wine. Frank managed a chuckle, a tired chuckle.

'Okay, Inspector Simenon. We checked for signs of her hitting her head somewhere – we didn't touch anything, just looked. And we noticed that her handbag was lying on the bathroom floor. White handbag, more the sort of thing a teenager would carry than a grown woman. We didn't touch it, nor anything else, as far as we could avoid it.'

Simenon took another sip of wine. He glanced apparently casually from Frank to Frieda.

'Yes, Inspector,' Frank said, 'it was my wife who pointed out that it was an unusual handbag for someone such as the victim to be carrying. Congratulations for guessing that. But, I repeat – je repetre – we are here on our honeymoon, and while we will give you all the assistance we can, some things come first. Vous comprends?'

Simenon nodded.

'Yes, I understand,' he said, sighing. 'It is as you say. It is unfortunate. You see –' He paused, as if hesitating in deciding whether to tell them something. 'You see, the young woman's name is Amelie Courbois. She is one of my officers. Not a very good one, I think. She was working undercover. She was supposed to be handing over a bag of heroin to a man we have been investigating. We had set up a large operation, many officers watching the hotel, cameras, cars, every possible contingency.'

'How many teams?' asked Frieda.

'Darling, it's not our case,' Frank said, stroking her arm. He turned back to Simenon. 'And then someone pre-empted the operation by hitting her over the head and taking the heroin?'

Simenon sighed again.

'It is worse than that,' he said. 'To quote the great Frenchman, Napoléon Bonaparte, du sublime au ridicule il n'y a qu'un pas. From the sub-lime to the ridiculous in the one easy steps, as I think you say in English.'

'Sublime,' corrected Frieda.

'Yes, just so. The sub-lime.' He gave another mournful sigh. 'You see, this is the wrong hotel. We had agreed not to follow her to the hotel, but to be there when she arrived. In case someone else was following her and spotted us. The entire afternoon we sit outside another hotel when it appears she is here.'

Frank and Frieda responded simultaneously.

'You have my sympathies, Inspector.'

'Personally I would be looking at restructuring the plan rather than interviewing tourists who obviously have no connection with the case.'

'That sort of thing happens to me all the time.'

'I presume that you have called in all your officers to sort things out.'

They looked at each other. Simenon half-smiled. Frank shrugged and grinned.

'But, of course, it isn't our case, fortunately,' he said. He turned to Simenon. 'How is she? The girl, I mean. Amelie Courbois, was it?'

'Oh, she will live. According to the hospital she has had the bang on the head, but it is not life threatening. She is young, and there is no sign of the brain damage, though how they tell this I cannot know. They believe that she will be well enough to be sent home within a few days.'

The police woman came back into the bar with a note for Simenon. Frank and Frieda watched as he read it, asking her an occasional question. Then he nodded as if to dismiss her, stopped, and held up a hand.

'You have not had the dinner?' he asked them.

'Not yet,' said Frank. 'And now you come to mention it, I'm starving.'

'I will have them send something from one of the local restaurants. It is late to be looking in the strange town for the restaurant.'

'That's very kind of you, Inspector.'

Simenon shrugged.

'All part of, what do you call it, the services?'

He gave the police officer a few instructions, she nodded and left, giving Frank another approving look, tinged with sympathy for a man who had yet to have dinner.

'It is the question with police everywhere, I think,' Simenon commented. 'Where do we find the next meal. But, tell me, this Wellbury of yours. It is a big town?'

'Oh, no. It's one of those places which hasn't quite decided whether it's a small rural village or a modern metropolis, so it's trying to be both without being either, if you see what I mean.'

Simenon raised his eyebrows slightly as if he found the description interesting.

'You have a lot of crime there? Drugs, perhaps?'

Frank smiled at the apparently idle question.

'No, I don't think we do. Most of our stuff is your normal day-to-day coppering. Not many crimes grande, as you might say.'

'You have a problem with drugs here?' asked Frieda.

'We are at the coast. It is not a large town, but drug dealers are always looking for new markets and new ways of getting their drugs into or out of the country.' He paused and drummed his fingers on the table. Then he leaned forward. 'There is one other guest staying here at the moment. A Mr James MacDavis, a Scottish man. have you met him?'

'No. We haven't met anyone apart from the owners of the hotel.'

'Mr MacDavis has come here at the same time every year, for a holiday, he says, for four years now. However, every year at this time I find myself with information about drug trafficking – supplies being brought in or taken out. Every year I find I am busy running from here to there, from there to here, chasing shadows, ghosts. This Mr MacDavis – you will recognise him, he has red hair, a pale face, a very pale face, white, a weak chin and what you call watery eyes, a nervous man. I do not trust him, around me he is always nervous.'

'Perhaps he's just one of those people who get nervous when the police are about,' suggested Frank. 'Most people are.'

'This is true. But I feel there is something more about this. You can tell by the look in a man's eyes. This one does not look you in the eyes.'

Frank was tempted to suggest that the Frenchman was letting his imagination get carried away, but decided that it was up to

Simenon to choose his own method of deduction. Simenon finished off his wine and stood up.

'I see that you have brought with you the saxophone and the clarinet. This is usual for the English way?'

'Probably not, Inspector,' Frank replied. 'The clarinet was my wedding gift to my wife, the saxophone hers to me. So they're somewhat special. And I was hoping to learn a little sax playing while we're here. I've never really had the chance to play the sax before.'

The way Frieda covered her eyes with her hand suggested that she did not think that this was a good idea.

'Ah, I understand,' Simenon said. 'It brings back for me the memories. I used to play the saxophone many years ago.'

'You could give me some tips, then,' suggested Frank. Frieda responded by shaking her head, hand still over her eyes.

'Perhaps, monsieur, if there is the occasion,' Simenon said. 'Well, bon chance and thank you for your time. I hope that the remainder of your stay will be more pleasant.' He smiled. 'Enjoy your loonymoon.'

As he was about to turn and leave the entrance doors burst open and a stern-faced woman with slim build and an aggressive bosom strode into the room. Everything about her spoke of sternness and efficiency, from her navy-blue skirt suit to her pulled-back hair. Even before reaching them she launched a barrage of volubility. Georges Simenon winced. He listened to her tirade with closed eyes. Eventually she had to pause for breath.

'Madame and Monsieur Summers,' Simenon said with hanging head, 'allow me to introduce my wife, capitaine, or Detective Inspector, Georgette Simenon.'

An Investigation Nouveau

There was a pause as Frank and Frieda took this in while Madame Inspector Simenon inspected them.

'My wife,' Simenon continued, a twitch in his mouth making "wife" come out as "wiff", 'is also an inspector, as I say. That is why I thought you were having the laugh, as you say. Fortunately she does not speak English.'

He turned to her and spoke, explaining the situation.

'Anglais?' she asked, interrupting him. He began again, using the words "police" and "inspector" before he was caught up short with another interruption. His hand gestures said "please, let me explain". Her body language said "Shut up and get on with it." When she was satisfied she turned to Frank with a delighted smile and delivered a barrage of French.

'She says she is charmed to meet an inspector from the English police force,' translated Simenon. 'She has long admired the professionalism of the English police.'

'Enchainte, madame,' said Frank, standing up and giving her a bow. 'And how long have you been barking mad?' Simenon glowered at him before translating something more polite to his wife. Her eyes opened in admiration and she clapped her hands together, speaking rapidly to Frank.

'She wishes to congratulate you on your wedding and hopes you will enjoy your stay. If you wish to make the visit to our station she will be happy to give you the tour.'

'Tell her thanks very much and –' began Frieda, also standing up.

'And we will do so at the first opportunity we get,' completed Frank swiftly. 'However, at the moment we are tired after a long day travelling and would like to make arrangements for the evening.'

Simenon translated this to his wife. She cut in, apparently berating him for taking up the time of a newly married couple who must be exhausted. Especially when the groom was such a handsome English police officer.

'We will leave you now,' Georges Simeon said, his jaw set grimly. 'Bon chance.'

His wife snapped something at him, smiled at Frank, and the Simenons left the room, she leading, he trailing. Frank and Frieda sat down slowly. Frieda noticed that the Simenon's wife's pencil skirt had a slit in the back. Not a deep one. Just enough to make movement of the legs easier. And to show anyone interested that they were pretty good looking legs.

'Phew! Poor bugger,' said Frank. 'I don't think she's a Georgette. More like a right Gorgonzola.'

'Promise me something, darling,' Frieda said. 'Promise me that we will never end up like that.'

'I think we should get a photograph of those two together. Take it out every anniversary and thank our blessings.'

'I'd have it on my desk at work,' Frieda replied, putting an arm around him and giving him a kiss on the cheek. 'With one of you next to it. To remind me of how lucky I am.'

They were interrupted by the arrival of their dinner. Whichever local restaurant had been told to provide the meal had obviously been given the order, "a little bit of everything, and make it a lot". Frank's offer of payment was declined: apparently the hotel was footing the bill as recompense for the "unfortunate events" of earlier.

'Not exactly their fault,' noted Frank, rubbing his hands and looking at the now crowded table in front of them. 'Right, let's tuck in!'

It was another thing Frieda intended to correct while she was about things, Frank's table manners. Not that there was anything really wrong with his table manners, but she had been brought up to believe that you shouldn't greet each new dish with "Yum yum!", nor finish a meal with "God! That was bloody good! I'm stuffed!" After all, there would be occasions when they would have to socialise with Chief Constables and their wives, and as their careers progressed this might extend to members of parliament, lords ... Well, perhaps the latter two groups were not the best examples of acceptable dinner-table propriety.

But right then, as she used her knife and fork in public as she had been taught to do, she decided to forgive Frank's fingers waving a drumstick for the moment. The food was excellent, and it made her realise that hunger had been another reason for her irritation. It was all too easy to forget about meals, and then to grab something on the hoof. For Frank it was a way of life. She, on the other hand, as her mother had told her – what hadn't her mother told her? – was now his wife, and it was her responsibility to make sure he was fed properly. She was not at all sure that she agreed with that. But perhaps it was one of those things you had to do if you were going to train a husband properly.

'Now that,' Frank said when he had finished, leaning back and licking his fingers, 'was bloody good! I'm stuffed!'

Frieda had to smile and agree.

'Ah, the landlady,' Frank said as the hotel proprietor entered, flustered. 'Bon soir, Madame Arneaux.'

'Madame, monsieur, a thousand apologies,' she said. 'I have had your luggage moved to another room. It is just as good as the other. Better, perhaps.'

'One without any attractive young women lying half-dead in the bath would be a great improvement,' Frank said as he and Frieda stood up.

'Pardon monsieur?'

'Oh, nothing, just a little joke.'

'Ah? Oh, please, to come with me. Ah, mon Dieu! What the day! Nothing such as this has every happened before! The girl, les flics. They are not nice people, those flics.'

'Ah, but we are also les flics,' Frank said as they followed her upstairs. 'We are police officers in Britain. En Grande Bretagne.'

'Ah, non-non. You are the – how you say – les poppies Anglais.'

'Poppies?'

'Yes, the honest English poppy.'

'Ah, bobby. Well, yes, I suppose you could say that.'

'English poppies are nice people. You can ask them for the direction, the hour. I was in England three months before. I do not know where I am. I ask the poppy, he guides me correctly. Politely. He smiles. Les flics – they are nasty men. You would not want your daughter to marry a flic. Now, here is your room.'

As they approached the door it was opened from the inside, and a young woman came stomping out, the same waitress who had served the wine. She was on the short side, broad and heavy set, and might well have been considered ugly had it not been for her youth and a wide smile on her honest-looking face. She carried a heavy, thick denim bag over one shoulder, almost as if she were a postwoman. She had earphones in her ears and was warbling a tune. Her face suggested that she thought that she was warbling quietly to herself, but the rather grating sound could be heard for some distance.

Madame Arneaux said something to her. The girl took an earphone out and Madame Arneaux repeated herself. The girl shrugged and appeared to apologise. Madame Arneaux shooed her away.

'Marie,' she explained to Frank and Frieda once the girl had left. 'She cleans for us. She is a niece – my husband's niece,' she added pointedly. 'Ah, pauvre enfant, she grew up on a farm, you see.'

Frank and Frieda looked at each other before turning back to her.

'She grew up on a farm?' asked Frieda. 'You say that as if it's a bad thing.'

'Mais oui, madame, it is trez, trez – bad. Ah, you see, farm people are simple people. This is not a bad thing of itself, of course, but – The carpets, they are a good example.'

'Carpets?'

'When Marie first came to us she believed that the only way to clean the carpets is to hang them outside and beat them with a big stick, as they did in the old days. To Marie it is a waste to use a vacuum cleaner when she can use her own arms.'

'Powerful arms, though,' murmured Frank.

'True, monsieur. Powerful enough to pull up the carpets

which were not meant to be pulled up – she thought they were sticking slightly. And then, the trolley, oh la la!'

'The trolley?'

'We have a trolley for the cleaning things, expensive, for it has to be small for the small passages, and it must have the lightness. She forgets it has a brake. A girl brought up on a farm, when something does not move, you push harder. So she pushes harder and breaks off a wheel.' She sighed. 'After that she carries everything in the bag you see. For us, it looks – not professional. But, she is happy, and the bag is cheaper than a broken trolley, so, we learn the compromise.'

'She does seem quite the cheerful sort.'

'Oui, madame, very cheerful. Very 'appy. Of modern things she is not in love, but that music thing, the, em-pee-three player? That she loves. It is all old music, music of the country, but for her it is better than a hundred orchestras. Such a pity she does not realise that she is always loud when she is listening. I tell her a hundred times, be quieter. A hundred times she apologises, she promises she will be quieter, then she forgets. Ah, la, la! She will never change!'

She shook her head at the sad simplicity of the farm girl.

'If there is anything you wish, please to ask me or my husband, or one of the other maids,' she said. 'Marie is very honest, she tries her best, but she – how do you say, listens literal?'

'Takes things literally,' Frank said. 'Oui, madame, nous comprehends bien. We know many people like that where we come from.'

'Merci, monsieur,' Madame Arneaux said, before looking around her, realising that this pleasant little chat was not getting the work done. 'Please to let me know if you need anything. I must go to look after things. Everything is in such mess, flics, bodies, I know not.'

She paused, as if remembering that she was supposed to be running a modern hotel, and the guests would not wish to know of any problems.

'But, of course, soon the flics will be gone and everything shall be peaceful again. You will have a happy holiday, the peace, the quiet, the sunshine. You have the honeymoon best in the world.'

Somewhere in the distance there was a clatter of something which sounded as if someone had just dropped a dozen pots and pans and then picked them up to repeat the process.

'Ah, Marie, mon dieu,' she muttered. 'Bon soir, madame, monsieur. Have the pleasant dreams.'

They watched her hurry away, Frank rubbing his jaw. Frieda recognised the sign. He was thinking about something. That was not a good sign. There was only one thing he should be thinking about, and that did not involve thinking.

'Attention, mon mari,' she said. 'This is your wife speaking. Come in, over.'

Frank scratched his head and grinned at her.

'Sorry,' he said, 'I was thinking of Simenon and his wife. Silly buggers. Why do people let their marriages go to pot like that?'

'I suppose you think that it's Mrs Simenon's fault.'

'Who's to say? Simenon seems a decent enough bloke. Who knows? But if he is a decent bloke, and she's the problem, why not just leave her?' He rubbed his jaw again. 'And, talking about Simenon, there's the other thing.'

'The other thing?'

'Marie can't hear anything with those earphones on. I can't help but wonder if that has something to do with things. The girl in the bath, I mean. I wonder if Simenon picked that up. Not to mention that bag she carries. Very handy to hide something in. Though of course that tends to suggest she was involved in some way, whereas not being able to hear suggests that she is innocent and missed something. Or perhaps someone hid the heroin in the bag without her realising it, and removed it later.'

That earned him a very special look from his loved one.

'That is enough, Frank, enough, okay? This is our honeymoon. Forget about it. Come on, let's get unpacked.'

'Zu befehl, mein fuehrer,' he replied, clicking his heels as she entered the room.

'That's not funny, Frank. Not in the slightest.'

He trailed into the room, his head hanging just as Simenon's had.

'That's not funny either, Frank.'

'How about this, then?' he asked, putting his arms around his waist. 'A new investigation.'

'Only so long as it's a thorough one. And do close the door first, Frank. And while you're doing that I'll check the bathroom. There are some investigations which should never be interrupted.'

You can't Always Get What You Want

Frieda could feel Frank drifting off to sleep as she lay in his arms. After the long day's travelling, the events of the evening, a good meal, a couple of glasses of calvados, and a celebration of their nuptials, she should have drifted easily and peacefully into sleep herself. But the image of Madame la Inspector Simenon kept popping into her mind, no matter how much she kept opening her eyes to get rid of the spectre. She knew that she herself could be tetchy at times – perhaps more than tetchy, and more than at times – and had indeed been snappish that evening. It didn't take much to imagine herself turning into a version of Madame Simenon. She tried not to see Frank in twenty years as Georges Simenon, but she guessed that Georges Simenon himself had once been not unlike Frank as he was now, with a ready grin and a mischievous sense of humour.

Yes, the image of Madame Simenon kept popping up in her mind. It kept popping up in her mind because of that navy-blue skirt-suit, the one with the pencil skirt with a small slit in the back. It looked precisely like the ones she wore at work. She suspected that she could name the label.

It was nonsense. There was absolutely no resemblance between the Simenons and the Summers. And there never would be. She would never turn into Madame Simenon. It wasn't going to happen. She was going to make a success of their honeymoon and create a stable foundation for a happy and loving married life, whatever it took.

Unlike her first marriage.

'This is going to be the best week of our lives so far. The girl in the bath was just a blip,' Frank said sleepily.

Frieda closed her eyes. She didn't know what was going to happen, but knew that, when Frank was confident that everything was going to be fine, it was a guarantee that it wouldn't be. That was his biggest problem.

'Darling,' she said, stroking his chest absentmindedly, 'what are you hoping to get out of our honeymoon?'

'A kepi,' he yawned.

The answer was so unexpected it took her a few seconds to react.

'A kepi?'

'Well, you know how people are always trying to nick a Bobby's helmet? I lost one that way, when I was in uniform, one New Year's Eve, in Trafalgar Square. I'm damn sure it was a French girl who nicked it, she'd been eyeing it up for half an hour before someone tripped me and it disappeared. I reckon it's about time to return the compliment.' He yawned again and gave her a kiss. 'Goodnight, darling, tomorrow's going to be just fantastic.'

She didn't reply, listening to him falling asleep.

She was full of plans for their honeymoon. Important plans. Crucial plans. They would get to know each other as man and wife, setting the solid foundation of the rest of their lives, loving strolls, intimate moments, bonding as man and woman in love.

And what did he want?

He wanted to nick a kepi.

Of all the things he could have mentioned ...

Her mother had been generous with her advice on what a wife should be. Most of it sounded as if it had come out of a

1950s manual on the perfect good little wife, with little relevance to the twenty-first century, but she had to admit that her mother had a very distinct way of putting things.

"Men have their own little quirks," her mother had said a few days before the wedding, in an unusual moment when they had been alone. She noticed her daughter's raised eyebrows and continued hurriedly and stiffly: "Not those type of little quirks, Frieda. It might be something quite simple, such as insisting on having his peas on the left side of his plate – your father did, only with him it was carrots."

At the time Frieda had initially wondered whether or not her mother was talking in code. She just knew that she would end up giggling if bananas came up. Instead she had asked weakly:

"Carrots, mum?"

"Yes, Frieda, I remember it well. We were courting – an old-fashioned phrase even in those days. Anyway, we were having dinner at a rather posh restaurant, posh for the salaries we were on at the time, and your father pointed out that the carrots were on the right when they should have been on the left. Now I filed that away and remembered it, so that when we were married I always made sure that the vegetables, especially peas and carrots, were on the left. Unless we were having a row, though, then I made sure that his carrots were on the right. He soon got the message. Mind you, I never had to do it more than once."

Frieda had no doubt that her mother would never have had to put the carrots on the right more than once.

"Of course,' added her mother, "you do have to point out every so often that you remember that they prefer having their carrots on the left, which is why you took care to put them there. An occasional reminder that you're constantly thinking of them. Otherwise they forget."

The trouble was that putting the vegetables on the side of the plate your husband preferred them was not a great deal of help as far as Frank was concerned. He wouldn't notice which side of the plate his peas or carrots were on, unless they were dressed in tuxedoes and tap-dancing the can-can. But she had taken her mother's point: in a long – especially lifelong – relationship, the little displays of thoughtfulness and care often made more difference than the great passions, which rarely happened. And especially reminding your spouse about each little display, just in case they failed to notice.

Another little piece of advice – or order – had been:

"And I don't want any phone calls, Frieda."

'Sorry, mum?'

She had probably said "Sorry, mum?" thirty times that afternoon.

"People these days seem to have the urge to telephone everyone they know as often as they can. A postcard would be more than sufficient for me. Remember that you're supposed to be a newly married wife. Every thought you have should be about your husband, not your mother or anyone else."

"But, mum, just a quick call to say that we've arrived okay?"

"No, Frieda, no. And stop saying 'okay', it's very common. What would Frank think if the first thing his new wife wanted to do was phone mummy? He'd feel left out, and I wouldn't blame him. No, Frieda, as I say, a postcard will be fine. In fact, a postcard will be better, because then I will have something to hold on to, something to look at in the future."

She paused to put her teacup down. "Think of it from your side. How would you feel if the first thing he wanted to do was phone home to mummy?"

They looked at each other, lips twitching. Eventually both broke out giggling at the idea of Frank wanting to phone home. It would be enough of a problem just convincing him to sign a postcard. It was the first time she and her mother had shared a giggle together since before her father died.

"But, mum, what if something goes wrong?"

"Well, darling, yes, if something goes wrong, yes, obviously you must call. But nothing is going to go wrong. And if it does, Frank will be at your side, he'll be far more capable of sorting things out there than I will be here. He will be your husband, after all."

Frieda couldn't help now but smile at that in their honeymoon bedroom. Something had gone wrong, and she and Frank were going to sort it out.

Frieda had wondered if her mother had been a good wife. To her surprise, when she thought about it, she realised that her mother had been a very good wife. On her own terms. Perhaps not a perfect mother, she still nagged her daughter as if she were a recalcitrant fourteen-year-old refusing to clean up her bedroom – and Frieda had never needed to be told to clean her bedroom, it had always been spotless, just as her father would have wanted – but she could not fault her mother as a wife. She had never scolded her husband, never nagged him, never upbraided him. But she had certainly known how to handle his carrots, from the sound of things.

In the semi-darkness Frieda could just see the outline of Frank's face, the slight difference in colour of the white quiff of hair.

'I will be a good wife to you, Frank,' she whispered to him. He turned on his side, towards her, stretched in his sleep, squeezed her, muttered, 'I love you,' and gave her an unconscious kiss on her forehead.

'I love you too, darling,' she replied.

But you are not, she decided, definitely not, going to ruin our honeymoon by trying to nick a kepi. We're in enough bother with the French police as it is. You will have to learn that, you, even you, Frank, can't always get what you want.

Such as ... She tried to remember an occasion when Frank hadn't got what he had wanted. She couldn't remember one.

'Not this time, my darling,' she whispered to a now fast-asleep Frank. And then she smiled and fell asleep herself. She was always happier when she had a plan. Even when that plan was about what was definitely not going to happen.

Her sleep was only occasionally interrupted by dreams in which Frank and Simenon sat drinking pints in Rick's place in Casablanca, swapping jokes and laughing. For some reason Simenon was loosely wearing a lord's ermine robe, his pork-pie hat strangely shrunken and hanging off his left ear; Frank had a kepi on his head. There was someone trying to interrupt them, but she couldn't tell whether that was Georgette Simenon or herself.

Wellbury. Monday. Morning.

Eric Johns Sees Clearly Now

The following morning, while the newly wedded couple still lay asleep in near-marital bliss, with only one occasionally stirring and muttering the word "kepi" with scorn, back in Wellbury the police station was running along its usual well-oiled and professional routine. Which is to say that not much was happening apart from Desk Sergeant Eric Johns beginning his morning shift by sitting in the strangely empty canteen with his usual strong, sweet cup of tea, cream bun, tabloid newspaper, and his own very special analysis of the world situation. And waiting for a victim to share that analysis with.

'Morning, Sergeant,' Constable Sam Nightingale said, sitting down opposite him. He looked up. She was not his ideal first-in-the-morning gossip partner. Samantha Nightingale was gay, that didn't bother him, he was an old (he preferred the word experienced) copper who had seen too much of life to worry about such trivialities. But she was also a plain speaker, and sometimes his take on life needed a certain amount of suspended disbelief. She was also, everyone in the station was well aware, a witch. An extremely attractive, red-haired and green-eyed witch, but that wouldn't make your life any easier if she decided to turn you into a frog. Not that he believed that she could turn him into a frog, of course, that would be silly. That was more your kind of metaphor. But metaphors can be nasty, dangerous things.

However Eric Johns took life as it came when he needed someone to exchange the most newly-minted tittle-tattle with.

'Heard the latest?' he asked in what he thought was a discreet whisper which echoed around the earless canteen. Sam returned his look with eyes which spoke of an interrupted night's sleep and preparation for some incredible rumour which would go beyond the boundaries of normal imagination.

'Probably not,' she said.

'It's Frank,' he whispered. 'Pete Phillips left me a note. He was on duty overnight.'

'It's Frank?'

'Yes. Silly bugger's already in trouble. Not married two days and it's already over.'

'What's over.'

'I told you. His marriage. To Fabulous. You know, I never thought I'd ever feel sorry for her – never thought I'd ever need to, but after what Frank's done ...'

Sam sighed internally.

'So what has Frank done?' she asked.

'Listen, keep it under your hat, but Frieda got back to their honeymoon suite – their honeymoon suite! – and found him in the bath with this French dolly bird.'

Sam looked back dispassionately, wondering why, when she had felt the need of human company, all she had been left with was Eric Johns. He was the only thing close to human in the canteen at that moment, but, even so, it was a bit much for a Monday morning after the weekend she had just had.

'The Inspector found Frank in the bath with a French dolly bird,' she repeated slowly. The statement was just so outlandish that she forgot to take Eric Johns up on his usage of the description "dolly bird". Not that she minded the phrase, she thought it was an accurate description of a certain type of woman, but Eric Johns presented such an old style of sexist approach it seemed almost a duty to take him to task whenever the opportunity presented itself.

The problem was that Eric Johns's statements normally had a

soupcon of reality in them. Another problem was that she could well imagine Frank in the bath with a hotel maid or someone looking up at Frieda and saying, "Look, I can explain ..." It would be totally innocent, of course, but Frank just had this amazing ability to get himself into situations which looked anything but.

'Now under normal conditions,' Eric Johns continued, 'the bride would punch the bridegroom and come running home to mummy. But this is Fabulous we're talking about.'

Sam had to admit that Eric Johns had a toe in reality there. Fabulous wasn't the type to run home to mummy. She wouldn't rip Frank limb from limb either, she would clinically dissect him and dispose of the parts in the appropriate recycling bin.

'No, you see,' Eric Johns nodded, casting a suspicious eye around in case one of the chairs had turned into an eavesdropper, 'we all know that Fabulous is a perfectionist. She can't stand being wrong or failing. I've never known her to be wrong. But' – he waggled a cream-stained finger – 'the thing is that she has failed. Her first marriage.' He nodded his head again to emphasise the point, since it was not the done thing to mention Frieda's first marriage at any great length, both because that had been to a fellow copper, and also because Frieda would not like it, and when Frieda didn't like something you left well alone. 'So there is just no way she is going to let this one fail.'

Sam rubbed her forehead. The reason for her tiredness was her partner, Martinique, or Martin as she called herself. Martin had been giving her the jealous-partner act ever since Frank and Frieda's wedding on the Saturday afternoon, and that seemed ages ago. Sam had danced twice with Frank, which Martin had decided was a sign that she was falling for him. Sam had enough problems with Inspector Summers without her girlfriend throwing a wobbly over him. She, Sam, had learnt to treat all superior officers with a polite distance. With most it was easy to remember that they considered themselves superior officers, they tended to remind you every chance they got. Frank was different. When in his boyish company it was easy to forget that he was an inspector. And, she had to admit, she did like him. But that was nothing for Martin to get jealous about, being gay didn't mean she couldn't have men friends.

She also liked Inspector Garold, now Inspector Frieda Summers – admired, as well as liked – which, she would have thought, was something for Martin to perhaps get jealous about, yet it was Frank Summers the silly woman was fixated on. She dearly hoped that Martin wasn't going to break down in tears and start talking about "that time of the month". Sam Nightingale had never suffered any mood or other changes on that score, and she had little time for women who turned it into a melodrama.

That morning she had walked into the station after parking her motorbike, grateful to have got herself away from Martin, wishing she had someone at the station she could share her problems with, but accepting that at least she would be able to get away from the hassle and spend time discussing Saturday's wedding and hazarding guesses as to what the lucky couple were doing at that moment, and what lovely late-summer weather it was to be having a honeymoon in. And now Eric Johns was removing even that idle occupation, replacing it with something very unwelcome.

'No, she'll never divorce him or anything,' Eric Johns said, 'she'll pretend it never happened. On the outside she'll still be the same efficient police officer, happily married and all the rest, but it'll still be a pretence. The thing is, though, we'll have to pretend we don't know anything about it.'

Sam tried to count up all the "pretends" that made. There seemed to be a maze of them, with no way out.

'Postcards,' added Eric Johns, nodding. 'You'll see.'

'Postcards?'

'Normally people send postcards while on holiday. They won't, because Fabulous isn't talking to Frank. Or she'll send one which is ambiguous. Or doesn't say anything. Or they'll each send one, Frank trying to make a joke of it. It'll be one or the other, you'll see.'

Sam rummaged through her handbag until she found a strip of headache tablets with one remaining tablet. She took it with a sip of tea.

'Headache?' asked Eric Johns sympathetically.

'I always get one when the visions become especially strong,' Sam noted, a slight twitch affecting her lips. 'It was bodies in the bath all weekend, the minute I closed my eyes. Naked bodies. All over the place.'

She smiled at him. She knew that both Eric Johns and Pete Phillips were nervous around her because they believed that she was a witch. How they managed to do that, she hadn't quite worked out – it appeared to have something to do with her describing her official religion as "Pagan" – but it did give her the opportunity of winding them up. If they thought that she had visions, she would give them visions. Loads of lovely visions. With auras. At that moment it appeared the only bright spot in the day.

Eric Johns licked his lips. Unusually for him, the question of whether Frank had been wearing any clothes in the bath with the young woman had not entered his imagination. And, had it done so, his attention would have been more on the young lady than Frank. But Sam's use of the phrase "naked bodies" brought to his mind a large bathful of nubile, almost naked, writhing young women. Having been happily married for so long such an image did not affect him, but he knew, from the pictures in the tabloids he favoured, just how such a picture could affect others. In Eric Johns's imagination, nubile, almost naked, writhing young women always wore carefully placed delicate lingerie to maintain their modesty.

'Visions, eh?' he said. 'Sort of like portents, is it?'

'Possible futures which can be prevented or encouraged,' Sam said, standing up. 'I'm not allowed to interfere with probability, of course.'

'No, of course not. But – well, you know, people as who don't have second sight – like his friends – they could try help things in the right direction, that would be okay, wouldn't it?'

'Oh, yes, certainly. In fact it's their duty.'

'Precisely, their duty.' Eric Johns paused before embarking on a new question. 'Do you have any advice on that score?' he asked. 'You know, avoid black cats, don't walk underneath ladders, that sort of thing?'

'I shall contact my familiar at lunch break, just for you.'

'Thanks, Sam, I'd really appreciate that.'

No, you won't thought Sam. Her headache was going quite quickly.

Eric Johns sat and pondered some more. This whole second sight and visions thing, it wasn't that simple. You had to know how to interpret things. Sam could obviously see things others couldn't, but she didn't always get them right. She had prophesized that Frank and Frieda wouldn't get married, for example, and that had been wrong.

An idea struck him. Everybody had their flaws. Sam's was that she got her visions mixed up. She had correctly prophesied that Frank and Frieda would get engaged. But she had got the wedding prediction the wrong way around. Her flaw was simple. She was a visionary dyslexic. She saw things, but sometimes in reverse. So the thing to do, on those occasions, was to reverse what she said and you'd be okay. Eric Johns nodded happily to himself. It all made sense. Sam was a part-time visionary dyslexic.

Yes, he could see it clearly now. All he had to do was work out was which was which. It wouldn't be easy. But it would be vital. The breakdown of Frank and Fabulous's marriage would affect the entire station. Something had to be done.

And he was the man to do it.

Normandy. Monday. Morning

Just The Two Of Us

Across the channel one of the subjects of this conversation was leaning on the bar, enjoying a coffee and chatting to the hotel proprietor. Frieda had sent him on downstairs while she did some "girlie things". Frank wasn't sure quite what that meant, but if she had some girlie things to do which she preferred to do on her own, he was quite happy to go ahead and indulge in a sociable chat over a cup of coffee with Monsieur Arneaux.

'C'est Lyons, je pens,' Frank said. 'Ils avez plus de la strikers, n'est-ce-pas?'

'Oui, monsieur. Lyons, c'est trez – ver' pretti,' replied Monsieur Arneaux, polishing a glass. It gave him something to do while pretending to understand what this Englishman was going on about. He personally had no idea, but the Englishman appeared happy enough. At least he seemed to know what he was talking about, which made one of them.

All in all Monsieur Arneaux was not the happiest hotelier about. He had been completely satisfied running a small family hotel where the guests were treated more as friends than customers. But now his wife had decided that they needed a more professional image. Hence the new kitchen. Hence the new restaurant. Hence the instructions to respond to guests politely and efficiently, not to lean on the bar chatting as if they were his old mates. He had a feeling that this Englishman was the type who would prefer that approach, but unfortunately he could not understand him. And what with his wife who might enter at any moment, and the business with the flics the evening before, and the girl in the bath, and this English couple perhaps suspects, or perhaps not, since they were English flics, Monsieur Arneaux was more nervous and confused than he had ever been. He was giving extra attention to the polished glasses he was polishing.

'On the other hand, Marseille, perhaps,' said the Englishman. 'Marseille est trez – trez solid defence.'

'Marseille, oui monsieur. C'est – ver' pretti.'

'Oui, exactement. Et Bordeaux, ils avez le bon goalkeeper, mais pas de strikers.'

'Ah, Bordeaux. C'est –' He struggled to think of an English

phrase other than "ver' pretti". 'Good wine,' he decided was about the best he could think of.

'A good win? Well, good for them,' Frank replied, smiling, taking a sip of coffee. While his face radiated confidence and bonhomie as usual, internally he wasn't quite sure whether he and Monsieur Arneaux were having the same conversation. For someone more than usually adept at communication it was extremely frustrating. He wasn't even sure if the phrase "I'm sorry, I don't understand" would be understood. He might find out that he'd ordered a light bulb on mouldy toast by mistake.

Upstairs Frieda was having a conversation of a different kind. She was reading a text message on her mobile phone. Not her usual mobile phone, that was lying in a drawer back in Wellbury. The one she now held had been purchased specially. It even had its own ring-tone to alert her to new messages, a silly tune, but one she liked: "It'll be just our little secret, just our little lonely lovely secret". All married couples have little secrets they keep from each other. Frieda's was the mobile phone. Frank hated mobile phones, almost as if he were allergic to them. He wouldn't forgive her if he discovered that she had brought one on their honeymoon. There was no chance of that happening. It would remain switched off at all times apart from a short spell each morning, while Frank was sipping coffee in the bar and she was "getting herself ready". Or doing some "girlie things", as she had phrased it, knowing that Frank would be quite happy, and polite enough, or shy enough, not to enquire what "girlie things" meant.

To make doubly sure that he remained unaware of its existence, there was only one person who knew the number, and that was her secretary, Tricia Leigh. Tricia had promised to text a short message each day. Just "All quiet" if there was nothing happening that might concern them. "All quiet", she had instructed Tricia, included burglaries, robberies, muggings, everything that might fall under the classification of "normal" police work. It was the abnormal she wanted to be aware of.

'For example,' she had told Tricia, 'suppose the police station has burnt down, and Bobby Stang has converted everyone to the worship of one-eyed purple wombats, and they're all patrolling the streets proclaiming the beginning of the age of Aquarius. That's the sort of thing I need to be aware of.'

Tricia had nodded. Bobby Stang was a quiet, innocuous constable, most unlikely to even think of attempting to convert anyone to the worship of one-eyed purple wombats, but stranger things had been known to happen in Wellbury.

'What about, say, the assassination of the Greek ambassador?' Tricia had asked. 'In Wellbury, I mean.'

'No, that doesn't qualify. That falls under "all quiet".'

'The American ambassador?'

Frieda had had to think about that for a few seconds. That sort of thing would have them returning to a town under media siege. Along with every single Chief Constable within a fifty-mile radius anxious to put their penn'orth in.

'No,' she had decided after careful deliberation, 'that'll be Percy's problem. That's also an "all quiet".'

'Right, so everything from assassination of American presidents down is Inspector Hanson's problem. You want to know of anything more serious.'

'No, Tricia, I don't want to know. I want to be aware of it

before we get back. The last thing I want is to know of it.'

Tricia had nodded and giggled. She understood the difference very well. As Frieda' secretary she had often been in the position, when other-worldly beings such as Chief Constables and Superintendents appeared, of being aware of things without knowing them. There was a world of philosophy between "I'm aware" and "I know", and it included the ability to deny the latter while not mentioning the former.

Frieda had justified the need for this communication channel by telling herself that it was not an inability to tear herself away from the office, but rather a means of ensuring that memories of their honeymoon were not suddenly overshadowed by returning to an unexpected crisis. It would be only too easy to get back to the station and let their marriage be overwhelmed by work. And they were married now, after all, even though it might still not feel entirely true. And it would still take an effort to make it work after the honeymoon. And she wasn't going to let their professional lives get in the way of that. And there was no reason that Frank needed to know about the mobile phone. So he wouldn't.

Now she read the message: "All quiet." It must have cost Tricia Leigh quite a bit of self-control not to add a joke, gossip, or just something such as "Hope all's well". Frieda too would exert the same self-control. She switched the mobile phone off without replying and buried it in her handbag. It would be switched on for less than a minute each morning. The rest of the time was to be dedicated to herself and her husband.

She went into the bathroom and checked her face in the mirror. She had largely cured herself of the habit of applying makeup as if it were war paint, and she had no wish to get back into it. Frank might wonder what "girlie things" might be if not makeup, but he wouldn't wonder long. There would always be something far more interesting to attract his curiosity. His only interest in makeup would be if it were evidence in a crime. Lethal lipstick, or murder by mascara.

As she gave her hair a final brush she noticed Frank's wash-bag on the ledge. It was the same wash-bag he had had ever since his days at boarding school. It was one of Frank's anomalies. He had hated boarding school, yet he had kept the wash-bag, now frayed and worn and really needing replacing. In a similar fashion his suits were always the epitome of smartness, yet his favourite jacket was an old leather thing with tears and patches.

Perhaps the wash-bag was his way of showing the boarding school two fingers. After washing he always carefully aligned his comb, toothbrush, and toothpaste – no doubt as he had been instructed to do as a schoolboy – and then tossed the wash-bag into the middle, scattering everything, as if to say, "There, that's what I think of your rules".

She smiled and moved the razor back into alignment. In doing so she knocked the wash-bag off the ledge onto the floor. She bent down to pick it up. A small bottle of tablets fell out. She picked the bottle up and glanced at the label as she was about to put it back in. She paused. It was a prescription label, and she thought she recognised the name of the tablets. It was the same as those Frank had been prescribed after his accident, a name she had then recognised because a fellow officer had once been prescribed them for extreme migraines after receiving a head wound. That officer had had to resign because of ill-health. As far as Frieda knew,

Frank had fully recovered.

So why had he brought the tablets along?

She shrugged and put the wash-bag back in place. Knowing Frank, the bottle had probably lain in the wash-bag ever since he had been prescribed the tablets, and he'd never bothered to get rid of them.

Then she cocked her head at the wash-bag, smiled, picked it up and tossed it back just as Frank always did. She turned, went back into the bedroom, picked up her capacious handbag, left the room, and tripped down the stairs, humming to herself.

It made her pause half-way down. When had she last done something like that?

Many years ago, in some forgotten life which someone else had lived.

Well, this was her new life. She was happy, the sun was shining, Frank was waiting, and she would hum to herself if she pleased. Frank had been right. This was going to be the best week of their lives, ever.

She passed Marie on the stairs, wished her a gay "Bon jour, Marie!" before continuing. Marie paused to take an earpiece out and return the greeting. She watched her skipping downstairs. She scratched her head. She was sure that she knew the name of the tune the Englishwoman had been humming. She just couldn't quite remember what it was. Then she shrugged and put her earpiece back in.

Normandy. Monday. Breakfast.

Breakfast For Three

'Ah, ici sont ma femme,' said Frank. 'Got everything, Free?'

Monsieur Arneaux's eyebrows rose appreciatively at the sight of a smiling Frieda in a loose summer cotton dress and blouse, her raven hair brushed loosely over her shoulders, her face innocent of any makeup, and innocent of any secrets.

'Bonjour madame,' the landlord said, discovering a new urge to improve his English. 'You sleep good?'

'Oui, monsieur, tres bon,' replied Frieda, giving Frank a suggestive look. 'Once my husband allowed me to get some sleep, that is.'

'Ah,' nodded monsieur Arneaux, scratching his head, understanding only the word "husband".

'I didn't notice any complaints,' said Frank.

'Who said I was complaining, darling? Now, breakfast. I'm famished.'

'Me too. Bon jour, Monsieur Arneaux. Auf wiedershein.'

'I think you mean "au revoir", pet.'

'Ah, yes, that's it. Keep getting my languages mixed up. Au revoir, Monsieur Arneaux.'

'Au revoir monsieur, madame.'

He watched them walk out, shaking his head and smiling. They seemed very happy, and, more importantly, he was now free of the threat of having to exchange social conversation in a language he found impenetrable.

'That English couple,' he said to his wife as she came in, 'I think they will be very happy together. She is pretty and the husband is a pleasant man. He was telling me about the places they have visited so far. Lyons, Marseille, Bordeaux, St Etienne. These English travel all over the place. And what a long honeymoon!'

His wife looked at him and shook her head in despair.

'Henri, I would think he was talking about football. Not even the English, strange as they are, visit so many places on their honeymoon. But they do like football.'

'Ah,' said Henri. He scratched his head again. 'A very pretty wife. A handsome couple. They will have a good marriage.'

'You have always had an eye for a good looking woman.'

'But of course. I married the best looking woman in all France, did I not?'

She looked at him and waved a finger.

'Be careful, Henri Arneaux,' she said, before walking away, smiling. It was nice having honeymoon couples at the hotel. Well, a certain type of honeymoon couple. Not the ones who had an argument and stopped talking to each other, making everyone unhappy. This English couple, however, were not that type. And now that that horrible business with the flics was over it looked like it would be a very happy week. Such a pity the new kitchen and restaurant would only be finished the following week. It would have been nice to celebrate the opening with a honeymoon couple. Though, with the way the builders worked, who knew when the kitchen would be finished? The English couple could be grandparents by that time!

'Hello,' said Frank, noting a sign outside a cafe with tables and chairs outside, 'Full English Breakfast. That sounds good. It's the only drawback about the French, they don't understand the need for a decent breakfast. Cup of black coffee, a roll-up, a Pernod, a croissant and that's your lot.'

'Scrambled egg on toast will do me,' Frieda replied. 'Shall we go in? Or sit outside?'

'Outside sounds better. Fresh air, watch the world go by. Unless madame prefers l'autre? To go inside, I mean.'

'Watching the world go by sounds appealing,' Frieda said, choosing a seat and checking that the table was as clean as it appeared. 'But do try not to mangle their language too much, Frank. I'm not convinced about the theory that they'll like you if you give it a bash.'

'Have to start somewhere,' he replied, dropping onto a chair. 'If I waited until I could speak it perfectly I'd never get going.'

As they sat a slightly plump young waitress came out.

'Bon jour, mademoiselle,' Frank said, making the girl blush for some reason. 'Un petite dejeuner Anglais et une scrambled eggs au toast, s'l-vous-pait. Avec deux cafe au lait, to begin with, as it were.'

'Oui, monsieur,' the girl giggled before hurrying away.

'I didn't say anything rude by mistake, did I?' asked Frank.

'No. But I think she was giggling because your French is so atrocious. And the fact that she's actually English.'

'My French atrocious? I haven't heard much of your French yet. And I bet you she isn't English.'

'I'll bet you she isn't French.'

'Hey, that's not fair. She could be Swiss French. She could come from Algeria or some French ex-colony. You said she was English.'

'We'll ask her,' Frieda said as the waitress returned with their coffees. 'Mademoiselle, est-ce vous etre Francaise?'

'Non, madame, je suis aux Canada.'

'See, Free?' said Frank. 'Canadian French, what did I tell you?'

'Actually I'm English Canadian,' the girl said.

'See, Frank, I told you she was English. You owe me ten pounds.'

'Now wait a minute, Free, first she isn't English, she's Canadian. And we hadn't agreed the bet anyway.'

'Frank, it's a bit rude to discuss someone as if she weren't here, you know.'

Frank shook his head.

'Typical. Changing the subject. Just like a woman, isn't it?' he asked the waitress, who burst into laughter.

'I'd guess you were here on your honeymoon,' she said.

'We are. What made you guess that?'

'Oh, I don't know. I was supposed to be getting married next June, so maybe I tend to think about things like that. You just sound like newly-weds.'

'Was supposed to be?' asked Frank.

'Oh, long story, it doesn't matter. It just had me thinking about weddings a great deal. I'm Catherine, by the way. Call me Cathy.'

'Pleased to meet you, Cathy,' said Frank. 'I'm Frank and this is the boss. Call her boss and you can't go wrong. I do, anyway.'

Cathy giggled.

'Don't mind him, Cathy,' said Frieda. 'I'm Frieda, by the way. But what you say is true enough. Before charmer boy here proposed to me I hardly noticed anything to do with weddings. Afterwards it seemed as if the world was full of people getting married.'

'What was your wedding like? If you don't mind me asking.'

'Best wedding in the world,' Frank said. 'I had the whole of the local police force out looking for me the night before.'

'You're joking!'

'Not at all. We're both police officers in a town called Wellbury in England. For some reason my best man – a detective sergeant – thought I'd disappeared. He was terrified he'd get the blame, so they invoked a special plan we have for dealing with emergencies, just to try to find me. All the silly bugger had to do was knock on my door.'

'And then, on the day,' continued Frieda, 'Frank and his father were on their way to the church and found their way blocked by an overturned lorry, with traffic jams building up all over. So they stole a traffic policeman's motorbike and came on that.'

'Be fair, Free, we didn't actually steal it, we just borrowed it for a short while.'

'And then the traffic policeman entered the church to demand his bike back just as the vicar had asked that question about anyone knowing of any lawful impediment to our marriage.'

Frank chuckled.

'The look on his face was hilarious,' he said. 'The entire congregation turned around to look at him. He went red and tried to tiptoe out, but his boots kept squeaking.'

'But after that it was pretty much plain sailing,' Frieda concluded. 'Until we arrived here to find a dead girl in our hotel bathroom. Well, almost dead, anyway.'

'Gee, that was you? I heard something about that on the news this morning. Uh, oh,' the girl said. 'Les flics. You can recognise them anywhere. I'd better get your breakfast.'

She disappeared as they turned around to find Georges Simenon approaching. He held a lead in his hand, attached to the collar of a young dog, just-past-the-puppy stage. Its bright, inquisitive eyes contrasted with Simenon's weary, cynical look.

'They don't seem to have a very high opinion of their plods,' Frank whispered. 'I've been into that breakfast place near my flat any number of times, and the waitresses have never run from me.'

'Yes, we need to discuss that at some stage, Frank,' Frieda replied. 'What we're going to do with your flat and improving your diet. That breakfast place, as you call it, is simply a greasy spoon cafe. It's not good for you.'

'Ah, be fair, Free, I only pop in once a week or so. Bon jour, inspector, grabbez vous une seat. And it's not as if I chat the waitresses up.'

'Bon jour, Inspector Simenon,' Frieda said. 'Voulez vous une cafe? Frank, you don't realise that they think that you are chatting them up.'

Georges Simenon sat down and regarded them with his chin in his hand, elbow on the table. The dog sat and cocked his head, looking from Frieda to Frank, as if watching a rather interesting game of tennis.

'I don't chat them up,' Frank said, 'I just try to be polite, exchange some idle banter, that sort of thing. Comment allez vous, inspecteur?'

'You may think it idle banter, Frank, but to that little girl, the blonde with the pale face and pony-tail, you're her hero.

Inspector, vous veux cafe noir ou cafe au lait?'

'She's just a kid, she'll grow out of it. How's the case going, Inspector? Anyway, how come you know about the girl with the blonde pony-tail? You've never been in there.'

'It just so happens that I walked past it one Saturday morning, Frank. I was going to pop in to say hello, but I didn't want to upset your fans. How's your officer, Inspector? Mademoiselle Amelie?'

Frank stuck his tongue out at Frieda and folded his arms. Georges Simenon waited until he was sure they had finished.

'Un cafe noir, s'il vous plait, mademoiselle,' he said to the waitress who had come with their breakfasts. 'It is kind of you to ask. La petite is doing well, better than expected. She is young and will have the fast recovery, I think. I must apologise for disturbing your petit dejeuner.'

'Inspector,' Frank said, tucking into his full English breakfast, 'I would play it exactly the same way. If I were in your shoes I'd also turn up at the most inconvenient time, just to keep my suspects off balance. Works for me every time. They eventually end up confessing to something. Not always what I want them to confess to, but you can't always have everything you want.'

He looked up at Simenon and smiled, his mouth chomping away. Georges Simenon gave him a baleful look and took out a cigarette. He looked at it miserably, popped it in his mouth unlit, and sank his hands into his pockets.

'Kojak sucked the lollipops to give up smoking,' he said. 'I suck the cigarette to give up the smoking. What the world has come to. My wife, she forbids the smoking in our house. That is something I come to live with. Then France, my country, forbids the smoking anywhere in public. Mon dieu, it is as if you English were to ban rosbif.'

'Have a waffle in syrup, it will take the urge away,' Frank suggested. 'I'm thinking of having one if I can find space after this. The waitress is Canadian. They must do waffles in syrup.'

Simenon made a moue.

'It is a problem. I smoke, they say I will die of the heart attack. I do not smoke, I eat, I get fat and die of the heart attack anyway.'

He looked at the dog, which looked back with bright eyes.

'This is Gaspode,' he said. Gaspode gave a brief bark to confirm his name. 'Gaspode is Amelie's dog. I bought him for her when it was a little puppy. She often said how much she liked puppies. Unfortunately Gaspode is no longer the puppy, and Amelie might like puppies, but she does not know how to look after them. She is not unkind, she is just – I think you use the word "simple".'

He sighed and looked at the dog.

'I am afraid, with Gaspode and Amelie, it is Gaspode who throws the stick and Amelie who fetches.'

Gaspode barked again, to indicate that he understood and agreed.

'But now I look after Gaspode. It is good. I get the exercise, Gaspode gets the food and exercise properly. Amelie will see puppies on the television and fall in love with them. They stay on the television, she is happy, she does not have to remember that she has to feed them each day.'

'That reminds me,' Frank said, 'I must try and catch some French television while we're here.'

'You come on the holiday and wish to watch the television?'

'Not all the time, Inspecteur, un peu. Just to get the flavour.'

'A very peu,' Frieda said. 'This is our honeymoon, remember, darling?'

'Ah, I knew there was a reason we were here,' Frank joked. 'Seriously, though, I reckon you can tell a lot about a culture by what they read and watch. Adverts especially. What is it they're trying to flog, to whom, and why do they choose to represent things the way they do.'

Simenon shrugged.

'Once upon a time that was true,' he said, 'but I have this fear that these days everything is becoming the same. Everything is becoming Americaine.' He sighed. 'There was a case once, when I was a young officer – there have been cases the same since, but this one I remember. A young man, seventeen, a boy in truth, killed his grandmother. He claimed that he was imitating what he had seen in a film, a French film, un film noire. There was much debate about whether films and such caused this behaviour in children, whether this should be allowed.'

'We have that sort of debate about once a year,' Frank said, as he tried to nail an errant mushroom. 'It's what we call an annual story. Something the newspapers and media dust off and bring out every so often. They never reach a conclusion, it's just a chance for them to use words like "horrific", with loads of exclamation marks.'

'Ah, perhaps this is true, the same happens here in France. But a few weeks ago, perhaps two months, I read the story of a similar crime – a jeune homme, who kills his ex-girlfriend because someone on the Internet told him to. Someone living in Australia. La! Not even a French crime. Now this madness is international.'

'I have a theory about that,' Frank said, causing Frieda to raise her eyes to the sky. 'It's similar to the Sixties.'

'The Sixties?' asked Simenon as Frank paused to enjoy a piece of bacon and baguette with his fingers.

'Well, everyone goes on about the Sixties being the decade of young love, flower power and hippies. Now I've interviewed lots of people who were young at the time, and almost none of them remember having that lifestyle.' He chuckled. 'The first real case I had in Wellbury involved a dead skeleton from the Sixties.'

'A dead skeleton?'

'Yes. But, anyway, getting back to the subject. The vast majority of people I interviewed from that period had the old pre-war worries, get a job, get married, settle down. That image of the Sixties everyone has only really happened in large cities like London, and then it was only mainly constructed by the media and what they call the beautiful people.'

'My husband has some interesting and unorthodox interview techniques, Inspector,' Frieda commented, smiling at Simenon who was still trying to come to terms with the idea of a "dead skeleton". 'He combines his professional duties with his interest in history. It isn't unusual for him to start discussing a certain historical period with a prisoner immediately after he's just arrested that prisoner.'

'It works, doesn't it, sweetheart?' Frank asked, winking at her as he wiped the last bit of egg from his plate with a chunk of baguette.

Frieda frowned at him, finishing her scrambled eggs. She signalled the waitress.

'Two waffles in syrup,' she said, 'one for me and one for the inspector here. The French inspector, not my husband. He's on a diet. And, Frank, try to remember that most people consider wiping your plate with a piece of bread not the best manners.' Frank shrugged.

'Their problem, not mine. I'm sure Epicurus would have done the same. He enjoyed a good nosh up.'

'Epicurus is my husband's hero, Inspector,' Frieda explained. 'Though I think he has his own interpretation of Epicurus's approach to life. Frank, he enjoyed a good meal and good company. I don't think he would have described it as a good nosh up.'

'He will do when I write the definitive guide to his philosophy,' Frank smiled. Simenon once again looked at them looking at each other, heads cocked, eyes twinkling.

'But this question of the Sixties,' he said, 'I do not understand.'

'Oh, that,' said Frank. 'It doesn't have to be the Sixties. It could be the Regency period. Middle Ages, possibly. Seventies, maybe. World War Two is also a good example.'

Simenon looked at him. Then he closed his eyes and pinched the bridge of his nose.

'It's all to do with the modern media,' Frank continued. 'They concentrate on stories which they think will sell. The trouble is that they try to give the impression that everybody is living exactly the same way – we're all becoming Americanised, films are turning youngsters into raving psychopaths, etc, etc. I don't know how history will record the days we live in now.

I doubt if any of us will recognise it. The truth is that the vast majority of people just don't live the sort of lives the media represent. They certainly don't where we come from.'

'Thank god for that,' said Frieda. She looked at Simenon. 'Sometimes I wonder if there isn't something wrong with Wellbury's water supply,' she said. 'We seem to have more than our fair share of strange people. Less than a month ago we were chasing a ghost and aliens in the local cemetery.'

'And we caught them,' said Frank.

'You caught the ghost and the aliens?' asked Simenon.

'The ghost turned out to be the vicar's wife chasing him with a thurible,' Frank said. 'The aliens were a couple of university students playing pranks.'

'Pranks?' asked Simenon, his blinking eyes suggesting that he was trying to work out which part of the conversation he understood least.

'Practical jokes.' Frank sipped his coffee and looked at the waffles in syrup Frieda was delicately eating. 'So, Inspector, what's your next move? As far as this body in the bath goes.'

'You were right,' Simenon said, turning to his own waffles in syrup, 'this does remove the craving. Perhaps I give up smoking, get fat and die of the heart attack. It sounds a better way.'

'Translation: mind your own business and leave me to ask the questions,' grinned Frank. Simenon shrugged.

'The truth is that I have no ideas at this stage,' he said. 'I have instructed my detectives to speak to their informants and remind them of what happens to anyone involved in an attack on a police officer, and anyone withholding information in such a case. I have officers with the photograph of Amelia

Courbois, interviewing people on the streets. The hotel staff have been re-interviewed. At the moment it is a case of asking questions, asking questions again, asking more questions, until we find an answer that will lead us to the truth.'

'What about the person who was supposed to be picking up the heroin?' asked Frieda. Frank raised his eyebrows at her.

'Not our case,' he murmured, looking at the sky.

'He,' said Simenon, 'turns out to be an entirely innocent tourist. Someone, I think, leads me up the guardian path.'

'Garden path.'

'Precisely. And now I am left with only the mystery of Amelie in the bath at your hotel.'

He put his fork down and wiped his lips with a handkerchief. There was a small piece of waffle on his plate. He tossed it to Gaspode who caught it in his mouth and chewed on it with the air of a connoisseur.

'It is a strange case,' Simenon said, looking at Gaspode. 'It is a small hotel. The only staff are the owners, monsieur and madame Arneaux, and the maid, the niece Marie. There are other maids, but they are not there yesterday. An hour before you arrived Marie was told to make sure that your room was ready and clean. This makes her the bit irritated, the room she had cleaned earlier that morning. It is already clean, why should she check it again? It appears that Madame Arneaux always worries that rooms are not ready just before guests arrive. Ironically, this time she was right. But we know, therefore, that Amelie was not in the room an hour before you arrived – which is helpful, since the people in the hotel bar remember her arriving two hours before, one hour before, half an hour before, five minutes, every time you could wish. They think she is a guest at the hotel, pretty, but nothing more.'

'Your average witness in a pub, or bar,' suggested Frank.

'Precisely. Their only interest in the time is whether the bar is to close soon. Now, Monsieur Arneaux, he chats with his friends in another hotel nearby, he has a strong alibi for that hour. Madame Arneaux, she is working in the bar, she is expecting your arrival, once again, a strong alibi, all the customers can see her.'

'Which leaves Marie.'

'Oui. Except Marie, once she has finished confirming what she knew, that your room is ready, comes down to assist Madame Arneaux. She is in the kitchen behind the bar, cleaning. Why she has to clean a kitchen which the builders will dirty the next day, she does not know. But Madame Arneaux sees her every few minutes. Even then, Marie is a peasant girl, she has the good heart, but not the imagination. Had she not an alibi it would be impossible to suspect her. Attack Amelie? Non, I cannot see it. If she attacked someone everyone in the hotel would know of it. Everyone in the town would know of it. She does not stay quiet about such a thing.'

'Let me guess,' said Frank. 'The room could only be gained by going upstairs, and the stairs were in full view of the people in the bar. And no one was seen going up the stairs in that hour.'

'You are correct, monsieur. There are the back stairs, the fire escape. But the door could not be opened without making the noise of the alarm.'

'Which you tested,' said Frieda, remembering the fire alarm of the night before.

'Yes. I like to test things. I like to test the small things that people tell me.'

'Including whether the steps on the staircase creaked. That was you jumping on them?'

'That is correct. But they do not make the creak. It tells me nothing. Someone could walk without being heard, yes, but without being seen? Non!'

'Bit of a sod, really,' Frank grinned.

'You seem to find it amusing, Monsieur Inspector.'

'Well, it leaves you with only two suspects. My wife and myself.'

Simenon nodded slowly.

'That, indeed, is my problem. And, with all due respect, Inspector Summers, your wife and yourself are the worst suspects I have ever had. Your credentials are impeccable. You are upon your loonymoon. You had no prior knowledge.' He sighed. 'But there is another problem. Of the hotel no-one had prior knowledge, not even myself. It was the wrong hotel.'

He paused in thought.

'Find the heroin,' he said, almost to himself, 'and you find the crumpet.'

'The crumpet?' asked Frieda.

'Oui, madame inspector. The crumpet. The guilty parting.'

'Oh, culprit.'

'Ah, the guilty parting,' said Frank, nodding. 'Wouldn't be surprised if he didn't turn out to be a cut above the rest.' And then he added 'Ouch!' as Frieda kicked him under the table.

'That is the English pun, inspector? "Cut" – "heroin"?'

'Er, you could say that. What about forensics? Have they come up with anything?'

'Nothing, they tell me. I have told them to go back and carry on until they find something.' He looked at Gaspode. 'Perhaps there is a pun there too. The word in English is "clean", is it not? When there are no forensics?'

'That's the one,' said Frank. 'Speaking of which, I need to pop into the little boys' room to wash my hands.'

Frieda watched him enter the cafe, managing to resist a comment about the usefulness of knives and forks in that respect.

'Tell me something, madame,' Simenon said, in a casual voice which might have managed to fool a two-year-old, 'your husband suffers from the headaches?'

Frieda looked at him before replying, a look that would have put another two-year-old in its place. She knew where the question came from. Simenon and his fellow detectives would have gone through their luggage, however unobtrusively. They would have noticed the bottle of tablets. It might have taken them a while to identify the English prescription, which was probably why Simenon was only asking the question now. First the missing heroin, then the prescription-only tablets. Drugs and more drugs. Even a junior detective would wonder if there was a link. And now Simenon had waited until Frank was away before dropping the apparently idle question into the conversation. It was rather fortunate that she had accidentally discovered the bottle. Otherwise she might innocently have answered the question in the negative, which could only raise suspicion.

'My husband was shot in the head on duty, Inspector,' she

replied. 'As far as we are aware he has made a full recovery. But the doctors say that side effects could appear at any time.'

Simenon nodded sympathetically.

'So that is the reason for the –' he waved a finger at his forehead. 'The white hair. A quiff, I think you say.'

'Precisely, Inspector.'

Simenon nodded again.

'It gives him the appearance sympathetic,' he said. 'Like a Byron.'

'Byron?' asked Frank, coming out of the cafe and catching Simenon's last words. 'You two aren't discussing Byron, are you? What a depressing subject. I've never understood why they call them the Romantic poets.' He sat down and took a sip of coffee. 'Romance and love should be all about being happy and having fun, not moping around and sighing deeply. Carpe Diem, that's the thing.'

Simenon gave the impression of a man trying to remember how to smile.

'I think I would agree with you, Inspector,' he said. 'We must do our best with what little the good Lord sends us.'

'Well, we wish you all the best, Inspector,' Frieda said, 'but, as Frank says, Carpe Diem. We have to collect our hire car and get on with our honeymoon.'

'Of course. I apologise for the unpleasantness, but I hope you understand.'

'Absolutely, Inspector,' said Frank. 'If there is anything we can do to help, please let us know. Right at the moment we intend to drive down to the beach for a stroll.'

'Ah, a romantic stroll on the beach,' said Simenon, standing up. 'The coastline is very pretty. Sometimes, living here, I forget that.'

'Well, partly a romantic stroll. We're starting with Omaha beach.'

'We're both what might be called amateur historians,' Frieda said. 'A honeymoon in Normandy seemed appropriate.'

'To prepare us for the wars ahead,' Frank joked. Frieda gave him a sideways frown. Simenon smiled.

'Perhaps that is what I should have done,' said Simenon. 'I am reminded of a saying from the great philosopher, Renan: Quand on a le droit de se tromper impunément, on est toujours sûr de réussir. I think the English is: if you are permitted to make the mistake, you will finally find the success. It is when the first mistake is always remembered that a man's life becomes the failure. Bon chance.' He nodded and walked away, Gaspode trotting alertly along at his side.

'First mistake, eh?' noted Frank, rubbing his jaw. 'I wonder what first mistake he was talking about. Professional, or personal?'

'None of our business, Frank,' replied Frieda, turning away from the sight of Georges Simenon's disappearing back. She looked at Frank. 'I feel almost sorry for him. He came on a fishing expedition and you fed him a bunch of red herrings. The Sixties and the dead skeleton.'

Frank winked at her.

'He's doing exactly what I would. Trying to pump people for information without appearing to do so. There's one difference between us, though.'

'And what would that be?'

'I'm better than he is. I'm going to beat him in this game. He's going to find himself going up a lot more guardian paths.'

Frieda shook her head at him.

'Darling, you have heard of hubris, haven't you?'

'Doesn't apply. Hubris requires the hero to have a fatal flaw. And I don't have one.'

'Really? Not?'

'No, I have so many minor ones there isn't space for a fatal one.'

'Well, that's true enough, darling.'

Frank made a face at her and then chuckled.

'Poor Simenon. He can't figure us out. Logically we're his chief suspects, but it doesn't make sense. So he's nosing around to find something that does make sense.'

'Suspects!' muttered Frieda. 'I'll give him suspects.'

'Not his fault. But we're not here to help him find the crumpet, are we?'

'We are definitely not. And I hope you aren't going to start mimicking him, Frank.'

'Course not, ma vie. Let's get on with our honeymoon. Forget about Simenon, Amelie and the rest. Pay bill, pick up car and on with honeymoon. I wonder if there's somewhere around here I can pick up a bucket and spade.'

'Just so long as you don't dig up a buried corpse while you're about it, Frank.'

He gave her a pained look.

'Who was it who found the body in the bath?' he asked.

'O, that woman that cannot make her fault her husband's occasion, let her never nurse her child herself, for she will breed it like a fool,' replied Frieda.

'Midsummer Night's Dream?'

'As You Like It.'

'Well, if you want to know how I like it, –'

'Frank!'

'Sorry, darling.'

Frieda sighed and took his hand.

'No, I'm sorry, darling. I think I'm still getting used to this idea of being on honeymoon, far from the madding crowd, all by ourselves.' She looked at him. She wanted to ask him about that bottle of tablets. She was sure that there was a perfectly innocent explanation to their being in his wash-bag. But it might bring back bad memories, and there was no place for those now. 'Come on,' she said finally, 'you can tell me how you like it as we walk to the car hire place.'

'It is interesting, though. How did someone get in and out without being seen?'

'That's enough, Frank. Do try to think about something else. Us, for example.'

Frieda was frowning as they left the cafe, hand in hand. She was trying to remove the image in her mind, the image of a staircase that someone had gone up and returned down without making the squeak or being seen.

And what "first mistake" had Simenon referred to? Or was that just another, French, red herring in exchange for Frank's deliberate meanderings?

No, she was not going to go down that route. They were

there on honeymoon, the start of their married life, not to get involved in foreign police matters. There was only one type of crumpet Frank was going to be allowed to get interested in.

And only one of them, too.

Normandy. Monday. Morning.

Postcards in Time

'Before we go anywhere or do anything,' Frieda said, putting on her sunglasses and checking the contents of her handbag as they strolled, 'we need to send some postcards. One to your parents, one to my mother, and one to the station. Come on, let's go find some.'

'Horrible things, postcards,' Frank replied with a grimace. 'Too small to say anything worthwhile, too large to get away with just a witty one-liner.'

'We'll just say that we had a wonderful journey – though tiring – and the hotel we're staying in is absolutely marvellous – which it is. Oh, and promise to bring back loads of photographs.'

'That should scare them off.'

'Now, Frank.'

'I know. What to write on the postcard: room came with a view and a beautiful bird in bath, stop. So good we ordered another, stop. Will tell you all about it when we get home, stop. If we come back, stop. Love to chat, but we can't stop, stop.'

'Really, Frank, it's not a telegram. And we aren't going to say anything about the – person in the bath. It's far too complicated to mention. And your parents will only worry.

And I don't think an inspector should be referring to a young woman as a bird. It's hardly professional.'

'Oh, come on, Free, it's too good a chance to give up. Imagine how it would get the station going.'

'That's exactly why we aren't going to do it, Frank. You know what they're like. Especially Eric Johns. It wouldn't surprise me if they let their imaginations get carried away with them and send a search party over here to rescue us from the French police.'

'You know, that could be fun.'

'No it wouldn't, Frank. Now, stop being silly and think of what you're going to say.'

'What about: Weather is here, wish you were all wonderful?'

Frieda sighed. She wondered if she wouldn't have been better off asking Frank's mother for advice on how to deal with him rather than listening to her own mother's 1955 theories.

And then she mentally paused and listened to what she had just said: "Now, stop being silly." It was exactly how her mother would have phrased it. Was she turning into her mother? Surely that only happened when people became parents?

Was she, in some weird way, treating Frank as her child? After all, he often acted like a little school boy.

'To be honest, I'd feel more comfortable writing a letter,' Frank mused.

'And you write letters all the time, do you?' Frieda asked, telling herself not to be silly. All men acted like schoolboys at times.

'Actually I used to write home quite often. At boarding school we had to write a letter every week – mine always contained hints about how bloody awful the place was. But after I left school and moved away to uni, and when I joined the force, I still wrote at least every other weekend. Then I got an e-mail address, the folks did too, so it seemed easier to e-mail.'

'So you e-mail every fortnight?'

'Well, no, it never quite worked out that way. I've always meant to, and it should be easier, but somehow it never happened. It just seems to be a different culture to letter writing – more ephemeral.'

Frieda glanced at him. He had his serious look on. The same look he acquired when investigating what he thought was an interesting case. It was almost as if he were going inside his mind, closing the door, and concentrating. She didn't mind him doing that when at work, but she was rubbermatted if she was going to allow him to do it on their honeymoon. Once they got back he could spend as much time as he wanted sitting in the garden drinking beer and gazing into the distance. Not now.

Oh, and it would be a glass of wine, not a beer. One had to have some standards.

'Darling,' she said, taking his arm, 'just a quick couple of postcards and then that's it? Okay? Just for little me?'

Had anyone at the station heard her describe herself as "little me" there would be chins bouncing off the ground. Not even Eric Johns's imagination could stretch that far.

'Hmmm? Oh, yes, absolutely. I'm sure we can think of something to say.'

They spent a little while strolling around the small shops, choosing the postcards. Frank, of course, was drawn to anything with a hint of innuendo or double entendre. Frieda managed to persuade him that such things would not be acceptable to his mother. They found a cafe and ordered a cup of tea while they completed the postcards. Frank pondered his, wrote a few lines, and then showed it to Frieda.

"Help! Help! I'm being held here by a maniac! Supplies running out; down to last hundred beers; send more beers."

Frieda looked at him.

'Frank, I get the impression that you aren't taking this very seriously.'

'Oh, come on, Free, the people at the station like a bit of a laugh.'

'Yes, I know they do. Frank, try to remember that you're an inspector now. I don't want any locker-room jokes about us and our – love life.'

'What are you talking about, Free?'

'Describing me as a sex-maniac. Really, Frank.'

If she were honest, she rather liked the idea.

'Where did I say that?' he asked, flummoxed. She read the card again.

'You implied it,' she decided, and returned her attention to her own postcards.

Frank wrinkled his nose and frowned. He wrote "Help! Help! Keep me in here!" a few times around the edge of the rejected missive. Then he sat and looked into the distance, chewing his pen like a baffled schoolboy doing his best but failing. Frieda ignored him. She knew he was doing it deliberately. In truth, she enjoyed it. That was the type of cosy thing that couples did. Suddenly he nodded, picked out another card, and began writing. When finished he showed the result to Frieda. She read it and sighed.

"Hotel superb; room so good we ordered a second. Natives are very friendly; even the local plods refuse to arrest us. P.S. Marriage is the last thing everyone should try. Life couldn't be better."

'Frank, "Marriage is the last thing everyone should try"? That sounds like you aren't enjoying it.'

'It means that you should keep it till the last, because after that nothing is better. Look, "Life couldn't be better." What's wrong with that?'

Frieda frowned. She knew what Frank was saying, she just wasn't sure how the others would read it.

'In that case I think you should say something such as "Marriage is so good it should be kept to the last as the best." Or something. Try again.'

He shrugged.

'Okay, Free, you write them, I'll sign them,' he said, leaning back and stretching his legs in an I've-done-my-best-and-now-can't-be-bothered pose.

Frieda felt a tickle of a tear come to her eye as she bent over the postcards and did as her master bid. Right then she hated the postcards, she hated Frank, and she hated herself. She knew she was over-reacting, but she couldn't help herself. Wanting everything to be perfect was a nice thought but a nasty expectation. It was one thing to issue orders at work; doing so in a marriage was only acceptable if one of the partners was the type to meekly obey, a description which fitted neither of them. She took a breath and finished the rubbermatting things off with a determined flourish.

'Right, that's that. Add your signature. We'll post them, and that's over.'

Frank leaned over and kissed her.

'Good,' he said. 'Now that's over with we can get on with the important stuff. Us together. You and me. And me and you.'

Frieda was so flustered with his attention that she efficiently stamped the postcards without thinking. Including his attempts at humour. And then they both posted them. Including the ones with his attempts at humour.

In a normal universe they would have arrived two weeks after the bridal couple had returned. As it was Frank's two postcards were destined to drop in front of Desk Sergeant Eric Johns on the Wednesday morning. Frieda's cards to her mother and the one to Frank's parents also arrived on time. Her own to the station never arrived.

That was delivered to a police station in a tiny, one-horse town in New Zealand. They still discuss it in the local pub on a Saturday evening.

Normandy. Monday. Morning.

Footprints in the Sand

'What was it that Wordsworth said?' asked Frank as they strolled along the beach, barefoot, hand in hand, their free hands holding their shoes. 'Heaven it was to be alive that time?'

'"Bliss was it in that dawn to be alive, but to be young, very heaven." I thought you didn't like the Romantic poets.'

'They had to get something right. Funny, really. You look at these gorgeous beaches, the country just inland, the rural idyll

– in those days, anyway. And then, June 1944, you have hundreds of thousands of young men coming ashore to wage war. You think about it, first they were stuck on board the landing craft for days before, seasick, it was raining, there was a heavy swell, the decks covered with vomit –'

'Thank you, Frank, I think I've got enough of that picture, darling.'

'Sorry. But then they have to charge across a beach with people being killed or maimed alongside, explosions, all the rest. And after they take the beaches, even then it's a long hard slog across Europe, death lurking at their shoulders every day. They're living in the open, mud, dirt, wet, the smell of unwashed bodies day and night, having to tolerate almost entirely male company, what humour there was must have been pretty crude – and then we end up with some romanticised idea that it was all terribly, terribly wonderful, a marvellous adventure. Is it me, or is there something wrong with that picture?'

'And gentleman in England now abed, shall think themselves accursed they were not here, and hold their manhoods cheap, whiles any speaks, that fought with us upon Saint Crispin's day.'

'Hah! Exactly! Henry V. I've always thought Monty Python should have done a sketch on that. Good old King Henry trying to convince a crowd of peasants to fight for him. "We must anon to France to go, to reclaim our lawful land." And a peasant replies, "Why?" So Henry scratches his head and says, "Well, it's this Salic law, innit? France belongs to me." And another peasant says, "Well, why don't you bugger off and ask for it back then, we've got the harvest to get in. And it's almost pub-opening time." '

Frieda smiled wryly.

'Do me a favour, darling,' she said. She stopped, dropped her shoes, turned to him and held his face in her hands. 'Promise me that, if they ever call for volunteers to go to war, you'll stay at home? With me?'

'It would have to be a pretty remarkable war to get me to volunteer to leave you, my sweet.' He smiled and gave her a hug. 'I know young boys are supposed to dream of becoming heroic soldiers at some stage, but I can't say I ever have. I think that's partly because dad is a historian. I knew more about the mud of Flanders by the time I was ten than most people do in a lifetime. Of course, mud to an ten-year-old is a good thing. Dad put me right on that score.'

'How did he do that?'

'He suggested I try digging a trench in the garden during the rain and living in it for a full day. Well, not suggested it, really, that would be going too far. From what I remember he said something such as, "Well, my boy, one of these days we'll try it as an experiment, shall we?" So, of course, I did, without telling him. Typical ten-year-old, I was going to prove I could do it.' He laughed. 'Just digging the trench was agony, but I finally made it. Or a small trench, anyway. Perhaps a foot and a half deep by three feet long. I had mum's broom as a rifle, one of the kitchen knives taped to it as a bayonet. And then, after fifteen minutes I was bored out of my skull. And it was raining. I managed to stay there for about forty-five minutes, until mum came home and found me.'

'I'll bet she was pleased.'

'Not that you'd notice. My trench intruded into her favourite flower patch. The digging was easier there.'

Frieda laughed.

'That is so like you, Frank.'

'And I was soaking wet and getting a cold. She was furious with me and with dad. I was in bed with a fever for four days. Mum used to come in with chicken broth, torn between giving me a lecture and making sure her little boy got better. Dad would slip in when she wasn't there to chat about things such as foot-rot and the men who made it back as amputees, brain damaged or shell shocked, men who would never experience a normal life.'

'A bit much for an ten-year-old, surely. Especially one in a fever.'

'Oh, not really. You see, dad believed in treating me as a small version of a grown up. And he would always end our discussions with something like "And that isn't going to happen to you, my boy". He really does believe that studying history is important to avoid repeating past mistakes.'

Frieda looked around. The beach. The surf.

'Young men dying almost every yard,' she said softly. 'I wish I could say that it will never happen again.'

Frank nodded.

'It will, somewhere, sooner or later,' he said, equally as softly, looking out to sea. 'But our children are not going to be involved in senseless slaughter.'

She looked at him. His jaw was set as it rarely was. She had always known that, beyond the easy-going image he liked to project, there was a steel to Frank Summers which the bad guys discovered at their peril. He looked back at her and grinned.

'The really, really ridiculous thing is, even knowing intellectually how terrible it must have been, there's still a little part of me that rather likes the idea of dressing up in a soldier's uniform and going off to war. Stupid, isn't it?'

'It's part of cultural indoctrination. Tribal myth. All those films, the stiff upper lip and the rest. The women hiding their emotions and bravely coping as the menfolk march off.'

Frank made a face.

'Far too serious,' he said.

'No, it isn't,' Frieda replied, taking his hand. 'Frank, let's be serious about us.'

She stopped speaking. He squeezed her arm.

'Free ... What say we sit down and watch the world go by?'

He took his jacket off and spread it on the sand.

'And before you say something about ruining the jacket, oh wife of mine, it's only a jacket, it can be replaced. The wings of time can't. Come on, Poppy.'

Frieda shook her head at him, smiled, and sat down. Frank took his place next to her and put his arm around her.

'I can't remember where I read it,' Frank said, 'some poem, I think. Something about using the quiet times to nurture strength for the difficult times ahead.'

'Sounds like Desiderata. "Go placidly amidst the noise and haste." '

'Could be.' He sighed and leaned back on his elbows. 'Aren't you glad we decided against Paris? We would have been rushing around from museum to museum, up and down the Eiffel Tower, taking photographs by the dozen to remind us of the memories we didn't have.'

'Talking of photographs,' Frieda said, taking a camera from her handbag and getting on her knees, 'I think I'll take one of you, now.'

'Ugh, no, Free!' he exclaimed, holding her arm as she began to stand up. 'Very bad luck that. I don't want single photographs. They make me think of the remaining partner left all alone, going through pictures of their loved one no longer there.'

'They do?'

'Absolutely. You must have done interviews with people when they bring out their photographs, saying something like "This is one of Gerald just the year before he died." It's never "This is Gerald and myself on that last holiday, we were so happy together." It's almost like a curse. It's always just the one person in the shot.'

Frieda looked down at him, a puzzled smile on her face.

'I never thought you'd be guilty of superstition, Poppy Summers.'

'Free,' he grinned, 'as far as you're concerned I'll believe in any superstition going. Give your old man a kiss.'

She put her hand alongside him, leaned over and kissed him.

'I'm going to start a diary,' he said, once they came up for air.

'A diary, darling Poppy?' she teased.

'For our kids, the little gobshites. Once they've grown up. I want them to know how much in love we are. It probably won't make any difference. I look at mum and dad and try to imagine them being young and in love, but it never works. I know they love each other, and me, of course, I just can't see them as young and in love like us.'

'It doesn't work, does it?' Frieda said, sitting down again, holding her knees and looking out to sea.

'Thinking of your mum and dad?'

Frieda nodded. Her mother had become, and still was, a bossy woman. Her father had died young. He was the one who had instilled a driving force to succeed in her. She had never been sure how different that might have been had they had a son alongside the daughter. In Frieda's confused and emotional recollection of those days, as her father weakened, clasped her wrist and struggled to tell her that happiness was more important than success, she dated the beginning of her mother's bossiness. Her father would never have tolerated such a thing, unless he was dying and had no option. To what extent her mother's determined control was latent and only awaiting her husband's illness to emerge, and to what extent it was a coping mechanism, a way of creating a distance, Frieda had never been quite sure. Nor was she sure that her father would have approved of her marrying Frank – before he became ill. Afterwards, she suspected, he might well – almost certainly would have – thought of Frank as an excellent choice. If choice it had been. The idea of marrying Frank still sat in her mind as being both inevitable and impossible. She wondered how long it would take before she woke up in the early hours thinking that she had been dreaming, and had to squeeze him to make sure that he was real.

What she was sure of was that she would never be able to imagine her mother and father as a love-lorn young couple. You might as well try to imagine Abraham Lincoln as a two-year-old having a strop, or Winston Churchill as a baby saying "Goo!" and chuckling happily up from his pram.

'Now, you see,' Frank said, 'if I had bought a bucket and

spade as I intended, we could have built a sand-castle and used it as a tripod to take a picture of both of us.'

Frieda smiled.

'You are determined to build a sandcastle, aren't you, darling Poppy?'

'Absolutely, my dearest Poppy. That and nick a kepi.'

Frieda stiffened, sat forward and looked out to sea.

'It's good that you know what you want,' she said. 'After all, isn't that what the manual says? It's better to have a plan, even if it's a bad one.'

Frank looked up at the back of her head.

'I can tell when you're upset, you know,' he said. 'You go all quiet and withdrawn, which is unnatural for you.'

'You mean otherwise I talk too much?'

'Whooah, wife! What's eating at you, Free?'

'Oh, I don't know, I suppose that perhaps I was thinking of the reasons most couples go on honeymoon. To celebrate being married. To explore their love for each other. To enjoy being together, just the two of them. Wanting to steal a kepi isn't something I've ever considered as being the purpose of going on honeymoon, but if that's what you want, that's what you want.'

He sat up behind her and put his arms around her waist.

'Free, if you think I'm not taking this seriously, you're wrong,' he murmured into her ear. 'I want us to enjoy being together too. I want us to explore our love for each other. I want this to be a honeymoon which we'll always remember as being the best start to our married life we could ever have. It's just that, I suppose, I take for granted that that's what we both want.'

'You do?'

'Of course,' he said, nibbling her ear. 'What else?'

She put her hands on his and leaned her head back into him. Of course he wanted exactly what she wanted. It was why they had married each other, after all. Frank just never stated what he thought was the obvious. Well, unless he was on a case. Then he always went back to the obvious. Too often a jumped conclusion at the beginning could derail everything. But he never seemed to use the same approach in his personal life, which had caused him all sorts of problems. Still, his personal life was hers too now. She would just have to make allowances, and remind him from time to time to state the obvious. Once a day for the first five years might do the trick.

She closed her eyes and smiled as he nibbled. She liked the thought that they would be together after five years, and then ten, twenty ... the rest of their lives.

May they live long and prosper.

She just managed to block the voice in her mind which suggested that the obvious question was: how did someone get into that hotel room without being seen? And, more importantly, what was it that had gone wrong in the Simenon's marriage? And what could they have done to avoid it?

After all, it could well be something that the Summers might need to avoid.

But if it involved a bloody kepi she didn't want to know about it.

Perhaps she could ask Tricia Leigh to make some discreet enquiries.

No. Definitely not. Definitely, definitely not.

Normandy. Monday Morning.

Stranger No. 1: Jacques

'I'm still going to nick a kepi, though,' Frank said in a little-boy voice, whispering in her ear.

Frieda sighed and turned around to him. Then she laughed and kissed him.

'My sweet, I'll buy you one, if it means that much to you. You silly noodle.'

'Can't be bought, Free. It has to be nicked.'

'Well, in that case I'll nick one for you, how's that?'

Frank's eyebrows rose.

'Inspector Summers! You naughty woman! What would the Chief Inspector say?'

'Nothing, so long as he doesn't find out,' she said, leaning over him. 'And he doesn't need to know about this either.'

Frank didn't have the time to ask what "this" meant before his lips were covered by Frieda's.

'I think perhaps we should get ourselves a hotel room before we frighten the horses,' Frank said.

'We've got a hotel room,' Frieda replied. 'Why don't we go back there for a siesta after we've seen the museums?'

'Coo-er, missus. Come on then. Let's get these museums out of the way then.'

As they leapt to their feet and Frank picked up his jacket a man appeared from behind a sand dune.

'It's one of Inspector Simenon's men,' Frieda said. 'Probably been watching us. Well, he can bloody well bugger off.'

Frank blinked. Frieda usually couldn't stand swearing of any sort.

'I don't think he is,' he replied, taking in the appearance of the man. 'He looks similar, but from the other side of the tracks, I would say.'

Frieda knew what he meant, but at that moment she had other things on her mind. She went back into detective mode, mentally ticking off the man's appearance. Blue denim trousers, ditto shirt, almost a statement that he was working class. But very expensive and tailored clothing, as if to tell the world that he might come from the working class but he was now a wealthy man. Heavy gold chain around the neck. Trousers too tight. Paunch hanging over them. Late-forties, mid-fifties. A mop of grey-black hair and large moustache, both carefully cultivated to appear dishevelled. Black beret. Pointed, polished brown shoes which suggested that they might be cowboy boots hidden under the jeans. All in all he didn't look as if he was there just for a stroll along the beach.

'Let's give it a test-drive,' Frank suggested. He turned towards the man.

'Bonjour, monsieur,' he called. 'Comment allez vous?' The man paused as if trying to appear surprised.

'You are English?' he asked.

'Mais oui. Nous sont aux Angleterre. Nous sont sur l'honeymoon.'

'You are on a loonymoon?'

'Bloody hell, can't any of the buggers speak French?' Frank muttered to a suddenly giggling Frieda. 'We're on our honeymoon,' he called out.

'Ah, I see,' the other man replied, strolling over. 'Congratulations.'

'Thank you. You wouldn't mind taking a photograph for us?'

'A photograph? But of course.' Frieda handed him the camera. 'Perhaps one with the cliffs behind you, and one with the sea?' he suggested.

'Just what I was thinking,' replied Frank.

The man took a couple of shots and they moved around for the seascapes. He seemed quite at ease with the camera. Once finished he came up and handed it back to Frieda.

'You have come at the best time of the year,' he said. 'Oh, forgive me, allow me to introduce myself. I am Jacques Pointer at your service.'

'Frank and Frieda Summers.' They shook hands, Jacques Pointer very formally with both Frank and Frieda as if he had studied an English etiquette manual at some point and was determined to do it by the book.

'I come here at least once a week,' the man said, waving at the beach and sea. 'My grandfather fought with the Free French during the war. He landed on this very beach on the 6th of June 1944 – the Normandy landings, you understand.'

'Yes,' said Frank, 'that's one of the reasons we chose this part of the coast. We're both interested in history. And we wanted somewhere quiet.'

'Ah, so? Well, that is very good, very good. You had a good wedding?'

'Very good,' said Frieda. 'Your grandfather sounds like an interesting man. What rank was he, if you don't mind me asking?'

'Ah, naturally I would wish him to be at least the colonel, but I am afraid he was merely what you would call a private soldier at the time. He did become sergeant by the time they reached Berlin, but by then there was only himself and two others of his original platoon. But it is, how you say, ancient history? Surely you do not wish to discuss such things today, on your honeymoon.'

'Well, actually –'

'Ah, non, non, of course not. But if you are on honeymoon you must have the honeymoon present.'

'Present, monsieur Pointer? No, really –'

'Please, call me Jacques. You see, I have the little aeroplane. This afternoon I take it for a flight, the engine, you know, it must be used at least once a week, so it is not the bother. And, as a little present, perhaps I can show you the country from the sky?'

'Well, that's very kind, monsieur, er, Jacques, but really –'

Jacques waved a finger.

'Non, you English and your politeness. To me it is no trouble, I fly whichever way, the engine must be used. If you do not like the flying, I understand. If you do, please say yes.'

'Seeing Normandy from the air sounds brilliant,' said Frank. 'What do you say, Free?'

'Well, yes, I would rather like that.'

'Bon! I will pick you up at your hotel after lunch – your half-past-two, non?'

'Half two sounds excellent.'

'Excellent, yes, excellent. Half past the two. Au revoir, madame, monsieur, et bon chance.'

He raised his beret, turned and walked away.

'I'm willing to bet that his grandfather was no more in the

Free French forces than I'm a canary,' Frieda observed as soon as he was out of ear-shot.

'What type of canary?' asked Frank.

'Frank, don't be silly.'

'Sorry. What makes you think he was lying? Apart from the obvious fact that he was?'

'Well, what was your impression of him?'

'I did notice that he was very enthusiastic to change the subject when I mentioned that we were interested in history.'

'Precisely. Within seconds he had us in Berlin with his dear old grandfather who had become a sergeant. As far from the shores of Normandy as possible. And in a Berlin controlled by the Russians.'

'Of course!' exclaimed Frank. 'I must be in holiday mode. This is Omaha beach. The Free French landed with the British, not the Yanks.'

'He could have been a liaison officer of some sort. That's why I asked about his rank. Dear old grandpa landed with his platoon. They wouldn't have had an entire platoon of liaison officers. Or liaison privates. The only way his dear grandpere landed on this beach is if their boat got very lost.'

'Frieda Summers,' he said with an admiring glance, 'I never suspected that you could be so quietly devious. I shall have to watch you.'

She laughed.

'I wasn't promoted entirely because I was a woman with a masters, Frank.'

'Ah. And there was me thinking you'd been promoted because you were such a beautiful and intelligent woman. Tell you what, hang about here while I nip up the ridge there. I want to have another look at our monsieur Jacques before he disappears.'

Frieda didn't hang about. She scrambled up behind Frank, her mind in a bit of a whirl. She was quite immensely pleased at being described as a beautiful woman. At the same time it went entirely against her philosophy. As a police officer looks should definitely never be brought into the issue, whether male or female: competence was the only question. On the other hand, she was now Frank's wife, and it felt extremely good to have your husband tell you that you were a beautiful woman. Your new husband. On honeymoon. Honeymoon, where you are supposed to be strolling along hand in hand falling ever more deeply in love, not scrambling up sand dunes to observe someone without being seen, as if you were on a stake-out. Especially as she wanted to get another look at Jacques Pointer just as much as Frank did. There was something not right about the man.

Jacques, not Frank.

'Interesting,' muttered Frank, lying down at the top of the ridge looking down to a road below. Frieda lay down next to him and they watched Jacques Pointer climb into what appeared to be a dilapidated old truck. Pointer drove off with a clash of gears, the exhaust blowing out a small explosion of black smoke almost as if the truck itself knew it looked old and battered, and was spitting contempt back at the world.

'I'll bet you his other car's a Mercedes,' Frank said as they stood up.

'Either that or a BMW,' agreed Frieda. 'But I think I'd put my money on a Mercedes.'

'Strange.'

'Very.'

'Not the local Godfather.'

'No. Too much of an individual, a loner.'

'Wealthy.'

'Smart dresser.'

'Clothes a little tight. Especially the trousers. As if he were trying to look twenty years younger.'

'But drives a beaten up old truck.'

The truck having disappeared they turned and looked at each other.

'Well,' said Frank, 'no doubt we shall discover a little more about our Monsieur Pointer this afternoon. I don't know what he's after, but he's definitely after something. That meeting was just way too much of a coincidence. And he made a very elementary mistake.'

'Agreed. He said he'd pick us up at the hotel. But he didn't ask the name of the hotel. So he knows who we are.'

'D'accord, madame. Which means that he almost definitely knows about last night and Amelie Courbois. Which is why he was here in the first place.'

'D'accord, mon mari. And now, Mr Summers, shall we forget all about Monsieur Pointer, Mademoiselle Courbois and the rest, and concentrate on us?'

'D'accord trop beaucoup, madame Summers! Let us continue our lovers' stroll. Whatever that might be in French. And then on to les musee.'

He paused, turned and looked out to sea, hands on hips.

'I was thinking of something I read about a German submarine during the war – U505, I think it was. Every time it set out it seemed to get clobbered in one way or another, and had to limp home. The sailors decided that it had a hex on it. What was really happening was that the Allies were getting sufficient Enigma decrypts to help plot the path of many of the German submarines. The Germans never even thought about the possibility, because they presumed Enigma was unbreakable. If they'd approached it logically, doubting everything, as Descartes advised, they might have worked it out. Instead they ended up believing that certain boats are hexed.'

He smiled and shook his head.

'So lovely and peaceful now,' he said looking at the sea below.

While he wasn't looking Frieda took a quick photograph. She suspected it might become a favourite, Frank looking into the distance, that little smile on his face, head outlined by the blue sky behind, his quiff lifting in the slight breeze.

'Come on, Free,' said Frank, turning to her as she slipped the camera out of sight, 'let's retrieve our shoes before the tide nicks them.'

When they returned to pick up their shoes they found Georges Simenon looking at the objects on the ground, Gaspode alongside him, head cocked to one side. Simenon turned as he heard them approaching. His previously frowning face broke into a smile.

'Thank the lord,' he exclaimed. 'I was concerned that someone had gone for the swim and not come back. I could not understand the two pairs of shoes.'

'You were looking for us, Inspector?' asked Frieda.

'No, no, I was taking Gaspode for a walk and myself for a think. We were both interrupted by these. But, all is well, we can continue our walking and thinking. Have a good day, Inspector and Madame Inspector.'

He gave a short bow and walked on, Gaspode trotting at his heels.

'Coincidence?' asked Frieda.

'Well,' said Frank, 'if it was purely coincidence, the only question is who will get more annoyed by the sight of each other – him of us, or us of him?'

He chuckled.

'Let's get to the museums. At least we aren't likely to be bothered by either the local cops or criminal fraternity there.'

'What you said about the U505, Frank,' Frieda said as they strolled on, again hand in hand, 'you weren't thinking about work, were you?'

Frank grinned.

'Not entirely,' he said. 'It also applies to life generally – and us specifically. I like to think we're both reasonably intelligent people. We're in love. So long as we approach things logically we should be able to avoid making the sort of mistakes others do. Such as old Simenon. Whatever his mistake was. We're going to be different.'

Normandy. Monday. Morning.

Frankie, Do You Remember?

'That's one thing,' Frank remarked as they walked around the battered but still solid olive-green Sherman tank in the car park at the front of the Omaha Beach Memorial Museum, 'if you've ever had something like this trundling around you, or had to drive one, it's not something you're likely to forget. As for that landing craft, and that rather nasty looking cannon over there, it's difficult to imagine that they were really once in action.'

'It's called a Long Tom,' Frieda said, reading from a guide book. 'One hundred and fifty-five millimetre calibre. The landing craft is an LCVP – Landing Craft Vehicles and Personnel, I guess. I must look that up.'

'I wonder if they still have one that works. A landing craft, that is. Be nice to take a trip. Maybe a landing on the beach.'

Frieda raised her eyebrows, considering the idea. Then she smiled and nodded at the thought.

'They probably don't, unfortunately, it would be fun. But I'm sure it would be well advertised if there was such a thing. Let's go inside.'

'What we need now,' he said as they strolled towards the entrance, 'is a rousing rendition of Beethoven's Fifth.'

'No, Frank, please, don't try humming it. Your version on the piano is bad enough.'

'There's nothing wrong with my piano playing,' he replied with a pained look. 'I just give it a bit more va-va-voom, that's all.'

She smiled and took his hand.

'Do you remember when you first came to Wellbury, darling?' she asked.

Frank blinked at the sudden question, thought for a few seconds, and then replied with a grin:

'I remember the first time I walked into your office, I was

expecting Medusa's mother-in-law in a bad mood. Pete Phillips did a good job of winding me up about that. Said you were a right ball breaker and that I'd be lucky to get out in one piece.'

'Did he really?' asked Frieda, her lips set. She knew that she was regarded as a strict disciplinarian – at the time it was exactly how she wanted the people at her then new station to see her, strict but fair. But "ball breaker" was going a little too far. Way too far. She would have to do something about Pete Phillips's attitude when they got back.

'Funny thing,' Frank noted, 'I said he was winding me up, but he really did believe it.'

'You don't think I'm – well, a – a little too strict?'

'A ball breaker? Course not, Free. You're a little softie at heart. Hello, a museum shop. And look at all those books. Let's have a quick shufti.'

Frieda wasn't sure that she wanted to be a little softie at heart either. Certainly not all the time. But she also realised that they were now talking about her, and she wanted to talk about him.

'I read your file before you arrived,' she said. 'it was – interesting.'

'Total pack of lies,' he replied. 'You know, I'm always amazed at the different number of books and videos and DVDs on the war. You would think that eventually they'd reach a limit.'

'You read it? Your report?'

'Yes, of course.'

'How did you manage that?'

'Oh,' he replied, his eyes caught by a more than usually lurid book cover, 'the one time at my previous posting I was called in for a bollocking as usual. My boss got caught up in a telephone conversation with some local politician. He had this habit of slouching in his chair, putting his feet up on the windowsill and looking out of the window while he was sucking up to people on the telephone – even used to pick his nose sometimes. I leaned over, picked up the file and read it through before he'd finished. He didn't notice. I managed to correct some spelling mistakes with a red pen while I was at it.'

Frieda would have gasped if she could. The trouble was that she could easily imagine Frank doing just that. It would have appealed to his sense of humour. And she imagined that, by the time he had finished reading the file, he wouldn't have given a damn. It was full of code words – "unorthodox", "unusual", "accident prone", "excessive zeal", "sometimes impaired judgement" – which identified the then Detective Sergeant Frank Summers as a dangerous maverick, a law unto himself, a loose cannonball who drank too much and often put in extra time in the cells convincing suspects to confess using less than acceptable methods. A man who had reached the top of his promotion ladder and wouldn't be going anywhere else. Apart from the dumping ground for such people known as Wellbury.

Frieda hadn't realised that Wellbury was a dumping ground for problem people. It was Detective Inspector Percy Hanson who had unwittingly informed her of this when he had innocently asked her, "So, what did you do wrong to get sent here?" It was the first and last time Percy had ever used such a chatty all-mates-together tone with her. When she had finished interrogating him as to his meaning he was allowed to leave to retire to his office and defrost on his radiator, where he informed Pete Phillips of the new detective inspector's nickname: Frigid.

Frieda, back in her office then, wasn't quite frigid. In fact she was close to spitting burning coals. She had worked hard to get where she was, and intended to go much further. She had invariably been top of the class when doing courses and exams. She had kept her relationships with other officers professional and objective. Everything was sublimated to the job. Efficiency. She accepted that there was invariably a good deal of politics going on, but she had avoided that as far as possible. When she had been promoted to detective inspector – a little later than some of the men at her own level who were never as good as her, to her mind – and been sold the posting to Wellbury as the place for an ambitious officer to make her mark, she had little realised that she was well and truly being conned. Finally a snippet of conversation overheard before the posting came began to take on a light quite different to the one in which she had originally viewed it.

"Garold," her boss at the time had said to a detective inspector in his office as Frieda had been passing. "That's a German name, isn't it? Frieda's also German sounding, isn't it?"

"Teutonic efficiency, guv," replied the other man.

"Well, efficiency should be rewarded, don't you think? Especially Teutonic efficiency."

"Dead right, guv. We could send her to Germany?"

Had Frieda stayed longer she would have overhead the sniggers that had followed this suggestion. Instead she had quickly moved on, neither approving of eavesdropping nor wanting to be caught doing so.

At the time she had blushed at what she had thought was unqualified praise. Only after she had drained Percy of definite proof that Wellbury was considered a dumping ground did she realise that, had she stayed around to listen to the rest of the conversation, she would sooner or later have hear her boss ask: "So what are we going to do with that bloody woman?"

Not one to rue the unfairness of life while the means of revenge were not to hand – and when they became so they would be used with clinical precision – she decided to continue with her determination to see that her section of the almost rural backwater of Wellbury would be the most efficient in the world. Beginning with the new detective sergeant she had been assigned, who, from his file was a law-breaking, whisky-drinking, tough-bitten, aged sergeant of the old school.

Thus it was that her first encounter with Frank Summers was one of confusion. Initially she had presumed that the nervous but smartly dressed young man with a winning smile who had entered her office had somehow managed to squeeze himself in ahead of Sergeant Summers. It was quite apparent that the young man would have the ability to charm himself to the top of the queue, and that Sergeant Summers was the type who would willingly postpone an interview with a senior officer, letting a younger and more impatient officer go in ahead of him. Summers was undoubtedly sitting slouched in a chair outside her office right at that moment, tie loose, shoes scuffed, probably unshaven. It was the ideal opportunity to both teach the young man in her office not to try it on with her, and to teach Detective Sergeant Summers outside her office that when Inspector Garold told him to report to her that was exactly what he would do.

Fortunately the young man had left her office door open. No doubt it was in the hope that the interview would be over quickly and he could get back to work. It meant that she didn't have to stand up to call in Summers sitting outside in her secretary's office. She fixed the young man with a stare that unequivocally told him not to even think of saying a word.

'Sergeant Summers!' she called out in a loud and firm voice.

The young man in front her blinked and took a step back.

'Er, yes, Inspector?' he asked.

She frowned at him and called out again:

'Sergeant Summers!'

The young man looked behind him as if expecting to find some hidden person, and then turned back to her.

'Um, I am Sergeant Summers, Inspector. Sergeant Frank Summers.'

She looked back at him dispassionately. Within minutes Detective Sergeant Frank Summers had made his first mistake. He had made her feel foolish.

When she had originally read his file she had gone for what she regarded as the meat, reviews, progress reports, ignoring such details as photograph and date of birth. Now she flicked through a few pages of the file idly. Not revealing that she was checking his date of birth. Not showing her surprise when she realised that he was only a few months younger than she was.

'Sergeant,' she said slowly, looking at him over her reading glasses, 'I want you to know that I run everything by the book.'

'Yes, Inspector.'

'By the book, Sergeant.'

A pause, as if he were trying to work out why this inspector was repeating herself like a pompous idiot. She was glad of the pause. It gave her a chance to try to work out how to stop sounding like the pompous senior officer she was doing such a good job of being.

'Yes, Inspector,' he replied finally.

'I expect my officers to report for duty on time, Sergeant.'

He gave a nervous look at his watch and looked around for a clock to confirm that the watch had somehow, unbelievably, stopped working.

'Um, well, sorry, Inspector, I could have sworn I was on time, my watch has been working perfectly for years, I don't know –'

'I don't mean today!' she snapped, realising that his interpretation of what she had said was perfectly justified. 'I meant as a general rule.'

'Ah, right,' he replied, giving his watch another puzzled look, as if apologising for doubting it, and asking it if it knew what the hell this strange woman was going on about.

'And I expect my officers to finish work on time too, Sergeant. No unauthorised overtime. No trying to cash in on the overtime budget. No going out for a few drinks, getting any bright ideas, and coming back to the station for informal interviews of suspects without their lawyers present.

Understand?'

He grinned, a flash of relief temporarily replacing the nervous puzzlement, his eyes lighting up with the mischievous look she was to come to recognise and regret.

'I can promise you, Inspector, I shall not work one minute longer than necessary. I'll even sign that promise with my very own signature.'

'I think we can do without the tautology, Sergeant,' she said, closing his file, putting it to one side and opening another. 'Dismissed.'

He left her office with an impressive fluidity. One second he was standing in front of her, the next she could just catch his voice saying something to her secretary in the outer office. Her secretary at the time – the one before Tricia Leigh – had replied with a chuckle, and then there was silence.

Frieda sat frowning at the door for some time after, that phrase running around her mind: "my very own signature". Coming from someone such as Desk Sergeant Eric Johns it would have been tautology. She was beginning to suspect that Frank Summers had meant it differently, that, if he didn't agree with something, he would quite happily sign it with someone else's signature, quite probably Michael Mouse's.

Or even, perhaps, her own.

She had expected Sergeant Summers to be a certain type of trouble. After that first meeting she had realised that he was going to be a different type of trouble, though she wasn't then quite sure what type it would be. She certainly never expected at that time that he would turn out to be the type of trouble which one day would be titled "My husband". It had taken her some while before things began moving in that direction, and even then that had been almost entirely subconscious.

She ignored the voice in her head that suggested that going undercover to a barbecue as Frank's girlfriend, which is what she had done during his first case in Wellbury, hardly required a Freudian interpretation.

'What did you do to get things like that on your file?' she asked, bringing herself back to the present, a present in which Frank was still scanning the books on offer with the look of someone working out good reasons to buy most of them.

'Oh, you know, a couple of unfortunate mix-ups. Plus my sergeant took a dislike to me before he ever saw me, and the inspector. They both came from working class backgrounds, they thought I was some kind of a toff. And they didn't like people who had been to university.' He chuckled. 'In a way I felt sorry for them, because by that stage it wasn't unusual to have working class kids going to university, that confused them. It wasn't the way the world should work, according to their way of thinking.'

'Didn't you feel angry towards them? Bitter?'

'I suppose I did, from time to time. But it's all in the past, they were dinosaurs even then, I'm sure they'll be retired by now, growing roses badly, spending the entire day complaining about how the world's gone to pot – and pissing off their wives who probably wish them dead, or at least not under their feet the whole day.'

Despite his joking tone Frieda sensed that Frank rather liked that image. His old tormentors spending their retirement being bossed around by their wives.

'How do you see us growing old, Frank?'

'Us? We'll never grow old, Free. Physically, maybe, but not

107

mentally. I shall still be making terrible jokes when I'm ninety, and you'll still smile at them and tell me how awful they are. I suppose it would be silly to buy anything here. We could get it cheaper on the Internet.'

'While I'm sitting in my armchair knitting, you in your armchair reading the newspaper.'

'Who knows? Maybe I'll be the one knitting and you'll be reading the newspaper. If there are still such things as newspapers by then. Perhaps all our news will come on a large screen on the lounge wall. Newspapers might be banned because they waste the earth's resources. Who cares? All that matters is now. All that matters now is that we're together.'

He gave her a kiss.

'You're a romantic at heart, aren't you, Frank Summers?' she said, squeezing his hand.

'I thought that's why you married me, Frieda Summers. Can't think of any other reason. Certainly wasn't because of my good looks or fortune, because I don't have either.'

She smiled. Suddenly it all felt right. Suddenly she hadn't a care in the world. She would be quite happy to spend the rest of her life in that moment. The sun shining outside, the blue sea, the golden beach, that little cloud just on the horizon, a little cloud of doubt in her mind.

'Frank – Jacques Pointer. Don't you think we should give him a miss? I mean, if he's involved in this heroin business – well, it isn't anything to do with us, and if he is a crook it could turn nasty.'

'Nah, Free, it won't turn nasty. He's just like Simenon, looking for information. Let's go have a look at the exhibits.'

'We could find ourselves driven to a deserted warehouse and

kept hostage.'

'Pointer's a loner. He doesn't have a gang of die-hards waiting in a warehouse to surround us. And he wouldn't try it on his own. He's just sniffing about. And he's not very good at it. I'd be more worried about Gaspode sniffing about than Pointer.'

Frieda thought about that. She had to admit that Frank did have a point. If Jacques Pointer was the head of a gang of criminals and wanted to get some information from them he wouldn't have arranged the supposedly accidental meeting on the beach. It would have been a squeal of wheels and their being tumbled into the back of a darkened van in a back street somewhere.

'And while he's looking for information,' Frank continued, 'we'll enjoy a view of Normandy from the air. We're going to get a lot more out of him than he's going to get out of us.'

He chuckled.

'You know, if he does have something to do with Amelie Courbois and the missing heroin, we'll be in the best position to work out just what is going on. On the one side we have Simenon giving us information without realising it, on the other our new friend Jacques Pointer. Between them we should get enough pieces of the jigsaw.'

'We are not going to get involved, Frank.'

'Course not, Free. Isn't there a section showing a depiction of everyday French life before the invasion? I want to see if it fits my theory that average people are pretty much the same everywhere, just that circumstances differ.'

'And if it doesn't?'

'Well, we'll have to rearrange it a bit then while no-one is looking. For the sake of verisimilitude, of course.'

Frieda didn't really believe that Frank would actually do any such a thing, but she kept watch on him to make sure that he didn't. He had a look in his eyes which reminded her of a little boy itching to take things apart to see how they worked. At least it helped to keep her mind off Jacques Pointer. The more she thought about the morning, the more she felt that the sensible thing would be to stay well away from both Simenon and Pointer.

Or, to be more accurate, to keep Frank well away from both Simenon and Pointer.

For just a brief second she wished that Frank had more usual pre-occupations, such as being a fanatical supporter of his chosen football club.

Normandy. Monday. Afternoon.

Waltz of the bumble bee

Jacques Pointer turned up at the hotel at the agreed time. The cowboy boots had been replaced by comfortable casual shoes. And true to their expectations he drove a Mercedes. A gleaming, purring, silver Mercedes which looked as if it had just had a wash and polish by a team of experts. His aircraft, on the other hand, when they arrived at the airfield, rather than a deserted warehouse, was in somewhat different condition. 'My little Bumble Bee,' Jacques said proudly. He noticed the surprise on Frank and Frieda's faces as they looked at a rather dirty, single-engined little aircraft with oil-stained streaks along the sides and wings.

'Oh, please, do not worry about those,' he said, a little embarrassed. 'They are just for the show, as you say. They do not come from the engine, I had to come out at night to put them there.'

'At night?'

'For show?'

'Ah, yes, er, for the show. You see, I have a cousin who, I do not know how to say this in English, but, well, for him everything has to be perfect. His bow tie must be straight. His shirts must be ironed just so. His trousers pressed precisely. He sees the speck on the shoe, he quivers. He too has the plane here. It is kept in a hangar, cleaned every day. I like to keep my little Bee with the oil stains close to his hangar. It upsets him. Even the name upsets him. It is English, oui?'

'Yes,' nodded Frank. 'You have what we would call sibling rivalry, only in reverse, as it were.'

'But the, um, engine,' said Frieda, 'and the wings, those sort of things, they're all in good order?'

'Oh, yes, madame, perfect order. After all, I have no wish to come crashing out of the sky. No, you have no need to fear, Bee is a strong little aircraft, and I am a good pilot. Please, get in.'

Frank climbed into the front seat alongside Jacques. Frieda sat in the seat behind Jacques, much less happy with the state of the aircraft than Frank.

'Dual control?' said Frank as he strapped himself in, looking at the joystick in front of him.

'Yes, monsieur.'

'Don't touch that, Frank,' warned Frieda, carefully checking that her own safety belt was tightly tied.

'Ah, flying is quite simple,' Jacques said. 'Look, you take hold of the joystick. You see the pedals at your feet?'

'Don't touch those either, Frank.' Jacques laughed.

'When we are in the air you fly her,' he said. 'But first let me take her off. Ah, a moment, some music. I always play the music when I am driving or flying. I burn my own CDs. This is the word, yes, "burn"?'

'As far as I'm aware,' said Frank. 'Why, I've never understood.'

Pointer raised his eyebrows as if to say "Yes? What a strange language!" and pushed a button. The sound of Johnny Hallyday came softly out of the speakers.

'It takes four CDs,' he said as they taxied towards take off. 'My cousin, his big shiny plane has a music player which takes one. So I have put in this, so I can tell him my little Bee has a music player which can take four. It irritates him.'

Frieda was concerned that Jacques might have decided to fly in a manner which would also irritate his cousin. But during the take-off and while ascending his physical manner changed from sloppy and carefree to that of a man comfortable with, and concentrating on, flying.

'There is nothing like flying,' he said once they had reached cruising height. 'The views, ah, beautiful! And the feeling of freedom, of tranquillity, ah!'

'It's gorgeous,' said Frieda. 'You can see the whole countryside. The beaches, the bocage ...'

'Biggest problem the Allies faced, the bocage,' said Frank, looking down. 'Looks very pretty from up here, but they were almost like solid walls to the troops below. Good defensive terrain.'

'Did your grandfather mention the bocage?' asked Frieda. 'I'm sure he must have. Having to face German troops armed with the panzerfaust and such, without being able to see them. Not knowing what lay around the next twist in the road ahead.'

'Ah, yes, my grandfather. Well, he saw such terrible sights – terrible, terrible. He never spoke of it ever again.'

'But he must have mentioned it if you know about it.'

'Ah, yes, but there is an explanation for that. You see – you would like to see Pegasus Bridge? We fly there.'

'Oh, go on then,' said Frank.

'Which unit was your grandfather in?' asked Frieda.

'Unit? Ah, I do not know. Details. Details. I have never been good with details. Numbers, names. But come, monsieur, I promised to let you fly a little. I think you will enjoy the experience.'

'That's okay, Monsieur Pointer,' Frieda said hurriedly, 'Frank doesn't want to fly, do you, Frank?'

'It looks like fun,' said Frank. 'And it looks quite easy.'

'It is almost as easy as driving a car,' Jacques said. 'I like this comparison. Because you must remember how it is when you first learn to drive a car. You make many mistakes. Maybe you think you will never learn to drive. Perhaps you fail your test. I failed five times. My cousin, he passed first time, with distinction, or so he claims. In France this is not easy, to fail. But then you pass. And you drive every day. Finally you do not even think about it. It is as natural as walking. Of course take-off and landing, they are different, but flying, it is like driving the car. But also you have the good drivers and the bad drivers.'

'I like to think that I'm a pretty good driver.'

'Come, monsieur, take the joystick and put your foot on the

pedal.'

Frieda closed her eyes.

'Hey, that's brilliant!' exclaimed Frank. 'See, Free, nothing to it.'

Frieda closed her eyes tighter and held firmly onto the door handle as the plane rocked and seemed to hit a speed bump in the air.

'Whoops!' said Frank. 'No, it's okay, I've got it.'

'Gently, monsieur, gently, you have to treat her like a young wo – like a young horse, to keep her under control, but gently so.'

'I've always thought of taking up flying,' said Frank. 'Can't afford it, though. Pity.'

'You cannot afford it?' asked Jacques, trying to give the impression that it was merely a polite question.

'We're both police officers, monsieur. You don't tend to earn enough to own an airplane.'

'Ah, yes? Police. In England?'

'Yes. A place called Wellbury. Nice little town.'

'That is interesting, very interesting. I too thought once of becoming the police officer. You must have interesting experiences, chasing criminals?'

'Oh, comme si, comme sa. A lot of it's rather boring, really. Criminals don't tend to be geniuses. Occasionally you come across something different, but it's unusual.'

'No drugs heists? Bullion jobs?'

Frank laughed. Frieda opened her eyes. Jacques was trying to circle towards his real interest. Frank was still flying the plane. That would explain the occasional strange side-to-side and up-and-down movement of the plane that she had felt. She shut her eyes again.

'No, I'm afraid not, Monsieur Pointer. Wellbury's too small to have a real drugs problem. You might find a few ounces of something if you're very lucky, but our criminals don't tend to deal in crates of the stuff. As for bullion robberies, no luck, I'm afraid.'

'Ah, I see. Perhaps I take the control back, we need to turn before we disappear over the horizon.'

'Okay,' said Frank, reluctantly handing the controls back. Frieda opened her eyes again and sighed with relief.

'You don't have much crime around here, I presume,' said Frank.

'I do not think so. I run a few businesses, we have little thefts, I read of fights on the weekend some times, but not the big crime. There was once the body found drowned on the beach, but that was many years ago. And it appears that it was an accident. Paris, that is where you find the grand crime. The grand government and the grand crime.'

'What sort of businesses?' asked Frank, looking out of the window. 'Hello, there's another little plane. Looks like he's coming up from the side.'

Jacques turned and briefly glanced back in the direction Frank was looking before returning his concentration to flying.

'Keep the eye on him for me, monsieur,' he said. 'He is close. He should not be so close. As I say, there are good drivers and bad drivers. I do not wish to be the accident of the bad driver.'

'He's flying parallel to us now. He's looking at us through a telescope. Wait a minute – bloody hell, that's a rifle.'

The glass in the window next to him starred. The next second their plane tipped to one side and began diving for the ground. The sudden movement caused Frieda to grab hold of the door handle again. Frank's head whipped sideways and cracked against the window. The CD skipped. The volume soared. Meatloaf began screaming about fires howling down in the valley below.

'What the –' Frank turned to find Jacques slumped over the joystick. He grabbed hold of the joystick in front of him for support as the dive became a spin. The thought came immediately.

'Free!' Frank yelled. 'Pull him back. I'm going to get us out of this dive.'

'Frank, you can't fly this thing,' Frieda cried, too busy with holding on to attend to Jacques.

'It's either that or end up as a blot of fucking strawberry jam all over the French countryside.'

He hauled at the controls, pulling as strongly and gently as he could from side to side, trying to get a response from the aircraft. After endless seconds it reacted, engine howling. The next thing they were spiralling straight up instead of straight down. The CD skipped again and Edith Piaf took over the bawling with "Non! Je ne regrette rien! Ni le bien! Qu'on m'a fait!"

'Right,' Frank shouted, sweat beginning to drip towards his eyes, 'I've got it now. Where is that little Fokker?'

'On our left, down below, a couple of hundred feet,' called Frieda, her face squashed against the window by the centrifugal force. 'Frank, you aren't thinking of doing anything silly, are you?'

'Right, here we go. Let's ask them a few questions in Braille.'

'Frank!'

'Hold on to Jacques, Free, his head keeps bumping around and getting in the way.'

Frieda forced herself forward against the bucketing flight of the plane and grabbed hold of the back of Jacque's seat. She managed to get a grip on his hair with her other hand. It wasn't much, but at least she was doing something. It was either that or hit Frank and tell him to stop being stupid. And right at that moment at least Frank was keeping their plane from dropping out of the sky. Or at least he had managed to avoid hitting the ground so far. Besides which the four-CD player had now skipped again and was playing Wagner. The Ride of the Valkyries. Loudly. Very loudly. Too loud to shout against it.

Frank tilted the aircraft to set it into a slight dive He was aiming it at the other plane. Bee seemed to understand the idea, but bucked left and right on the way. Frieda wanted to cry out. But she knew that he was following one of his core beliefs. It wasn't what you intended to do that was important. It was what the other person thought that you were going to do that was important. And even at that distance she sensed a puzzled look coming from the other plane. They did not know who was piloting the aircraft bearing down on them in what appeared to be crab-like sidesteps. They didn't know what his intentions were. But they could undoubtedly see that they were in grave danger of being hit.

'Right you son of a bitch, take this,' Frank yelled. He coerced Bee into the attack. The plane rolled, shuddered and jarred, but vaguely followed his intentions. The other pilot took one look at the aircraft behind and turned into a dive. Frank followed. Within a minute both aircraft were barely above ground level. The pilot in front desperately jinked for cover. Bee desperately tried to stay airborne. Suddenly they seemed to hit an air pocket. Meatloaf returned to rage that he would be gone when morning comes. Frank pulled at the joystick and their plane lifted and swung to the right. The pilot in front looked at his rear-view mirror and turned around to see why. He immediately looked back to the front for any obstacle he hadn't seen. There was a low-flying tree just in front. He pulled desperately into a curve upwards. Up and away from Frank and Frieda. The turns slowly brought each plane around. They were now flying directly towards each other.

'Frank, we're going to hit him!' Frieda yelled. 'Pull left!'

'I think he's going to pull left,' Frank called back. 'I'll break right.'

Frank was right in one sense. The other pilot broke to his left. But it was Frank's right. They continued on their collision course.

'Pull left, Frank! Pull left!'

'I am bloody pulling flucking left!'

Frank tried to haul Bee gently to the left. Meatloaf screamed that if he gotta be damned he wanna be damned. The two planes came within fifty metres of each other. The other pilot pulled the nose of his aircraft up in an attempt to gain height. For a second the nose was pointing vertically. Then the engine coughed, died and the nose sank. At thirty metres it was back directly in their path. At twenty it had dropped just below. They passed about five metres above it as it plunged towards the ground. The pilot frantically over-compensated and swung it around from side to side. Finally it hit the ground in a field. It slithered for a while before commencing a series of circles and eventually coming to a stop.

'That'll teach you to mess with the Blue Baron, sunshine,' Frank breathed, his eyes bright. Bee was heading upwards again, with a nod to left and right as she went, and a little bump for the CD player. Edith Piaf returned with "Non! Rien de rien! Non! Je ne regrette rien!"

'Darling, I was going to suggest you come to earth.' Frieda paused to take a breath and get a firmer grip on Jacques's hair. 'But I have a horrible feeling that that might be our main problem.' She took another breath. 'Darling, would you terribly mind trying to fly straight and level? This going up and down all the time is making me dizzy. I'm not sure how long I can keep lunch where it's supposed to be.'

Frank almost giggled. He had a mad look in his eyes. The sweat was now pouring down his face.

'Ah, straight and level, good point Free. I'll do my best. Come on, Bee, you can do it!'

He grinned as he eased the stick forward and the plane assumed a more horizontal flight. Relatively horizontal. Each sudden left swing was compensated by a radical right swing in the air. From the ground it would have appeared that Bee was attempting a waltz.

'God! That was fun!' he said.

'No, Frank, that wasn't fun. That was bloody terrifying.'

'Ah, come on, Free. Just the way you drive your Range Rover sometimes.' He giggled again.

Frieda thought of all sorts of replies. Such as she only did that sort of a thing in an emergency. And she didn't always take corners on two wheels. And this wasn't a Range Rover, it was an aeroplane.

'Frank, two points. One, I'm not in the driver's seat at the moment. And, two, I don't think that parking this thing is going to be a simple process. It doesn't appear to have a reverse, for a start.'

'Ah, yes. Landing. Jacques said that that was the difficult part. I keep wanting to step on the brakes, which would not be a good idea.' He exhaled, wiped his brow with the back of his wrist and then quickly grabbed the joystick with both hands as the plane bucked violently. 'You know, it's at times like this that I wonder what old Epicurus would have said.'

'And what do you suppose he would have said right now?'

'Why on earth did you want to do something so bloody silly as to get into that ridiculous little machine, I would imagine. Look, Free, the sea's over there to our left. I reckon our best chance is to try for a landing on the beach. I'll see if I can't break the wheels off as we come in so that we slide in rather than go arse over tip.'

Frieda was reminded of something Frank's mother had said of him: "There isn't anything he doesn't believe he can't do until he tries." Unfortunately trying and failing here would not be quite the same as attempting to do a somersault and landing on your backside on the grass.

Slide in rather than go arse over tip?

She could imagine the arse over tip conclusion more easily than the sliding in.

'Frank, why don't we fly in circles for a while and see if we can get some help over the radio?'

'Good thinking, Free. It will also help burn off petrol. Don't want to have to bring this baby in with too much on board.'

Frieda looked at the side of his head. She appeared to be thinking of punching it. The only two things which held her back was that her one hand was desperately locked on the back of Jacques's seat as she bumped up and down in her seat, the other was still grasping Jacques's hair.

'Thank you for that insight, Frank,' she shouted. 'And to think I was only worried about being killed during crash landing. Now I can worry about petrol exploding at the same time. You don't have any other delightful scenarios to share, do you?'

'We'll probably be okay, Free,' he yelled.

'Probably?'

'Well, it can't be that difficult, can it? I'm not saying it will be the smoothest landing anyone has seen, but if you think about it, all we really have to do is watch our shadow as we approach ground. That will tell us how close we are. Whoah, Bee, calm down, calm down.'

Frieda leaned forward and studied the side of his face. She recognised the look. It was the one he always wore when he didn't have a clue, but was desperately hoping something would turn up. Somehow at that moment she would have preferred the confident look.

'Aren't you going to try the radio?' she suggested.

'Okay,' he called back above the noise. 'I'm just a little worried about taking one hand off the controls. They keep jumping for some reason. Maybe the ailerons got hit. I don't suppose you could reach the radio from where you are?'

'I don't think so. I can try, but – is there any chance that you could switch that infernal noise off? Give the blasted thing a clout.'

Frank risked hitting the CD player quickly with his fist before again grabbing hold of the joystick. Suddenly Johnny Hallyday calmed and soothed the air once more with his own version of blues and rock. There was a groan beside Frank.

'What's that, Free?'

'That wasn't me, Frank. I think Monsieur Jacques is coming to.' She peered at the Frenchman's head. 'It's a crease wound, Frank! I think he might be alright. We must have missed him groaning under that music.'

'Well, slap him round a little. We need the bastard awake long enough to land this bloody thing. I mean this lovely airplane. Sorry, Bee, you're a lovely little plane. A lovely, lovely, gorgeous little plane. Just stop bloody jumping around the whole time, for Christ's sake!'

'He's calling for someone called Emily. Monsieur Pointer, wake up. Come on, wake up!'

Jacques groaned again. Frieda shook his shoulders roughly. Then she slapped him hard around his head.

'Eh? Eh?' he demanded, his eyes blinking open.

'Wakey, wakey, monsieur,' Frank called. 'We need you for a few minutes to land this thing. After that you can nod off again.'

'Eh?' asked the Frenchman.

'You know, this is an excellent time to ask him a few questions about Amelie Courbois and the heroin,' Frank suggested. 'Before he regains consciousness fully and realises what's happening.'

Frieda stared at him in disbelief.

'Frank?'

'Yes?'

'Just concentrate on keeping the fucking plane in the fucking air, okay?'

'Yes, my sweetness.'

'Monsieur Pointer!' Frieda shouted directly into Pointer's ear. 'Wake up! Now! Allez!'

'She didn't mean that, Bee,' Frank whispered to the plane. 'She doesn't normally use language like that.' Bee acknowledged this by nodding her nose up and down. Jacques turned to look at Frieda, his eyes wide.

'You?' he asked. He looked at Frank. 'What has happened?'

'Would you like the full story or just the summary?' asked Frank.

'I think the summary will be sufficient,' Frieda said. 'Monsieur Pointer, you remember there was another plane flying alongside us?'

'Another plane? What plane? Where are you? Where am me?'

'Okay, we'll keep this simple,' Frieda said quietly in his ear, in the tone of voice teachers have used for centuries to terrify pupils. 'We are in your plane in the sky, the Bumble Bee, understand? You were shot. It isn't serious. What is serious is that Frank here has never flown a plane before in his life, and doesn't know how to land it. So the question is, are you going to land this thing properly, or do you fancy the excitement of seeing if my new husband has a guardian angel looking after him – and the rest of us?'

'A guardian – I do not understand.'

'Monsieur Pointer,' Frieda said slowly, 'take the controls of this blasted thing and land it. Comprenez vous?'

Monsieur Jacques blinked and then gave a brief nod, wincing.

'Land this blasted thing,' he said, and slowly took the joystick in his hand. He looked out the window and muttered to himself. He looked ahead and did some more muttering. Still muttering, he checked the instruments in front of him. Finally he nodded.

'I know where we are. At the moment we are headed towards Portsmouth. Or perhaps the end of Ireland. We need to turn around.'

'Good idea,' said Frank. 'We haven't finished our honeymoon, and our clothes and stuff are back in Normandy. Anyway, I don't think British customs like unscheduled flights popping up on their radar screens. The RAF might get a little upset too.'

'French customs are the same, Monsieur Inspector, I do not think we have flown too far out for them to become suspicious, but we may have some flics waiting at the airfield for to ask us the questions.'

'Oh, I wouldn't worry about that, monsieur,' said Frank, breathing out and closing his eyes for a second, stretching and flexing his wrists and hands. 'I think I can guarantee that there will be some flics at the airfield wanting to ask us lots of questions. And I bet you the buggers won't have brought any refreshments along. I could do with a nice cuppa right now.'

'Eh?'

Frieda looked down and noticed that they had just passed over the coast and were again heading inland. The trouble was that she recognised none of it.

'Monsieur Pointer,' she interrupted, 'you do know where

you're going, don't you? I don't want to cast doubt on your abilities, but you are sure you know where we are?'

'Mais oui, madame, certainly.' He pointed at a device attached to the screen in front of him. 'Satellite navigation. I could never read the map properly. My cousin, he is good with maps. There, you can see the airfield ahead, a few kilometres away.'

'Well, the flics will be there alright,' muttered Frank as he spotted two cars far below heading towards the airfield, the front one with blue lights flashing on its roof, and no doubt siren going. 'So, tell me, monsieur Pointer, why would someone want to shoot you down?'

'Me?' asked Jacques in surprise. 'They were not shooting at me, they were shooting at you.'

'Oh? And why were they shooting at us, then?'

Jacques gave him a quick side glance which showed that he thought Frank was obviously mad, and dangerously so.

'I must concentrate on the landing,' he said, 'other than that I know nothing. Nothing. You understand, nothing. I understand nothing.'

'Ah, the good old rien,' murmured Frank. 'There's a lot of that going around.'

Jacques brought the plane in to a bumpy landing, swearing and muttering under his breath. He taxied it close to its stand, switched the engine off, closed his eyes and sighed with relief. He wasn't alone. Both Frank and Frieda leaned back in their own seats and closed their eyes.

'Well, thank flip for that,' said Frank.

'At this rate I am going to take up swearing again,' said Frieda, 'on a serious basis.'

Jacques appeared to be saying the rosary quietly and very, very fast. Frieda opened her eyes, leaned forward and checked his head.

'I think you need to see a doctor,' she said.

'Ha! Doctor? Non, I –' He turned and saw Frank. 'Yes, doctor,' he decided, 'I will see the doctor. Toute suite, as you say.'

He opened his door, dropped to the ground, stumbled, and then scuttled off on unsteady legs.

'Strange man,' commented Frank, watching two uniformed police officers step in front of the hurrying Jacques. He opened his door and dropped down. 'Come, my Poppy,' he said as she opened hers. He held his arms up for her.

'I'm okay, Frank,' she said. 'A little shaken up, but okay.'

'I'm not. I need someone to lean on,' he said, putting his arm around her shoulders. She looked up at him, smiled and put her arms around his waist. She could feel his muscles, both taut and trembling.

'Let's go sit over there,' said Frank, motioning towards some old chairs next to the hangar, used, presumably, by mechanics when taking a break in the sun.

'I see our friend Inspector Simenon is here,' Frieda said as she helped Frank to the chairs. Simenon was leaning against a car bonnet, arms folded, with Gaspode sitting alertly at his feet.

'I'll order tea when the waiter comes,' Frank said as they sank into two chairs. 'Deux the, s'il vous plait, garcon,' he called as Simenon walked slowly up, hands in the pockets of his coat.

'I have asked the mechanic to get some tea,' Simenon said. He looked at them before slumping into another chair, opposite them. 'So, monsieur inspector, madame inspector, you have had an exciting afternoon.'

'Bloody marvellous,' said Frank passing the back of his hand over his brow, head back, eyes closed. 'We came here on our honeymoon. First we find ourselves in the middle of a drugs operation, then we get shot at in a light aircraft. I'm thinking of writing to the Times to commend this place as an ideal honeymoon resort. More excitement than you can shake a stick at.'

'What is going on, Inspector?' asked Frieda. 'Are you going to tell us, or are you just going to shrug your shoulders and practice looking inscrutable?'

Simenon looked as if he were about to shrug his shoulders, then changed his mind.

'I do not know,' he said. 'Nothing like this has ever happened before.'

A nervous mechanic came up with three mugs of tea, handed one to each, and left quickly with a worried glance at Simenon. Simenon nodded his thanks without looking at the man and took a sip.

'Were they shooting at you, or Jacques?' he asked, almost to himself.

Frank and Frieda looked at each other and then back to Simenon.

'You know Jacques?' asked Frieda. Simenon nodded.

'Oh, yes. We have been – what is the word, acquaintances? – since we were little children. Not quite enemies, not quite friends – perhaps amicable enemies.' He smiled. 'For years I have tried to find a reason to arrest him. For years he has smiled at me and been insolently polite. Cocked the snuck, as you say.'

'Cocked a snook,' corrected Frieda.

'Yes, cocked the snuck. But, as the great Buffon once noted, *le genie est une longue patience*. Or as you say in English, patience is a virtue. My time will come.'

'He's a crook?' asked Frank.

Simenon shrugged.

'For some around here that is like asking whether a man breathes. He has businesses, legitimate, no doubt he breaks tax laws, but that is not for me, the tax. But he does not involve himself with things like drugs, that is not his style.' He took another sip of his tea and admired the chipped mug. 'Tell me, how did you meet him?'

'We bumped into him purely by accident on the beach. He claimed he was taking a stroll where his grandfather had landed during the Normandy invasion. His grandfather was with the Free French forces.'

Simenon smiled thinly.

'If you put together all the grandpères who served in the Free French and all the grandmères who were in the Resistance there would not be space enough for them in all France. And if you looked for a collaborator you would find that both of them fled to Argentina and no-one knows any of their relatives.'

'And which was your grandfather?' asked Frank. 'Free French or Resistance?'

Simenon gave him a cool look.

'He was a police officer, Inspector. Just like I am today. And just like I am today, no doubt he was often puzzled and confused, unsure and uncertain.'

'Jacques Pointer,' said Frieda. 'You know him. Why would he arrange to bump into us?'

'He is Amelie's uncle. Amelie has a large family. They are all proud of her, and protective. Jacques has little love for most humans, but for Amelie I think he would do anything.'

'Anything?' asked Frieda.

'Ah,' said Frank, 'the family. A bit like the Sicilians, the Cosa Nostra and such.'

'Non, monsieur, just a very big family who like nothing better to fight amongst each other, unless an outsider joins in, in which case they all fight the outsider before returning to fight amongst each other again.'

'And we are the outsiders?' asked Frieda.

'I think that is what Jacques wanted to find out,' Simenon said. 'Are you just a couple on honeymoon, as you say, or are you from some criminal gang who have tried to kill their little Amelie? If the first, they have no wish to hurt you – they do not pick the argument with innocent tourists on honeymoon, especially not innocent English police officers. If the second ... they will not stop until they have their revenge.'

'But why would anyone want to shoot at us?' asked Frieda. 'If they weren't sure about us?'

'Why would anyone want to shoot at Jacques?' asked Simenon.

Frank put his mug down and leaned forward, rubbing his temple.

'The question is, why would anyone take off in a light plane and take pot shots at another plane with a rifle? If you're trying to kill someone, it's a pretty inefficient way of doing it. It isn't even an efficient way of scaring someone. Your chances of actually hitting the other aircraft are almost nil – Jacques was incredibly unlucky to get hit. Normally you'd be able to float around the sky thumbing your nose at anyone trying it on. A light aircraft is just not stable enough a gun platform. One second the rifle would be too high, the next too low. It would be all over the place. There are much better ways of doing that sort of thing.'

Simenon put his own mug down and rubbed his cheek.

'What you say is true.' He frowned. 'Yes, a good point. A very good point.'

He frowned again, looked at the grass, rubbed his cheek again, looked at the sky.

'What about the other plane?' asked Frieda. 'Have they recovered it?'

Simenon nodded.

'Two young men, no serious injuries, as far as I know, very, very lucky young men.' He stood up. 'Allow me to drive you back to your hotel. And then I must find out who and what these two young men are.' He looked at Frank. 'Unless you would like to accompany me?' he asked. 'Perhaps you might like to see how we French interrogate suspects? We have a saying about that.'

'No,' said Frank, standing up. 'Thank you, inspector, but non. Definitely non. We are here on our honeymoon. It's very kind of you to offer, but we have more important things to attend to.' He turned to Frieda. 'What do you say? Back to the hotel, a shower, a drink or two, and then a stroll around to find a restaurant for dinner?'

'Yes,' said Frieda, standing up and smiling at Frank, ignoring her stomach which was not at all interested in dinner. The drink or two sounded very welcome to it though. 'That sounds perfect.'

'Allons,' said Simenon, 'I give you the lift then.'

'That was very nice of you, darling,' Frieda whispered to Frank as they followed Simenon. 'You would have liked to sit in on the interview, wouldn't you?'

'Not a chance,' Frank whispered back. 'They'd yak on in French, I wouldn't understand two words, and I'd be bored as hell within five minutes. We'll get much more out of Simenon when he's finished with them.'

Frieda's smile changed into as much of a pout as Frieda's face could ever manage. Frank could at least have pretended that he was sacrificing a juicy interview to be with his wife.

Still, at least they could get away from French police work, be by themselves, and she could get on with the important stuff, such as training Frank in the right way to be a husband. Away from blasted little aircraft and blasted little Frenchman who claimed their blasted little grandfathers had blastedly landed on Omaha blasted beach. And blasted little French inspectors.

She excused Gaspode. It wasn't the dog's fault.

Though she had to admit to herself that, when Simenon had suggested it, she had wanted to be in on that interview. Not just for the experience, but also to have a word or two with the two young men. But again, Frank was right. If they didn't speak English there wasn't much point. Better to wait until Simenon had finished with them.

'Anyway,' continued Frank, 'I'm not sure if I could manage to interview them without thumping them. The bastards almost killed us.'

Frieda glanced at him. He was rubbing the side of his head again. His face was pale.

'Are you okay, Frank?'

'I'm fine, Free. Just a twinge of a headache. Too much sun, or something.'

'Are you sure? I've got some headache tablets in my handbag.'

'Thanks, I could do with a couple.'

Frieda rummaged around until she found the tablets and a bottle of water. Frank took two and immediately swallowed them. His lack of hesitation and lack of a throw-away comment surprised her. She stopped and took his face in her hands.

'Darling, you've got a bump on the side of your forehead. When did that happen?'

He felt the side of his temple.

'Oh, must have happened when Jacques was shot. I cracked it against the window. Nothing serious.' He gave her a less than convincing smile and kissed her. 'A long hot shower, a couple of Calvados, that'll do the trick.'

Frieda squeezed his arm. She too was looking forward to a long, hot shower and a drink. And if Frank wasn't feeling better after the tablets and a shower she was going to start getting worried. She could almost recite the doctors' varying predictions after Frank had been shot. One thing they all had in common was the idea that there might be, or might not be, or could be, they couldn't say, but, well, unforeseen side-effects. And if he received another head injury, who knows? But it was an interesting case. Very interesting, from the professional viewpoint.

As forward planning she got Simenon to give her his card. She wasn't expecting Frank to get worse, but, if he did, she wanted someone who could speak French at hand. Simenon might be a pain in the neck, but he could have his uses.

What was really beginning to worry her was the bottle of tablets in Frank's wash-bag. A suspicion was growing that the idea that Frank has just left them there and forgotten them was just not true. He had downed the headache tablets she had given him with the manner of someone far too used to them.

How well, she asked herself, do I really know my husband?

Normandy. Monday. Evening.

Like a dream

'Pick a restaurant, any restaurant,' Frank said as they strolled hand in hand past open cafes in the evening dusk. His mood was relaxed, almost back to his jaunty self. Frieda could even feel that his muscles were relaxed. It had been a false alarm, she concluded, nothing more than a headache to be expected after what they had been through.

'I fancy a fish dish,' she said. 'Seeing as we're so close to the sea it should be fresh. Hold on, Frank, let's have a look at this menu.'

They stopped to read the menu chalked on a board.

'Ah, the famous moules marinieres,' Frank said, 'otherwise known as marinated moles.'

'Frank, it's not marinated moles and you know that.'

'I know, I know. It's a story from the First World War. Rations were scarce, and a newly arrived colonel from England saw moules marinieres on the menu, complained about the disgusting French eating habits and said there was no way he would eat mole.'

'That sounds like one of those apocryphal stories. It's a bit dark inside.'

'Probably based on something which did happen, though, I would imagine. Doesn't look too dark.'

They both peered inside the cafe. Each table was lit by a small lamp, leaving most of the rest of the restaurant in semi-darkness. It was about half full, or half empty, according to a person's viewpoint. Suddenly Frieda grasped Frank's arm and pulled him away.

'I think we'll find somewhere else,' she said.

'It wasn't that dark.'

'No, just light enough to see two diners right at the back, in a corner. I only noticed them because a waitress moved a lamp next to them.'

'And they were?'

'Madame Simenon and A N Other. Very pale face, youngish. Red hair. Looks a bit like a slice of Brie with a wig on.'

'Not Mr Simenon, then?'

'Precisely. And even if it was, would you really want to take the risk of her coming over to explain in French how much she admires British police officers.'

'God, no. We're supposed to be honeymooners, not police officers.'

'Or even loonymooners.'

'Now I can live with being a loonymooner.'

They found a restaurant along the street which met with Frieda's approval and which contained no signs of French detectives.

'I've been thinking,' Frank said after they had placed their order.

'Yes, my sweet?'

'Do you think we should move to another part of Normandy for the rest of our honeymoon? There's bound to be plenty of spare places at this time of the year. Get away from Simenon and the rest of this mad bunch.'

Frieda thought about this as the waitress placed her order of tuna steak in front of her.

'I don't know,' she said. 'On the one hand it sounds appealing. On the other, we have booked the week, and we'd probably have to pay a forfeit of some kind if we gave up the room. And it would mean losing a day or two, looking for somewhere else, travelling, booking in again. And despite all the problems I like the hotel we've got. Madame Arneaux and her husband are very pleasant people.'

Frank nodded, popped a butter-soaked baby potato in his mouth, smiled at her, chewed while making appreciative noises, and swallowed.

'Just what I was thinking,' he said. 'The business on Sunday night was a pure coincidence. Simenon has probably sorted out whatever nonsense was caused today – a case of mistaken identity, I reckon. We're centrally situated here, the restaurants are great, we don't have much driving to do. We probably won't be disturbed again. After all, you know how people always complain about how long it takes us to investigate a case. By the time Simenon wants to have another word we'll have been back in Wellbury for a month or two.'

Frieda looked at him. She was well aware of the complaints about Wellbury's response times. They invariably landed on her desk. It was a question of having too few resources to handle situations that could change on an hourly basis, if not faster. At any other time she might have felt defensive about such a comment. But Frank was right. The French police no doubt faced similar problems. Might as well look on the bright side and enjoy themselves.

Frank was almost right. They managed to get to the coffee stage before being interrupted.

'Oh, dear. Don't look now, Frank, but we're about to have a visitor,' Frieda said, frowning at the entrance.

Frank's eyebrows rose, but he didn't turn around.

'Qui est-ce?' he asked.

'Gorgonzola,' Frieda replied. 'She must have spotted us through the window.'

'Avec le Brie?' asked Frank.

'Non, pas de Brie. Which is interesting. I wonder why that is.'

Before Frank could reply they were assaulted by a gush of voluble French as Madame Simenon arrived at their table. Frank stood up.

'Madame Simenon, enchainte,' he said. 'Vous etre bien?'

'Mais oui' was all either caught before she was off again, gabbling about something which appeared to involve delightful English policemen.

'Er, care to join us?' suggested Frank when she paused for

breath, indicating a chair for her to sit down on. She shook her head emphatically.

'Non, non, vous etre sur loonymoon, nest-ce-pas? C'est Anglais, loonymoon, oui?'

'Oui madame, certainment.'

There was another short burst of French, followed by a kiss on each cheek for Frank, and then Madame Simenon waved a hand and disappeared.

'What the flip was that all about?' asked Frank, sitting down slowly, as if he had been suddenly assaulted by a large handful of lumpy marshmallows which had then flown off into the night.

'Curiouser and curiouser,' Frieda noted, taking a sip of wine. 'Maybe she fancies you.'

Frank rubbed his jaw.

'Free, remind me that we're here on our honeymoon. Remind me that we are not going to get involved in anything that smells of detective work.'

'We're on our honeymoon, darling. We're not here to get involved in detective work.'

'Good. Because I can't help but think that Madame Simenon was blowing smoke. She reminds me of a case I was investigating once. Something to do with porn shops. I kept bumping into this bloke who immediately began talking about politics, very loudly. It didn't take much to work out that he was trying to hide something.'

'Mrs Simenon suspects we have seen her, and instead of a quick wave or similar innocent reaction, breezes in to overwhelm us with delight?'

'Something like that.'

'What was the man you kept bumping into trying to hide?'

'Turned out that he was visiting his boyfriend and he didn't want his wife to find out. I felt like strangling him when I discovered that. He had me running in circles investigating him when he was perfectly innocent.'

Frieda smiled.

'Perhaps you should ask Madame Simenon whether she's got a secret girlfriend on the go. That would be interesting.'

'More like impossible with my French and her lack of English. Come on, Poppy, let's pay up and head back for an early night, what say?'

'I'll race you.'

They didn't quite race. Instead they strolled along in the warm Autumn evening, hand in hand. They tried strolling along with Frieda's head on Frank's shoulder, but had to conclude that the human body wasn't advanced enough for such perambulatory style.

'Tell me something, Frank,' Frieda said.

'Anything, my sweet.'

'Did your father give you any advice about marriage?'

Frank paused.

'Well, in a way,' he said.

'In a way? What sort of way?'

'Well, I thought I'd better ask him. I've always thought that my folks have a very happy marriage, so I decided I'd ask him what the secret is.'

'And what did he say?'

'Well, you know my dad. He sort of blinked, as if completely surprised by the question. Then he scratched his head. Then he blinked again. Anyway, he finally said, "Good point, Frank, good point. Good question, yes. I suppose I really should be giving you some advice, shouldn't I? Pitfalls to avoid. That sort of thing. Yes. Hmmm." '

Frieda giggled at the impression. She could imagine Frank's father saying just that, a look of bemused concern on his face.

'So he sat there thinking for a while. And then suddenly his eyes lit up and he looked at me, beaming.' Frank softened his voice to imitate his father's. '"Keep mum, my boy," he said, "Keep mum." And he looked ever so pleased at having come up with that.'

'Keep mum? That sounds a bit ambiguous.'

'Well, yes, possibly. But I think he put it in a nutshell. You're mum, and I have to keep you.' He squeezed her hand. 'For me that says it all.'

Frieda squeezed back. She wasn't quite sure that she understood the concept. In a strange way it sounded right, but she preferred to have things properly defined. Logically ordered. Still, they had the rest of the week to get Frank's mind logically ordered. Just so long as there weren't any more silly incidents such as being shot at while in an aircraft or finding young women in the bath.

No, whatever Frank wanted, they were not going to get in another aircraft that week. No planes, no hot air balloons, hang gliders or any other arbitrary methods of transport which Frank could find in order to make their lives more interesting and more dangerous. Being married contained sufficient dangers and perils without Frank adding to the brew.

And if there were to be further bodies in the bath, so to put it, she would make sure that Frank was the one to discover them. After all, he was the one who was supposed to come up with these problems, not her.

Somehow, strolling hand in hand in the balmy evening air, with the faint aroma of sea-air and the perfume of some late-flowering plant, it was impossible to think that there had been a body in the bath, nor that they had been in that plane that afternoon. It felt as if it were some distant bad dream. Especially with the thought of what the week still held in store. Caen's attractions, the cathedral at Rheims. Wonderful, wonderful days of just being tourists with no responsibilities. Honeymooners in love.

She sighed. It felt like being a teenager again. Without the angst.

Normandy. Tuesday. Breakfast.

Favourite things

Frieda listened to Frank's muffled footsteps disappearing down the stairs, dropping from one step to the next as if he were a happy little schoolboy. She smiled, delved into her handbag and took out her mobile phone. She switched it on and waited for it to report any new messages. The only thing she expected was "All quiet." What she didn't expect was the one she found herself reading.

"Everything normal. Source code-named The Cream Cake Man reports that you found Lover Boy in bath with gorgeous young woman. Please advise whether or not to encourage source to develop this theory."

Frieda giggled and tapped in a quick reply:

"Confirm girl in bath, but not Lover Boy. Encourage the Cream Cake Man, if any encouragement needed."

Frieda was well aware that The Cream Cake Man, aka Sergeant Eric Johns, was known for his ability to make mole hills out of flat earth, and then transform the freshly manufactured mole hills into mountain ranges, volcanoes, and a number of unusual and unexpected geological and apparently solid formations. Normally she would have stamped on such an example of this straight away, but, she decided, she was not in charge of the station at that moment, and she felt like a bit of fun. It would be amusing to hear details of his constructions when they returned, and to see how he attempted to reconcile what he had earlier imagined with the more mundane reality. How he had picked up details of Amelie would also be an interesting question. It was just a good thing that he was unaware of the basic details of yesterday's exploits. He would have herself and Frank on a Tintin-like voyage to the moon.

She pressed the send button, made sure the mobile phone was definitely switched off, buried it at the bottom of her handbag, and went off to catch up with Frank. She wished she could share the chuckle with him. Well, he would just have to wait until they got back. His face would be a picture.

'So, where shall we enjoy breakfast today, my love?' asked Frank as they strolled out of the hotel entrance.

'We should choose a different place, I suppose.'

'Oh, I don't know. That place yesterday was ideal. The waitress was very friendly, food was excellent. I don't see why we shouldn't go there every day. Make it our special little breakfast spot. We could go back there every year, a reminder of the best times of our life.'

Frieda smiled. She liked the idea. Frank, she had realised, did understand the purpose of a honeymoon. Just the two of them and their special places, memories to keep them together in the years to come. He just wasn't very good at saying it when he should have done. And so far they hadn't been very successful at it. But that was going to change.

'Let's do that, darling,' she said.

'And the same table outside, of course. And if anyone else is sitting there we'll take another and scowl at them until they leave.'

Frieda giggled. She knew that that was exactly what Frank would do. Fortunately there was no-one occupying their special table.

'Ah, bon jour, Cathy, ca va?' asked Frank as the waitress stepped out of the cafe, tray in hand with two coffees.

'Bon jour, monsieur, bon jour madame. Trez bien. Et vous? How's the honeymoon going?'

'Couldn't be better, Cath. As Churchill once said, there is nothing like the excitement of being shot at and missed.'

Cathy's eyebrows rose.

'Someone shot at you?' she asked.

'Someone took a pot shot at the pilot of a plane we were in,' Frieda said. 'I doubt if they were aiming at us.'

'Ah, come on, Free,' said Frank, 'you make it sound far too boring. I bet I could get a better story out of it than that.'

'I bet you could. But you aren't going to. It's breakfast and we're on honeymoon, and you aren't Indiana Jones.'

'A body in the bath on your first night,' noted Cath, 'shot at while in a plane the second day. I can't wait to hear what happens next.'

'What happens next, Cath,' said Frieda, 'is that we're going to have a quiet little breakfast followed by a quiet little visit to Caen. Oh, you don't know if there's a pet shop around here, do you?'

'A pet shop?'

'Yes, I'm thinking of buying a lead for lover boy here, just to make sure he doesn't get into any more trouble.'

'You know what I think?' asked Frank, lounging in his chair.

'Do tell, darling.'

'I think I will have an omelette. A nice, large, cheese and mushroom omelette. With toast. And a touch of tomato sauce.'

'Really, Frank, tomato sauce? I'm sure the omelettes here don't need any such thing.'

'Actually, the chef does a really good omelette,' said Cathy. 'But I'll bring a bottle of tomato sauce anyway. I know we've got one somewhere. We keep it for tourists, but they never use it. Well, only rarely.'

'I think I'll also have an omelette,' said Frieda. 'Not as large as Frank's, and definitely no tomato sauce.'

'You know,' said Frank, after Cathy had left, 'talking of pet shops, well, I know we're supposed to leave everything behind for the honeymoon, but I can't help but wonder how little Squish is doing.'

'I know, darling, I keep thinking about her. But she'll be fine, Tricia will spoil her rotten. She might not even want to come

143

back to us afterward.'

'Nah, Squish would never do that.' He rapped his fingers on the table. 'I wonder when Simenon will turn up.'

'Simenon?'

'Probably just as we've started tucking in. That's the way I'd do it. All smiles and "Oh, don't worry about me, you just carry on, meanwhile I have one or two questions", that sort of thing.'

Frieda frowned.

'If he does I shall make a formal complaint,' she said.

To Frank's surprise they completed an enjoyable breakfast free of Simenon and Gaspode.

'Come to think of it,' Frank said as he slowly stirred his post-breakfast coffee, 'there is something that rather intrigues me.'

'Caen, Frank. Little streets, cobbled alleys, wonderful little shops, two people strolling hand in hand. That's what we're going to do this morning. The marina, the abbeys, that sort of thing. Intriguing thoughts will have to wait.'

'Hmmm.'

Frieda sighed.

'Okay, darling, I know you'll be useless for anything until you say it, so say it and get it over with. What is it?'

'Cathy,' said Frank.

'Cathy?'

'What she said yesterday – "I was supposed to be getting married next June" – wasn't that it? I wonder what happened.'

'Frank! That is none of our business.'

'Oh, yes, I know that. I'm not going to pry or anything, but I can't help but wonder.'

'Good, you can wonder all you like, so long as you don't pry. Now, shall we pay the bill and stroll out for a saunter?'

They paid the bill and strolled out for a saunter. They gave the perfect appearance of a newly married couple in love. You would never have spotted the faint irritation Frieda was feeling.

She also wanted to know what Cathy had meant. After all, it could have relevance to their marriage. What if Cathy had done something which she, Frieda, needed to avoid at all costs?

She wasn't going to pry. Definitely not. But you never knew which way an innocent conversation would go. Did you? After all, what harm could it do?

Normandy. Tuesday. Morning.

From Paris, without love

'I wouldn't mind retiring to a place like this,' Frank said after they had spent a little time looking at the various offerings in an estate agent's window and debating the affordability of a little cottage which apparently had a view of the sea. Frieda had spotted the little shop and suggested a five minute browse before they left for Caen. 'But I'd also like to retire to somewhere like Cornwall or Devon – and a little place in Spain would be nice. On the other hand, Wellbury's the real place I'd see us retiring, if we ever get to that stage.'

'How do you mean, if we ever get to that stage?' asked Frieda, suddenly having alarming images of them separated, or one of them having died.

'Oh, you know, the way things are going these days, retirement will be made illegal soon. We'll all be forced to carry on working until the day before we kick the bucket. They'll have special clinics you'll have to attend once a year, to calculate how much longer you've got. "Mr Summers, according to our calculations you may retire in two years, three months and four days. Our tests show that you will die at five twenty-two the following morning. Congratulations." And they'll be staffed by Filippino doctors because the government and the NHS will have stuffed things up so badly all the British doctors have emigrated elsewhere.'

'A bit of a morbid thought, Frank.'

'True. But, anyway, coming back to retirement cottages. That means we'll have our main home in Wellbury, with a cottage here, one in Devon, one in Cornwall, and one in Spain. Do you think that's enough? Perhaps we should also have one in the southern hemisphere. New Zealand, that sounds good.'

'It sounds good, yes. Did you have any plan on how we're going to afford such a plethora of living establishments? Winning the lottery, perhaps? Three or four times should do it.'

'Just day-dreaming, Free. After all, that's what honeymoons are for, isn't it?'

Frieda was about to reply that she was glad that Frank had his mind on what a honeymoon was for, and to take the chance to nudge that mind in the right direction, when a woman suddenly exited a narrow alleyway close by.

'My goodness,' said Frank.

It was Madame Simenon. She hesitated for just a split second as she recognised them, before launching herself into a volley of French containing, as far as Frank and Frieda could discern, phrases such as "Mon inspecteur", "Mon brave", "Frank Summers", "Terrifique" and "quiche". She opened her arms wide, threw them around him, hugged him, kissed him four times, twice on each cheek, and then gave him a final bear hug before striding off.

'You wot?' asked Frank of her disappearing back. 'What on earth was that all about?'

'Well, you certainly seem to have gained a fan,' noted Frieda. 'Perhaps the fact that she doesn't understand a word you say has something to do with it.'

'In that case, the sooner I learn French the better. I'm all for Anglo-French relations improving, but that entente was a little too cordiale for my liking.'

'You know, darling, I don't want to puncture your ego, but I rather got the impression her little outburst was not, as it might have appeared, a strange attraction to yourself, but was in fact a little performance to distract our attention. A smoke screen, as you so well put it last night.'

'I think you might just be right, Free. Shall we have a look down this alleyway? There might be some interesting little shops to look at.'

'Some interesting little shops which might give us a clue what Madame Simenon was doing? And why she was so flustered when she bumped into us?'

'The thought hadn't crossed my mind.'

'Yes it had. Come on.'

They walked into the alleyway. It opened out after a short while into a street of shops and then houses. Towards the end they could just see a slim man with red hair, wearing a brown jacket and fawn-coloured trousers walking rapidly away. He disappeared around a corner. They quickened their pace without thinking. When they got to the corner they found a street empty of any people, especially a slim man with red hair and wearing a brown jacket and fawn-coloured trousers.

'I'm pretty sure that was the same man as the one in the restaurant last night, our Mr Brie,' Frieda said as they turned back.

'Well, well. A furtive assignation in the darkest corner of a secluded restaurant. A meeting in a back street, after which each goes in opposite directions. Presuming that was what happened.'

'It would be a remarkable coincidence if they hadn't met each other here. There aren't any other streets either could have suddenly and co-incidentally have popped out of.'

'And he doesn't look local. He doesn't walk like a local. He's got a city stride. A man in a hurry.'

'I wouldn't have called it a city stride. But definitely not the easy stroll of a countryman who measures time in seasons rather than days.'

'So,' said Frank, 'who is he, and why is our Madame la Inspecteur Simenon meeting him somewhere they aren't likely to be seen? A little love affair? Or perhaps he's some form of informant?'

'Mrs Simenon? A love affair? I can't see that happening. As to informant, possibly. Someone who used to live in a large town, spent a while in prison, came here for peace and quiet, and was convinced by the local police that a little information from time to time would buy him that peace and quiet.'

'Unless he's a copper himself. Works for the Surete in Paris.

They're worried about the drugs down here, he's sent down as an undercover operative, and he's given Madame Simenon as a contact.'

'Without telling Simenon himself?'

'Maybe. In fact, quite possibly. After all, Simenon likes to give the image of a tired old bull-dog of a copper who's prepared to break a few rules to put the bad guys in jail, but what if he's bent himself? We only have his word that Amelie Courbois went to the wrong hotel by mistake. Maybe it was a deliberate mistake. Maybe Simenon sent her there.'

'But then Amelie would have spilt the beans afterwards. Unless she was also in it.'

Frank nodded.

'Good point. I'd like to have a few words with Amelie. From what Simenon said she's a bit of an airhead, but she can't be that bad. Not if she's chosen for undercover police work.'

Frieda stopped and turned to him.

'Frank, did you just hear what you said? You're speaking as if this was Wellbury and you were on the case. We are supposed to be on honeymoon, if you haven't forgotten.'

Frank looked at the ground and made a face. Then he looked up at Frieda and grinned.

'You want to work it out just as much as me,' he accused.

'Yes, darling,' she replied, taking his arm and walking him on, 'but let's get our priorities right. This is our honeymoon, that is, you and me, husband and wife. We will never have another one, so let's make the most of this one.'

'Absolutely, my sweet.'

They walked back in silence for a few yards until Frank said:

'She's not that bad looking when you come to think about it,' noted Frank. 'Madame Simenon, I mean.'

'What?'

'Well, I remember –' Frank paused as he realised that what he was about to say – "I remember the first time I saw you thinking how good looking you'd be if you didn't frown so much" – was probably not the most diplomatic comment to make, and changed it to: 'I remember the first time we saw her, she was having a go at Simenon, looked a right shrew. Take that away, let her smile a bit, and she isn't unattractive.'

Frieda pursed her lips. She could see what Frank meant about Madame Simenon. She just wondered whether, during that slight pause he had made, he hadn't been thinking of someone a little closer to home. Someone who also wore navy blue skirt-suits at work.

They continued in silence until about ten yards from the alleyway leading back to the street when a man with a scarf across his face jumped out in front of them. He was holding a long, shining kitchen knife.

'You! Handbag! Now!' he shouted. The performance was let down a little by the way he staggered and tried to regain his balance after jumping out and by the way the scarf muffled his shout. Bloodshot eyes looked nervously from Frank to Frieda and greedily back to Frieda's handbag. He seemed to realise that he had given them far too much space and began edging forward, knife out, right foot forward.

'Oh, for crying in a bucket, what now?' muttered Frieda. She then shrieked. It was the first time Frank had heard Frieda shriek. It sounded just like the kind of fake shriek a very bad actress would shriek. The man's eyes widened nervously at the sound.

'Oh, darling, he's got a knife! Oh, darling, what shall I do?' she asked, moving back and away from Frank.

'Handbag!' insisted the masked man, now wearing a slightly puzzled look. Frank moved back and away from Frieda.

'My, it is a big knife, isn't it?' he said in his best my-goodness Wodehouse tone. 'Monsewer!' he shouted, 'Monsewer, avec allez, la junga din bot-bot mugga nut!'

'Eh?' asked the masked man.

'Darling,' said Frieda, by now standing opposite Frank with the other man in the middle, 'you take it, I think I'm going to faint.'

She tossed her handbag over the man's head to Frank. Frank caught it and looked at the man who was half turned and completely confused.

'Handbag!' he insisted.

'You don't parley le Anglais by any chance, do you?' Frank asked. 'Sorry, darling, it's your handbag, you look after it,' he said, throwing it over the man and back to Frieda who caught it expertly.

The man staggered around to face a woman, something he seemed more confident about. He managed "Le hand—" before a kick from Frank hit him in the back, just where his kidneys were. He managed an "Urgh!" before the handbag he was after hit him in the face from Frieda's side, followed by a kick just below his kneecap. He collapsed on the ground, pleading, in a foetal position.

'Now, my friend,' Frank said, taking the man's right arm and forcing it up behind his back while Frieda scanned the street for any possible co-muggers, 'nous avez une question or deux, et vous, mon ami, sont going to answer them, capisch?'

Frieda sighed. A couple of shop owners and local tenants had poked their noses out, but seeing Frank holding a man in an arm-lock, and the look in Frieda's eyes, told them that these were les flics, and they had better not get involved.

'Police!' Frieda called, smiling as best as she could, waving her warrant card and praying that no-one would actually check it, otherwise she was going to be in deep trouble back in England.

'Oui,' shouted Frank. 'Nous sont polizei!'

That convinced the onlookers. They had deep cultural memories of German police. They would have preferred to blow up these two on a dark and lonely road one night, just as their grandparents had done to the Boche, but it was neither dark nor lonely, and the best for them to do was to go polish the basement floor and pretend they had seen nothing. Besides which, did you see that smile the woman flic gave? Enough to freeze your soul on a hot summer's day. They were the worst, those women flics.

'Frank,' Frieda said, turning her attention back to him and the man, 'I don't think he can understand you.'

'No problem. Monsieur, vous voulez avez les poissons coucher ce soir, mon ami?'

Frieda gave another sigh.

'Darling,' said Frieda, 'I don't think "do you want to sleep with the fish" translates quite directly into the French. And I suspect that it's an Americanism anyway.'

'Oh, I don't know, he seems to be getting the message.'

'That's probably more because he thinks you're trying to rip his arm off.'

'Rip his arm off?' Frank leaned forward and spoke into the man's ear. 'Listen, mon ami, if I was trying to rip your arm off I'd be beating you with the wet end by now, comprendez? C'est ma femme, you little son of a bitch, ma femme, get it?'

'Calm down a little, Frank,' Frieda said. 'He's not worth a charge of assault.'

The truth was that Frieda's own heart was pumping fast. Much as she had put on a blasé performance, the shock had sent her adrenalin soaring, and she could see now that Frank was just the same. A drunk thug with a knife was probably more dangerous to himself than anyone else, and had no chance against two trained police officers, but he could still do quite a bit of serious damage before he was put down. Had it happened back in Wellbury they would certainly not have approached the man in such a way. It would have been stab-proof vests and a van load of police officers all the way, and if he didn't drop the knife the Tasers would be used. From a safe distance.

'Bugger,' said Frank, pricking up his ears. 'Is that sound I hear the sound of a French police car?'

A siren was coming closer. There was no doubt it was coming towards them. An unmarked car stopped at the entrance to the alleyway and Georges Simenon stepped out. He strolled up to them with a resigned air, Gaspode alongside.

'I heard on the police radio that two foreigners were being mugged, a man and a woman,' he said, prodding the man kneeling on the ground with his toe. 'For some reason it seemed unnecessary to ask who the two foreigners were.'

'Do you know him?' asked Frank. Simenon rattled off a question at the man. He sneered weakly and spat. Gaspode barked. Frank twisted his arm a tadge. Frieda took out a steel nail file and began filing her nails idly, looking into the man's eyes with such an expression of pure innocence it was terrifying. The man's pain-stricken eyes went from her eyes to the nail file and locked on it. He answered Simenon's question rapidly. Simenon searched in the man's pockets until he found a wallet. He leaned idly against a wall and began flicking through it.

'He says he was asked to do a job down here. He lives in Paris. He asks to be taken into custody. I think he feels safer with the French police. I have this impression that he regards the French police as cruel friends, but the English are barbaric enemies. Apparently you threatened to mate him with a fish.'

'Tell him,' said Frank, staring down at the man's head, 'that my grandfather was Scots, my grandmother Welsh, and my great-grandfather Irish and we all hate the fucking French for deserting us when we were fighting for our independence. And tell him,' he added, giving another twist, 'if he ever even thinks of pulling a knife on my wife again I will kill him.'

'There is not the need, Inspector. I think he gets the general idea, as you say. His documents appear to be correct. If they are false they will tell Paris even more. I think you can hand him over to the French police.' He raised an arm and two uniformed police officers came running. The man seemed to be grateful to have handcuffs clipped on his wrists and led away. He gave Frieda and Frank one last fearful backward glance.

'So, Inspector, Madame Inspector, you live an interesting life, not so?'

'Inspector Simenon,' said Frieda, 'we are here on our honeymoon. So far we have found a body in the bath of our hotel room, we have been shot at while in a light aircraft, and now someone has tried to mug us. With all due respect, Inspector Simenon, enough is enough.'

Simenon grimaced.

'I understand, and I apologise, Madame la Inspector. I wish I could give you some good news, but I am afraid I have only the bad news for you.'

'Bad news? What? Such as the French riot police have ransacked our latest hotel room and destroyed all our luggage – by accident, of course. Or something worse? Maybe your military police have found something to be interested in? Well, Inspector Simenon?'

'Calm down, Free,' Frank said, wiping his brow with the back of his hand.

Simenon raised both hands in surrender.

'Your supposed attackers yesterday, the ones who shot at the aeroplane,' he said.

'Let me guess,' said Frieda, 'they were from the French air force and it was a case of mistaken identity.'

'No, I am sorry, they were not. We know who they are. They have been very co-operative. Unfortunately they are also very irrelevant.'

'Irrelevant?'

Simenon shrugged.

'They are each the son of a wealthy family of politics,' he said. 'As can happen in such cases, they have grown up thinking that they can do anything and get away with anything – with impotency, I think you say.'

'Impunity,' suggested Frank.

'Yes, that is the word, imputency. These two, they live the life of fast cars, drugs and young women. Yesterday they are at the chateau of one of their families, alone. They take some drugs, they have the great idea of going hunting. But to go hunting on foot, this is the idea boring. So they decide to borrow an uncle's aircraft – they have both had lessons in flying – and hunt from the air.'

He sighed.

'According to their statements, which are not worth the paper they have signed them on, as they are still too drugged to make much sense, they spotted a pigeon, which they shot at. At the very next moment, the pigeon's mother, a huge white eagle which filled the sky, fell down from the heavens and attacked them.'

Frieda and Frank looked at him. He studied his nails.

'We were shot at by two young drug addicts who thought we were a pigeon?' asked Frank.

'I'm afraid so, Inspector.'

'Not the mafia?' asked Frieda.

'I'm afraid not, Inspector.'

'No local Corsican band of brothers?' asked Frank.

'No, Inspector.'

'Just two drugged up punks?'

'I'm afraid it is as you say. Wealthy punks.'

They looked at him in silence for a while.

'What a cheek. I feel like asking for my money back,' decided

Frank.

'Pardon?'

'My husband was trying to make a joke, inspector. He does that quite often – tries, that is.'

'Seriously, Inspector Simenon,' Frank said, 'they were just a couple of over-rich little brats high as kites? It was a pure coincidence?'

'I'm afraid so, monsieur Inspector. However, allow me to assure you, this is not normal.'

'Well, thank Christ for that,' muttered Frank. 'I thought Wellbury was a strange place, but at least we don't have people mistaking a light aircraft for a pigeon, or a pigeon's mother eagle.'

Suddenly he chuckled. It turned into a low, ironic laugh which lasted some seconds.

'God, Free,' he said once he had recovered, 'we'd better not mention this back there. You know how daft some of them are. We'd have reports of house-sized pigeons attacking people in the woods within days.'

Frieda smiled reluctantly. She knew only too well how true it was.

'But,' said Simenon, sensing a good moment for departure, while he had a breathing space in which to leave before he was put on the spot again, 'I must now have words with our little mugger. I shall have news of what he says for you by this afternoon.'

He doffed his hat politely.

'This afternoon?' asked Frieda, surprised. 'That's a bit quick.'

'Madame La Inspector, perhaps we have different methods in

la belle France. But, be that as it may, our friend is ready for questioning, his fear will aid us. As the great La Fontaine once said, Qui craint de souffrir, il souffre déjà de ce qu'il craint. In English that is, he who is afraid of suffering is already suffering what he is afraid of.' He shrugged. 'Or perhaps it is just me. I do not like it when a French thug attacks visitors, I put more effort into the case.' He smiled sadly. 'Especially when the visitors are on their loonymoon. Madame, monsieur, au revoir.'

'Au revoir,' called Frank. 'If you want us, we'll be in Rheims.'

'Enjoy the city,' Simenon called back.

They watched him walk away, a certain stomp to his gait which boded ill for the new prisoner. Frieda put her arm around Frank's waist, and he put his arm around her shoulders.

'Rheims?' she asked. 'Now that wouldn't be trying to send him on a wild goose chase while we're actually in Caen, would it?'

'Exactly,' replied Frank. 'Him and any other bugger he happens to come across and just by chance let slip that we're off to Rheims.'

'But we're nowhere near Rheims .'

'Good,' he said, smiling, giving her a hug. 'The further away the buggers go the better.'

'Darling,' she said, after a pause.

'Yes, my sweet?'

'You were – how can I put this – a little rough with that man? The mugger? It wasn't quite standard procedure, was it?'

Frank thought about this for a while. Or tried not to think

about it. The problem was that old Epi had never left any notes about how to feel and act when your wife was in danger. Not just your wife. The woman you loved, the woman you were looking forward to spending a lifetime with.

'He was threatening you, Free,' he said softly. 'I won't have that. Never. Not ever. Anyone tries that, he's going to have to kill me first.'

Frieda looked up at him and smiled. She rather liked the idea of having a strong man next to her, looking after her. For the moment, of course. She was not about to turn into the good little wife any time soon, theirs was going to be a relationship of equals.

But, just for the moment it felt good. The way expensive Belgian chocolate felt good. An occasional treat.

'I could do with a good cuppa,' Frank said, grinning, and suddenly turning back into the normal Frank. 'What say we pop over to that cafe and see if they don't offer mugs of char?'

Frieda's nose twitched. It was another thing on her list of Things To Train Frank In. Namely, that tea should come in cups. Not necessarily delicate cups, but definitely not over-brewed mugs of char.

But it could wait.

'Good idea, darling.'

The proprietor of the cafe did not think it a good idea. Firstly he did not want these German police in his cafe. Secondly they appeared to be trying to tell him that they were flowers, namely poppies. Thirdly, it seemed that they were actually Anglais, which was possibly worse. Fourthly, the young man with the strange quiff of white hair asked for tea in a language which sounded as if it might have been French, but the Bon Dieu only knew where such French was spoken.

And as for the hand gestures the young man made when describing the tea they wanted, well, if these were Anglais then they had found a new approach to the life noire, and long may they keep it to themselves. In the end he provided them with strong mint tea with plenty of sugar. The Algerians liked that sort of stuff, and, the Bon Dieu also knew, they were just as mad as the Anglais.

'Lovely stuff,' said Frank, sipping the sweet tea. 'Russian tea. Very few people know how to make it properly.' He smiled at Frieda. 'I'm glad they didn't come up with a good old English cuppa, you know. Much better to enjoy the local fare.'

Frieda smiled back at him, her chin cupped in her hand.

'I love you, darling,' she said.

'And I love you too, darling,' he replied, smiling back.

Inside the cafe owner sighed and carried on dusting a corner which had last been cleaned twenty years ago. He had chosen the unusual vantage point because it gave him the opportunity to eavesdrop. With his limited knowledge of English all he could work out was that these two mad Anglais were in love.

Having seen how they had handled that drunk mugger, all he could do was thank the Bon Dieu that he was neither Anglais nor in love. Obviously either condition entailed insanity of one degree or another. He prayed that, whatever madness they were going to do next, they would do it far away.

Normandy. Tuesday. Afternoon.

It's that man again

After a day free of further incident, spent wandering around the sights of Caen in pure tourist-cum-loonymoon mode, with only the serious debate of which restaurant to choose for lunch to cause a slight concern, they drove back to their hotel late that afternoon as the sun began to consider packing up his bags for the day to allow the moon to take over. As they parked they noticed Simenon's car parked facing away from them, with Simenon sitting on the bonnet, his back to them, his feet planted on the bumper, tossing pieces of biscuit for Gaspode to catch. Gaspode carefully chewed each biscuit, giving it due attention for its taste and texture, and then waited until he was ready before barking for the next one.

'I'll give him that,' Frank said as they walked up, 'he doesn't bother to hide himself.'

'I think you quite admire him,' said Frieda.

'I suppose I do, in a way. He's approaching this just the way I would. Moving from potential suspect to potential suspect, revisiting witnesses, listening to their stories over and over until he gets the feel of what's reliable and what isn't.'

Frieda was tempted to point out that the difference between Simenon and Frank was that Simenon appeared in no danger of ending up injured, which Frank seemed to manage without trying. But that might bring up memories best forgotten. And she was rather happy to realise that she hadn't felt any irritation when Frank had spoken of how a case should be run. She would have run things quite differently, but she no longer thought that her way was better. Just different.

Though it had to be said that her way was almost invariably …

'Bon jour, Inspector,' called Frank as they stepped out from their car. 'Or is it bon soir already?'

Simenon turned around and stepped down from the bonnet, putting away the biscuits in his pocket. Gaspode seemed to accept that biscuit time was over, and looked towards Frank and Frieda, barking a greeting.

'Almost the evening,' Simenon said. 'You seem to have brought the good weather with you. I feel as if I am getting the tan. You too look as though you have been enjoying the sun.'

'It has been good weather,' Frank replied. 'The sea's a bit cold for swimming. We dipped our toes in yesterday and almost froze them off.'

'Ah, that makes you the real tourist. No local would think of swimming. Not even in the summer. The Mediterranean, yes, the Atlantic, no.'

'Not even Gaspode?'

'Ah, Gaspode is a strange dog. He does not like the sea. The beach, yes, not the sea. And he enjoys the bath with shampoo. But it must be the right shampoo. I use the wrong shampoo and he barks at me to say non. Fortunately he does not require the expensive shampoo.'

Gaspode gave a short bark to confirm this.

'But I am not here for the discussion of the bath for the dog. I have news. Your attacker has revealed his mission. Apparently they, the people who hired him – whoever they might be – believe that you have the heroin Amelie was to have handed over.'

'They think we have it? Why on earth would they think that?'

'You know the criminal mind, Inspector Summers. To them a – is "bent copper" the phrase? – is something they understand, something they wish to believe in.'

162

'You have a point. Some of the most gullible people I've known have been crooks. Suggest that there's a whiff of something dodgy about something and they'll fall for anything. Still, they'd have checked up on us. Easy enough to confirm that we really are two newly-wed police officers from Britain. You'd have to have a pretty suspicious mind to believe that we deliberately chose this hotel so that we could get involved in a drugs transaction.'

'I think it more likely that they believe that you stumbled on the heroin accidentally and decided to keep it.'

Frank grinned.

'Which is exactly what you thought – and perhaps still think.'

Simenon smiled slightly.

'I am holding my options open until further evidence comes to light.'

'Who exactly are "they", Inspector?' demanded Frieda. Simenon shrugged.

'The man who attacked you – who tried to attack you – is a petty thief from Paris. He is not a natural mugger. He has confessed to drinking much cheap brandy before he could achieve the courage to approach you. From what he says he was promised money if he got the bag of heroin from you, which, for a reason I do not understand, was supposed to be in your handbag, madame.

'That doesn't make any sense.'

'Precisely. Further, he does not know the name of the man who approached him. But he was given a small amount of money, with the promise of much more, and a train ticket. I think he thought that he was now, as you say, into the big time.'

'He doesn't know the name of the man who approached him?'

'No. This is unusual, but not unknown. What you call, in English, a cut-out, I think. It protects the identity of the man paying, but it does not guarantee the quality of the workman. Our prisoner, for example, was given detailed written instructions on what he was required to do. Unfortunately he is almost illiterate. He had a friend read him the details and then he threw away the paper. All we can know for certain is that someone believes that you have, or might have, the heroin.'

'And they're prepared to send men with knives after us to find it.'

Simenon grimaced.

'I think you need to take care, Inspector, but not to worry. I think I know who would have sent the man, and I do not think you are in real danger. The knife, the mugger, I suspect that that was not requested.'

'Oh, good, just unreal danger, then?' suggested Frieda. Simenon's eye twitched.

'I understand your feelings, Inspector. I will speak to who I think is responsible. I do not think it will happen again.'

'Why don't you take him in for questioning?' suggested Frank. 'Until Saturday, anyway.'

Simenon smiled.

'Because we do have laws about that, Inspector. And because I am not fully certain. You see, the man I am thinking of – he does not employ idiots such as the one who tried to mug you. But I will speak to him. I will know if it is him. He will never admit it, but I will know. Talleyrand once said, la parole nous a été donnée pour déguiser notre pensée – we use our words to hide our thoughts. But I can see behind those words. I cannot prove the thoughts, but I can see them.'

'You know,' said Frank suddenly, 'the person you need to consult is the chef.'

'The chef, Inspector? I am afraid I do not understand what you mean.'

'Well, everyone knows that le chef has his own secret sources,' Frank replied, chuckling quietly.

Simenon looked puzzled. Frieda uttered a groan and closed her eyes.

'I apologise, Inspector, but I still do not understand.'

'Don't worry, Inspector Simenon,' said Frieda. 'My husband has his own unique sense of humour. What's the name of the man you suspect?'

'Ah, naturally I cannot tell you, as you would not tell me. But, if I am right, and if it is he, he will do nothing further, that I can promise you. Do not worry, Inspectors, I believe there will be no further problems. Adieu.'

They watched him get into his car with Gaspode, wave, and drive away. Frank pinched the skin between his eyes.

'No further problems,' he quoted. 'Got any more of those Thunderbolts, Free?'

'Thunderbolts?'

'Headache pills. I feel another one coming on.'

Frieda took out the strip and gave it to him.

'Thanks, love.' He noted the concern on her face and smiled. 'Don't look so worried, Free, it's just a little headache. Even I get them. I bet you that even Epi had them from time to time.

In fact I bet he got them quite often. Can you imagine trying to explain to people the benefits of a quiet, rational life while they're running around getting all excited about gods and deep philosophical questions? Must have been a right pain.'

Frieda smiled and stroked his hair into place. There was a troubled look in her eyes, as if she was trying not to think about something.

'Do me a favour, darling,' she said.

'Anything, oh my dearest, sweetest heart.'

'Warn me before you come out with any more puns like that. So that I can make sure I'm not there to hear them.'

Frank chuckled.

'That's my revenge on Simenon for coming out with those bloody quotations every five minutes. Talleyrand this, Voltaire that. Makes me want to head-butt him. Well, yes, to be honest I'd prefer to have a stock myself, of English philosophers, to give him as good as he gives us, but I can never remember the damn things at the time.'

Frieda nodded.

'He does seem to have a fund of them, doesn't he?' She looked back to where Simenon had driven away. 'I hope he's right, that there won't be anything else,' she said. 'I think we've had enough excitement for ten honeymoons. And this is the only one we're going to have.'

'He'd better be right. Anyone else tries it on I am going to rip their bloody arms off. And shove them somewhere painful afterwards.' He smiled weakly at her. 'As Epi might have said in his younger days. When he was still working on his philosophy of life.'

'I think we can trust Simenon's judgement, Frank. He seems to know his own patch.'

'Do you? Trust his judgement? Or in fact anything else about him? That he's on the side of the angels and capable?'

Frieda paused.

'If not he's going to regret it,' she decided.

Wellbury. Tuesday. Evening.

Girls' night out, 1.

'Things have been so quiet since Frank and Frieda left,' noted Doctor Susan Pleadle, Wellbury's pathologist and one of Frank's former girlfriends. She was sitting in the Hangman pub with Detective Constable Gertie Gregson, another former girlfriend of Frank, known as Gertie for her propensity to break out in fits of giggles, quite often at the most inappropriate time. 'I know it's only been a couple of days, but ... You haven't spoken to Tom recently, have you, Gertie?'

'No,' replied Gertie mournfully. 'And I suppose you haven't spoken to Wilf?'

'No, Wilf hardly ever calls.'

Tom was Gertie's elder brother who had escorted Susan to Frank and Frieda's wedding. Wilf was Susan's younger brother who had escorted Gertie to the same wedding. "Escorted", much as a dog on a lead could be said to escort its owner.

'Men just don't realise that they should call if they're serious,' Gertie complained. She took a sad sip of her gin. 'That's if they are serious, of course. And Wilf did ask me to that

French film, and I said yes, even though he's an Arsenal supporter.'

'Tom seemed interested,' Susan said. 'I mean, we went for walks, and there was that Medieval demonstration, and he said he likes badminton.' She paused. 'Gertie, you're Tom's sister, you should know how he thinks. Did he say anything to you?'

Gertie wriggled her nose.

'The thing is, Sue ... well, he did say a lot, but I wasn't really listening.'

'You weren't listening?'

'I was thinking about Wilf. You're his sister. I don't suppose he said anything about me?'

Susan had to consider this, and come out with the truth.

'I'm afraid I wasn't really listening. I was thinking about Tom.'

'Great pair we make, then.'

Both sighed simultaneously.

'Men,' said Gertie.

'Men,' agreed Susan.

'They just don't take things seriously.

'I suppose some men do. Or is that a myth, like the unicorn?'

'A myth, I reckon. I'd like to believe it, but ... experience tells me ... it's just a myth.'

Susan scanned her memories of boyfriends. She came to an abrupt halt at the one who had died the day she believed he was going to propose to her. Then she fast-forwarded to her last one.

'Not all men. Frank would,' she said, downing her gin.

They paused for a moment.

'No, Frank wouldn't,' they agreed.

'Especially not if he were on an interesting case,' said Gertie.

'Poor Frieda.'

'Wilf really didn't – I mean, you know, say anything, did he? Before he went back to London? Anything at all?'

'He did complain a lot about unfeeling Man United supporters, if that's any help.'

Gertie sighed. It had been a point of disagreement between herself, a Man United supporter, and Wilf, an Arsenal supporter.

'Could be worse, Gertie,' Susan said. 'Imagine if you were a Tottenham supporter and he an Arsenal supporter. Then you wouldn't have any chance.'

Gertie made a moue.

'Don't seem to have much chance at the moment.'

'You really like Wilf, don't you?'

'You mean, apart from the fact that's he's good looking, has a great sense of humour, isn't afraid of his feminine side, and is also studying with the Open University, so he understands the problems I face – well, apart from that, yes, I do like him, as it happens.'

'Tom also has a good sense of humour,' Susan said defensively.

'That's the problem. I see Wilf as a charming, handsome man, you see him as your little brother who used to irritate you by being childish. You think Tom is a hunk, I just think of him as a stuffy older brother who was always telling me off for being naughty.'

'Doesn't make much difference, I suppose. Well, sod them. If they can't be bothered to pick up a phone to say hello, well – sod them. Tell me about this business with Frank again, I'm not sure I understood your text message.'

Gertie grinned.

'Okay, the first thing to remember is that this comes from Eric Johns, and he got it from a note Pete Phillips left on Sunday evening – and Eric Johns has lost the note, so we don't have even that to go on. But, according to Eric Johns, Frieda got back to their honeymoon suite on Sunday evening and found Frank in the bath with a young French girl. So she's not speaking to him – Frieda, that is, not the French girl – but she doesn't want the marriage to fail, so she's pretending that nothing has happened – except that they're now in separate rooms, and she's not talking to Frank apart from when she absolutely has to.'

'Hmmm, I can imagine Frank landing up in a bath with another woman, it's the sort of thing he's good at. But there'd be a perfectly innocent explanation. He did that to us a couple of times when we were going out with him, remember?'

'Oh, yes. What I can't imagine is Frieda getting that upset at it – not once he'd explained whatever strange reason had caused it. Or the idea that she'd quietly pretend that nothing had happened, that's just not like her. But that's Eric Johns's version, and he's decided that it's up to us to pretend we know nothing about it when they get back. Not to mention anything if we find Frank's back at his flat and Frieda is back at her house, that sort of thing. Just pretend everything's normal.'

'I don't know. I can see Frieda doing that. Imagine having being married once and it fails, and then you get a second chance and that fails on your honeymoon? I think I'd pretend to the world that nothing had gone wrong, but I'd make sure he lived in the kennel and did what he was told.'

Gertie made a face. She couldn't imagine doing anything like that. She would have half killed both husbands and thrown them out. Before going on to the third, and making damn sure he was trained properly.

'Anyway, I don't believe it,' she said. 'But Eric Johns should be careful about interfering in Frank's life. You'd have thought he would have learnt by now.'

'And Frieda's.'

'Pity we don't know what's really going on.'

'You know how pompous Eric Johns can be when he thinks he's doing the right thing, when he gets into the I'm-older-than you mode.'

The idea that Eric Johns might be serving as a male proxy for their displeasure with their non-calling boyfriends did not enter their minds.

'There's Tricia and Sam.' Gertie waved to the other two who had walked into the pub. Sam made a gesture indicating a refill. Gertie gave a thumbs up. In short order Tricia and Sam joined them with fresh drinks. Sam had that effect on people. She tended to get served faster. It was something about her eyes.

'I was just telling Susan that you were the first to speak to Eric Johns,' Gertie said, once they had seated themselves and passed the refreshers over.

'Aarggh!' cried Sam. 'Do not mention that man's name. Please.'

'Bad day, Sam?'

'Yesterday I had him sermonising before the first cup of tea. Today he gave me the full benefit of his golden rules for a happy marriage. The first of which is, apparently, that a woman must be a good little wife. As if I'm going to give a toss.'

'Er, Martin not coming?' Susan asked.

'It's girls' night out,' Sam said. 'Which means no partners of either sex.'

The others looked at her as she sipped her brandy. She noticed their glance.

'Okay, okay, while it's just us together, Martin's throwing a wobbly. She thinks I'm secretly having an affair with a man. Jesus, give me strength. And you know who that man is? Inspector Summers, for Christ's sake.'

They looked at each other.

'Frank!' she cried. 'Inspector Frank Summers! I mean, really! As if I could find him attractive in that way.' She paused as she realised that she was in company with two ex-girlfriends of Frank, and some diplomacy might be required. 'Look, I'm sorry, I shouldn't have said that. I shouldn't have put it that way.'

They all, to certain degrees, protested against this idea. The protests had no effect, bar one.

'Miaaouw,' said Squishy, emerging from the pocket of Frank's jacket which Tricia had brought in and put next to her. Tricia helped the kitten onto the table. Squishy looked blearily around, and then stumbled towards Sam, rubbing herself against Sam's fingers.

'Oh, dear, dear, Squishy,' Sam said, stroking the kitten. 'You know, don't you?' She looked around the table. 'Look, I'm not a witch, as Eric Johns thinks, though I do follow, more or less, the idea of Wicca, but – well, cats are strange. They seem to understand when someone, a human, is having a problem. They always seem to gravitate towards someone who – someone who isn't feeling sure of themself. Maybe that's because they know they'll get hugs and strokes, and possibly even fed. I don't know, I can't even, normally, stand cats. But Squish – well, you're special, aren't you, Squish?'

'She's missing him,' Tricia said. 'I let her sleep next to me in bed, on Frank's jacket. She kneads it a few times, she knows it's bedtime, then she looks at me as if to say, "Well, where is he?" It makes me want to cry, poor thing. I do tell her that he'll be back, soon, but I don't think she understands.'

'Don't worry, little Squish, Frank will be back before you know it,' said Susan, reaching over to stroke the kitten. 'And he'll have loads of interesting stories about young women in baths, but I think you might be a little young to hear those.'

'Ah,' said Tricia, 'I've had news about that from the other side.'

'The other side?' asked Sam, scratching Squishy under the chin. 'Don't tell me that you're psychic, Trish, one witch is enough for a police station. Though, then again, it could be quite useful in winding Eric Johns up. He's been asking for it.'

'No, I meant the other side of the channel. Mrs S – she's Mrs S now, of course – says to encourage the Cream Cake Man in his delusions. She says the story about the woman in the bath is correct, but not about Frank being in the bath. She'll tell us all about it when she gets back, but we might as well have a bit of fun with a certain desk sergeant.'

That gained all of their attention. Even Squishy appeared to perk up.

'There really was a woman in the bath?' asked Gertie.

'Yes. But how or why, I don't know. Frieda didn't have much time, she only sent a short text message on her mobile phone.'

There was a sudden silence. Glances were passed.

'Frieda took her mobile phone with her?' asked Susan.

'Not her usual one. She doesn't want every Tom, Dick and Harry able to contact her. She bought a new one just for the purpose. But don't let anyone else know, it's top secret.'

'I'll bet it is,' breathed Susan.

'Does Frank know she's got it?' asked Gertie.

'I don't know. Does it matter?'

Gertie and Susan looked at each other.

'Well,' said Gertie slowly, 'Frank has what you might describe as a phobia about mobile phones. Perhaps not a phobia, as such, but he does hate them. He once described them as the invisible chains of modern self-imposed slavery. Then he started quoting William Blake, something about handcuffs. I didn't understand it, but he really does hate them. Mobiles, I mean. In fact, I don't think the word "hate" describes it. He loathes them. With a passion.'

'That's a bit over the top, isn't it?' suggested Tricia. 'I'd feel lost without mine.'

'Some phobias have a basis in existence,' Sam noted. 'When I was eight we lived in Botswana for about a year – my dad was an engineer, and he had a contract there. One day I was bitten by a snake – we were living on a farm at the time. Anyway, I

174

was absolutely terrified, they have some nasty specimens out there. The farm workers all got together and discussed the different ways I might die. Whether it was one of the venoms that attack the nervous system, or the blood supply, or whether my flesh would just rot off. Cytotoxic, haematoxic – I forget the name for the other. Anyway, after half an hour one of them produced the snake which had bit me, it turned out that it was quite harmless, and they'd just been teasing me. Ever since then I've absolutely loathed snakes – and farm workers, as it happens.'

'Neurotoxic,' said Susan. 'The venom that attacks the nerves. God, Sam, I don't blame you. What an awful thing to do to an eight-year-old child.'

Gertie giggled.

'I think Frank was probably once interrupted by a call on a mobile while having a passionate snog with a girlfriend. I think that would probably put me off the things. If I was having a passionate snog with a boyfriend, I mean,' she added quickly, blushing slightly, and trying not to look at Sam.

'One of the men in my last station was discussing his weekend in the locker room with the door open one time,' Sam said, apparently not noticing. 'I just happened to overhear a bit where he was describing how he had just got this girl's top off, a girl he had met that evening, he was just trying to undo her bra, when his mate rang up to ask if he wanted to go out for a few beers. From what I heard next it ruined the evening. Though he didn't quite put it in those words.'

This was met by a chorus of laughter and grimaces.

'Something I haven't quite decided,' said Susan, 'is, if I'm in a restaurant on a date, and my partner's phone goes off, and he answers it and starts chatting away, do I slap him first and walk out, or just walk out? I mean, after all, we're supposed to be there on a romantic date, aren't we?'

'Oh, yes!' exclaimed Tricia. 'That is so rude! Even if it isn't a date, even if you're just having lunch with someone.'

'I'm always surprised how people react when you arrest them and take them down the station,' Sam said. 'You take away their wallet, their watch, all the rest. But when it comes to taking their mobile phone away, it's almost as if you're taking their life support system away. They act like babies, most of them. And then there are the ones who insist that you can't take their phones away. One of them threatened to sue me for torture, once.'

'The question is,' put in Susan, 'does Frank know she's got it? If he does, all well and fine. If he doesn't, and he finds out – well, I think they might just have the first argument of their married life. And it'll be a biggie. Oh, yes, that will be a biggie. Knowing Frank.'

'I wouldn't blame him,' said Sam. 'After all, a honeymoon should be about just the two of you. Taking a mobile along – it's almost like saying that the other person isn't good enough company.'

'Frieda just wants to stay in touch in case anything serious goes wrong,' Tricia said, defending her boss. 'She won't get involved, but she wants to know if she's going to come back to any crisis. Which, in Wellbury, is entirely possible. She could get back to find that some new religious group have decided that the devil lives in the sewers, and they're digging them up to find him. Or seventeen circuses have booked into town and you can't walk because the streets are clogged up with fire-eaters.'

They all nodded. That sort of thing was entirely possible in Wellbury. And you would want to be prepared, rather than step off the train and have to walk around open drains, or find that all the taxis had been block-booked by troupes of clowns.

'It rather comes back to whether or not Frank knows about it,' Susan said. 'If he does, fine. If he doesn't, and he finds out ...'

'It is,' said Sam, putting her finger on it, 'not a question of mobile phones. It's a question of trust.'

'If Frieda doesn't want him to know then he won't find out,' Tricia said.

'This is Frank we're talking about,' said Gertie. 'You can't hide that sort of thing from him. It isn't that he goes looking for anything, he just has this bad habit of stumbling into things.'

'Such as women in the bath,' suggested Sam.

'Exactly.'

'Well, my money's on Frieda,' Tricia said. She started as her handbag made a noise. She opened it and took out her mobile phone. She sighed. 'Bloody Jeremy! I told him tonight was girls' night.'

'Something serious?'

'Serious? No, he's just sent a text message to tell me he loves me. Oh! He can be so irritating at times!'

'Well, we are a right shower, aren't we,' noted Susan. 'Sam's having jealousy fits from Martin. Tricia's having problems training Jeremy. And Gertie and I seem to have struck out with bloody Tom and Wilf.'

'Oh, well,' sighed Tricia, 'at least we know a lucky couple just across the Channel who, right at this minute, are probably finishing a candle-lit dinner before indulging in a little legal romantic how's your father.'

'Lucky buggers,' noted Gertie. 'Still, no sense in moping. There's work to be done. What are we going to do about the Cream Cake Man? I fancy some fun.'

'Let Operation Cream Cracker begin,' said Sam, slamming down her glass and smiling at the others. They all smiled back.

Normandy. Tuesday. Evening.

Quelle Question!

The lucky couple just across the Channel were indeed enjoying a romantic dinner in a lovely little restaurant, to the sound of someone softly playing the accordion in the background. The romantic how's your father wasn't the next immediate item on their menu, though.

'I'd like to have another look at that room where we found the girl, Amelie,' Frank was saying.

'Darling, the French police will have picked it over. If there was anything to be found I'm sure they would have found it.'

'Yes, I know. But you know how it is. Revisiting the scene of a crime can jog something in your memory.'

Frieda did not reply immediately. She also dearly wanted another look at the room. At the same time she couldn't help but feel that it was distracting them from their real purpose, that of being on honeymoon, of having a holiday and getting to build that firm foundation of being husband and wife.

'Darling, would you mind if I asked you a question?' she said, deciding to steer things in their proper direction.

Frank blinked. It wasn't like Frieda to be so delicate. If she had a question to be asked she asked the question. Anyway, why should a wife ever hesitate asking her husband a question, or a husband a wife?

Although, come to think of it, there would no doubt be some questions best left unasked. Probably ones involving what the husband discussed when out with the boys, or what the girls talked about on a girls' night out. If only because it might turn out to be depressingly mundane.

He chewed thoughtfully for a few moments, swallowed, turned his attention back to the meal, and said:

'No.'

'Oh, please, darling, just a little question.'

He grinned at her.

'No,' he repeated.

She pouted back.

'Very well, then, I won't.'

'Just teasing, Free. What's the question?'

'No, I shan't ask it.'

'Oh, go on Free.'

'No.'

Frank put his knife and fork down and looked at her. She continued her enjoyment of her meal without returning the look.

'Hokay,' he said, shrugging his shoulders and picking up his knife and fork.

They carried on eating in companionable silence, just as if they were any other happily married couple. This continued until Frank risked a peek at Frieda just as she did the same to him. Both giggled.

'Now we're being silly,' Frieda said.

'Yes, we are. Nice, isn't it?'

'It is.

'Go on, what was the question.' To Frank's amazement Frieda blushed slightly. He began to wonder if it wasn't the type of question best not asked in the middle of a reasonably crowded restaurant. Especially as the accordion-player had paused for a break, and they could probably be overheard by one of the couples nearby.

'Well, I was wondering. Which side of the plate do you prefer to have your peas on, left or right?'

Frank blinked several times. He prided himself on rarely being surprised at what life might throw at him. Baffled, confused, perplexed, yes, often; surprised, rarely. But "What side of the plate do you prefer your peas to be on"? What sort of a question was that?

'Free, that's a very unfair question to ask your husband,' he replied once he had decided that he had not misheard her. 'Or anyone, for that matter. I mean, I've never even wondered whether I had a preference for the location of peas on my plate. Never mind left or right, there's top and bottom, too. And now, I have this horrible feeling that I will spend the rest of my life worrying about whether I do have a preference, and if it says anything about me.'

'I'm sorry, darling.'

'Thinking about it, if, for example, I'd just ordered a plate of steak, chips and peas – and eggs, of course –'

'No, eggs would be too much. Steak, chips and peas is sufficient. More than sufficient. Especially if the peas are done properly.'

'Hmm, you might be right. Depends on the size of the steak. Let's say it's a small fillet steak, tasty, but leaves enough space for a fried egg. Fried in butter, of course.'

'Hmm, even so I think I'll skip the egg.'

'Okay – oh, with bread and butter on the side. White bread, naturally. Thick white farmhouse bread, and lashings of real butter.'

'Frank, you're being greedy now. You'll never have a good night's sleep if you over-eat.'

'Well, never mind the bread and butter, they aren't on the plate. So, we've got fillet steak – to the right; chips, in the centre.' He thought for a moment. 'Yes, the peas have to go on the left. Definitely.'

'Interesting. My father always had his peas on the left. Although that was actually carrots. Do you think that's a man's sort of thing?'

Frank's knife and fork paused again. He was faced with answering three questions: peas, carrots and "a man's sort of thing".

'I'm not sure that the concept of anything being a man's sort of thing is entirely valid,' he said, frowning at a piece of potato which was rather enticingly cavorting with some melted cheese. 'Too much danger of stereotyping and generalisation, wouldn't you say?'

'You can generalise without stereotyping. Take Pete Phillips as an example. You could predict pretty much ninety-five percent of the time whether he would think something was a man's thing or a woman's thing.'

Frank speared the piece of potato and associated melted cheese. Frieda was right about Pete Phillips. On the other hand he wasn't overly happy about extrapolating anything out of that. And, anyway, how could the positioning of vegetables say anything about male or female characteristics?

"Your honour, I noticed that the suspect had his peas on the right, which immediately identified him to me as a well dodgy character."

"And quite right, Inspector Summers. No gentleman would allow his peas to be on the right."

'Okay, Free, which side of the plate do you prefer your peas to be on? Or carrots.'

Frieda shrugged.

'It really doesn't bother me,' she said. He dropped his fork.

'Now, Free, that's not fair. You can't just say that it doesn't bother you.'

'Why not?'

'Well ...' Frank struggled to come up with a reason, failing totally. 'Putting the peas to one side for the moment –'

'On the left.'

'On the left, if you wish. Putting that to one side –'

'Would it really bother you if they were on the right?'

'No, Free, it would not bother me at all. However –'

'What about top or bottom?'

'Frieda, I don't care if they're left, right, top, bottom or sideways. Now –'

'Or mixed in with everything, like a stew?'

Frank put his knife and fork down again.

'You're teasing me, aren't you?'

She looked up from her plate and giggled.

'Just a bit.'

'Okay, try to be serious for just a second. Are we going to have another look at that room, or not?'

'Of course we are, darling.'

'Good.'

Frieda paused.

'What about beans?' she asked.

Madame Arneaux was manning the counter of the bar when they returned to the hotel. She greeted them with a smile, and several of the regulars nodded acknowledgement. Frank leaned towards Frieda as they approached the counter and whispered into her ear.

'Two blokes, dark suits, sunglasses. Corner towards the left.'

'Yes, I saw them. Very suspicious.'

Frank smiled at Madame Arneaux.

'Bon soir, madame,' he said. 'Vous etre bien?'

'Bon soir, monsieur, très bien. You have a good day?'

'Oui, madame, très jolie. I wonder if we couldn't ask a favour. Would it be possible to get the key to the room we were originally supposed to have?'

'I think I lost my engagement ring there, madame,' Frieda

said, having quietly pocketed the same item. She raised a hand showing only a wedding ring.

'Oh, la-la, madame, I understand. To lose the engagement ring – this is a disaster enormous. Oh, la-la! Should I lose mine! I shall get the key immediately.'

She went into the kitchen and returned with the key.

'The key, madame.'

She leaned over.

'I do not wish to make you anxious, but please to make sure your door is locked if you are not in your room. There are two men in the corner who appear very – suspicious, yes?'

'Dark suits, white shirts, black ties, sunglasses,' said Frank.

'Oui, monsieur. You notice them?'

'Oui, madame. Nous sont les poppies British. We notice everything.'

Madame Arneaux smiled at this and moved away to serve a customer. These English police. They were so polite yet so ... quiet and efficient. They noticed everything. And so handsome! The English woman was a flic, but an Inspector, and she was so smart!

Madame Arneaux was very practical apart from a weakness for English magazines about how to decorate your house, and how to dress. Madame Summers was an English Lady. She wondered where she shopped.

Frank unlocked the door and they entered the room. It was almost entirely bare. No sheets on the bed, the cupboard doors open, showing empty shelves. Even the door to the small drinks cabinet was open.

'They've pulled up the carpet,' Frieda noted. 'Didn't do a very good job of putting it back properly.'

'Just like us, I suppose,' Frank mused, 'no money in the budget to pay for a carpet fitter, so they do it themselves.' He wandered over to the bathroom and looked at the white floor tiles now stained with a number of different police footprints. 'Why was she in the bathroom? She's here ostensibly to hand over some tagged heroin. What was she doing? She's not in here to take a bath, or to go to the loo. So why isn't she in the bedroom, sitting on the bed and waiting for Mr Mug to turn up?'

'Touching up her makeup? Checking her appearance in the mirror?' suggested Frieda.

'Could be. So she's looking in the mirror and someone whacks her from behind. Someone hiding in the bathroom, I reckon. Behind the door.'

'That would make sense. Otherwise the other person would have had to have followed her in. She wouldn't be likely to calmly look in the mirror to see if her clothes were askew or her eyeliner needed refreshing if she knew there was a strange man watching her. And this bathroom is too small. The other person would be right behind her, far too close for comfort.'

'Unless that person was someone close – boyfriend, lover, husband.'

'Hmmm.' Frieda nodded. 'That is a possibility. But if that's the case then what is he doing here?'

'What if we're looking for a she? Amelie says, I'm just popping into the bathroom to check my make-up, the other woman follows her, chatting away about boyfriends or perfume or something? Something innocuous to Amelie.

185

Would she feel uncomfortable having another woman looking at her?'

'Possibly not, though I wouldn't feel comfortable with someone that close. Frank, without knowing what type of person Amelie is, we could end up going in circles. She might be the modern sort of girl who thinks doing their make-up in public is nothing to be embarrassed about.'

Frank nodded.

'True. But it narrows down the possibilities.'

He looked around the bathroom.

'Free, let's try going through it again. You walked in here, you had your toiletry bag with you. What did you do then?'

'I walked in. I didn't notice the handbag at first – I almost stepped on it. I thought it strange. I put my toiletry bag on the top, next to the basin, caught sight of something in the bath, pulled back the shower curtain, and there she was, lying in the bath.'

'I tell you what, let me get out of the way. You walk over and do exactly what you did on Sunday night.'

Frank stood back by the door while Frieda repeated her actions of two days earlier. When she had finished Frank folded his arms and shook his head to indicate that her actions had not given him any new ideas.

'So she's been knocked over the head and fallen into the bath,' he said. 'Her head's towards the taps. Our attacker then pulls the shower curtain across. Tell you what, get into the bath and I'll be the attacker.'

Frieda raised her eyebrows.

'You want me to get into the bath and pretend I'm Amelie

lying unconscious?'

'Look, I'll do it.'

He pulled the shower curtain back, climbed into the bath and lay down, head towards the taps.

'She was like this, if I remember correctly. More or less on her side, hands up towards her head, underneath, almost as if she were having a snooze.'

'Not quite, Frank, she's a lot shorter than you. She didn't have her legs sticking out the other end.'

'Well, yes. Yes, her knees were tucked in, weren't they. Mmmm.'

Frieda waited as he looked at the side of the bath in front of his eyes, pondering.

'Any thoughts?' she asked.

'Yes, I was wondering why some people find it enjoyable having a bath together in a bath made for one. Sounds bloody uncomfortable to me. Free, draw that shower curtain across, just like it was when you walked in.'

Frieda pulled the curtain across, masking Frank from her sight. She listened.

'Frank, stop pulling those faces,' she said.

'How do you know that I'm pulling faces?'

'You always do when you're trying to think and don't have any answers.'

'No, that's when I don't have the questions. I don't mind not having the answers, because I can always look for them. It's not knowing the questions that really irritates me. But I do have one now.'

He pulled the shower curtain back and looked up at Frieda.

'Spot anything strange about this set-up?' he asked.

Frieda looked around, knowing that Frank had noticed something, determined to spot it herself without having to ask. After a while she gave up.

'Okay, clever-clogs, what is it?'

'I should have noticed it straight away. It's blindingly obvious when you think about it.'

Frieda cocked her head at him in a "You have ten seconds to live" pose.

'We don't have a shower curtain in our bathroom in the other room,' he said. 'We have a bath, and a shower just like the one behind you, but no shower curtain in the bath. And there isn't a shower head above this bath. Or attached to the taps.'

Frieda looked. Frank was right. Separate shower cubicle behind her. Separate bath. Two taps. Shower curtain draped into bath, but no shower head over the bath.

'So why the curtain?' she asked.

Frank pushed the curtain to one side and heaved himself out of the bath.

'It's an anomaly,' he said. 'Remind me to ask Madame Arneaux tomorrow. There's probably a perfectly reasonable explanation. No doubt a French custom of some form or other.'

'You think it could be significant?'

'Probably not. But it's the only unusual thing I can see.'

He looked at the curtain. He pulled it back across the bath. And then opened it again.

'Our anonymous friend clobbers Amelie over the head,' he said. 'One blow, side of the neck, just behind the ear, so he or she is probably a professional – either that or lucky, because Amelie goes out like a light. He – or she – then picks her up, dumps her in the bath, pulls the curtain across, and makes their getaway without being seen. Which, once again, inclines me to think that we are dealing with a professional. It isn't easy getting out of a building like this without anyone seeing you.'

'You seem to be quite good at it. I can't count the number of times I've gone down to your office to find that you've disappeared, and no-one saw you go.'

'That's because I had a lot of practice at my last station. My inspector there hated my guts, so I thought the less he saw of them the better. There's just one problem. The handbag.'

Frieda nodded.

'The attacker goes to all the trouble of putting her into the bath and pulling the shower curtain across, but leaves her handbag lying on the floor for anyone to see as soon as they open the door.'

'The good old case of being disturbed and rushing things. I don't think. That only turns out to be the case every twentieth time.'

'It would fit with the facts. Marie cleaned the room less than an hour before we arrived. She would have noticed the bag, investigated, and found Amelie. So that means Amelie was attacked within an hour of our arrival, after Marie had finished cleaning. The attacker must have known that we – or someone like us – were due to arrive. At the very least they would have expected it. So, they've put Amelie into the bath, drawn the curtain, they pick up her handbag to get the heroin, hear a noise of some sort – possibly a nearby door opening –

possibly even us – drop the bag and exit as fast as they can.'

Frank frowned at the bath as if irritated that it couldn't speak to him. He looked around.

'The handbag was on the floor right there, wasn't it?'

'Yes, a couple of feet from the basin.'

Frank stretched out a hand to where the handbag might have been had it been on the top, next to the basin, and then pulled it back as if he was pulling out a small packet. He shook his head and went down on his haunches.

'It's too far back,' he said. 'If Amelie had put it next to the basin, then our Mr X coshes her right on the spot, catches her as she falls, dumps her in the bath, grabs the heroin out of the handbag, drops it on hearing something – it would have fallen next to the basin, not in the middle of the floor.'

'Unless they dropped it as they left.'

Frank nodded.

'That makes sense. It would have fallen just there.'

He sighed.

'The question is, where's the heroin at this stage? Let's say it was in her handbag, nowhere else for her to have it. She takes it with her into the bathroom. The other person, having put her into the bath, grabs the handbag, grabs the heroin, drops the handbag, and slips out. All fine and dandy. The only problem is, the people out there, the main suspects, haven't got it, they're still looking for it. So whoever did for Amelie isn't one of them.'

'She might have strapped it to her leg. Or even under her blouse.'

Frank looked up to her and raised an eyebrow.

'No,' said Frieda, 'I don't think it was. She wasn't wearing the right sort of clothes. And her clothes hadn't been interfered with.'

'White blouse, white dress, white shoes,' noted Frank, looking at the floor. 'She likes white, our Amelie.'

'You noticed?'

'Red belt. Probably plastic, but expensive looking. Red earrings. Red lipstick. Belt had a brass clasp. Very shiny, maybe plastic or chromium, but again, that ring of expensive. Or, at least, taste.'

'She knows how to dress. And you have a good memory of her lying in the bath.'

'That's because you told me she was dead. I have a very good memory for corpses.'

He tapped the edge of the bath while Frieda frowned at him.

'Where's the heroin?' he asked. 'That's the important question.'

'Unless the heroin wasn't here in the first place.'

Frank rubbed his jaw and grinned ruefully.

'You're right, there are too many questions and we aren't in a position to get them answered.' He stood up and turned a frown towards the basin.

'Before you turn around, Frank,' Frieda said, standing close behind him.

'Yes?'

'What am I wearing? Right now?'

'Right now? Free, be fair –'

'Without looking, Frank. What am I wearing?'

Frank sighed.

'You want me to be honest, Free?'

'Perfectly honest, Frank.'

He sighed again.

'Free, you're wearing that strange black dress, I don't know what it's called, it isn't the little black number, because it goes across almost in little pleats, or whatever they're called, over your breasts, which makes me just want to take you and ravish you, and the skirt part of the dress is also pleated, so it whirls around as you move, making you look as sophisticated as can be. Your shoes are black, with that crossover strap which shows off your ankles to perfection. Now, can I turn around?'

Frieda considered this. It was probably as perfect a reply as she could ever hope for.

'What earrings am I wearing?' she asked.

Again he sighed.

'The gold ones. With the diamond insets. The same ones you were wearing when we got married.'

Frieda considered that. Frank had remembered what earrings she had been wearing when they had said "Yes" in front of the altar?

Those were the same gold earrings her mother had worn when she had married. She remembered her mother saying, "Now don't be a goose, Frieda. You need a good pair of earrings, and these are the ones your grandmother wore when she got married, just as I did when I got married to your father."

To think of any more questions for your husband regarding

your apparel would undoubtedly be goose behaviour.

Either he was very perverse, or he was perfect.

'Can I turn around now?' he asked. 'Because, if you're going to interrogate me on the lingerie front, I'm afraid I was hoping that would be a surprise later.'

'The question is, who is lying?' Frank asked after they had got into bed.

'You're thinking of our Monsieur Simenon?'.

'That's exactly it.' He rolled over on the bed and looked at her. 'What if he's a bent copper making sure that we take away the right impressions? What about his wife, who appears to turn up on the right occasions? Their apparent problem marriage. Is that a front?'

'Frank, that's one too many marriages at this moment. Right now I'm only interested in ours.'

'Good point,' he said, turning over, away from her. 'Let's sleep on it.'

'What?'

He turned back.

'Just teasing, Free. Give your husband a kiss. We are on honeymoon after all.'

Later they lay in the dark, holding each other tightly.

Frieda was thinking vaguely how silly she had been, how her Frank was obviously The Right Man.

Or, in his case, The Right Frank.

She really should trust him more.

Frank, as he floated off towards sleep, would have echoed

those thoughts about his Free.

But a tiny voice at the back of his head said, "Good thing her mum told you about those gold earrings she gave Frieda, innit? Otherwise you never would have noticed."

'Bollocks,' he muttered.

And then they both dreamed about shower curtains. Frieda's were a tasteful pink, and hung down neatly. Frank's were multi-coloured and kept blowing in the wind.

Normandy. Wednesday. Morning.

Curtains: shower curtains

Once Frank had bounced downstairs Frieda took out her mobile phone and switched it on. "It'll be just our little secret, my sweet, just our little lonely lovely secret" alerted her to a new message.

"Nothing new from Cream Cake Man, but he's developing what he's got quite nicely. Please, please send more titbits to feed him if there are any. Everybody sends their love. Love, Tricia."

Frieda frowned. She wasn't quite sure she liked the sound of "Everybody sends their love." It suggested that others knew that Tricia was in contact with her.

Still, that could only mean people such as Gertie and Susan, and she was happy enough with that. She tapped her fingernails, uncertain as to whether or not to give a brief mention of the previous day's attempted mugging.

Downstairs Monsieur Arneaux was busy with his usual morning entertainment of polishing glasses.

'Bon jour, Monsieur Arneaux,' Frank said cheerfully as he

entered the hotel bar. 'Ca va?'

'Bien, monsieur Summers, très bien,' the other man replied warmly, confident that he could manage so long as the Englishman stuck to simple enquiries such as that one. Even so his glass polishing speeded up. 'Et vous?'

'Très biens, monsieur, très biens.'

'Une cafe normale, monsieur?'

'Oui, monsieur.'

Frank paused as he watched the man pour his coffee. Talking around a subject in English in such a way that the suspect didn't realise what was happening was second nature to him. Doing the same thing in French was likely to be slightly more difficult, even if the other man wasn't a suspect. Not that Monsieur Arneaux was entirely off the list. He might have an alibi, but that didn't mean that he wasn't involved, after all, he would know the hotel inside out. But, apart from a certain strange nervousness, the Frenchman seemed such an unlikely criminal his name would remain on the list only through standard procedure.

'Ah, merci, merci,' Frank said as Monsieur Arneaux placed the coffee in front of him. 'Monsieur, une question, s'il vous plait.'

'Une question?' This sounded like the sort of thing Monsieur Arneaux did not want to get involved in. Even a simple question in the Englishman's unique approach to the French language was likely to result in a large amount of confusion.

'Oui. Les rideaux douche.'

Monsieur Arneaux paused before speeding up his polishing until it threatened to break the sound barrier.

'Riddo dushe?' he asked

'Oui, dans le bain.'

'Dance le bane?'

'Oui, mais pas de douche head – porquois?'

Monsieur Arneaux took a slow but deep breath.

'Pardon, monsieur?'

Frank scratched his head. He had this horrible feeling that he might be translating just a wee bit too literally. That was the curse of carrying only a small dictionary. It might give you enough to ask which way to the Tuilleries, but they tended to be lacking in how to ask important questions about shower curtains and baths which lacked the associated shower head.

'Shower curtains,' he said slowly, reluctantly abandoning his foray into French for the more widely used speak-very-slowly-in-English-to-Johnny-Foreigner approach. Usually it would be "slowly and loudly", but there were certain limits.

'Ah, shower curtains,' Monsieur Arneaux said, his face a mixture of relief at finally understanding this polite but incomprehensible Englishman, and sadness at something else. 'Je regrette, monsieur, je regrette. Ah!' He threw his hands up in the air to show just much he regretted. Then he put a finger to his watch to indicate time. 'Samedi,' he added, 'samedi, très ... unfortunate.'

Frank nodded politely. Apparently the answer to shower curtains was Tuesday.

He took a sip of his coffee. The answer to shower curtains was Tuesday. That could be important. Very important. It was the type of thing that turned out to be the vital clue which lay at the heart of the case.

Just such a pity he didn't have a clue what the man was on about. He decided to try a different track.

'Ce samedi?' he asked.

'Oui! Oui!' exclaimed the other man. 'Ce samedi. Mais, dimanche, ah, dimanche, no?'

Right. So it was supposed to have been Tuesday, except for Sunday. Perhaps you only got shower curtains if you booked into the hotel on Sundays – possibly only on Sunday evenings. But even so, what about the shower head?

This could turn out to be a really tricky conversation.

Monsieur Arneaux had similar thoughts. He decided that the best approach to a tricky conversation was to change it to something he could handle.

'You have good night?' he asked. 'The meal good? You sleep well?'

'Oui, oui,' replied Frank. 'Vous avez la cuisine grande, n'est ce pas? A la francais?'

Frank thought that he was complimenting Monsieur Arneaux on French cooking. Monsieur Arneaux wondered why this Englishman was asking him, or certainly appeared to be asking him, if he had a large kitchen. A large French kitchen. All in all that kitchen was giving him far more trouble than he had ever expected.

'It is so-so,' he said. He was pretty confident about this English phrase, "so-so". He had been reliably informed by his wife that "so-so" meant neither good nor bad. Neutral, even. "Are you well?" "So-so." "Is the weather good?" "So-so." "Did you enjoy doing your tax returns?" "So-so."

'Ah, mais non, non, c'est superbe!' answered Frank,

astonished that a Frenchman such as Monsieur Arneaux should not extol French cooking to the skies. Usually it was the opposite. 'Votre cuisine, c'est très, très superbe.'

Monsieur Arneaux risked a glance at this Mr Frank. He was enthusiastic, friendly – perhaps mad? Why did he insist that they had a large kitchen? And now a superb kitchen?

First shower curtains, now kitchens?

Perhaps English kitchens were very small?

Still, there was one way to satisfy the Englishman. Let him see the kitchen.

'You wish?' he asked Frank, opening the door behind him and motioning into the kitchen.

Frank blinked. Presumably Monsieur Arneaux was going to show him how bland French cooking was. It was not something he had expected. But he was curious to see exactly how Monsieur Arneaux was going to manage this. He walked behind the counter and followed the other man into the kitchen.

'La,' said Monsieur Arneaux, indicating the size of the room. It had a look of a restaurant kitchen which had just been cleaned by a conscientious housewife after the builders had finished the previous day, a certain mixture of smells of plaster, paint and washing-up liquid.

'C'est so-so, n'est ce pas?' he asked.

'I suppose you could put it that way,' agreed Frank. 'You need a couple of roasts or something to give it the right smell, though. The aroma, oui?'

Monsieur Arneaux smiled politely. He hadn't understood a word, apart from "roast", and he wasn't going anywhere near that. Some English got very upset if you mentioned roast beef. His cousin had had a bad experience in somewhere called Weston Super Le Mare.

'Yes, yes, très bon,' Frank continued, wondering why Monsieur Arneaux was standing there saying nothing. Wasn't he supposed to be saying something about French cooking?

To Monsieur Arneaux's relief Marie chose that moment to come crashing in through the door to the back garden. Had the scene come from a silent movie it would have been unremarkable: buxom, smiling peasant girl enters, hooks her bag on the back of the door in one single practised movement, pauses at the sight of the two men. With the sound on it was a series of bashes and crashes, accompanied by Marie's loud trilling of whatever song she was listening to on her earphones. It gave Monsieur Arneaux an excuse to admonish her. It was only natural that he should do so. And while doing so, he could not, unfortunately, attend to the Englishman. He was just reminding a bemused Marie for the third time that she must learn to be quieter, yes, quieter, definitely quieter – had he mentioned the need for quiet? – in a hotel, it was not a farmyard, was it? – when his wife entered the kitchen carrying a pile of clean laundry. She looked from her nervously communicative husband to a bemused Marie and then to a puzzled Frank, who was leaning against a table trying to follow her husband's speech.

'Henri!' she cried, silencing him. She turned to Frank. 'There is a problem, monsieur?'

'Ah, non, madame, pas de problem. Je – I was just wondering about the shower curtains in the room we were going to have. The one that had the body in the bath.'

'Ah! A thousand apologies, monsieur. Your new room would

have had the shower curtains – Henri was to fit them on Tuesday. But, mon dieu, that terrible business on Sunday, and we had to give you the other room before it was ready. A thousand apologies, monsieur, it was a great tragedy. But,' she continued as an idea struck her, 'Henri can fit the shower curtain while you are out, today, if you wish.'

'Non, non, madame, please do not go to any bother. I was just wondering why there is a shower curtain and no shower head.'

Madame Arneaux considered this point.

'But there is the shower,' she suggested. 'Opposite the bath.'

'Yes, yes, there is the shower. However, in England, we normally only have a shower curtain if there is a shower in the bath.'

'Ah, je comprends. Non, monsieur, the curtain is not for the shower, it is for the privacy. Perhaps the wife is having the bath, and her husband needs to wash his hands, if she wishes the privacy she pulls the curtain across. If she does not wish the privacy, then, no pulling.'

'I see,' said Frank. 'Yes, that makes sense. Er, that's a French custom, is it?'

'Non, monsieur,' Madame Arneaux replied with a proud smile. 'It is my idea. I am in England four months ago, I stay with a friend. I see the shower curtain and the shower in the bath, and I think, this is a good idea. Curtains for the privacy.'

'Une idee très bons, madame,' said Frank. 'I wish I'd thought of that. Very nice.'

And absolutely nothing suspicious about it. Another possible clue swept away.

Bugger.

Upstairs Frieda had decided not to recount their latest adventures. She was even beginning to become concerned about suggesting that Tricia should encourage Eric Johns. It could easily end up with people saying things such as "But you told me", and then stopping to wonder how the other person had known whatever it was they had told. All in all something best left alone. She sent Tricia a quick message: "Off to Rouen this morning. Having best of all possible honeymoons. Will bring back loads of photographs."

She switched the mobile phone off, put it right at the bottom of her handbag and went to brush her hair one last time. In the bathroom she looked at Frank's wash-bag. I must, she thought, ask Frank about those tablets.

And then she went downstairs to find Frank with Monsieur and Madame Arneaux in the kitchen discussing shower curtains.

'So that explains the shower curtain,' Frank said as they approached their favourite breakfast restaurant. 'Pity. I had hoped it might have told us something. Still could, though.'

'Not a bad idea as far as privacy goes,' Frieda said, sitting down at what was now "their" table. 'Especially when you've got an old hotel which wasn't designed to contain showers and baths.'

Frank smiled.

'I remember when I was a kid, the folks insisted we go away at least once a year. No cheap flights in those days. Shared bathrooms down the corridor in some hotels which would be condemned by Health and Safety these days. Great fun for a kid. Bonjour, Cathy, ca va?'

'Bonjour, monsieur, madame,' replied Cathy. 'Coffee to begin with?'

'Coffee sounds good. Free?'

'Yes, please.'

'And then,' Frank said as Cathy went back inside, 'I think I shall have a healthy breakfast for a change. Poached eggs on toast. With lashings of butter.'

'Mmm. I haven't had poached eggs in ages. Might skip the lashings of butter, though.'

'You know what I think?'

'If it has anything to do with the case of the missing heroin, then, Frank, no.'

'Hokay.'

Frieda let ten seconds pass before giving in.

'Okay, Frank, what is it you think?'

'You know what they say: cherchez la femme. Maybe it was a crime passionel. Nothing to do with drugs.'

'Do you get many of those?' asked Cathy, emerging with two coffees on a tray.

'Yes, it happens often enough,' said Frank. 'Though most crimes of passion are quite boring from the point of view of detection. They tend to be done on the spur of the minute, and it's normally obvious who did what.'

'I suppose I'm not the passionate type. Otherwise I know one man who might end up being found at the bottom of a wine barrel.'

'You mentioned you were supposed to get married next June,' said Frieda. 'That's the man, is it?'

'Yes. Old story, I suppose. I met him at university in Toronto. He was French, good looking, charming. Great sense of humour. I never expected him to think of me – that way, if you see what I mean. I'm not exactly a film star, the folks are just normal folks trying to live a normal life, paying the mortgage, saving for retirement, taking out the garbage, that sort of thing. Anyway, we got together and I thought that that was that. I was pretty pleased. I've never been the kind of girl who dreams about falling in love. To me finding a man who you would be happy to spend the rest of your life with was, I don't know, pretty much like hoping to find a decent house you can afford, I suppose. You know you don't want a mansion, you just want somewhere comfortable you can call your own.'

'And then he turned out to be a facade rather than bricks and concrete?'

'Sort of. He had to go back to France. He promised to write, but he never did. I got a chance to come over here. I went looking for him. I think I was just pissed off with him more than anything. Turned out he was from a wealthy family with vineyards and everything. I arrived the day before he was due to get married. He hadn't told me that he was engaged to someone else from his set. I had the great pleasure of telling everyone what a shit he was. I knew they'd all think I was some cheap little tart who didn't deserve any better, so I said that I wasn't angry that he had shagged me, just that he had lied to me. I asked his fiancée if she was happy to be marrying a man who had no honour. Then I left before they could throw me out.'

'Did it make any difference?'

Cathy smiled.

'They called the wedding off, so I imagine it did. Anyway, here I am gassing about myself when you folks are waiting for your breakfasts.'

'I do love the fascinating tapestry that is human nature,' Frank said when she had left with their orders. 'I have this suspicion that Cathy would have shacked up with her Frenchman quite happily for a limited period if she had known he was engaged. It was his lying about it she couldn't take.'

'You would approve?'

Frank shrugged.

'Each to their own. If it makes happy and doesn't hurt, let people do what they enjoy.' He grinned. 'Having said that, I have no doubt something will crop up to prove me wrong. Life's like that.'

'So it's okay for him to have an affair even though he's already engaged?'

'Ah, there you go, you see. Perhaps his fiancée was the old-fashioned type who believed in staying pure until marriage, but expected her husband to sow his wild oats. The contract being, as it were, that she never found out about them. On the other hand, maybe she was just as bad as him. Maybe Cathy's appearance was an excuse to give up on a marriage she didn't really want? Who knows?'

He smiled at her.

'I always find such things fascinating,' he said, 'but most of the time you should never get involved, unless you're asked to – and that should come written down in triplicate. Otherwise it just ends up as interference. And there is only one priority to my mind, and that is you and me. Anyone interfering with us – well, there will be severe consequences.'

Wellbury. Wednesday. Morning.

A Message in a muddle

Eric Johns sat on his stool at the reception counter of Wellbury police station, moodily regarding two postcards in front of him. Constables Ken Edgars and Sidney Feeler came through the entrance doors sharing a joke.

'What's up, Sarge?' asked Ken Edgars. 'You look as if someone stole your elevenses.'

'Worse than that, my lad.' Eric Johns held up the postcards. 'Confirmation. Frank and the Inspector. See this? "room so good we ordered a second."'

The two men looked at each other.

'Er, what's that mean, then, Sarge?'

'Can't you see? Plain as the nose on your face. They've got separate rooms. Frank has been kicked out of the conuptial bedroom. And see how he's signed them – "Frank and Free". That's code you know, psychological code. Means he's telling the truth, only in a unconscious sort of way, you know?'

Ken Edgars and Sidney Feeler glanced at each other again. Their faces showed clearly that they didn't know.

'Mark my words,' continued Eric Johns, missing the looks, 'it can only get worse. I knew a couple just like that, had a blazing row on the first night – she found him in bed with one of the bridesmaids. Totally innocent, it was, but they had separate bedrooms for the rest of their lives. She never spoke to him in their home, treated him like dirt out, never let him go anywhere on his own, no pub, he had to give up his allotment.' He nodded to emphasize his point.

'I didn't know Inspector Summers had an allotment,' Sidney Feeler said after a pause.

Eric Johns sighed.

'I didn't say he did have. Listen, son, you'll just have to take my word for it. It'll be treading on eggshells when they get back. Treading on eggshells.'

The bemused looks on their faces were interrupted by the entrance of Inspector Percy Hanson.

'Eric, you haven't seen – ah, postcards, they'll be from Frank and Frieda. Let's have a look.'

Eric Johns handed them over reluctantly. His face showed surprise as Percy chuckled.

'Good old Frank, eh? I'll take these through to the canteen and show them around. You can pin them up on the notice board after.'

Eric's eyes bulged.

'I don't think he realises what's going on,' he said after Percy had gone.

It was said to an empty reception. Ken Edgars and Sidney Feeler had followed hard on Percy's heels. The choice between Eric Johns's ramblings and a warm cuppa was easy.

Anyhow, they knew they would get his version of things later on. They always did, sooner or later. The more polished editions were always better. And better taken in at a distance.

Normandy. Wednesday. Morning.

Oo est lospital?

'Now, Frank,' said Frieda as she drove them towards Rouen, 'no more adventures. No more taking flights to be shot at, no more muggings. Comprendez?'

'Oh, je comprendez alright. It's just that we hardly planned on those sort of things. I'm quite happy to forego such little experiences. The problem is whether the nutters who seem to think we have a stash of heroin comprendez that.'

'Well, if they follow us they will discover that we are just a boring honeymoon couple visiting the local sights. The cathedral first. Fortunately most criminals find cathedrals boring.'

'If Simenon pops up he'll probably find it fascinating. If he could ever show a sign of being fascinated about anything, that is.'

'If he turns up I'll give him a lecture, and it won't be about the Normandy landings, Rouen, Caen or Monet.'

'Come, on, Free, he's just doing his job. Anyway, we don't have to worry about him. It's the idiots who seem to have let their imaginations get carried away. Two British police officers arrive on honeymoon and suddenly they're heroin smugglers. Apparently we got married purely for this purpose. We also chose the hotel specifically for that reason, never mind the fact that Amelie Courbois wasn't even supposed to be there. Or we just happened to stumble on the heroin and suddenly decided to branch out into the drug trade. Despite the fact that we're coppers and we'd know the place would be searched top to bottom within minutes of their coppers arriving.'

Frieda pursed her lips in a way Frank had come to recognise.

It was the face she showed when she wanted to do something but had a feeling that she shouldn't be wanting to do it.

'Amelie,' he murmured.

'Amelie?'

'You know,' he said, tapping the map on his knee, 'we could pop into the hospital on our way. It isn't that far. We could take a little detour.'

'No, I suppose it isn't, really,' agreed Frieda.

'And it would be bad manners not to pop in to say hello. After all, we have been introduced in a way. Although admittedly she was unconscious at the time.'

'Frank,' Frieda said, doing a U-turn and pointing the car towards the hospital, 'if we get into more trouble because of this I shall blame you.'

'Ah, so that's my role in married life. I wish someone had warned me beforehand.'

'Frank, we didn't have to get married for you to get the blame. You used to get it before we were married.'

'True.'

The hospital turned out to be a modern white building standing in the centre of well-tended gardens.

'Doesn't look like the NHS,' noted Frank as they walked up the entrance path. 'Unless it's newly built.'

'Maybe she has wealthy parents.'

'Or a profitable side-line in something or other.'

'Flowers,' said Frieda, nodding at a little shop next to the front door. 'We should take her some flowers. One of those fuschia plants should do the trick.'

'Ah, so that's what fuschias look like. I've been meaning to look that up. Pretty, aren't they?'

'Frank, you're not telling me you don't know what a fuschia looks like, are you?'

'Not until now. Roses, okay, gladioli, yes, nasturtiums, normally, after that it kind of becomes a blur.'

'Well, I suppose this isn't the time to start teaching you, let's pay for the fuschias and get inside.'

Inside the reception area everything was shining, white and very quiet. A single nurse sat on a stool behind the reception counter, tapping something into a computer. She smiled as they walked up.

'Bonjour, mademoiselle,' Frank said to her, 'nous cherchon Mademoiselle Amelie Courbois. Elle sont ici, n'est-ce pas?'

The nurse's smile instantly disappeared and was replaced with a baleful look, full of misery for the early morning.

'Famille?' she asked.

'Ah, non, pas de famille,' Frank replied. 'Non, mademoiselle, nous sont polizei.' The nurse missed the sigh that Frieda gave.

'Polizei? Allemande?'

'Mais non, mais non, nous sont aux Angleterre. Nous sont les poppies British, n'est-ce pas, vous comprehends?'

'Poppies British?' the nurse asked weakly, in the manner of one for whom the end of the working day would preferably have come at least an hour before.

'Les English poppies,' agreed Frank. 'Mais – Mademoiselle Courbois? Ou sont elle?'

The nurse closed her eyes, shrugged, re-opened them and

pointed down a corridor.

'Là!' she exclaimed, and returned to her computer in a manner that stated that any further conversation was out of the question.

'As an experienced police detective trained in observation I would say that this young lady is not having a good day,' Frank whispered to Frieda as they walked away.

'I would have said that it was probably the way you try to attack the poor French with their language, Frank, but I'm tempted to agree that she was already having a bad day before you turned up. Shall we find Amelie?'

'Well, okay, my French isn't perfect,' Frank said with a hint of hurt schoolboy in his tone, following her down the corridor, 'but at least I try. '

Frieda made a mental note not to keep having a dig at his enthusiastic approach to French. Not too often, anyway.

They walked into the first ward that appeared, presuming that the "Là!" of the reception nurse did not extend, to her great regret, any further than that. Inside what turned out to be quite a large ward they stopped in amazement. They were greeted with a scene of a family outing. A large group of mainly middle-aged and elderly men and women appeared to have taken over the ward. They surrounded a bed in which a young woman, presumably Amelie, in a white night-dress could just be made out. She was sitting up with her legs tucked underneath her, with two older women in black alongside her dominating, each trying to impose some edible delicacy on the patient who was quite clearly in radiant health. It resembled some family picnic, with radiating circles of eating, debating, arguing relatives, including two or three younger couples in various stages of romantic relationships. At the far end, beyond the beds, a little girl with a bedpan was chasing a little boy.

Other patients in the ward appeared to have welcomed the invasion, which was perhaps not surprising, as the food they found thrust upon them gave off the distinctive aroma of something homemade, local and spicy, a far remove from a normal hospital menu. Various open hampers showed bottles of wine which had been liberally distributed. Not only that, but it gave the other patients a ringside seat at family gossip and scandals, and allowed them to repay this largesse with intimate details of their own ailments and incisions. The loud hum of chatter suggested that the members of the invading party were responding with commiserations and bigger and better stories of their own trying health.

'Why does the phrase "tactical withdrawal" come to mind?' asked Frank softly. 'Before they realise that we're here.'

'Possibly because of that other phrase, "overwhelming odds"?' murmured Frieda.

'Maybe we should come back when it isn't so busy – outside of visiting hours.'

'I have a suspicion that this is outside visiting hours. No wonder that poor nurse was looking harassed.'

They turned around and were about to tiptoe out when they found their path blocked by Simenon. He wore the tired smile of a man about to share his miseries with someone else.

'Bon jour, Inspector,' Frank beamed. 'Comment allez vous aujourd hui?'

'Good morning, Monsieur Inspector, good morning Madame Inspector. You are here to see Amelie?'

'We thought we might pop in briefly to say hello,' Frieda replied. 'We weren't expecting such a crowd. We thought Amelie would be on her own.'

'Amelie's ancestors come from further south, almost part of Spain,' Simenon replied. 'For them family is important. Come, allow me to introduce you.'

'Well, she looks as if she's busy —' began Frank, but Simenon led them towards the bed. The crowd of picnickers fell silent, watching their approach suspiciously. They failed to greet Simenon in such a forceful manner that it was obvious that they knew who he was.

'Notice our friend at the back there?' whispered Frank in Frieda's ear.

'Yes,' she murmured back. 'Jacques trying to hide. A bit difficult with that bandage he's got around his head.'

'Now I wonder why he's worried about being seen.'

Any reply from Frieda was prevented as they got through the crowd and arrived at the bed on which Amelie sat. She was a young girl with jet-black hair, glowing cheeks, large innocent dark brown eyes and long eyelashes. She wore a white night-dress more suitable for someone ten years younger, or a few sizes smaller, definitely for someone without her heaving bosom. It was a bosom to be proud of, high, full and bursting, and held a fascination for both the women and men around her. This was just as well, for Amelie appeared totally unaware of having such an attribute. Indeed, it was almost as if her bosom were a separate being, contending for attention and highly indignant at being attached to someone whose bright, sparkling, energetic eyes showed a total lack of any independent mental activity behind them whatsoever.

'Amelie, this is Inspector Frank Summers and Madame Inspector Summers,' Simenon said. The two older women fell back, out of distrust rather than respect for Simenon and the foreigners. Amelie clapped her hands in delight.

'Mr Frank!' she exclaimed in delight. 'Mrs Frank! You saved my life! How can I ever thank you? Ah, Mr Frank!'

Frank found himself dragged forward to receive four ecstatic kisses, two for each cheek in sequence. Amelie turned to Frieda to repeat the process and found a fuschia plant in the way.

'We thought you might like some flowers to cheer you up,' Frieda said.

'Oh!' exclaimed Amelie in delight, taking the little pot-plant, 'gooseberries! My favourite!' Without turning from Frieda she handed the fuschia plant to the nearest relative who managed to catch it before it dropped. She then grabbed Frieda and repeated the process of ecstatic embraces, before turning back to Frank and taking his hand while looking soulfully into his eyes.

'My family will be very glad to meet you,' she continued without pausing nor appearing to need to pause for breath, possibly because her heaving bosom managed that on its own. 'This is my grandmother, and this is my grandmother, and over there is uncle ...'

Even with a better explanation than Amelie's confused but voluble presentation Frank and Frieda would never have been able to remember the names or occupations of Amelie's extended family, but it appeared, at the final count, that she had six cousins present, eight aunts, seven uncles, a handful of great aunts and uncles, and five or six grandparents, at least one of whom had been a mayor at some point.

The relations, most of whom appeared to understand nothing apart from their names, relaxed and began to take a friendly interest in these two English, as if the introduction had somehow given them a legal claim on them. If they were okay with their Amelie, blessed child, then the family were prepared to allow that they might not be entirely evil foreigners, even though they had turned up with that Simenon.

One of the grandmothers next to her leaned forward and whispered in Amelie's ear, nodding towards Frank and Frieda. Amelie replied with another burst, this time in French, apparently explaining who they were..

Both grandmothers cried out. One leaned over the bed and grabbed Frank's hand to kiss it, the other took Frieda's as compensation and kissed that.

'They say that they will give prayers for you for saving my life,' Amelie translated. 'They will light many candles for your happiness and long life. They were so proud when I tell them I am going undercover, and then so fearful when I was attacked. And now they are grateful to you for saving my life and for coming to see me in this terrible hospital.'

'And do not forget to mention that they are on their loonymoon,' Simenon said with some satisfaction.

'Loonymoon?' asked Amelie in confusion.

'Honeymoon,' Frieda corrected. Amelie's eyes sparkled with happy tears and she again clapped her hands.

'But that is wonderful!' she said. 'I must give you a kiss!' She again attacked both Frank and Frieda with passionate and somewhat over-intimate kisses, before turning back to her relations and explaining this new reason for her delight. All of them were now fascinated in the English couple. Saviour of their Amelie, and newly-wed! Could life be better?

While the women Oohed and Aahed over this wonderful gift of both a hero, a heroine and a great romance, one of the great uncles sealed this new friendship by offering Frank a slice of dark sausage, along with a grunted comment recommending it. It was a signal for all the older relations to dive in with their contributions, edible, potable and voluble. Amelie managed to shush them after a heated exchange. Frank and Frieda were left holding slices of sausage in each hand. Another uncle proffered two glasses of red wine as if they were religious offerings, explaining, they presumed, how this was the best wine ever made in all the world.

'Ah, thanks,' said Frank, 'but it's a little too early for us. It's one of those British customs, never get – never drink before midday.'

Amelie explained this to the uncle in a tone that suggested she was rebuking him for insulting their English guests. After all, everyone knew that the English were strange, it wasn't their fault, but that was no need to go around offering them wine before midday. The uncle shrugged and passed the second glass to an aunt, before enjoying the first glass himself.

'Your English is very good,' Frank noted.

'I speak seven languages flawlessly,' Amelie said with a great deal of innocent pride. 'French, of course, English, Spanish, German, Dutch, Italian, Polish, Greek, and Swahili. '

'Seven?' asked Frieda.

'Swahili?' asked Frank.

'I had a few days with nothing to do and got bored.'

In the silence that followed this casual remark a small man in his mid-fifties managed to slip through the crowd and get next to Frank and Frieda. He was a fussy looking man with a waxed moustache, wearing a turquoise waistcoat and a yellow bow tie. He looked like a cross between Hercule Poirot and Salvador Dali.

'Mr and Mrs Summers,' he began, 'please, I beg to introduce myself. I call myself Xavier Dubons – aargh!'

This sound of suddenly emitted air was a result of someone else elbowing him roughly aside. It was the head-bandaged Jacques, beaming broadly.

'My friends!' he exclaimed, 'you are twice our saviours. Madame, I kiss your hand most avidly –' he kissed Frieda's hand most avidly '– monsieur, I shake your hand most deeply –' he shook Frank's hand most deeply. 'Ecoutez!' he called to the assembled throng, all of whom had gathered closer for this new amazing development. Some of the other patients demanded that their beds be moved nearer so that they could share in this latest revelation.

'Ecoutez!' repeated Jacques, following it with a speech in French which passed Frank and Frieda by, but which involved quite a bit of chest thumping by Jacques, hands going up and down in a way that suggested he thought he was an aeroplane, plus a moving and tearful appeal to the ceiling which indicated that he was thanking God for sending this man and this lady just to deliver him and his family from evil, especially the little ones. By the time he finished there wasn't a dry eye in the ward. Everyone was clapping and demanding to kiss Frank and Frieda, and also that they may be allowed to present this bit of sausage or that bit of pie, oh! you have no drink! Try this excellent red, it is the best. You don't? Ah, well, I will drink it for you. Your health!'

'I tell them,' gasped Jacques, 'how you save my life.'

'But –' began Frank.

'I tell them, there I am, in my plane, about to die, about to crash, to crash alone, perhaps to fly into the sea to drown. I tell them, these are my last minutes on the good God's earth.'

'Well, technically speaking –'

'I tell them, no man should die like this, shot by his cowardous enemies, alone, far away from his family, many miles above. They below, unconscious that he is going to death, perhaps never to be even found. No, this is not the death a man should face.'

'Well –'

'And then, I tell them, and then! Mon Dieu! Mon Dieu has sent His angels to look after me. With me I have two people I have met only that morning, walking along the beach, strangers I did not recognise as angels.'

'That's a bit –'

'Yes, and even English angels! And while I am unconscious, while I lie helpless, the plane dropping towards my final end, this angel takes control of a plane when he cannot fly, and this angel looks after me and binds my wound.'

'Er –'

'And he cannot land the plane, so he flies in circles until I am recovered, recovered just to the point where I can guide him down. C'est une miracle!'

At last Jacques appeared to have run out of breath. Frank and Frieda might have had a chance to say something had the backup team not taken over.

'Ah, Monsieur Frank!' exclaimed Amelie, tears running down her pretty little face. 'Madame Frank! On Sunday you save my life, for this alone you are heroes to us all. On Monday you save my uncle's life. How can we ever repay you?' She threw her arms around Frank and gave him another series of kisses

'Well, that's very kind of you,' said Frank as quickly as he could, trying to disentangle her arms, 'but I must point out that we take Wednesdays off. If anyone needs saving today they'll just have to put it off until tomorrow.'

'Oh, Mr Frank!' squealed Amelie, sitting back and stuffing her knuckles into her mouth. She took them out to explain to the others this joke the witty and self-deprecating – and handsome – and a bridegroom – English gentleman had made. There was a chorus of "Ah, Monsieur Frank!" from the audience.

One of the grandmothers clapped her bony hands sternly and addressed everyone. There were general murmurs of agreement as she spoke.

'Ah,' whispered Simenon, 'they speak of having a blanket in your honour.'

'A blanket?' Frank whispered back.

'Yes, the blanket with the food and drink.'

'Ah, a banquet.'

'Just so, the blanket.'

'Let's hope it won't be a wet one.'

'No, no, the forecast is for sun for the next few days.'

'I will organise this,' Xavier Dubons declared, poking his head underneath Jacques arm. Jacque's other hand pushed his face back.

'Oh! A wedding breakfast!' exclaimed Amelie.

'I will take care of everything!' exclaimed Jacques. 'We shall have a celebration and a wedding breakfast.'

'Oh?' asked Frank. 'Who's getting married?'

'It is for you, and your wife!' Jacques continued. 'The doctors say that Amelie may not leave here before Sunday – what do doctors know? We shall have a celebration on the Saturday.'

'Well, that would be tremendous, really, but I'm afraid we have to leave on the Saturday.'

'You do? When?'

'Well, midday, I'm afraid, but thanks anyhow –'

'This is not the problem. The celebration we start at ten.'

'Er, we have to be at Calais by one.'

'We start the celebration at nine. And we drive you to Calais. All of us.'

Frank looked at Frieda with a cheerful smile on his face. Only Frieda recognised the desperation in his eyes.

'What a marvellous idea,' he said, his lips twitching.

She smiled back. She had understood. The way a wife gets to understand the little signs a husband might make. In Frank's case this meant: "Saturday is a long way away. Let's get the hell out now while we can."

'Well, we'd better dash,' he said to Amelie. 'Things to see, people to do, that sort of thing.'

A clutch of relatives, led by the grandmothers, realising that they were about to lose such interesting and unusual guests objected to their leaving so soon. Frieda leaned over and took Amelie's hand.

'You have all been very kind to us, Amelie. But I now I ask the privilege of a new wife, that I may have my husband to myself for a while.'

Amelie stuffed her little handkerchief in her little mouth, blubbed shortly at this romantic request, and translated it to the others. It was met with a mixture of responses, the men mainly making crude suggestions, the women nodding and saying, yes, this is right, a young wife must have time with her husband.

And how politely the English Lady put it. Certain French men could learn a lesson or two from the English.

'Allow me to escort you out,' said Simenon, taking Frieda's elbow. 'Otherwise you will be here all day long.'

Amelie turned suddenly to Simenon and burst into a pleading question. This was followed by an abrupt interjection from one of the old women, one obviously critical of the detective.

'Ta-ta-ta!' exclaimed Simenon. He patted Amelie's hand and assured her and the women in a sing-song voice. 'And now,' he finished, 'we must go. Monsieur Inspector, Madame Inspector?'

They left with the others making a little corridor for them, insisting on shaking their hands and kissing their cheeks. Simenon followed, a cynical smile on his lips and an amused look in his eyes.

'Blimey!' said Frank as they reached safety outside the ward doors, 'I'm not sure I didn't prefer being shot at in a plane.'

Simenon chuckled.

'I suppose I am fortunate,' he said, 'I do not have the burden of being liked by them.'

'Any particular reason they don't like you?'

He shrugged.

'During the war, with the Germans in charge, thievery became patriotic. And that family became very patriotic. Their children have carried on the tradition. There are more criminals in there than any other room in Europe. They do not like a policeman.'

'Just a minute,' said Frank. 'Didn't Amelie say something about how proud they were she was going to be working undercover? Was that before or after she was attacked?'

'Before, I am afraid. I expected it, but I thought that they would never get involved with drugs. It is as if they have certain standards, and for them drugs are – how do you say, lower class? Now, however, I have no lack of suspects. It is most aggravating.'

'But surely none of them would have harmed her?'

Another shrug.

'An accident? who knows?'

'You don't think Amelie might know who it was?' asked Frieda. 'That she's keeping quiet because of family loyalty?'

'Amelie? No. Amelie would not tell me, but she would have an argument with whoever it was. A very family argument. She would be very loud and annoyed for, oh, at the minimum five minutes. I leave it to your imagination what would happen when the others found out.'

He nodded in a determined way.

'But I shall find out what is going on. As the great La Fontaine once said, rien ne pèse tant que un secret. There is nothing more trouble than a secret.'

Frank's mouth twitched.

'Jacques is one of her uncles, you said?' Frieda asked quickly.

'Yes. I don't think that meeting on the beach or the invitation to go flying was an accident. He wanted to find out more about you.'

'Would you say that he's decided that we are just innocent tourists? Or was that a bit of a show in there?'

'With Jacques it is difficult to know. I think perhaps he decided that he would pretend to love you as much as the rest of that family. With them you do not disagree with the grandmothers unless you are very certain. And Jacques likes to present a certain image, of being perhaps confident. Or not exactly confident, I am not sure of the word in English –'

'Savoir faire?' suggested Frank. 'Good old English phrase, that.' Simenon's mouth twitched.

'Amelie seems to be recovering well,' noted Frieda.

'Ah, that is not only youth, but Amelie's – simplicity, is perhaps the word, non?'

'That bit where you went "ta-ta-ta",' Frank said, 'you were re-assuring her about something?'

'Ta-ta-ta?' asked Simenon, wryly mimicking him.

'Just before we left,' Frieda said. 'You patted her hand.'

'Ah, that. Yes, she is worried about her handbag.'

'Her handbag?'

'Yes, it is now evidence. What of, what for, I do not know. But evidence. She was worried she might have lost it forever. I assured her that it is in the exhibits room, she will have it back toute-suite.'

And probably against regulations, thought Frank.

'It's a special handbag?' asked Frieda.

'Oui, madame, I knew you would understand. It is a gift from Amelie's grandmother for her sixteenth birthday. It is her very first young lady's handbag, you could say.'

'Which grandmother was that?'

'The one on the right, of course. Now, however, if you will excuse me, I left Gaspode with a porter outside the kitchens. For some reason they do not permit innocent dogs in hospitals.' He paused as if a thought had suddenly struck him. 'As I say, they are very close that family. You are honoured, I think. They would do anything for you, now that they think you saved Amelie's life – which you did, of course. She was very near death. Tremendously near. A few more hours and she might not have lived, perhaps seconds, only, think of that!'

He paused in his exaggeration and smiled.

'But whether their friendship is better or worse than their non-friendship, of that I am not sure.'

He walked away, chuckling.

'I swear if he ever comes to Wellbury ...' muttered Frank. Frieda did not reply. She had noticed a harassed-looking doctor trying to hurry anonymously by. There was something she wanted cleared up.

'Pardonnez moi, monsieur le doctor,' she said, stepping in front of him to make sure that he acknowledged her presence.

'Er, oui, madame?' he replied looking beyond her as if desperately seeking an escape route.

'Mademoiselle Amelie Courbois,' Frieda said, 'vous connaitre, oui?'

The doctor closed his eyes.

'Mademoiselle Courbois,' he almost whispered. 'Oui, madame?'

'Elle a, er, Frank, where's that dictionary? What's French for heart-beat?'

'I doubt it has that in,' replied Frank, taking the dictionary from his pocket. 'Let me see now ...'

'Vous etre Anglais?' asked the doctor. 'I mean, you're English?'

'Oui, monsieur le doctor,' replied Frieda.

'Well, so am I. You wanted to know something about Miss Courbois? I don't want to sound rude, but I am in a little hurry. Much as I would appreciate the chance of speaking English for a few minutes again, I really must get on.'

'She has a very slow heart-beat, doesn't she, doctor?'

The doctor shook his head sadly.

'She has low blood pressure. So low, for anyone else, I would be worried. But our Mademoiselle Amelie ... how can I put it? Other people develop faster rates of heart beat with the stress of modern life. It's one of the banes of the medical profession. Advertising, television, the Internet, people are constantly bombarded with new things, with advertisers exhorting them to buy the latest car, politicians demanding this, the newspapers shouting crisis and chaos. Our Mademoiselle Amelie is special. Her thought processes are so simple that she does not require a great deal of blood supply to her brain. To be quite honest, with that bunch of relatives she has, it's probably a good thing.'

'So she would have a very slow heart beat if she were

sleeping? Or unconscious?'

The doctor nodded enthusiastically, as if Amelie were a special case.

'It would be so slow to make it easy to miss it. In fact she reminds me of stories I've read of isolated tribes in Africa back in the nineteenth century. Apparently some of them had so few worries, their lives were so fixed in custom, that it was difficult to find a heartbeat while they were asleep, they had a rate of about one or two beats a minute. I've often wondered how true those stories were, but Miss Courbois appears to support the possibility that one or two might have been.'

'Thank you doctor, that's very helpful.'

'That's all?'

'Yes, thank you.'

'You're not relatives? Cousins? Second or third cousins? Something like that?'

'No, fortunately not.'

He sighed in relief.

'That's unusual. Can't seem to turn a corner without discovering more of them. Anyway, must shoot. Good luck.'

Frieda turned to Frank as the doctor hurried away, looking left and right in case any more of Amelie's relatives should suddenly pop out and accost him with demands of diet or prescription for their poor little brave child.

'See, Frank? It was a mistake even a doctor might have made. Thinking that Amelie was dead in the bath.'

Frank smiled and kissed her on the cheek.

'I never doubted it,' he said.

One of the problems with Frieda was that she always had to

be right. They were opposites in that respect. Frank didn't mind how many battles he lost, so long as he won the war. Frieda insisted on winning every battle, irrespective of how the war was going. Though it wasn't entirely a defective strategy: it made others more amenable to surrendering at the first opportunity.

'Free, you didn't inspect that handbag, did you?' Frank asked as they came out of the front doors into the sunshine.

'Of course not. It was part of the scene of crime.'

'Pity. I was wondering if it could have held a secret compartment.'

Frieda nodded.

'Containing a packet of heroin, yes, that thought had occurred to me. I don't think so, though. It was too soft. Imitation white leather, a bit scuffed. Unless the heroin was very loosely packed.'

They pondered in silence for a few moments as they walked.

'Now if this was Wellbury ...' Frank began.

'We'd sign the handbag out and inspect it ...'

'But if we asked Simenon if we could see it ...'

'He should refuse. We would.'

'Even if he isn't involved in some way.'

'There is one way we could have a look,' Frieda suggested.

'There is?'

'Remember Mrs Simenon offering to show us around their station? We might just end up in their evidence room. Where the handbag should be.'

Frank closed his eyes and shuddered.

'I don't want to even think of that, Free.'

'What? You aren't going to be a little scaredy-cat, are you now, Inspector Summers?'

'I'm not a scaredy-cat, Free, as far as that woman goes I'm a terrifiedy-cat.'

'Strange. She seems to like you,' Frieda said, stressing the "you".

'Free, there are some sacrifices which are just too costly. Anyway, we're supposed to be on our honeymoon, not solving a case for the French. Their case, their problem. Bad manners to get involved.'

'D'accord!' said Frieda.

Much as she had been falling prey to her own professional instincts and Frank's curiosity. It was time to get back to the more important matter of their honeymoon.

'Let's get on to Rouen.'

'What a waste,' Frank said as they walked in the direction of the car-park.

'A waste?'

'She has a brilliant talent for languages, all of it useless. You can't use her in an interview because she'd believe whatever your suspect said without thinking about it. He could be lying his head off and she wouldn't have a clue. She would never be able to spot those nuances that tell you someone's telling porkies. If she came across someone holding a smoking gun standing over a dead body who told her that he wasn't there at the time, she'd believe him. And write a report saying so.

That would be hilarious in court. Even worse she'd quite happily blab out things which are supposed to be secret. Telling her family that she was working undercover … And Simenon knew she would. That just does not make sense.'

Frieda had to agree, but couldn't help but feel that it wasn't right to write Amelie off as "a waste".

'She'd make a good translator,' she said.

'Not a political one. If the US president told the Russian president he was a dumbass, Amelie would translate it precisely, poor girl. And she'd know the right word in Russian, even if she didn't understand it.'

'She's very pretty, isn't she?'

Frank gave a wry smile.

'Yes, if you like the brainless, soppy-eyed type. I love it when you give me a soppy look and tell me you love me, but you wouldn't want it twenty-four hours a day, now would you?'

'Of course not, darling,' Frieda replied, wondering when she had ever given Frank a soppy look. Told him she loved him, yes, but a soppy look? She made a mental note to check the next time. She wanted to be able to remember how to do it. It might come in useful.

If you couldn't be soppy with your husband, who could you be soppy with?

'Now there's a question,' Frank said, stopping suddenly, looking nowhere thoughtfully.

'Frank?' Frieda pleaded, recognising the look. 'Please don't do that, my sweet. We're on honeymoon, let's do something honeymoonish.'

'Why does Simenon keep her on? She's useless as a copper.'

'She's probably very good with paperwork, darling. Now let's –'

'Paperwork. Hmmm.' He rubbed his jaw. 'You could be right. Hmmm.'

'Rouen, Frank, Rouen. That's where we're going now.'

'You're quite right. Sod it, let us on to Rouen.'

'He seemed a little depressed today,' noted Frieda as they walked on. 'Simenon, I mean. Behind his obvious enjoyment.'

'Gets too tied up in his work, as far as I can see.'

'Do you think it's right – keeping Amelie on just because she makes him feel good? If that is the case.'

'Can't say I blame him, with that harridan he's married to,' Frank replied, missing the hard look Frieda shot at him. 'I wonder if they're having it off together. Simenon and Amelie, I mean.'

'As opposed to having it off separately?' Frieda suggested, a thin edge to her voice which Frank had learnt to recognise as a sign that Frieda was less than happy. He smiled, turned to her and kissed her.

'You're absolutely right, my sweet,' he said, holding her shoulders. 'I'm not being a very good husband, am I? Here I am, letting this business take over our honeymoon. Come on, let's do something loonymoonish. Let's relish Rouen.'

He took her hand and they continued walking.

'There's something wrong with them, though, that's certain,' Frieda said.

'Who?'

'The Simenons. They make sense as a couple whose marriage has – well, gone sour, I suppose. They just don't fit as a couple of police officers.'

'Now, Free, are you sure you aren't judging them by your own high standards? If we had a tiff I'm sure you'd carry on being as efficient and objective at the station as ever. I don't think everyone could do that.'

Frieda bridled at the suggestion. It was too close to suggesting that she was a frigid ball-breaker.

'So, you expect us to have tiffs, do you?' she asked, in the tone of someone embarking on one.

'Course we will, Free. Goes with the territory. But the great thing is that we then get to kiss and make up, along with – Oh, hell, no, not that!'

Frieda looked at him, surprised.

'You don't want us to make up?'

'Look, down there, about a hundred yards, to the left, the green Citroen.'

'Rubbermats!' said Frieda, turning in the direction Frank was pointing and recognising the vision of Madame Simenon castigating a uniformed police officer.

'Lovely gardens these,' Frank said, pulling Frieda behind some bushes. 'I think we should take a closer look. It's probably a short cut anyway.'

'I think you're right, darling,' Frieda replied as they moved away, hunched over.

'Tell you something, though, Free. I could never, ever imagine kissing and making up with Gorgonzola. Suicide would be the more obvious and pleasant option. No wonder Simenon looks so haggard.'

Frieda looked at the back of his head, wondering whether he

was trying to tell her something.

They made it back to their car without being seen by Madame Simenon. But they did almost fall over two men appearing to be working on the gardens, weeding. It was just their dark suits and sunglasses that suggested the men weren't in their natural setting.

Wellbury. Wednesday. Lunch.

Percy is puzzled

Detective Inspector Percy Hanson replaced his telephone, a mildly puzzled look in his eyes. It was one of the reasons that he had been transferred to Wellbury. Detective inspectors at his previous station had been expected to shout very loudly and thump tables equally loudly, not to look thoughtful. Thinking was all very well so long as you kept it out of your work life. Save it for the wife and the roses.

He tapped a pencil on his desk a few times. Much as he hated admitting it, he was missing Pete Phillips. His detective sergeant was a pretty unimaginative blundering fool most of the time, but at least he was someone Percy could talk to or bounce ideas off – and ideas tended to bounce off Pete Phillips much as water bounces off a duck's back. But he was someone to talk to, better than the coat stand at any rate.

Percy was feeling lonely in the absence of Pete Phillips, Frieda and Frank. Especially Frank. Frieda made him nervous. Frank often made him confused, but never nervous. He was quite prepared to tolerate Frank's endless chases through mazes which often ended up in a cul-de-sac. In fact he enjoyed them. But tolerance had been regarded as another vice at his previous posting.

He decided to wander down to the canteen for a cup of tea and see if there was anyone there he could have a natter with without it appearing unusual. The canteen was reasonably crowded, but mostly with constables with whom he only had a passing relationship, not anyone he could discuss a delicate matter with. He had hoped Gertie or Tricia would be there, a cup of tea and a chat with either would have been unremarkable, but they weren't to be seen.

There was always Eric Johns, who would talk to anyone and everyone, or more accurately, at them, but Percy had heard enough of the rumours going around the station to know that the last person he wanted to talk to was Eric Johns. Fortunately the sergeant wasn't amongst the crowd, a rare event at lunchtime, but welcome all the same.

In the end Percy got his cup of tea and wandered over to a table where Sam Nightingale was sitting alone, eating a hamburger and reading a magazine. For some reason he liked Sam. Apparently Sam was supposed to be both a witch and a lesbian, but Percy had lost any few prejudices he might have had a long time before.

'Hello, Sam,' he said, sitting down. 'Everything okay?'

'Yes, sir,' replied a wary Sam Nightingale. She distrusted senior officers on principle, but the little she knew of Percy inclined her to rate him as mostly harmless. The biggest black mark against him was that he was Pete Phillips's immediate superior. To her Pete Phillips was like a rather stupid and untrained hunting dog. With sergeant's stripes.

'Tell me something, Sam, do you know if Frank can fly?' Percy asked.

Sam had been about to take a bite of her hamburger and try

to ignore Percy as far as possible. She was halfway into an interesting article about a motorbike trek across the roof of Africa, and had just concluded that she could continue reading and eating while responding to Percy with the minimum attention consonant with being reasonably polite to an inspector. Now, she realised, after such a question, it would be impossible. She put the hamburger down.

'How do you mean, Inspector?'

'Don't let me interrupt your lunch, please. I've just had a very strange telephone call from a French inspector – I presume it's the same one who spoke to Pete Phillips, or from the same station. He wanted to know if Frank could fly – fly a plane, that is. I have to admit that it isn't a question that has ever occurred to me before. I don't suppose you know?'

Sam considered the question while taking a bite of her hamburger. She chewed for a while, and then swallowed before answering.

'Well – working on the basis that flying lessons aren't cheap, and the average police officer isn't the best paid person in the country, I would tend to doubt it. But it is possible, I suppose. Inspector Summers ... does come up with some surprises from time to time.'

'That's what I thought. I told this French chap that I thought it unlikely, and he asked whether Frank could learn very quickly, if he was under pressure, such as being shot at.'

'What?'

Percy nodded.

'Well, precisely. It's the sort of question the Americans would call coming out of the left field, or right barn, or whatever it is their strange questions come from. God knows where strange

French questions come from. I said that Frank was definitely a fast learner, and asked what was going on. He said it was just a rhetorical question, and not to worry. And then he said merci, au revoir, and that was that.'

Sam looked at Percy. He was gazing at his teacup with the look of an honestly baffled man. He looked up at her.

'You don't happen to know what's going on?' he pleaded. 'I've heard some very strange rumours lately. I presumed that they were the usual nonsense, with a perfectly reasonable explanation, once you find out what it is. But this just sounds very strange. More strange than the usual stuff.'

Sam felt sorry for Percy. But she had an oath of secrecy to the girls.

'I haven't a clue, I'm afraid, sir.'

He put his teacup down. He picked it up. He put it down again. He tapped it with his teaspoon.

'The thing is,' he said, 'I like to know what's going on. Not necessarily so that I can do something about it, just so that I'm forewarned, as it were. I don't want to find myself putting my foot in it when Frank and Frieda get back. If I'm sitting on a volcano about to erupt, well, that's bad enough, not knowing anything about it is a bit much.'

He sighed.

'Mind you, I don't believe a word of it,' he said. 'That's my main problem. I can't believe it. Knowing Frank and Frieda – well, it just doesn't sound right. It doesn't fit. It really does just not fit.'

'I'm afraid I can't be of much help, sir.'

'Well, if you do hear anything, Sam, do me a favour and let

me know. Just one thing,' he said, leaning forward and speaking in a low voice, 'whatever you do, don't let Eric Johns find out what I've just told you.'

'I won't, sir. Trust me, I won't.'

'Thanks, Sam,' Percy said, standing up and wandering out of the canteen and back to his lonely office. Neither he nor Sam had noticed a desk sergeant sitting down at a table nearby, with a plate of cream buns and a cup of tea in his hands.

Eric Johns hadn't caught the last bit about making sure that he never found out what the other two had been discussing. But he had caught a few words of the rest, and his fertile imagination was already at work with the first bite into a cream bun. What he had heard made obvious sense.

In the office she shared with Frank Gertie was on the phone.

'Susan? Gertie here. I just called to let you know that your brother isn't as useless as we thought he was. Right at this moment I'm looking at a vase containing a dozen red roses, delivered to reception half an hour ago, with a Man United badge in the middle.'

'A Man United badge?' asked Susan. 'It must be serious, I've never known him go that far before. Though I'd be surprised if he actually gave up Arsenal.'

'Oh, he isn't giving up Arsenal. There's a note attached. He says that he will never betray his own club, but he's willing to admit that there is at least one decent Man U supporter. After that he rambles on a bit about something in first class. Here it is: "I've trailed the highways and byways of First Class, searching for a hint of my beloved, I've even trod silently through conferences law, but not a sign of her I saw; I look through a mist, and ask myself, do you really exist?" Any idea what he's on about?'

'God knows. He's always been into writing poetry which doesn't make any sense even when he explains it. I've often wondered if one of us were adopted, we seem to have such different interests. But at least you seem to have got things sorted. Who knows, maybe I'll meet the man of my dreams sometime. Knowing my luck it will be in my dreams, and only in my dreams.'

'Ah, but that's not all the news I've got for you. I received a telephone call an hour ago. Want to know who it was from?'

'Who?'

'Guess.'

'Oh, Gertie, I'm no good at guessing. Frieda, I suppose.'

'Don't be silly, Susan, why would Frieda call?'

'Well, I don't know. It wouldn't be Sam or Tricia, they'd just walk into your office.'

'No, not Sam or Tricia. Someone closer to home, you might say, my home.'

'Gertie, I really don't know. Who was it?'

'Okay, I'll tell you. My older brother.'

'Tom called you?'

'Yes, he said that he'd realised that he should be taking more interest in his little sister's life, and he thought he might pop up to Wellbury for the weekend, if that was okay. He remembered that there were some nice walks around, and could do with some fresh air. And then he asked, trying to sound ever so ever so casual, how you were doing.'

'He did?'

'He did.'

'And you said?'

'Well, I told him I'd have to check the roster, I might be working this weekend. I told him I'd call him back this afternoon. I thought I'd have a word with you and see if you were interested, if not I'll call him and tell him I'll be working the whole weekend. I'll tell him that you're going out with a gorgeous Italian you met last week. Shall I do that?'

'Don't you dare, Gertie Gregson!'

Gertie giggled.

'Okay, okay, just teasing. But listen, he's pretty useless with women. He's always been too shy. The sort of bloke who wouldn't think twice about diving into a rugby scrum, but hasn't a clue when talking to a woman. So we'll have to make a plan, otherwise he'll spend the entire weekend tramping around the hills, hoping that he might just bump into you by accident.'

'Any ideas?'

'I'll phone Wilf and thank him for the flowers. I'll tell him that Tom's coming up for the weekend to see you, that the three of us are going to go out for dinner, movies, that sort of thing, that we're looking for someone to make up the forth, but everyone else is busy this weekend, and would he be available? Sort of offhand, if you see what I mean.'

'Wilf will see straight through that one. He always knows when he's got a girl interested. Which, in his case, is most girls he meets.'

'That doesn't matter. So long as he knows he's on a leash.'

'That will have to be some leash. Okay, call me back when

you know.'

'Tell you what, how about drinks after work? We can have another girls' night. Tricia's probably got to go out with Jeremy but Sam might be available.'

'Two nights in a row? And why not?'

'Six o'clock. See you then.'

Normandy. Wednesday. Afternoon.

It's that woman again

'I can see why Monet tried to paint it so many times,' Frank said as they stood and looked up at the west facade of the Cathedrale Notre-Dame in Rouen. 'It makes my eyes water just trying to take it in. I can imagine the architects being told, "Think Gothic. And when you've done that, double it. And then quadruple it. Research everything Gothic and make the old stuff look like plain wallpaper."'

'Four hundred years to build, and then almost destroyed during one bombing raid in 1944,' Frieda said, browsing a guide book.

'I told you. Didn't you believe me?'

'I was concentrating more on driving, Frank.'

'Let's go have a look at that stained glass window – St Julian the Hospitaller. Accidentally murdered his parents, according to that book. I bet you it wasn't an accident. Maybe we can solve the mystery.'

'Or maybe we should just stroll along like normal tourists and take in the atmosphere instead,' Frieda said, taking his hand. 'Come on, Poppy, dearest, let's wander around it first before going in.'

They strolled along, Frieda trying to watch where she was going while still browsing the guidebook. Several times they found themselves wandering off, away from the cathedral, but, as both agreed, they weren't in any hurry, and there were many interesting shops they passed.

Just then Madame Simenon came out of one of the shops. She just managed not to drop her large shopping bags before recovering with an over-excited smile. Once again Frank was subjected to a barrage of bonhomie, including the regulatory bear hug and kiss on each cheek, before she disappeared down the street.

'She does seem to like you,' observed Frieda.

'I wish she'd find another way to show it,' Frank replied, rubbing the small of his back. 'Her shopping caught me right here. I don't know what was in it, but it had a sharp corner. Several, I think.'

'Joan of Arc was burnt at the stake in Rouen. Maybe Madame Simenon is her reincarnation. Here to wreak revenge on Englishmen.'

Frank scowled in the direction Madame Simenon had taken and pinched his nose.

'Strange that she should suddenly appear here,' he noted. 'I wonder if she and Simenon aren't working together, pulling a good cop, bad cop trick.'

'Which one's the bad one? It can't be Simenon. And his wife always wants to hug you.'

'That was a lot of shopping. She doesn't strike me as a big shopper. Or maybe I'm wrong. Maybe she's just stocking up on the latest fashions.'

Frieda's guess was that Madame Simenon was very similar to

herself in terms of clothing apparel: good quality, clean lines, no fashionable nonsense, and nothing floral or gaudy.

'You know,' she said, 'I was thinking I might buy myself a frock while we're here. Something unusual. Perhaps something with flowers on it. Something French.'

Frank blinked his eyes.

'But first let's get back to the cathedral. I want to have a look at the nave.'

'I wonder if we won't bump into our friend MacDavis.'

'And then the Lady Chapel. And the Library staircase. And, Frank?'

'Yes, my darling?'

'If Mr MacDavis should happen to appear, remember that we don't know him. We haven't been introduced, and we don't want to be introduced. We aren't interested in him, comprehends?'

'What if he turns out to be stuck on top of the cathedral spire?'

'We'll take a photograph and move on to the next tourist attraction, darling.'

Wellbury. Wednesday. Evening.

Girls' Night Out, 2

'Sorted,' said Gertie, giving Susan a thumbs up as they met at the entrance to the Hangmans. 'Wilf said that he'd give you a call to see if he could crash at your place for the weekend. Tom's going to be sleeping on my sofa bed in the lounge.'

'Wilf's already called, and I said, yes, he could.'

'Wilf's a cheeky bugger, though,' Gertie said as they made their way to the bar, 'said that he was looking forward to the weekend so that he could discuss Arsenal's chances in the coming season with Tom.'

'Strange. He's always teased me – things like calling me Big Sis, that sort of thing – but he's never teased his girlfriends. He's always been very particular about that.'

'I'm not his girlfriend yet, he's still going to have to earn that. G and T as usual? I mean, how would you feel if Tom immediately decided that you were his girlfriend, just like that?'

'I wouldn't object, to be honest. I've reached the age where a stable relationship followed by getting married and settling down is the next thing. Either that or nothing. Running around after new boyfriends, all the hassle of new relationships – it loses its appeal after a while.'

'Mmm,' replied Gertie, taking a sip of her G and T. It hadn't quite lost its appeal for her, but she had reached the stage of wondering whether it wouldn't be a lot easier if one could simply go down to the supermarket to choose a boyfriend. Off the shelf. With a returns policy and warrantee. Even if the original packaging had been thrown away.

'Now that's good timing,' Tricia said, arriving with Sam and Squishy.

'Two more G and T's coming up,' said the barmaid.

'We'll be getting a reputation,' Susan said, once the drinks arrived and they had sat down at a table. 'I've never been sure whether it's a good thing that the bar staff know your usual, or whether you're turning into an old soak.'

'Definitely a good thing,' said Gertie. 'Saves time and hassle. I thought you'd be out with Jeremy tonight, Trish?'

'I told him that we were having another girls' night out because he disturbed last night's one.'

'Poor little Jeremy,' said Sam. 'I feel sorry for him. He always seems a little lost.'

'He'll be okay, once I've got him trained properly. Now, down to business. Have you heard the latest?'

'I'm pretty sure I haven't,' said Susan. 'What is it?'

'Well, there are two parts. The first part is that Uncle Eric the Elder – also known as The Cream Cake Man – has revealed the latest in his version of the French connection. According to him, Frank was fleeing the hotel where they're staying when Frieda shot at him, and told him to get back inside and not try anything that silly again. She's determined that everyone will think that there's absolutely nothing wrong with their marriage. Frank's not going to get anything out of it, of course, but he isn't going to get out of it either.'

'Ye gods,' breathed Susan. 'Where on earth does Eric Johns come up with this stuff?'

'Did he tell you this himself?' asked Sam.

'No, that's linked to the second bit. Allison and Harry told me. I asked them if they believed such nonsense. They didn't quite say yes or no, I don't think they were interested in whether or not it's true. So I asked them where Frieda was supposed to have found this firearm she was using. According to Uncle Eric almost all Frenchmen have hunting rifles, and the owner of a rural hotel would definitely have one. Frieda just borrowed it for a while.'

'It can't be true, can it?' asked Susan. 'I mean, okay, obviously it isn't, but where did Eric Johns find the little wisp of an idea on which he's created this fantasy, and what was that wisp?'

'Good question, Susan,' said Tricia. 'I'm afraid I didn't have a chance to ask the cream cake man, but there is the second part to all this. Uncle Eric has taken it upon himself to organise a surprise welcome back party for the bridal couple – presumably all guns to be handed in at the door. It is, apparently, now our duty to welcome them back in such a way that they don't realise that we know that they have a problem. Solidarity. One big, happy family.'

'Frank's going to kill him when he finds out,' said Sam.

'If he's lucky,' said Gertie. 'If Frieda gets her hands on him first – well, I don't even want to think about that.' She paused, and then added, 'But I wouldn't mind watching.'

'The thing is,' said Tricia, 'that's why Allison and Harry came to speak to me. They were planning on going away for the weekend, but now Eric Johns has more or less ordered everyone to be at the Blue Bliss on Saturday evening at six for a welcome back party, pretending that we all firmly believe that there are no problems in the happy marriage of our dearest colleagues, even if we do know there are. Allison and Harry were more interested in getting away than becoming involved in Frank and Frieda's affairs, that's why they weren't really interested in how true the rumours are.'

'That's the problem,' said Gertie. 'Eric's always had a vivid imagination, but up until now he's kept it relatively quiet because Frank or Frieda would have stepped all over him – as they have done before. Pete Phillips might have kept him in check, but he's not here either. And Percy's run off his feet, being the only senior officer around, so he doesn't have the time to get involved.'

'Wait a minute, wait a minute,' said Sam. 'Tricia, you said that Allison and Harry said that Eric said that Frank was fleeing the hotel?'

'Yes.'

'Funny sort of a word to use,' noted Gertie. 'The only time I've ever heard anyone describe someone as fleeing has been in court. And then I think that was a programme on the telly anyway.'

'That's just it!' cried Sam. 'Okay, let me tell you something. I was sitting in the canteen at lunch today, minding my own business as usual, when Percy drops by for a chat. I thought it rather strange, but, looking back, he wanted someone to talk to, someone he could trust not to spread things around too much. He probably chose me because I was sitting by myself, but that isn't important. You see, he had just had a call from a French policeman wanting to know if Frank could fly a plane.'

'Fly a plane? Frank?' asked Tricia.

'Knowing Frank, he'd have a good go,' said Gertie. 'Go on, Sam.'

'That's just it, you see. Percy says, no, he doesn't think Frank knows how to fly a plane. So the French policeman asks, is Frank a quick learner? Would he be able to learn to fly a plane if someone was shooting at him?'

'What?'

'What?'

'What?'

'So Percy says, well, yes, he probably would, but why is the French man asking such questions? And the French policeman says, thank you for your co-operation and goodbye. Well, that's more or less it, as far as I can remember.'

'How bizarre,' said Susan.

'Oh, it's bizarre, all right. But, think about it. Now Percy asked me not to mention it to anyone, especially Eric Johns, and I made sure I didn't. But what if someone overheard part of the conversation and passed it on? Somehow "flying" gets changed to "fleeing", throw in the idea of someone shooting at Frank, and you've given Eric Johns the recipe for a new mental magic carpet.'

The others nodded. It made sense. As far as anything so far made any sense.

'Tricia,' asked Susan, 'Frieda hasn't mentioned anything to you about anyone being shot at?'

'Well, no, but we haven't actually spoken, you see. I leave a text message on Frieda's mobile in the evening, she reads it the next morning and sends a reply. Apart from the body in the bath bit, from me it's mainly been "Everything okay in Wellbury, hope you're having a fabulous time". And from her side it's mainly "Everything as perfect as possible, will tell you all about it when we get back". As I said yesterday, she just wants to know if there's a crisis, apart from that she wants to use it as little as she has to.'

'"Everything as perfect as possible",' quoted Sam. 'That's a bit ambiguous, isn't it? What's wrong with "Everything perfect"?'

'Please don't go there, Sam,' said Tricia, 'we've got enough problems with the cream cake man's imagination without trying to psycho-analyse Frieda's five second text.'

'I agree,' said Gertie. 'But I think we need to let Frieda know about the latest rumours, and especially Uncle Eric's planned surprise reception.'

Tricia shook her head in disbelief.

'It certainly sounds like the sort of crisis Frieda would want to be kept aware of. Though I doubt whether it's the type she was thinking about when she bought the phone.'

'She's going to be livid,' Gertie said in a sing-song voice which suggested that she might just be looking forward to the event.

Normandy. Wednesday. Evening.

A Chance Encounter

'So, my dearest, same restaurant or a different one?' asked Frank as they strolled along the boulevard amongst the scattered evening pedestrians, people on their way home, going out for a drink, or just chatting idly with friends.

'Let's see if we can find one that looks as inviting,' Frieda replied. 'If not, and there probably won't be one, we'll go back to ours.'

Frank was tempted to point out that Frieda had said exactly the same thing the previous evening, and they had ended up back at their original choice. But, after all, that was part of the idea about having time just to saunter and look in shop and restaurant windows, not to have anything to rush back to, or be continually thinking about anything you had to do the next day or week or month.

He felt that, all in all, the day had been, even counting the visit to the hospital and Madame Simenon's appearance, extremely enjoyable and worry free. They hadn't even been hooted at by indignant French drivers, let alone been shot at or attacked.

But he had no intention of pointing that out. Reminding the gods that they had not yet upset someone's day was not a wise move.

'It's been a lovely day,' said Frieda, inspecting the contents of a dress shop. 'You know, for the first time I feel that we really are on honeymoon. Just the two of us together, no-one else interested in what we were doing, nobody trying to interfere. That skirt looks rather nice. A casual type of formal. Or a formal type of casual. What do you think?'

'Well, well, surprise, surprise,' murmured Frank looking along the pavement. Frieda followed his gaze and sighed. Georges Simenon was walking towards them, the bright-eyed Gaspode trotting at his side, happy to see them again.

'Bonjour, inspector,' Frank said with a large, welcoming smile. 'Comment allez vouz?'

'I am well, Inspector. Madame l'Inspector. And yourselves?'

'Très bien, Inspector, très bien. Hello, Gaspode, you're looking as happy as always.'

Gaspode agreed with a short bark.

'He needs the walk, I need the walk, it is a fine night,' Simenon said. 'Very enjoyable. I have forgotten how pleasant it is just to take the evening stroll, not to worry about work, not to worry about anything. To talk to Gaspode, who seems to understand perfectly. He is very intelligent.'

'We just co-incidentally appear to have chosen the same walk,' Frieda noted. Simenon gave her his lugubrious look.

'You think I am here on the porpoise?' he suggested. 'In that case I fear you must blame Gaspode. When we reach the corner I ask him, do we turn left, turn right, or go ahead? Perhaps he realised you were here and wished to say hello.'

Gaspode barked again as if to confirm this.

'And when Amelie gets out of hospital Gaspode will go back to her?' asked Frieda.

'No, I think not. Amelie is a good girl, but she has not the concentration for looking after a pet. The attention span, as you say.'

'Elle est la mademoiselle très – beaucoup,' said Frank, as they began strolling again, Simenon and Gaspode falling in step alongside. 'No, wait a minute, what's the word for beautiful?'

'Belle,' said Frieda.

'That's it. Elle est très belle, n'est ce pas, inspector?'

Simenon gave Frank his usual battered-beagle look.

'You wonder why I keep her as my officer,' he suggested. 'You think she is beautiful, but the little stupid?'

'Ah, mais non, inspector,' Frank lied fluently, fooling absolutely no-one. 'She's very good with languages, isn't she? Quite incredibly so.'

Simenon gave him another foul look.

'This is true,' he said. 'She speaks many languages fluently, and learns others quickly. Talking is something else she is good with. That apart, she is entirely inefficient. She files papers away incorrectly. She is always late or early. She believes whatever anyone says implicitly, no matter how untrue they might obviously be. Her memory – tchah, a fly has the longer memory.'

'My goodness,' said Frank, 'fancy that.'

'So you wonder why I do not fire her? Transfer her? Bien, mon ami, I tell you. It is simple. She makes me feel good. When I am tired she brings me the coffee and smiles at me with those eyes, already I feel better. When the day has been long and I have had to share the same room as some scum I question and I feel the dirt over me, she smiles that silly smile and I feel it is not such a bad world. She is a good person. She believes the world is a good place.' He sighed and looked up at the sky. 'Mon jeune ami, you are young. Me, I have worked long as a police officer. I am getting old. Cyclical, that is the word, yes?'

'Cynical,' corrected Frieda.

'Ah, pardon, yes, cynclical. Madame inspector, you, you are English, you are efficient, perhaps you think I am soft in the head, or perhaps you are the angry feministe who thinks a young woman should not be treated so. Perhaps you are right, who knows? One day I answer the bon Dieu, I hope He says, Georges, I understand, a man should have the one ray of sun in his life. Mais, pardon, I use your time. You wish no doubt to be on your – loonymoon. Monsieur, madame, au revoir.'

Frank and Frieda watched him walk away, Gaspode trotting happily alongside.

'You know,' said Frank, 'I think he was being honest about that being a coincidental meeting. I don't think he expected to bump into us. Not that time, anyway.'

'What makes you say that?'

'He didn't have one of his bloody quotations ready.'

Frieda smiled.

'He did seem depressed,' she noted. 'More depressed than usual, that is.'

'Maybe he was reminded of his own honeymoon,' Frank replied, missing Frieda's sudden look. 'Or maybe he had really managed to forget about work for five minutes, until we suddenly appeared.'

He stood musing for a while as Frieda hunted around in her mind for a way to ask if Frank was suggesting their honeymoon could ever be comparable to whatever had happened on the Simenons' honeymoon.

'And then there's the other possibility,' Frank continued. 'Perhaps he is the guilty parting, and had managed to forget about everything for five minutes. Then we suddenly appear to remind him, and he knows that we, unlike the others, have our suspicions.'

He nodded at the thought.

'And if that is the case the best thing to do is look at this in terms of cuisine.'

'Cuisine?'

'Yes. Let him stew in his own juices while we go for dinner. Our restaurant, shall we say?'

'Our restaurant it is. Let's take the long way around. And let's hope Gaspode doesn't.'

'You know, Free,' said Frank once their order had been taken, 'I think we need to set some rules for our marriage.'

'Rules?'

'Yes, rules. Such as, we have to go to the cinema or theatre at least once a month. Or a concert. You know what it's like in our job. Things get hectic, there's always something you just have to do, you put things off. Then you look back and you haven't done anything like that for an entire year.'

Ah, that sort of rule, thought Frieda. She agreed. She knew extremely well how easy it was to let work take over. And it showed that Frank really was thinking ahead about their marriage.

'I think that's an excellent idea, Frank. How do we implement it, though?'

'Oh, I don't know. At the start of each month circle a couple of weekends as just for us. Something like that.'

Frieda nodded. She suspected that it would be her job to do the circling. Still, she was the better planner.

'And no shop talk at home. Home is our time.'

'That might be a little difficult, Frank.'

'I don't think so. A fifty pence fine whenever one of us mentions work.' He smiled at her. 'I'm not sure what I would spend the money on, though.'

Frieda smiled back. She enjoyed a challenge like that. And intended to make sure that it was Frank paying in, not her.

'And having people around for some grub every so often,' Frank continued. 'Epicurus was very hot on that.'

This time Frieda frowned at him.

'I'll agree with the concept, Frank, though I think our ideas of execution might differ.'

'Execution?'

'Epicurus would not have brought in a crate of beers, ordered a huge pizza delivery and had his buddies around to watch the football on a Saturday afternoon.'

'Ah, but that's exactly what Epi would have done. That was his philosophy, the ideal life. A little wine – the beers – some good food – the pizza – and the company of good friends and intelligent conversation.'

'Frank, my sweetheart, a little wine, yes, not a crate of beers. Intelligent conversation amongst friends, yes, not shouting at the television to tell the ref that he's blind and he enjoys solitary sex. And Epicurus would never, never have ordered double pepperoni with extra cheese and garlic. A simple cheese and tomato with a dash of herbs, yes, double pepperoni with extra cheese and garlic, never.'

Frank considered this, his mouth twisting as he tried to find a weak point in the argument.

'I like pepperoni,' he said finally, defensively. 'And garlic's good for you. Anyway, it's not as if it's every weekend, in fact it's hardly once a month. After all, how often do I get an entire Saturday afternoon when I know I can relax and do nothing? And the Chief Inspector normally joins in, so it's not as if it were the lads having a booze up, now is it?'

Fortunately their order arrived to interrupt the conversation. Frieda liked the Chief Inspector and trusted his judgement. If he considered it acceptable to occasionally spend an afternoon drinking beer and watching football then perhaps ... She would see.

'I was thinking, Frank,' she said, picking up her knife and fork, 'the first thing we need to do when we get back is start looking for a new home.'

Frank was tempted to ask whether they shouldn't unpack first, but decided it best not to make a joke. Instead he just said 'Hokay,' and attended his food.

'It's important, Frank. I know you think it's silly, and I know you probably wouldn't think of it, but it is important that we find ourselves somewhere which is ours, both of ours.'

'Well, Free, if that's what you want.' He chewed thoughtfully. 'Did you have anything special in mind?'

'Somewhere in a good suburb, with parks and a decent school nearby.'

'Lords Acres?'

'Don't be silly, Frank, we couldn't afford somewhere in Lords Acres.'

'The problem is, with house prices today, even if we sell your place we probably wouldn't be able to afford to buy it two days later, never mind anything better.'

'Our place, Frank.'

'Okay, our place, then. You know, what we want is some beaten up old place which needs a lot of work doing on it. Buy it cheap, fix it up.'

Frieda looked at him. He had never, as long as she had known him, expressed an interest in any building activity whatsoever. Which was unusual for Frank. He was the kind of man who could find an interest in almost anything, especially if there were a hint of criminality about it, and in her experience people in the building trade were the types who interpreted the law in very flexible ways.

'Have you ever done any DIY, Frank?' she asked.

'I used to help dad a few times when I was a kid. And then mum would call a builder in a couple of weeks later to do things properly.'

'That isn't exactly confidence inspiring, Frank.'

'I'm sure it can't be that difficult.'

Frieda wanted to groan. This was pure Frank.

'What about electricity?' she asked.

'Apart from electricity. I mean, obviously with something like electricity you have to get in someone who knows what they're doing. Apart from simple things like changing a plug or that sort of stuff. I can do that, no problem.'

Frieda closed her eyes briefly. Even she knew how to change a plug.

'How about plumbing?'

'Well, okay, plumbing too. Initially. For the big things. And even then it shouldn't be too hard to pick up a trick or two while watching. Changing a washer is easy enough. If you remember to switch the water off first.'

'Laying carpets?'

'Isn't that normally included in the price?'

'Frank, is there any DIY you can do?'

'Wallpapering can't be much of a problem.'

'How about plastering?'

'And painting – anyone can paint a wall.'

'You don't know the first thing about plastering, do you, Frank? It's extremely difficult to get the right finish. A decent plasterer can earn a very good wage.'

'Well, we'll have to find a place that doesn't need too much plastering then. Anyway, I'm sure Vic Brown will know a few plasterers willing to do the job for a reasonable amount.'

Frieda shook her head in disbelief. Vic Brown was a failed crook who had appointed Frank his hero, and would do anything for him. He just wasn't very good at doing the anything very well. She could imagine the results if he was allowed to contribute to any enterprise.

'What about carpentry?' she asked.

'Ah, now I did some carpentry at school. So, yes, I could probably handle the basics.'

'The basics?'

'You know, how to saw a straight line. That sort of thing.'

Frieda put her knife and fork down. She wiped her lips and looked at Frank.

'So, Frank, let me see if I've understood this properly. Between us the sum of our knowledge about building issues is that one of us knows how to saw in a straight line. And, darling, you know I love you, but I somehow have this little doubt about even that – sawing in a straight line. And you think we should find some old house, some old house which is falling to pieces, and rebuild it ourselves?'

'It makes more sense to do it that way than just moving for the sake of moving. If we buy another place the same as yours, in good repair, we'll just be handing over money to estate agents for no reason whatsoever.'

Frieda's eyes glowed the deep red fire of hell for a few seconds. She loathed estate agents, and Frank knew it. It was rare for her not to be able to be objective about any group, but when estate agents entered the conversation reason left. She took a few moments to compose herself.

'Just promise me one thing, Frank.'

'Of course, my darling.'

'I mean it, Frank.'

'Me too, Free. What is it?'

'Promise me that you will never, ever, ever agree to buy somewhere without asking me first. Not even if I'm – if I'm out of the country, on a conference or something, beyond reach of communication. Not even if it's the perfect house, and the seller is demanding an immediate answer. Not even if the price is half what it should be. Not even if it comes with a swimming pool and tennis courts. And a little stable housing sweet-looking little Shetland ponies.'

Frank rubbed his jaw as he considered the possibility of a swimming pool, tennis courts and sweet looking little Shetland ponies.

'On one condition, Free,' he said.

'Oh? And what's that?'

'That you promise me the same.'

'Now this is what I will remember,' Frank said as they strolled back towards the hotel in the moonlight, his arm around her shoulders, hers around his waist.

'It's a beautiful night.'

'It is indeed. Just made for newlyweds. I had it ordered specially. You can't get this over the Internet, you know.'

Frieda smiled. She was feeling pleasurably tired. Normally she would have considered it far too early to think of going to bed, but that was because normally she would still have her head full of all the things that needed to be done at the station. But now they were on their honeymoon, it had been a warm, long day, and the prospect of an early night appealed.

'Do you fancy a nightcap, or shall we just head off to bed, darling?' she asked.

'A nightcap sounds like the perfect end to the day,' Frank replied. 'A little brandy in an old French hotel with the regulars sitting around discussing the weather. Probably complaining that it's too hot for the time of year, and that it means that it will be a long and cold winter, something like that. You know, just the way Wellburians do.'

She smiled again. Winter. Christmas. Their first Christmas together as man and wife. Then she stopped suddenly and pulled him back.

'Frank! It's the ginger-haired man.'

'Coming out of the hotel. Well, well, All of a sudden he doesn't seem too worried about us seeing him.'

'Pretend you haven't noticed him.'

'Haven't noticed him? He's coming straight towards us.'

'Mr and Mrs Summers – or Inspector and Mrs Summers?' asked the man with a sniffle in his voice and a burr in his accent. His eyes were red and looked as if he had been crying.

'Inspector and Inspector Summers,' replied Frank.

'Ah, yes, of course, sorry, I – ah-tshoo!' The man took out a handkerchief and blew his nose. 'Sorry, blurddy hay-fever. I'm fine in the heather of the Highlands, but my sinuses go crazy over here. I'm Jamie MacDavis, by the way. I've been meaning to say hello ever since you arrived and found that girl in your bath. I don't normally speak to other British people on holiday just because they are British, but I suppose it's like having an accident. You want to offer any help you can give, even if just to be polite.'

'That's very kind of you, Mr MacDavis,' said Frieda.

'Fortunately things seem to be under control now, no more bodies in the bath,' said Frank. 'Do you come here often? Do they normally have bodies in the bath waiting for guests?'

'Oh, aye,' said MacDavis, sneezing again. 'Every year for the past four years. The first time was a pure accident – late booked holiday, I noticed it in the travel agent's window. Since then I've booked early each year. I hear that you spoke to an Inspector Simenon. Or should I say, you were grilled by Simenon.'

'Yes. You know him?'

'I met him the first time I stayed here, in a different hotel. Some jewellery went missing and he came to investigate. A verra rude mun. '

'Did they find it?'

'Find it? Find what?'

'The jewellery.'

'Och. I don't know. I wasn't interested, to tell the truth. I'm more of an out-doors man. Jewellery, that sort of thing – havena the time for it.'

'You go walking while here, I presume,' suggested Frank.

'Aye, all over, wherever and whenever I can. I prefer the beauty of the Highlands, mind, but around here is pretty enough. Well, if yere nay neeed of help I'll bid ye weel and make on. There should be enough moonlight for an hour or so yet.'

'Interesting,' said Frank as the man strode away. 'He suffers from hay fever here, but not in the Scottish Highlands. Strange that.'

'It could be psychological, or ...'

'Yes, that's it, the "or". Or perhaps he's been sniffing more than the pretty flowers which grow in the fields.'

'A bit late in the season to be suffering from hay fever caused by pollen.'

'Difficult to say. It could be something silly – an allergic reaction to the furniture polish they use over here.'

'True. But why come here every year when you know you'll spend most of the time blowing your nose?'

'That Scottish accent seemed a bit put-on, don't you think? I would say that our Jamie MacDavis merits a little closer inspection, wouldn't you?'

Frieda thought about this. The detective inside her replied with a definite "Yes". The new wife inside her reminded her that it was Wednesday evening, they only had three days left of their honeymoon, and she had yet to engage her husband in a serious discussion regarding their future marriage. For "discussion" read "training".

'Frank,' she said, 'let's forget all about it for this evening, shall we? It's Wednesday, almost Thursday, and we haven't even started our honeymoon, not with all this nonsense going on. Just for tonight let's enjoy being together, by ourselves. Shall we?'

'You're right, Free,' Frank said, his schoolboy grin appearing. 'Sod the others. If Simenon turns up again we'll set Gaspode on him.'

'And if Mrs Simenon turns up?'

'I don't know, I'll be hiding underneath the table.'

Normandy. Thursday. Morning.

I'll be calling you-oo-oo-oo

In the hotel room the following morning Frieda read the message on her mobile phone with the same disbelief that Tricia had shown the night before. Frieda had always known that the cream cake man's imagination could be entering deepest space before an earth rocket had even begun to take off, but this was pushing the boundaries of another universe.

She sat and tried to think of a response. The cream cake man had to be stopped, there was no doubt about that. And punished for having the temerity to interfere in her marriage.

How to do that was another question.

She would have to find a quick reply to Tricia, giving as much information as necessary to dispel the rumours, without Tricia having to reveal their daily communications. If the station found out then Frank would find out, and it would be on their return. Frank would blow his top, and Eric Johns would, ironically, be able to claim that there was some truth in his belief that she and Frank were having problems.

Correction. Frank would not blow his top. He would draw within himself and suffer in hurt silence, which would be far worse than him blowing his top.

She checked her watch. She should already have been on her way downstairs. Quickly she typed in the message:

"Cream cake man to be stopped at all costs. Apart from revealing communications. Do not reveal comms."

What else could she say?

"Flight confirmed. Other incorrect."

She started as she heard footsteps coming along the passage. She recognised the sound. They were Frank's footsteps.

She pressed the send button and dropped the mobile phone into her handbag. Then she stood up and walked to the door, opening it just as Frank reached it.

'Everything okay?' he asked. 'I was beginning to wonder if you had gone out and forgotten about me.'

'Ah, no, Frank, I just couldn't find, um, my nail varnish. The bottle rolled underneath the bed somehow.'

'It didn't leak, did it?'

'Leak? What didn't leak?'

'The nail varnish. I read somewhere that it's almost impossible to get out of a carpet. No, wait a minute, I think it might have been that you can use nail varnish to get something else out of a carpet.'

'No, no, it didn't leak, it's fine. Let's go have breakfast, shall we?'

'Excellent idea, I'm starving.'

'No change there, then.'

'Well, there is, really. When I'm at work breakfast is usually a cup of tea. It's only on holiday when I find myself having a full breakfast. I reckon it's all this fresh air and exercise. Especially the night exercise.'

'Mr Summers! Really.'

'It's okay, Free, we're married, we're allowed to say things like that. In fact, I think it might be mandatory.' He sighed and put his arm around her as they walked downstairs. 'If old Edith Piaf was lucky enough to regrette rien – which I doubt – there aren't many others who can say that. But one thing I will always be able to say is that I will never regret marrying the woman I love.'

Frieda put an arm around him and squeezed. Apart from the fascination with nicking a kepi, which, thankfully, he appeared to have forgotten, Frank seemed to have got this honeymoon idea more or less right. In a strange way this whole business with Amelie and the heroin was actually a godsend. Other couples probably came home with memories of museums or swimming pools and palm trees, without really having grown closer. Their honeymoon, she felt, was bringing them closer every day.

There was one thing she had forgotten to do. Which was to switch her mobile phone off. Inside her handbag it hummed to itself, calling out to a nearby transmitter, saying hello, asking if there were any calls to take.

Wellbury. Thursday. Breakfast.

Let it be

'Could we have a word, Sergeant Phillips?'

Pete Phillips looked up to discover that a deputation consisting of Tricia Leigh and Gertie were standing in front of his desk. He was somewhat disconcerted that he had not heard them coming into the office. More than disconcerted, a little irritated.

Pete Phillips was not, in fact, a very happy detective sergeant. He had returned the night before from Wales, where he and his family had gone for three days' holiday with his in-laws. He had been looking forward to some hill-walking with his father-in-law, and that had indeed happened, and had been most enjoyable, despite a persistent drizzle. It was the evening and morning meals which had been the problem. His wife had continually regaled her parents with details about Frank and Frieda's wedding, which had been bearable as far as that went. The problem was that his wife insisted on reminding everyone that he and Frank had been fellow sergeants, and now Inspector Summers was just that, an inspector, despite having a shorter service period than the man she had married. She didn't quite get around to bewailing the fact that she had married a loser, but no doubt she was just working her way up to it.

Ironically it was Frank who had helped him a couple of years previously when his marriage was foundering. At the time he had thought that Frank was the best mate a man could have. Now he wished Frank had kept out of it. If he had, he, Pete Phillips, might have been happily divorced, instead of being lumbered with a two-year-old daughter who seemed to have a permanent whine caused by colic, and a wife who had a permanent whine caused by god knew what.

But no doubt she would get over it, once she had a new hairdo or something, or Frank and Frieda had returned and they became a normal married couple instead of the happy honeymooners, and they no longer figured so deeply in his wife's thoughts. In the meantime he could escape to work, and hopefully some tasty and interesting arrests.

Unfortunately that was not to be. He had arrived at work early to find that the desk he had so carefully and earnestly cleared of paperwork before leaving was now again covered with the stuff, all generated by his boss, Inspector Percy Hanson. Pete wished he could blame Percy, but with Frank and Frieda away they were severely short-staffed, so it was only to be expected.

Not having anyone to blame made it even worse.

And now Tricia and Gertie stood in front of him, looking suspiciously like two people who weren't about to lighten his load. Much as he liked both of them, he had no time for a constable and a secretary giving him extra grief.

'What is it?' he asked. 'I'm busy, as you can see.'

'Just a couple of quick questions, Sergeant,' Tricia said. 'You took a call from a French police officer on Sunday night?'

Pete nodded. He vaguely remembered the call. It felt as if it had happened six months before.

'Can you remember what the French policeman said?'

Pete shook his head.

'Look, love, it was late in the evening, we were all tired and still had a few hours of shift to go. I wrote everything down as clearly as I could and left the note in the log.'

And I can't speak French, and the Frog wasn't that hot in English, he felt like adding.

'It's important, Sergeant,' Tricia said. 'Can you remember anything?'

'I told you, love, I wrote everything down. I didn't try to remember precisely because I wrote it down. Understand?'

'Yes, Sergeant, only Sergeant Johns has lost the note.'

Pete sighed. He had been very careful about getting that note right. And he had left it there for Percy to read, not Eric. Putting it in the log had been a mistake. The only thing you could trust Eric not to lose was food. Mainly because he could eat it faster than he could lose it.

'Do you remember something about a bath?' asked Gertie.

'Vaguely. Look, all I remember is that some Frog copper

wanted to confirm that Frank and the Inspector were who they said they were, okay? The Frog made some joke about a woman in a bath or something. I presumed that it was some French sense of humour. I logged the call and left the note for Percy in case anything further came up. If Eric got hold of it and lost it, well, you'll have to speak to him. I've got more important things to do.'

'There is a slight problem, Sergeant Phillips,' Tricia said. Pete groaned.

'And I suppose you're going to tell me,' he said.

'I'm afraid that certain rumours have arisen, rumours that Inspector Summers and Inspector Summers have – are having marital problems. Those rumours are a direct consequence of misunderstandings leading from the message you left last Sunday.'

Pete put his face in his hands. His initial thought was, "Good, let Frank feel how crappy a marriage can be", but that had gone as soon as it had arrived. Instead he now had a feeling that he was about to be involved in deep trouble caused by Eric Johns's unique ability to re-arrange the cosmos in an illogical fashion and with very strange colours. And the cherry on the cake was that it would involve Frank and Frigid. To get on the wrong side of one was stupid. To get on the wrong side of both didn't bear thinking about.

'Whatever it is,' he said from behind his hands, 'I don't wish to know. If Eric has decided to go out to sea in a rowing boat and pull the plug, I'm not going to be the second oarsman. I do not wish to know, okay? Now, if you don't mind, I have a lot of paperwork to get through, and my wife is expecting me back for tea tonight, sometime before seven at the latest. And if I turn up late – I am not going to be late. End of story.'

Tricia and Gertie looked at his bowed head as he returned to the paperwork. They glanced at each other and withdrew into the corridor.

'There goes our only hope,' said Tricia.

'I wonder if he hasn't got the right idea,' mused Gertie. 'Keep our heads down, let Eric Johns have his silly welcome back party, hope nothing goes bang, and, if it does, make sure we're nowhere close.'

'Something will go bang. Think about it. Frank and Frieda return to find they're expected to attend a surprise welcome back party. They'll both be tired as it is. Frank will wonder what's going on, especially with this lot. In the meantime Frieda knows what's going on, and dearly wants to strangle Eric Johns, only she's got to pretend she doesn't know anything, just as everyone else is pretending they don't know that Frank and Frieda's marriage is effectively over, even though it isn't. Frank will find out, and he's likely to be furious. Frieda then has to pretend that it's news to her and that she's furious And of course she is furious, but not surprised. So, there we all are, in the private members' bar at the Blue Bliss, Frank has just punched Eric Johns out cold, Frieda is giving everyone a great bollocking, with promise of more to come. And just when you think things can't get worse, Frieda accidentally says something which Frank picks up on and realises that she knew all the time. Got the picture so far?'

Gertie did. Only too well. She searched for a flaw, any flaw.

'Frank wouldn't punch Eric Johns,' she said.

'After he's helped screw up his marriage?'

Gertie sighed.

'For that he'd punch Eric Johns,' she admitted.

'So, failure is not an option.'

'Trish, you've been watching too many movies.'

'No I haven't. But it's a good question: what would Humphrey Bogart do?'

'Stop the Cream Cake Man?'

'That's it! That's it, Gertie! We just have to nobble the Cream Cake Man for a few days.'

'Great,' said Gertie. 'Any ideas on how we're going to do that? Put a laxative in the pecan pie?'

Tricia smiled.

'That isn't a bad idea, you know. But do we go for the pecan pie or the raspberry fool?'

Normandy. Thursday. Morning.

Jailhouse Rock

'Oui, Madame Simenon,' Frank said into the telephone, sitting at the bar counter of the hotel. 'Aujourdhui, c'est parfait. In une hour's time, then?'

He listened.

'Tres bon, madame. Au revoir.'

He smiled at Frieda as he put the telephone down.

'Sorted. We've got an hour for breakfast, then allez a la station de plods.'

'She understood you?'

'Of course she understood me. What do you expect?'

Frieda blinked her eyes and tried not to shrug. She had understood Frank's side of the conversation because she

267

understood both what he was trying to say and his novel approach to translation. What she couldn't understand was how any French speaker could have a clue.

'Bon,' said Frank. He waved to the landlord behind the bar, busier than ever with glass-polishing. 'Au revoir, Monsieur Arneaux, nous allez pour le petite dejeuner.'

'Bon appetit, monsieur,' replied Arneaux. He shook his head as they left. From what he had understood of the one-sided conversation it appeared that the Englishman had told the other person that he was coming to inspect their private areas. At least it had meant that he was not the one being subjected to a very confusing conversation. He was developing a fear of early mornings when the Englishman came down. He had mentioned it to his wife, but she had just laughed and told him not to be silly. It was all very well for her, she could speak the abominably confusing language fluently.

Still, at least the morning trial was over.

'Are you sure that she understood?' asked Frieda as they walked out.

'Absolutely. Perfectly.'

They walked in silence for a few yards until Frank turned to her, grinning.

'After the first sentence she put on someone who could speak English,' he said. 'They kept translating my French back to English to make sure they'd understood. Then they translated it back into French for her.'

'So that's why you kept saying "Oui" all the time.'

'Absolutely.'

'Frank Summers, you are the most – oh, I don't know, what's

the word for supreme blagger?'

'Ah, come on, Free, be reasonable. No bloody good if we let them speak English to us all the time, we'd never learn anything, would we?'

Frieda smiled and took his hand.

'No, darling, you're right, it wouldn't be any good.'

Frank would never know it, but her real joy was that he had used the word "bloody" without thinking about it. Her first husband had used swearing as an additional aggressive weapon. It had imbued her with a loathing for even the mildest form of swear word. She would still never use any such word herself – well, certainly not under normal conditions – but the fact that she could accept Frank doing so, and be untroubled by it, showed that things were definitely moving in the right direction.

'Looks pretty much like any cop shop,' Frank murmured as they entered the police station. 'Just not as friendly as an English one.'

'Are English police stations friendly places?' asked Frieda. 'Or is that just because we're used to them?'

'With Eric Johns on the desk? Wellbury has to have one of the most welcoming receptions in the world. Or, putting it another way, he's the least frightening desk sergeant I could think of. I remember when I first walked in he was trying to hide the cream cake he was eating.'

'He was eating a cream cake on desk duty? I thought I'd made it quite clear that I wouldn't tolerate that sort of thing.'

Frank grinned. Frieda hadn't stopped Eric Johns from

indulging his sweet tooth while on duty, just made him better at hiding things.

'Perhaps this place looks that bit more foreboding because of whom we're coming to meet,' he said.

'Cheer up Frank. Why don't you say something such as, "I only regret that I have but two cheeks to be kissed for my country"?'

'Free, really. A double entendre in a French police station? What is the world coming to?'

Frieda blushed slightly. She hadn't even thought of the possible double meaning.

'Bonjour,' Frank said to the young policeman manning the desk. 'Nous sont inspecteurs Summers. Nous sont ici pour parlez avec Inspecteur Simenon. Madame Simenon.'

'Madame Simenon?' asked the young officer in surprise.

'Oui,' Frank replied confidently.

'Moment.' The young man picked up a telephone, dialled a few numbers, and had a short and respectful conversation with someone. 'Madame Inspecteur is gout,' he said, replacing the handset.

'Gout?' asked Frieda.

'Oui, madame. She is gone to – to – ah, que est-ce, Anglais ...'

'Parlez francais, officeur,' suggested Frank. 'Nous parle le bon francais.'

'I should arrest you for a lie like that,' said a voice behind them. They turned to find Georges Simenon, the usual sad smile on his face.

'Inspector!' exclaimed Frank in simulated warmth. 'Sorry to hear that your bon madame has gout.'

'Non, inspector Summers, she has not the gout. I think Francois here was mixing "gone" and "out" and arrived at "gout".'

Frank chuckled.

'We could invent a new language,' he said. 'Beat the teenagers at their own game.'

'My wife apologises for not being able to meet you as agreed,' Simenon said. 'But I am happy to take you on a tour of our little offices. I hope you will not be too bored. Please, follow me. Is there anything particular you wish to see?'

'Not really, Monsieur Inspector, I tend to prefer general impressions, get the feel of a place. What about you, Free, anything special you'd like to see?'

'No, no, I agree, a general feeling.'

'Well, let me show you the cells first. Most visitors wish first to see the cells. Prisoners, on the other hand, prefer not to.'

Frieda tried her best to show an interest in the cells. It was not too difficult. There were shared concerns, and Frieda questioned Simenon on every one she could think of. She was standing in the middle of an empty cell with Simenon at the door, when he noticed Frank peering through the inspection hatch of another cell several yards away.

'Something interests you, Inspector?' he asked, coming up beside him.

Frank nodded at the man in the cell.

'Looks like he went to a fancy-dress party and had several too many,' he said. Simenon looked in.

'Ah, no, that is Father Anthony. That is not fancy dress, he is a real priest. Every Wednesday he drinks too much, argues a lot, and then we put him in a cell overnight. The next day he feels terrible and apologises much.'

'Every Wednesday?'

'Yes. I think it is his weekend, you could say.'

Frank nodded. He looked sideways at Simenon and then glanced towards the cell Frieda was still inspecting.

'It's the missus,' he whispered to Simenon, 'she's dedicated to her career. When we went to Fiji she wanted a look at the local police stations, to see if they did something different, or better. The cells were apparently quite different.'

'I understand, Inspector. My wife is much the same. Personally I would rather avoid anything to do with police work when on holiday, but there is a type of woman who cannot let go.' He paused. 'Though when I was in Fiji I had chance to visit the police station. It is strange. I do not remember there being cells there.'

'I wouldn't know. I managed to find an excuse not to go. Well, actually, I had a touch of food poisoning. I think it was the peas. Speaking of peas, inspector, do you like them? Peas that is.'

'Peas? Well, yes. A little of sugar, a touch of salt, butter ...'

'What about carrots?'

'Yes, carrots too, again, just the hint of sugar, some butter, real butter, of course –'

'Which side of the plate do you prefer them to be on?'

For a moment Simenon's mouth hung open. It was not a question he had ever considered before.

'Well, that's been very interesting,' Frieda said, coming out of the cell. 'Now, do you have special operations rooms, or do you set them up when necessary?'

Simenon shook his head to clear it of the image of a plate of peas and carrots.

'We have one running at the moment. Allow me to show you.'

They moved off while Frank lingered to take one last intrigued look at the black-clad man in the cell. Having a drunken debate with a priest appealed to him. Or should that be "having a debate with a drunken priest"? Either way it could not but help enhance his understandings of the mysteries of life. In his current state Father Anthony resembled a man in despair, but Frank rather suspected that, after a couple of drinks, he would become the life and soul of any party.

'It's my husband,' Frieda said in a low voice to Simenon. 'He's incurably curious about how other people live and work. He'll probably be bored within a few minutes, as soon as he realises that there isn't much difference in the way we approach things.'

'I understand, Inspector. My wife is much the same. Personally I would rather avoid anything to do with police work when on holiday, but she can never stop her curiosity.'

'Yes, when we went to Hawaii he insisted on visiting the police station there. He especially wanted to see the forensic laboratory.'

'Hawaii. Yes, my wife did the same when we were there. Though I do not remember seeing a forensic laboratory.'

'I don't know. I refused to go. Instead I sat in a restaurant on the beach and had the most wonderful local food. Mostly rice and vegetables, best I've ever tasted. Mainly peas. Do you like peas, inspector?'

Simenon blinked. Peas again?

'Yes, I like the peas.'

'And carrots?'

'Carrots, too.'

'Which side of the plate do you prefer them on?'

Again Simenon was left with his mouth slightly open.

'Right, let's have a look at this operations room,' Frank said, coming up to them.

'Please to follow me,' Simenon said in a less than confident tone. He was still thinking about peas. He had yet to decide on the question. He had hoped that it could be deferred until he was back in his office, alone. It was not an easy question to answer.

By the time they completed their visit to the operations room he had recovered his sad bonhomie. He then showed them around several uninteresting offices, the latest coffee machine, showed them where the toilets were, took them on a tour of the officers' locker rooms, the little room that housed the cleaners' equipment, and even a little attic which gave a good, if dusty view of the street. After that they began to descend the stairs.

'I think that is everything,' Simenon said. 'Unless there is something I might have missed?'

'No, can't think of anything,' Frank replied. 'What about you, Free?'

'No, I would imagine that covers everything.'

'You are sure?'

'Absolutely, Inspector Simenon. Time we were on to Giverny.

Monet's place.'

'I am an idiot!' exclaimed Simenon, slapping his forehead. 'I almost forget. We have not been to the evidence room.'

'Is it an interesting evidence room?' asked Frank, looking very bored.

Simenon shrugged, somewhat confused.

'It contains evidence,' he said.

'What say, Free, shall we have a look at the evidence room? Or have you had enough?'

'Oh, go on then, I know you'll enjoy it Frank.'

'Only if you will, Free. I'm quite happy to give it a miss if you've had enough.'

'No, you'll only keep mentioning how much you would have liked to have seen it if we miss it, Frank. Come, Inspector, lead the way. Just for my husband.'

Simenon led them down to a basement room, shaking his head from time to time and almost muttering to himself.

'It is very old fashioned,' he apologised, opening the door to a large room containing metal shelving loaded with a variety of objects bound in plastic. 'We hope one day to have the barcodes and scanners and databases which tell us exactly where every single item is, but at the moment we can only afford the old paper labels and plastic bags.'

'Lovely things, computers,' Frank said. 'The problem is that they only know what you tell them. Give them duff information and they'll be passing it back forever, or until a human realises that something is wrong.'

'This is very true. In the old days it was paperwork. A certificate of birth would give a man an identity. So long as the bureaucrat had the piece of paper to tell him who this man was, he existed, even if he could not be seen. No certificate, and the man could stand naked in front of him and the bureaucrat would deny his existence. Today it is computers. If something is not on the computer it does not exist.'

'So what case is this handbag involved in, Inspecteur?' asked Frieda, picking up a brown handbag.

'The wife loves handbags,' Frank said. 'She's always buying them. Ouch!'

'Sorry, darling, was that your foot I stepped on?'

'That, is, I am afraid, merely lost property now. It was discovered after a man was seriously injured in a bar fight. Later we discovered that it belonged to an American tourist who apparently returned to America a few days later. So, no link to the fight, and no tourist to return the bag to. All we know is that her name was probably Elaine or Nancy. Unfortunately we do not have the manpower to search for tourists to return handbags to.'

'Here's another one,' Frank said, 'up here. Looks like a young girl's handbag.'

'Ah, no, Inspector, that is an extremely expensive handbag, fashion of the highest class. In the Rue Faubourg-St Honore it would cost you around eight thousand euros.'

'Eight thousand euros for a handbag? You're joking!'

'Not at all, Inspector. I know something about these things. You see, at one stage I collected handbags, antique handbags. I had two important examples from the Napoleonic era.'

'You collected handbags?'

'Yes. They are fascinating objects, a combination of the practical and the aesthetic. Unfortunately I allowed my wife to convince me that a French police officer who collects handbags is unlikely to receive many promotions. We are still what you call macho in many ways.'

'Interesting hobby,' commented Frank.

'It was interesting. These days I regret not continuing, and not worrying so much about promotion. However, c'est la vie. But you have reminded me, I promised Amelie that I would rescue her little handbag. It is in the third row, I think.'

They followed him along the racks until he stopped and picked up a little white handbag in its own plastic bag. He took it out of its wrapper.

'Isn't it still evidence?' asked Frieda.

'Strictly speaking, yes,' replied Simenon. 'Speaking unstrictly, Amelie has been begging me to let her have it back, she says it was given to her on her sixteenth birthday, and it is her most prized possession. How, I do not know, for she has many such little trinkets which are also her prized possessions. Here, madame,' he said, giving Frieda the handbag, 'see for yourself, it is the handbag almost of a little girl.'

'Wow!' exclaimed Frank, turning away from them. 'This is more like it! A set of kitchen knives. Let me guess, a domestic quarrel that ended in murder and the burying of the victim's body deep in the woods?'

'No, Inspector, it is a case of shoplifting. The culprit refuses to admit his guilt, so we keep the evidence for the moment.'

'Oh. Well, what about this?' Frank continued, moving away, keeping Simenon's eyes off Frieda, who was delving into the white handbag. 'An old typewriter. Used to type a suicide note. Except forensic evidence suggests that the typing was done by a left handed woman, whereas the suicide was a right-handed ninety-year-old man who couldn't type anymore because of his arthritis.'

'You have a vivid imagination, Inspector. I'm afraid you might note from the fact that this is not tagged or covered in plastic that it is not, in fact, evidence. It is an old typewriter which was used in the station. One of the officers wishes to keep it as an antique, but he is storing it here until his new flat is ready.'

'Pity. I preferred my version. Don't you have any really interesting evidence, Inspector? Murder, blackmail, tricky cases?'

'I am afraid not. There used to be a dead rat in the corner, but that died of natural causes and was disposed of.'

'Ah, well, pity,' Frank said, picking up Frieda's shake of her head. 'I suppose that's that, then.'

'I suppose that is indeed that,' Simenon said, turning and taking the handbag from Frieda. He smiled sadly. 'You did not find a hidden compartment?'

'Er, hidden compartment?' asked Frieda.

'I searched myself, but I am not au fait with modern ladies' handbags. I thought perhaps a younger and feminine eye might see something I had missed.'

'Er, no, it doesn't appear to have any hidden compartments. Perhaps – an X-ray?'

'No, that showed nothing.' He sighed. 'So, once again back at the first square. No suspects, apart from all of Amelie's family, none of whom would hurt the hairs on her head, and no heroin.'

'No guilty parting and no crumpet,' noted Frank.

'Quite so, Inspector. A moment, I must sign this out.'

'Logically it has to be Marie,' Frank said, after Simenon had finished his paperwork and the three of them walked back to reception. 'Whoever attacked Amelie had access to the room, and was able to leave it without anyone remarking on it. And they had to have a way of carrying the heroin without it showing. Even a small package would have made a bulge in a suit pocket. Marie, on the other hand, always has her bag of cleaning stuff with her. So, she sees Amelie enter the room, follows her, hits her over the head – let's face it, she's strong enough – takes the heroin from Amelie's handbag, pops it into her postman's bag, and leaves the room whistling. I know she doesn't look the criminal type, but what other explanation is there?'

'And how much money would you be willing to bet on that, Inspector?' asked Simenon.

'How much? Approximately or precisely?'

'Approximately, Inspector.'

'Doesn't make any difference, the figure would be the same. Bugger all.'

'Bugger all?'

'Nothing, Monsieur Inspector. It's the only logical explanation, but it's also the wrong explanation. It doesn't fit.'

Simenon smiled.

'Then your money is safe, monsieur. You see, the packet of heroin was covered in red paper which was coated with a substance the nude eye cannot see, but which leaves its trace wherever the packet goes. We checked mademoiselle Marie's big blue bag. There was no trace.'

'She could have two bags.'

'She might, but she does not. We also checked up on her history, as you would. She is what she appears to be, a simple farm girl. There is only so many times you can dream of solutions to facts before you have to accept that they are facts.'

Frank grinned.

'I've just realised. That's one of the reasons your lot took so long on Sunday evening. You were checking our luggage for traces of this chemical you put on the heroin.'

'I am afraid so, monsieur Inspector.'

'And you didn't find any.'

'That is what puzzled me,' admitted Simenon. He held out a hand. 'I will bid you good afternoon. This afternoon I am off duty. No doubt we shall meet tomorrow again. Bon jour, Monsieur Inspector, Madame Inspector.'

'I'm getting to like Simenon,' Frank said as they walked to their car.

'He's an interesting man,' replied Frieda, with a certain lack of enthusiasm.

'You don't like his methods.'

'No, I don't. I would never have run this case this way.'

'It's almost exactly the way I would have run it.'

Frieda had to smile. He was quite right. She would have run everything as tightly as possible while he bumped from suspect to suspect in an apparently random fashion, probing stories like a dentist might probe a suspect tooth, until something gave. And once something gave and the suspect was safely in police custody that suspect would come under Frieda's efficient discipline, where any hope of a slip up by a grinning Frank Summers disappeared entirely.

'I wish you would stop limping, Frank, I didn't step on your foot that hard.'

'I have very tender feet.'

'I'll drive this afternoon, then, shall I?'

Frank grinned. He always got out of driving when he could avoid it. He believed that you couldn't think and drive at the same time, and he had had sufficient disagreements with lamp posts to prove the theory. Never mind drivers in a hurry who seemed to think it unreasonable that he should fail to notice that the lights had turned green while in deep cogitation. Getting out to explain to them that he had been thinking did not, for some reason, go down too well.

'I'll bet you the answer is staring us in the face,' he said.

'Giverny, Frank. Giverny, Monet and lilies.'

'Mais oui, ma cherie. But I still bet you that the answer is staring at us in the face.'

Wellbury. Thursday. Lunchtime.

The Odd Couple

'Good holiday?' asked Eric Johns, putting his tray down and sitting opposite Pete Phillips in the canteen. He was glad that Pete was back. He had missed having someone of his own rank to chat to. And it felt as if he had had to shoulder responsibility for absolutely everything for the past few days.

Now he could share the load.

'So-so, I suppose,' Pete Phillips replied. Normally he enjoyed Eric Johns's company, but now he had a shed-load of work to finish before the end of the day, and he had a horrible feeling that Eric Johns was going to bring up the business of the telephone call on Sunday night. He had no wish to add that to his list of things to worry about.

'You don't sound as if you enjoyed it that much.'

'Oh, most of it was okay. Just little Jenny seemed to be crying the whole time, and the missus wasn't in the best moods.'

Eric Johns was about to use this as an excellent prompt to bring up the subject of the unfortunate honeymoon couple when Pete suddenly continued.

'Somebody showed me some jokes about marriage,' he said, latching on to the first idea that came to mind to forestall Eric Johns's conversation. 'They were quite good. There's this one where this bloke says, "My wife is an angel", and the other bloke replies, "You're lucky, mine's still alive".'

Eric Johns paused. His own marriage was a shining example of a happy marriage, as he was entirely willing to explain to any young constable having difficulties, but he hesitated at taking the same approach with Pete Phillips.

'And then there's this little boy who asks his father, "Dad, how much does it cost to get married?" And the father replies, "I don't know, son, I'm still paying."'

Pete Phillips chuckled.

'There were quite a few more,' he added, 'some really good ones. I'll see if I can remember them. There was a really funny one about a mother-in-law and a lemon, but you need to get the punch-line just right.'

'You want to be careful about spreading jokes like that,' Eric Johns said in as much of a whisper as he could, 'especially after Sunday night.'

'Sunday night?' Pete Phillips asked reluctantly, realising not for the first time that when Eric Johns wanted to pursue a subject the only way to prevent it was to make sure you weren't there. And he hadn't finished his lunch, so disappearing was not an alternative. Though a diet was beginning to sound attractive. An Eric-Johns-free diet.

'That message you got from the French police. About Frank and the Inspector having a bust up.'

That stopped Pete Phillips. When Tricia had spoken of "marital problems" he had presumed that it had been some tiff or other. "Bust up" sounded far more serious. It also sounded nothing remotely like the little he remembered of the message he had taken.

'Now hang on, Eric, who said anything about a bust up?'

'You did. In that note you made.'

'I did?'

'In black and white.'

'I don't remember that. What did I write? Where's the note?'

'It's disappeared,' Eric replied. "Disappeared" sounded better than "I lost it". It also suggested alien forces at work trying to destabilise things. 'I think someone – I don't know who – someone realised that leaving it lying around would mean that the whole nick would find out, and neither Frank nor the Inspector would want that.'

Needless to say almost the entire nick now believed, via Eric Johns's idea of secrecy, that Frank and Frieda had permanently split. While staying together for appearances' sake.

'The thing is, Pete,' Eric Johns continued, 'we have a kind of duty to support them. You, especially.'

'Me, why me?'

'Well, it was you who took the phone call, wasn't it?'

Pete Phillips could see the logic in that. It was called shooting the messenger. He couldn't remember what the conversation with the French officer had been about, apart from something about a woman in a bath. It had been late, he had been tired, and now it was almost four days and a holiday away. Eric Johns must have been awake and fresh on duty when he read the note, so Pete could only presume that what Eric said was correct.

But really, it was unfair. He had been Frank's best man, and that had almost been a disaster. Once Frank was securely married he thought that he could relax. Now it seemed that he was been dragged back into Frank's problems unfairly.

An idea struck him.

'Well, that was four days ago,' he said, 'I'm sure they've patched it all up by now. No need for us to worry unnecessarily. I'm sure they're having a great time.'

Eric Johns shook his head mournfully.

'I wish that were true, Pete, I really do. But I'm afraid we can't ignore the facts.'

'The facts?'

'You know they're sleeping in separate rooms? Frank had to move out the very first night.'

'He did?'

'And the Inspector took a pot-shot at him when he tried to slip away the one night.'

'She what?'

'Keep your voice down, Pete. She probably wasn't aiming at him. I reckon it was just a warning shot. Over his head, like.'

'A warning shot?'

'Yeah, we don't want to make things too melodramatic. You see, basically, the Inspector's determined that the marriage won't fail. Or, to be more accurate, that people won't think it's failed. You know what she's like.'

Pete Phillips thought that he did know what Frigid was like, and pretending there wasn't a problem didn't sound like her. She was more the type to drag a problem out of hiding and hang it in full view of everyone until it became embarrassed and ceased to be a problem.

However, that was, admittedly, when it was to do with a professional problem. She would never bring a personal problem to work, so what Eric Johns said made some sense. A very little, but some.

'Anyway, the thing is, it's up to us, both as colleagues and friends, to support them. Be there for them, if you know what I mean.'

Pete Phillips did not agree. If Frigid was pissed off the best place for a man to be was anywhere else.

'And the best thing we can do now,' Eric Johns continued, 'is to make sure that they don't know that we know that they have a problem.'

Now Eric Johns was making much better sense.

'So I'm organising a surprise welcome back party for them.

Nothing major, just a few drinks at the Blue Bliss on Saturday.'

Now Eric Johns wasn't making any sense at all.

'Eric, how is having a surprise welcome back party going to help matters?'

'Well, if we knew they were having problems, we'd leave them alone, wouldn't we? We wouldn't throw a surprise welcome back party, would we?'

'Well, exactly.'

'Yes, so when we do throw a surprise welcome back party they'll think we haven't a clue. We'll all pretend that we don't know a thing.'

It was not the first time that Pete Phillips felt himself a powerless victim in the coils of Eric Johns's anaconda-like logic.

'Well, I suppose a few quiet drinks won't hurt anyone,' he said slowly, with the horrible thought that his experiences told him that a few quiet drinks were almost invariably the beginning of major trouble. A lot of the arguments between himself and his wife had started with a few quiet drinks. Normally when he had popped into the pub for a few quiet drinks after work and come home to find his wife demanding to know where he had been.

'They'll be a bit knackered after the journey home,' Eric continued. 'What with the ferry, and the trains and all. So we'll keep it down to about an hour, I reckon.'

Pete liked the sound of that. He could tell his wife that it would only be an hour, hour and a half max, and if it was going to be in the private members' bar at the Blue Bliss she and little Jenny could come along if they wanted. She was always complaining about him leaving her with the child to go drink with his mates. Well, on this occasion, she could come with. She enjoyed having a natter with some of the other wives. And there was the children's play area at the Blue Bliss for Jenny. Jenny was always much better when she had kids of her own age to bully rather than her father. All in all it was sounding better and better.

'We'll let them have a drink to start off with,' Eric continued, 'then we'll pop up and give a couple of short speeches, a few more drinks and some polite chat, and then we all go home, and leave Frank and the Inspector thinking that everything's normal, and none of us has the slightest clue.'

'Here, wait a minute, Eric, speeches?'

'Nothing to worry about, Pete. Just a short word of welcome back. I know most people are scared of giving a speech, but this will just be a few informal words to people we both know. Of course, I've actually taken a course in giving speeches, so it doesn't worry me. I know a few tips on how to calm the nerves, so don't worry.'

Pete bristled. He thought he was quite good at giving a speech. He had had to do so on a number of occasions, such as at Frank's wedding, and Eric Johns's patronising suggestion that he might need "a few tips" rankled.

'Giving a speech doesn't worry me,' he said. 'And the tux is just back from the dry-cleaners, so that isn't a problem.'

Eric Johns nodded as if the idea of wearing a tuxedo was something he had planned on. The thought hadn't struck him before, but it appealed. It would give the occasion just the slight touch of formality it needed.

'We'll have to work on the speeches,' he said. 'Make sure we don't repeat what the other has said. Keep them down to five minutes, maximum.

Pete was pretty sure that he could manage a short speech with a maximum length of five minutes. He had often held an audience in stitches of laughter for three times that length when he had been a member of the rugby club and they had been celebrating.

'I know,' he said, 'I'll include a couple of jokes. That always goes down well.'

Eric Johns blinked. He wasn't sure that Pete Phillips's idea of a good joke might go down that well.

'Just none about husbands and wives having a hard time. Or mothers-in-law.'

'Pity, I'm sure I can remember some good ones. Now what was that one about the mother-in-law? It had a lemon in it, I'm sure. Or was it an orange?'

There were a number of ears which overheard that conversation, try, as most of them did, not to. Eric Johns had a voice which could be easily tuned out at normal speaking volume, but when lowered seemed to drive itself into your brain no matter how you might try to avoid it. Sam Nightingale had been yet again interrupted in her study of the rally across the top of Africa. In a way she sympathised with Pete Phillips, for she had no time for whining women or whining children herself. But if the man didn't have the sense to walk away and keep out of Eric Johns's plans he would have only himself to blame.

Wellbury. Thursday. Teatime.

Tea for more than two

Eric Johns carefully aligned the log book with the corner of the desk in reception. He prided himself on keeping what he called a "tidy ship", though the closest he had come to nautical matters were his annual holidays at Brighton. To put it bluntly, and, considering his imagination, quite surprisingly: he was bored. Crime had been very slow that week. He had missed the opportunity of using his scintillating wit on both members of the public reporting crime, and the miscreants being arrested for crime.

Thus it was that, when the front doors opened, he stood up as straight as he could and prepared to unleash his charming best for whichever old-age pensioner it was who had arrived to report the theft of their purse or wallet, when they had, of course, merely left it at some shop or other.

His charming smile froze.

'Sergeant Johns!' Frances Summers exclaimed. 'How are you?'

'Very well, Mrs Summers, very well. Afternoon, Professor Summers. And yourselves?' he replied, wondering what on earth Frank's parents were doing at the police station, hoping it was nothing serious.

Oh, dear sweet saints alive! Had they got wind of Frank and Frieda's disastrous honeymoon?

'Oh, very well. We've just been doing some shopping – we're looking after Frieda's house while they're away – well, I suppose I should say Frank and Frieda's house now – anyway, we thought we might pop in and say hello while we're here, see if there's any news of the happy couple. We did get a postcard, now where is it?' she asked herself, rummaging in her handbag.

Well, thank heavens for that! Frank's parents were obviously still blissfully unaware.

Postcard! thought Eric Johns. Those postcards were pinned to the notice board on the wall to his right. If Frank's parents read them they couldn't help but realise that something awful had gone wrong. Whatever happened they must not read them!

He smiled as best he could, sidling out from the reception counter, trying to make his movement seem perfectly normal as he backed towards the notice board and leaned against it, blocking the view of the postcards. Fortunately Mrs Summers was engrossed in her handbag, and Professor Summers was looking around with a vaguely bored and lost air, as if his thoughts were somewhere else.

'Ah, here it is,' Frances Summers said, taking out a postcard. She looked up to where Eric Johns had been, puzzled to find that he had disappeared. She turned to find him leaning at an unusual angle against the wall, arms akimbo, a weak smile on his face.

'It's such a nice picture of the hotel,' she said, moving to where Eric Johns leaned, showing him the postcard. He took it and smiled his appreciation, left arm still akimbo.

'Lovely,' he said. 'I'm sure they're enjoying themselves.'

'Oh, yes, I know they are. You see what Frieda has written? "Everything perfect. Taking loads of pictures. Will bore you to tears when we get back." Isn't that lovely? They're too busy to write very much, which is such a good sign. And Frank's added his signature with a little smiling face. Frank always used to be very good with writing letters, but never postcards. And you know, I've always found that it's the wife who ends up writing, sending Christmas cards, that sort of thing. Men just seem to lose the knack after they get married.'

'Very true, Mrs Summers, very true,' said Eric Johns, a man who had rarely sent a Christmas card prior to becoming married, and not once afterwards. He would have liked to have said something better fitted to his usual sociable manner, but his back was beginning to ache with the strain of appearing relaxed while leaning against the wall with several muscles complaining that they weren't designed to be where he was trying to keep them.

'Still, I'm sure they're both having an absolutely wonderful time,' Frances Summers said, returning the postcard to her handbag. 'I don't suppose you've heard any news? I'm sure Frieda must have sent a postcard, I'm sure she would. Frank will probably have sent something not quite polite, if he bothered to find the time, he does let his sense of humour get carried away sometimes.'

'Well,' said Eric Johns as slowly as he could, 'they did send a postcard, yes, though I'm not sure where it is right now, naturally everybody wanted to read it. I'm sure I –'

Fortunately for him they were interrupted by Pete Phillips coming through the front door.

'Hey, Eric, I've got another one!' he called. 'This bloke puts an ad in the newspaper saying "Wife wanted". Next day he gets a hundred replies: "You can have mine".'

He chortled at this, and idly looked at whoever it was who had come to report a crime, or make an inquiry.

'Oh, bugger,' he muttered. 'I mean, ah, hello, Mrs Summers. Professor Summers.'

'Sergeant Phillips, isn't it?' asked Fances Summers with the smile of a mother who remembers the names of her son's friends and colleagues, even if she had only met them at the wedding.

For a moment Pete Phillips was tempted to reply that he was actually Inspector Percy Hanson. Anyone. Constable Sam Nightingale, perhaps. Just a bloke delivering bread. Percy took that moment to come through the internal door.

'Ah, Pete,' he said, 'there you are. I've been waiting half an hour for you – Mrs Summers! Professor Summers! Good to see you. How are you keeping?'

'Oh, very well, Inspector. I was just saying to Sergeant Johns here how we've just been shopping and thought we might pop in to see if there was any news of Frank and Frieda. They did send a postcard, and I don't suppose you've heard any more, but we thought we'd pop in on the off chance, as it were.'

'Yes, yes, we received two postcards,' said Percy. 'One from Frank and one from Frieda. Quite funny, they are. They must be around here somewhere. Eric, you must know where they are.'

'Er, still doing the rounds, sir, I think,' Eric replied, maintaining his "I am perfectly relaxed" stretched stance against the notice board.

'See if you can find them, Eric. Mrs Summers, Professor Summers, why don't you come in for a cup of tea? We could even show you around the station if you like. Things are quite quiet at the moment.'

'A cup of tea sounds wonderful, Inspector. Frank showed me around before the wedding, but Frank – my husband here, Frank – hasn't seen it.'

The idea seemed to perk Professor Summers up.

'Yes, that sounds interesting. I haven't seen the inside of a police station. Well, not since before we got married. And that seems so long ago. I wonder if the cells have changed much. Of course we were students then.'

That statement left everyone apart from Frances Summers standing with open mouths.

'Well, Sergeant Phillips,' said Percy once he had recovered, 'why don't you take Professor Summers on a quick tour of the station – including the cells – and I'll take Mrs Summers to the canteen.'

'Yes, sir. Professor, if you'll follow me?'

'And Eric,' Percy continued, 'find those postcards and have them brought to the canteen.'

'Yes, sir. If at all possible.'

Eric sighed with relief as the others left. He staggered back to the reception counter and sat on his stool. Whatever happened, Frank's parents must not see those postcards. They would only be upset by them. It shouldn't be too difficult. All he had to do was put them away somewhere and claim to have been unable to find them.

But where? Percy was in one of those moods where he would insist on them being found. Percy might not be the best at tracking a criminal down to the ends of the earth, but as far as social niceties went he could spend a week locating someone's preferred choice of marzipan.

And then Eric Johns had a brainwave.

What if he found two postcards which looked almost the same? Wrote some innocuous message on each and produced those? A little bending and buckling would distort the pictures, and, anyway, one hotel looked pretty much the same as another. Especially if they had had an unfortunate drop into a bucket of water along the way.

He went to the notice board, unpinned the post cards and put them in a drawer. Then he put his jacket on and waited for a constable to turn up.

'Ah, Steve,' he said when Constable Steve Right entered a few minutes later, 'look after the desk for me for a few minutes. Won't be long.'

Steve Right was about to point out that he was supposed to be on tea break, but Eric Johns had disappeared before he could say "But, Sarge". He sighed and sat down behind the counter, hoping the sergeant wouldn't be gone more than a few minutes, but, knowing Eric Johns, not believing it. Gertie walked in.

'Hello, Steve. Percy wants to know where those postcards are. The ones Frank and Frieda sent. They were on the notice board.'

Steve Right scratched his head and opened a few drawers.

'Here they are,' he said. Gertie took them.

'Frank's parents are here,' she said, 'so we have to be on our best behaviour and at least try to pretend that we're professional and polite police officers.'

'That might be difficult,' commented Steve. 'What with Percy and all. He'll probably fall over a waste paper basket or something.'

'You should have more respect for your senior officers, Steve,' Gertie replied, walking away with the postcards while giggling.

Steve Right sighed to himself as he watched her leave. He had not revealed a very close secret to anyone, not even his girlfriend.

Steve Right had a deep and passionate crush on Constable Gertie Gregson.

Frances Summers was enjoying herself immensely. Along with a refreshing cup of tea had come freshly baked scones, with cream and home-made strawberry jam. That was a special treat supplied by Agnetha in the canteen kitchen for very, very special guests, and not necessarily ones of high rank. It had been known for an officious chief constable to be offered stale biscuits with his mug of stewed char, and also for a charming and gentlemanly old man temporarily resident in the cells to find himself enjoying some of the best cream cakes ever made in the world.

The tea had come in a floral patterned teapot with dainty floral teacups to match, another sign of important status. It was, in fact, the special tea service Agnetha reserved for Inspector Garold – now Inspector Summers, of course. Mrs Frances Summers was Inspector Frank Summers's mother, and Inspector Frank Summers was Agnetha's private favourite, next to Inspector Garold-Summers (a name Agnetha had settled on to avoid confusion). And now Mrs Frances Summers was mother-in-law to Inspector Garold-Summers, which made her doubly worthy of the best Agnetha could provide.

Strangely enough, Frank Summers, even when the tea set was in use, was given a mug. Some things you just had to accept, one of them being that Frank Summers and delicate tea cups were not made for each other. Though now, perhaps, he could be trained in the correct manner of handling such an item.

Possibly.

Agnetha had high hopes of Inspector Garold-Summers, but she was, at heart, a realist.

Frances Summers was unaware of all this protocol, but she knew that she was being treated as a special guest, which was immensely gratifying. But, more than that, she was sitting having a natter with the polite Percy Hanson, the adorable young Tricia Leigh – with the cute kitten Squishy, who had submitted herself to thirty seconds' fussing before seeking refuge in Tricia's arms – and the stunningly gorgeous Sam Nightingale, who had politely tried to leave, but who Frances had intercepted by exclaiming, "Sam! How are you?" and following that up with an unstoppable flow about Frank, Frieda and postcards, and before she knew it Sam was sitting down having a good old gossip.

And Gertie would be back with the postcards shortly to add to the group. Wellbury was a very nice place, and Frances Summers was already on first name terms with the local shopkeepers near to Frieda's – Frank and Frieda's – house, but she was missing her old friends back home, the daily gossip, cups of tea, discussion of the weather, the latest news, and all that goes up to make a happy little community. Gertie, Tricia and all the others at the station were almost like old friends, and she could indulge in a natter about her favourite subject, her son. Even better, she now had two favourite subjects, Frank and Frieda.

'I can't wait to hear what they've been up to,' she was saying. 'I know a mother's love is supposed to be blind, but I also know my little Frankie too well. He'll get up to some mischief. He always does, you know. Ever since the day he could crawl he was making mischief. Nothing bad, of course, he always means well, but he always gets himself into trouble one way or another.'

She took a sip of tea, seeming to miss the exchange of looks between Tricia and Sam. She had been about to embark on a description of one of Frank's adventures as a toddler, but instead turned to Tricia, smiled sweetly, and asked:

'I don't suppose you've heard from either of them? I don't think Frank will have thought in the slightest of getting in touch, and it is their honeymoon, after all, but I just wondered if Frieda hadn't e-mailed, or whatever it is that people do these days.'

Tricia was saved a reply by Percy's smiling reply.

'No, Mrs Summers, apart from the postcards, nothing. As you say, it is their honeymoon, they're probably too engrossed in each other to think about anyone else. I know I was, when I was on honeymoon. The time just seemed to fly. My wife was most upset with me when it got to the last day and we realised that we'd written fifteen postcards and forgot to send a single one. I'm afraid we posted them anyway, and blamed their late arrival on the postal system.'

'Oh, dear, that was naughty of you. Still, probably better that way.' She sighed. 'It's all so different, these days, though, isn't it? My goodness, when I married Frank's father – well, we honeymooned in Cornwall. We couldn't afford to jet around the world the way you can today. Goodness, yes, when I think of how much a flight to New York cost in those days. Not that we wanted to go to New York, you understand, Cornwall was quite far away enough then. And I remember the farmhouse we stayed in. It didn't even have a telephone. If we had wanted to call someone we would have had to walk to the village and use the public call box. These days, of course, it's so easy to stay in touch, what with mobile phones, this Internet thing, goodness knows what else.'

'Inspector Summers has a bit of a phobia about mobile phones,' Sam said. 'I think he might be allergic to them.'

'Really?' asked Frances Summers. 'Well, I knew that he wasn't too good with a normal telephone – using one to call his mother to let her know that he was well, that sort of thing, but mobile phones? He's always been very technologically minded, or whatever the phrase is. He was always taking things apart to find out how they worked. And quite often he was able to put them back together again.'

'Got them!' cried Gertie as she came up to their table, waving the two postcards. 'Here you go, Mrs Summers.'

'Oh, thank you very much, Gertie! You are a dear!' She delved into her handbag for her reading glasses, extending the pleasure of looking at the postcards in front of her as she carefully extracted the spectacles from their case. 'Now, let me see. Oh, yes, this is definitely Frieda. Such a sweet girl. I think she was just made for Frank, she's so sensible. And such a sweet young girl.'

A couple of coughs were muffled around the table at this description.

'Their handwriting is very similar,' Frances Summers noted. 'But I suppose that's because of working together. And this is Frank's one. Yes, dear little Frank, he's never lost that schoolboy humour, you know. Oh, I can see his cheeky little face smiling up at me now!'

Her pleasurable reminiscences were interrupted by the arrival of Pete Phillips and Professor Summers.

'Quite extraordinary,' Professor Summers was saying. 'It's a very old and simple mechanism. Tried and trusted throughout the ages. The Greeks used the very same principle, you know. The Ancient Greeks, of course.'

'That's okay, Professor Summers,' Pete Phillips replied, a confused look on his face. 'We'll get the locksmith in, he'll know how to sort it out.'

'I can't understand how it happened. Most peculiar.'

'A problem, Pete?' asked Percy Hanson.

'No, sir, nothing that can't be fixed. Only –'

'It's quite extraordinary. In theory it can't happen.'

'Professor Summers was looking at the locking mechanism on one of the cells,' Pete Phillips said.

'Victorian, of course, but I presume you know that. But the principle has been with us for centuries. Quite amazing.'

'And Bobby Stang was standing inside, and somehow, er, the lock seems to have jammed.'

'Don't be silly, Pete, you can't jam those locks. It's impossible.'

'That's exactly it,' Professor Summers said. 'Precisely. They are designed never to jam. And such a simple design that, in theory, it can't happen. But there you go.'

'I'll just go call the locksmith,' Pete Phillips said. 'Bobby should be on tea break as it is. We should get him out quite quickly.' He hurried away before Professor Summers could say anything else about the impossibility of jamming the lock, and before he got his hands on anything else that was theoretically unbreakable.

'Frank!' called Frances Summers. 'You haven't been fiddling

again, have you? Really, I can't leave you alone for a moment! Now come sit down and have some tea, dear. I'm sorry, Inspector Hanson, my husband tends to do this sort of thing all the time.'

'Not at all, Mrs Summers. It's really a bonus, if you think about it. If something can go wrong we need to know about it. Better that it should happen in the middle of the day rather than at two in the morning.'

Just then Eric Johns entered the canteen waving two dripping postcards above his head, an unusual exercise for the portly sergeant. He stopped abruptly at the sight of Mrs Summers holding the two postcards she was never meant to see, angrily remonstrating with her husband. Professor Summers was obviously totally stunned.

'It should never have happened,' he was saying. 'Technically it's impossible.'

'Well, it has, and that's that,' replied his wife.

'Are you okay, Sergeant?' asked Percy Hanson, eyes wide at the strange sight of Eric Johns apparently imitating a ballet dancer, holding two sodden pieces of cardboard.

'Er, fine sir, fine. I was just looking for, um, Bobby Stang. Yes, that's it. Bobby Stang. Postman's just dropped something off for him.'

'He's locked up in the cells. Be a good chap and go look after him.'

'Right sir.' he turned and left, trying to bring his arm and the postcards down as if it was perfectly normal behaviour.

He had been too late! Frank's parents knew the awful truth! This was going to be more tricky than he had originally thought.

In the canteen Professor Summers absent-mindedly stroked Squishy, who had come across to him as soon as he had sat down.

'It's very puzzling, isn't it, little Squishy?' he said. Squishy purred. This human wasn't quite Frank, but there was something about him that reminded her of Frank. If that was so, maybe he had brought Frank along. Maybe Frank was somewhere close?

'Well, the least said the soonest mended,' Frances Summers said, deciding that she wasn't going to let her husband upset what was a thoroughly enjoyable little gathering. She returned her attention to the postcards.

'I do wonder what they're up to at the moment,' she continued. 'I do hope Frieda isn't letting him get away with anything. It must be so difficult. I know I always forgave him anything when he gave me that cheeky little smile of his. Such a sweet little boy he was. And is, of course.'

Normandy. Thursday. Afternoon

Onion Riots

'We know that it almost definitely wasn't Marie,' Frieda said as she drove. 'It wasn't Monsieur Arneaux, he was having a chin-wag and a drink with his friends. It wasn't Madame Arneaux, the regulars in the bar confirm that she wasn't out of sight for more than a minute or so. No-one else was seen going up or down the stairs at the time. Our Scots friend wasn't in – he doesn't have an alibi as such, he claims he went for a walk and can't remember where exactly or what the time was. That doesn't matter, because two or three people saw him go out before Amelie arrived, and no-one remembers him returning, so it's pretty certain that he wasn't there. So, who did it?'

For a moment Frank wished that his own constable, Gertie, had been driving. Gertie loved driving, however dangerously, and she was quite happy to leave Frank to cogitate, think out loud, mutter to himself or whatever he felt like as he tried to think things through to a logical conclusion. She might offer suggestions, but she never tried to out-think him – at least, not at the rate Frieda was doing. Having Frieda question his conclusions at the end of a day, when he had had time to work things out, or at least decide that he had insufficient evidence to come to a conclusion, was one thing. Having her next to him the whole day firing off possibilities every other second was preventing him from being able to follow a thread for long enough to decide anything.

In fact, thinking about it, the reason that Gertie didn't interrupt his thinking was that her particular approach to driving required a lot of concentration on the road.

'Are you listening, Frank?' asked Frieda.

'Yes, my sweet, I am listening intently.'

'Don't lie. You didn't hear a word I said.'

'I heard every word, my angel. And I agree with every word. But I'm also trying to think.'

'Oh, I do apologise for interrupting the great detective's thoughts. I'll keep my mouth shut like a good little wife, shall I?'

Frank didn't reply. In fact he was trying hard not to think, to just let his mind loose so that it could patrol whatever little they knew, hunting out something which didn't fit.

'There's something wrong with our Mr Jamie MacDavis,' he

muttered.

'I'm sorry, darling, have you come up with a brainwave that your little wife might understand?'

'I said, there's something fishy about MacDavis. And Madame Simenon, come to think of it. And if there's something fishy with Madame Simenon, then there's something fishy about Georges Simenon.'

'Not Amelie? Or Jacques? Or Monsieur Dubons?'

'I'm pretty sure that Amelie's just the airhead she appears. Jacques and Dubons are just crooks. The entire family are crooks of one sort or another, but I'd imagine it's mostly tax evasion, maybe a bit of selling stuff which fell off a truck. I think they're more interested in the image than anything else. I can't see them getting involved in drugs, not hard drugs.'

'Which helps us how?'

'It doesn't,' said Frank, closing his eyes and folding his arms. 'The trouble is we've hit a brick wall and we've got to find a way around it. Sometimes ignoring the main suspects and looking at the periphery allows you to spot a gap in the wall.'

Frieda was tempted to say that, since she was obviously disturbing the master detective, she would shut up and let him think. But she had a keen eye and ear for that sort of contradiction: if she was disturbing his thoughts then saying so would only disturb them further and prevent him from thinking. It was the sort of petty comment she hated in other people, and she was not going to let herself get away with it. She concentrated on the road and tried to think of some other comment to make. Her concentration was aided by coming to an intersection in the middle of a small town. Their decision had been to avoid the main roads as far as possible, and it now appeared as if it might not have been the best one.

'I don't remember reading about an onion festival,' she said, bringing the car and his thoughts to a stop. He opened his eyes to find that the street ahead was blocked immediately in front of them by a line of uniformed police officers wearing kepis, and beyond them by a number of parked tractors draped with bunches of onions.

'Doesn't look like a festival,' Frank noted. 'Looks more like a demonstration. Their police don't appear to be too happy about it. I'll ask them if they're going to be long.'

He hopped out of the car and strolled over to the police officers.

'Bonjour, officers. Que c'est que going on?'

They blinked at this unexpected and unintelligible question, looked at each other and then back at Frank. One snapped something at him, indicating with an officious wave of his hand that he should return to his vehicle and stop asking questions.

'Je sui Inspecteur Summers,' he replied, taking out his wallet and showing his warrant card. 'Polizei,' he explained.

This thoroughly discombobulated them. Apparently this strange man speaking some foreign language was a German police officer whom they might just have to be polite to. It was bad enough having to be polite to their own officers. Doing so to foreign ones was a duty too far. The one who had spoken drew himself half to attention and gave a reluctant salute.

'C'est un festival de onions?' asked Frank. 'Des legumes, those thingies.' He pointed towards the tractors, and they followed his hand, eager to have something to be able to pretend they were considering, hoping that another would say something.

'Le tractor,' nodded one. The others rapidly nodded their heads in agreement. 'Tractor,' muttered another, to confirm that what they were looking at were tractors.

'Inspector Summers,' said a voice behind Frank, 'please have pity on our police officers. They are only trying to do their duty. They are not paid to be confused by an English inspector.'

'Inspector Simenon!' Frank exclaimed. 'You do turn up in the most unexpected places.'

Gaspode barked agreement. While Simenon was still wearing his battered suit, rain coat and pork-pie hat, he had discarded his tie.

'I could say the same of yourself, Monsieur Inspector. As I told you earlier, this afternoon I am not on duty. I was on my way to visit with my parents when, what a surprise, I find the road blocked and there you are with Madame Summers.'

'Any idea what's going on?' Frank asked.

'A demonstration. Come, let us retire to the cafe over there for a coffee. We can better enjoy the show from there. Perhaps Madame Summers could park your car while we order?'

They turned to find that Madame Summers had already parked the car and was about to join them.

'Bon jour, Inspector. Ca va?'

'Bien, madame, merci. Et vous?'

'Tres bien, Inspector. Que est-ce le problem?'

'A demonstration, madame,' Simenon said as they sat down at

a table outside a cafe. 'Farmers. They are protesting at prices. It is not unusual at this time of the year. It is not planned, I think they become bored and have a demonstration as they might have a game of boules. They block the intersection and enjoy themselves watching the discomfort of tourists.'

'Inspector Simenon was on his way to see his parents,' Frank said. 'Pure co-incidence we bumped into him.'

'You do not believe me?'

'Of course we believe you, Inspector,' Frieda assured him. 'Is this demonstration likely to last long?'

'Ah, no. Fifteen minutes more, perhaps, at most. They make a point, local television take the pictures, then it is over and we continue our different ways.'

'You're going to see your parents?'

'Precisely. Now I am not at work. Now I do not think about work. Now I have the pleasant drive through the countryslide. I sit in the garden pretty and sip tea. I assure maman that I am eating properly. I agree with papa that the world is not as good as it was in the old days. Maman tells me all the local gossip, who is going out with who, how much the priest is drinking, who is not speaking to their neighbour because the chickens have got out again, and so forth. Then I say au revoir and have another drive through the pleasant countryslide back to my home. I do not think of work.'

'Countryside,' corrected Frieda automatically.

'Yes, as I say, the countryslide,' Simenon replied, looking up as the cafe proprietor came towards them, a disapproving look on her face. 'You wish the tea or the coffee?'

'Tea for me,' Frieda said. She looked at Frank who was sitting hunched forward, his elbows on his knees and his hands clasped together, watching the bored police watching the bored demonstrators watching the bored police. 'Frank? tea or coffee?'

'Hmm? Oh, er, coffee, please.'

Simenon raised an amused eyebrow at Frank.

'I think, perhaps, it is hard to learn how to leave work behind, madame,' he suggested. 'For a police officer, that is.'

'That isn't normally the case for this one,' Frieda replied. 'If anything it's difficult to get my husband to concentrate on work at the best of times. He gets bored very easily, don't you, Frank?'

Frank didn't reply. His eyes had a lost gaze.

'Well, I am not at work this afternoon,' Simenon said with some feeling. 'I sit here as the spectator civilian. I drink my coffee and amuse myself watching these gendarmes and the onion farmers.'

'The heroin is the key,' Frank said.

'Onions,' said Simenon. 'I wonder where they came from.'

'It was heroin, Inspector?' asked Frank. 'Not just some white powder made up to look as if it were heroin?'

'Potatoes, they come from the Americas, this we know.'

'Because if it was just white powder, whoever it was would have thrown it away as soon as they found out. But if it was heroin, they'll still have it.'

'And turkeys, these too come from the Americas. But in English they are called turkeys because people thought they came from Turkey. An interesting fact.'

'Inspector, would Amelie be able to tell the difference between, say fine sugar and heroin? Any white powder?'

'But onions? Where did they come from? Have there always been onions in Europe, or were they brought in, from China, perhaps. So much we think of as European originally came from China. Or perhaps Africa. There is always something new out of Africa. Now, who was it who said that? A Roman, I believe. Or was it one of the Ancient Greeks? Perhaps, even, though it would be impolitic to say so, it was an Egyptian?'

Frank looked at Simenon with the face of someone who has realised that, no matter how long he goes on, he is just not going to get an answer.

'Remind me to ask you again tomorrow,' he said, leaning back and taking a sip of his coffee. 'When you've got the countryslide out of your brain.' Frieda glanced at him. She recognised the look on his face. If Simenon wouldn't answer his questions Frank was going to find a different route to enjoy his own sense of humour.

'Perhaps it was just the seed,' Simenon continued. 'Perhaps the onion seed came upon god's good wind, and settled in the soil.'

As if to demonstrate how the onion could have arrived in Europe, one came flying over the heads of the police officers and hit Simenon in his ear. His eyes opened wide and his speechless mouth hung open for a few seconds.

'Murder! They throw les oignons at me? On my day off! Non!'

'That's a bit of a bummer,' said Frank. 'You would think they'd have the courtesy to wait until you were back on duty.'

'This is too much!' cried Simenon, standing up. 'Too much! I go to the countryslide, I do not get attacked with onions!' He strode over to the line of police officers, pointing at one of the demonstrators and giving orders.

'Simenon's lost it,' noted Frank.

'I'd say that he knows who threw that onion, and it's personal. It was meant to hit him.'

'Yes, but he's going about it the wrong way.' Simenon was ordering one of the police officers to arrest a man. The police officers adopted the attitude of people who know that their superior officer is making a mistake, and don't wish to be part of that mistake. A few minutes longer and everyone could leave in peace. And there were far more demonstrators than police officers.

'They aren't prepared for a riot,' noted Frieda. 'No shields, no body armour. They look more as if they were going to a presentation. Those uniforms look old-fashioned.'

'If Simenon doesn't watch out he's likely to land up in the thick of it.'

'No, please, not now, Frank.'

'He'll be right in the soup shortly.'

Frieda sighed and sipped her tea.

'You could say he's dicing with death. It'll all end in tears, you watch.'

An onion came flying over. Frank reached up and caught it without looking, flinging it back with a lazy air. It hit a demonstrator in his mouth.

'I wish you wouldn't do that, darling,' said Frieda.

'Do what?' asked Frank. 'Return his property?'

'No, catch it in that casual, I'm-not-really-trying manner. It is very irritating to us mere mortals, you know.'

'It's the Buddhist approach. Attaining your target by not aiming directly at it.'

'Frank, please do not bring Buddhism into it. The French police and onions are quite sufficient.'

'It's a bit like tying your shoelaces.'

Frieda would have closed her eyes had not the melee been so close.

'It's good weather for it,' she said instead.

The French police officers were backing away from the demonstrators. One of them tripped and fell at Frieda's feet.

'This is betting a bit close,' Frank said. 'Go and play over there, you lot, this is the spectators' area.'

The crowd of police officers and farm workers failed to notice this request. Frieda and Frank were now in grave danger of being overrun with police officers, farm workers and onions.

'Where's Simenon got to?' asked Frank. 'This is his bailiwick. He should be sorting things out. Letting law and order go to pot like this, I don't know what the world is coming to.'

'He's probably taking pot luck with the person who threw the first onion.'

'Well, if he isn't going to do anything about it, I will.'

'Frank, do you think that's wise?'

A police officer and a man in blue dungarees began wrestling with each other three tables away.

'Okay, okay, that's enough.' Frank said. He stepped onto a chair and called out: 'Ecoutez moi! Come on, you lot, ecoutez moi!' There was a brief pause in the melee. They looked up at him. They were about to shrug and ignore him when he pointed.

'What's that silly bugger doing now?' he asked. They all looked around.

Simenon, followed by a loping Gaspode, was chasing a small man around the tractors. The man was wearing a red shirt, blue work trousers and an unidentifiable piece of material on his head which appeared to resemble a hat or a cap. Simenon was putting his best into it, but the wiry little man showed the lined and tanned face of someone used to outdoor work and exercise, whereas Simenon had the pallor of a man too used to office desks, car seats, and perhaps too much coffee and a diet of take-away food. As he lolloped alongside Gaspode occasionally looked from Simenon to the little man as if enquiring whether he should catch up with the man. Perhaps, if it weren't too unhygienic, to bite him.

One of the farm workers watching cheered the little man on. One of the police officers cheered his superior. The farm worker turned to him and gabbled a question. The dirty bank notes which appeared in his hand showed that he was suggesting a little bet. The policeman shook his head and waved his hands emphatically. He might support his superior, but he wasn't going to be silly enough as to bet on him.

'Damn, they've disappeared,' said Frank as Simenon and his target ran around a corner. One of the farm workers looked at his watch and uttered an exclamation. Frank caught words which sounded suspiciously like "lunch" and "the wife" as the workers rapidly left.

'Well,' said Frank, stepping down and sitting down, 'that's the way to clear a farm riot. Wait until it's lunchtime and their missus is waiting for them to get home.'

They watched as the gathering quickly dispersed. Tractors started up, men ambled quickly away, the farmers and farm workers waved to the police and called humorous adieus, along with certain hand gestures which might have been misconstrued by the uninitiated. The police watched until most had gone, had a quick discussion between themselves with much wiping of brows, and apparently decided that they were already very late for being somewhere else. A few taps on breasts suggested that someone, if not all, was late for the awarding of a medal. Within minutes Frieda and Frank were sitting alone outside the cafe.

'Well, that was fun,' Frank commented. 'I think we need a fresh round, though, my coffee's gone cold.'

'I wonder what happened to Inspector Simenon?' Frieda mused, signalling to the waitress for fresh drinks.

Simenon re-appeared, coming round a corner, panting, puffing and almost stumbling, a bright gleam in his eyes, a rag in his right hand. He managed to get to them and sank into a seat. Gaspode sat alertly upright next to him, as if he now knew what to do next time, and fortunately it did not involve his jaws coming into contact with a dirty trouser leg.

'Now I have him,' Simenon wheezed.

Frank looked around.

'You do? Where?'

Simenon coughed, tried to say something, failed, and waved the rag.

'I have his hat!' he exclaimed.

They looked at the rag. It had obviously never been washed. Its condition was such to either keep a forensics lab busy for six months or to evacuate the area immediately and quarantine it for two years.

'What you might call solid but unstable evidence,' Frank noted. 'Are you sure that thing isn't live and ticking?' Simenon shook his head, waved the rag again, and gasped for breath.

'It is his lucky hat!' he roared.

'Lucky you haven't died from something contagious?'

'You do not understand, Inspector Summers! While I have this Alfons will not do anything. Without his lucky hat he knows he will fail. He dare not even tie his shoelaces for fear of tripping. He will come to me on bended knees, begging for his hat.'

'Shoelaces?' asked Frieda weakly. 'Not shoelaces again.'

'Alfons?' asked Frank.

'That – that miserable little wretch who threw the onion. Ha! He thought he could hide behind the others and throw the onion at me? Non! I have arrested him many times in the past. He has escaped jail many times because he has a clever lawyer. But now, now he is beyond the law. Now I have his hat!'

'Superstitious type, is he?'

Simenon had managed to control his breathing, getting his blood pressure down from over the top to just very, very high. He waited until the waitress had delivered their fresh drinks, took a sip of coffee and looked at Frank.

'Inspector Summers, if you scratch a Frenchman you find a superstition. You have read of the problem we have with secularism? Some people think France is a Catholic country. The truth is, it covers thousands of years of myths and superstition. The French took in the Catholic religion because it has so many superstitions itself. They just added them to their own.'

Frank nodded.

'Superstitions, eh?' he murmured.

'Now, Frank, stop that,' said Frieda.

'You have an idea, Inspector?' asked Simenon.

Frank sighed.

'No, I'm afraid not. It's just that your lot sound just like the lot we have back in Wellbury. You remember we told you about the ghost and the aliens?' Simenon nodded.

'I remember. I thought that perhaps you were exaggerating. Now I wonder.'

'Oh, no, it's all true. It's not so much that something happens and people let their imaginations run riot, more like their imaginations are already on riot level and looking for an excuse to go crazy. It can be useful.'

'And you were thinking perhaps of such a use in this case?'

'Hoping, more than thinking. If Amelie had been killed, her ghost might have come in quite useful.'

'Frank!'

'Yes, I know, I wasn't wishing that Amelie had been killed, just wondering if we could use their superstition to twist a few mental arms, as it were.'

Frieda looked from Frank, glumly thinking what a pity it was he couldn't come up with an idea, to Simenon, glumly thinking what a pity it was he couldn't come up with an idea.

'Well, if you two want to sit around moping, I shall go and enjoy myself,' she said. 'It won't be the same having my honeymoon on my own, but it will be a lot better than having to sit around with a pair of depressives.'

'Tien!' exclaimed Simenon, standing up. 'You are right, madame. I interrupt your honeymoon, and I forget all about my afternoon. Thank you for reminding me. I go to my parents. Au revoir and bon chance.'

'Before you go, Inspector,' said Frank.

'Oui?'

'I know you don't want to think of the case at the moment, but it's worth remembering something: sometimes it's not the answers which are important, but the questions.'

'I am aware of that, Inspector. But now I leave for the countryslide.'

'Consider the question, Inspector, consider the question. For example, what would you say if I asked you where Napoleon kept his armies?' Frank said. Simenon paused.

'Well, it depends on which campaign, of course. When he was thinking of invading England they were quartered at Boulogne, for instance.'

'No, no, think of the question, Inspector, think of the question: where did Napoleon keep his armies?'

Simenon raised his eyebrows and shrugged.

'Very well, Inspector Summers, where did Napoleon keep his armies?

'Up his sleevies, of course,' Frank replied, and collapsed in laughter. Simenon looked at him in bafflement. Frieda sighed.

'Don't forget your, er, trophy, Inspector Simenon' she said.

Simenon nodded, as if grateful to have an excuse not to ask where this 'sleevies' was.

'Ah, yes, Alfons's hat. That is not work. That is pleasure.'

'Interesting form of pleasure,' Frank muttered as Simenon walked back to his car, Gaspode trotting alongside. 'Enjoy the countryslide, Inspector,' he called out.

'I will. Enjoy your loonymoon, Inspectors.'

'Countryslide indeed,' said Frank. 'And you talk about me butchering the French language.'

'He's only doing it to wind you up, Frank,' said Frieda. 'I thought you would have realised that by now.'

'He is?'

Frieda sighed again.

'Darling, for a detective who is supposed to be one of the better ones, you can be really obtuse at times.'

'Cheeky bugger,' Frank muttered. 'Well, in that case, I think I shall return the favour. I might not be good at many things, but winding Simenon up – well, I'm sure I can do it. In fact, it's a challenge. Winding Eric Johns up is too easy. It's time I took on someone more worthy of my abilities.'

He didn't notice the twitch in her eyes as he spoke of Eric Johns.

'Darling,' she said, 'it's Thursday afternoon. We only have the rest of today and tomorrow. Can't we just forget about Simenon and the others? And no mention of anyone at the station. Just us two, far away from all madding crowds.'

'You know, you're right, Free. Sod it. Just the two of us.' He smiled at her. 'Have I told you lately that I love you?'

'Just so long as you don't sing it, Frank,' she replied, trying to hide the blush creeping over her face.

The waitress collected their cups and saucers as they left. The interesting looking Englishman with the attractive white quiff in his hair was humming a song. She was sure she knew what it was, but for the moment couldn't quite remember.

For the rest of the afternoon customers left humming a song to themselves, trying to remember the words, wondering what the title was, frustrated that they couldn't remember. Simenon spent the afternoon frustrated that the only atlas his parents had, one that he had used as a schoolboy, showed no town or region that an Englishman might pronounce as 'Sleevies'. His mother seemed to recall an aunt who married someone from a village with a similar name, a village close to the border with Belgium, but his father was sure it had to be in Italy somewhere.

Frank and Frieda managed to get through the afternoon in Giverny pretending that they had forgotten all about Amelie and the heroin. And for a few hours Monet and a lack of Simenons made Frieda feel that they were at last enjoying their honeymoon as they should.

Normandy. Thursday. Late Afternoon.

Xavier Dubons sings

'Trying to take Italy was a mistake, I reckon,' Frank said as they drove back towards the hotel. 'They should have stayed in Sicily and let the Germans keep troops in Italy just in case. Far better to have gone for the underside of France earlier.'

Frieda treated Frank's views on history with respect. Not because they were Frank's but because they almost certainly came from, or were inspired by, his father. Frieda had no automatic respect for rank. To her a chief constable or a superintendent meant nothing by virtue of their title. Each person had to gain respect by themselves. She had no truck with the idea that it was the uniform that was respected, not the person.

The one exception to this was the rank of Professor. When she had been at university, you could question a tutor, criticise a lecturer, even deride and insult them to a certain degree if either not to their faces or done in a polite way. But not Professors. Professors were demi-gods, only occasionally visible in their academic gowns, delivering incomprehensible and immutable truths.

And Frank's father was a Professor.

Their first meeting had been a disaster. At the time it had been preying on her mind for weeks. It had been crucial that Frank's father should like her. Frank and his father were very close, and she wanted to be seen as a welcome addition, not an intruder. With the first meeting due to occur the day before the wedding she had been as nervous as she had ever felt, and had immediately put her foot into it. It was only the following day that she realised that Frank's father had been equally as nervous, and had thought he had put his foot into it. After that – at least after Frank had definitely said yes, and they were definitely and absolutely married – she had had time to relax and begin to think that Frank's father was probably the most adorable father-in-law she could have.

Even if he was a demi-god.

'Is that what your father thinks?' she asked now as she parked the car a short way from the hotel entrance.

'I think he has his doubts,' Frank laughed, getting out of the car. 'Whenever I mention World War II he manages to change the subject to Carthage and Hannibal in about two sentences. He is interested in the subject, but it's not his main field. I think he's worried that he doesn't have enough information to reach a firm conclusion.'

'The problem with sitting in Sicily,' Frieda said, having established that she was not in danger of becoming a heretic through disagreeing with Professor Summers's judgement, 'is that the Germans would have bombed it to pieces. And the Allied supply lines from North Africa.'

'I don't think their air force and navy were up to that at that stage. I think they would have lost more aircraft and naval vessels than the Allies would have suffered casualties. And they'd have their major battalions in the toe of Italy waiting for the invasion, while the Allied troops would have been pushing into southern France. The German troops in Italy would have been cut off the same way those in Norway were. No food. No ammunition replacement. No petrol supplies. And living in a country becoming increasingly hostile to them.'

Frieda wrinkled her nose at this idea. The problem was that it really needed to be tested in depth, with historical data and the ability to judge the effect of a number of theoretical possibilities, including the damage done to the German and Italian economies, transport systems, Allied losses through various causes, etc, etc. Which meant some form of war game. And there just wasn't room in the house. If she showed any weakness they would both end up with the lounge and any other spare room resembling a child's play room following a particularly strenuous party.

It was not so much that that worried her, but the inevitable cleaning up. Should Frank's parents visit and find such a scene, Frank's father would no doubt be on his hands and knees immediately, engrossed in the study. Frank's mother would be little impressed. It was silly. Her own mother could, and did, criticise her for hours, and she managed not to take too much notice. Frances Summers would rarely utter a word of dissent, whatever she felt, yet because of that Frieda dreaded doing anything to upset her.

They were almost at the hotel entrance when a man stepped suddenly out from a shop entrance, blocking their way. Before he realised what he was doing, Frank's fist shot out and just stopped as he recognised the little man in the natty waistcoat and yellow bow tie.

'Inspector Summers! I apologise,' cried Xavier Dubons. 'I did not mean to disrupt you.'

'You should be careful,' Frank said, breathing harder than he would have liked, 'jumping out at people like that, Monsieur Dubons, or you'll be the one who gets a surprise. Our experiences so far of people surprising us haven't been that good.'

'Ah, yes,' Dubons said, running a finger around his collar. This disturbed the line of his yellow bow tie, and he put both hands up to re-adjust it. That meant that he dropped his elegant walking stick. 'You see,' he said, stooping to pick up the walking stick, 'I have a confession to make. A mea culpa. Yes, that is it, a mea culpa. A very much mea culpa.'

'A confession?' Frank asked as the man quickly beat his breast solemnly three times, but not so as to disturb the line of his waistcoat.

'How can I put this? It was a misunderstanding. Yes, a misunderstanding.'

'What, precisely, was a misunderstanding?' asked Frieda.

'He was not supposed to do that. Non, that was a

misunderstanding. An unfortunate misunderstanding.'

Frank and Frieda looked at each other.

'Who was not supposed to do what, Monsieur Dubons?' asked Frank.

'I gave explicit instructions. Explicit. Indeed, I wrote them down and sent them by the first post. First class.'

'Monsieur Dubons, what are you talking about?'

'Why, the man who tried to mug you.'

Another look was exchanged between Frank and Frieda. The last thing Xavier Dubons resembled was a kind of Godfather.

'You hired the man who tried to mug us?'

'Non! Non! Non! I hired a private detective to find out if you had the heroin. He sent down that fool. He was only supposed to find out if you had the heroin, nothing else. I said it might be in your handbag, thus a mistake is made. A tragic, tragic mistake! Please, I insist you believe. It was a tragic mistake! Tragic!'

'But why did you think we had the heroin?'

'You were the ones who found Amelie. The heroin is gone. It seemed logical.'

'And what business is it of yours anyway, Monsieur Dubons?' asked Frieda. 'Even if we did have the heroin, which we don't, it's a police matter.'

The man gave a little shrug, adjusted his bow tie, dropped his walking stick, and picked it up, disarranging his bow tie again.

'Amelie is my niece. She is under the suspicion. I know she would never do such a thing, but Simenon – he suspects everyone. I wanted to clear my little niece's name. She is very dear to me.'

'Just as a matter of interest, Monsieur Dubons,' Frank asked, 'if you had found that we had the heroin, what would you have done?'

Dubons blinked his eyes. Then he straightened his shoulders and puffed out his little chest.

'I would have informed the chef of Simenon's course.'

'His chef?'

'His chief,' translated Frieda. 'His boss.'

'You would have told Simenon's boss,' Frank said slowly. 'Not Simenon himself?'

Xavier Dubons looked as if he considered this a most reprehensible suggestion.

'Simenon? I do not trust that man. No, I trust that man not at all. I run businesses in a very legal manner, but Simenon? For Simenon there must be something illegal if I make a profit.'

'Nor his wife? Madame Simenon. She's an inspector too.'

'His wife? She is quite mad. Once, at a gathering, a party, as you say, she touched me on ... It is quite impossible to say. Perhaps she had been drinking. But she is quite mad. Quite definitely mad.'

Frank looked at Frieda and raised his eyebrows as if to say "Well, he's got that right." Dubons took out a yellow handkerchief and patted his brow.

'Please,' he said, 'I ask you to allow me to make the recompense.'

'Recompense?'

'Mais oui. What happened, it is a terrible mistake, a tragic mistake, but I feel responsible. I must make the recompense, the ammendations.'

'Monsieur Dubons, perhaps the best amends you could make would be to explain things to Inspector Simenon.'

'What? Impossible! I would rather freeze in hell over! No, it is your good selves I injure, purely by accident. Only to you can I make the recompense.'

'With all due respect,' said Frieda, 'I don't think we want the recompense. I think we've had enough without the addition of the recompense. We're supposed to be on our honeymoon. We've discovered Amelie in the bath, we've been shot at, and attacked by a mugger. That's enough.'

'Ah! I understand, Madame Inspector, yes, I understand. But, please, think of me. My honour, this is important to me. And you have saved Amelie, this is more important to me. I have mistaken, by accident, but I have mistaken. I must make the correction. Please, I beg of you. I never beg of anyone, but to you, I beg of this.'

'Monsieur Dubons,' said Frank, 'you know that we are British police officers. I don't think that there's any recompense that you could make which we could accept. We do have certain rules, you know.'

'Ah, you think I mean the money? Mais, non, that is not correct. That is the crudity of Jacques Pointer. Moi, I offer merely a service, just a little service.'

'A service?'

'Oui. The little service. Now, on Saturday you come to the celebration breakfast, this is so? And then you return home, a long journey, to Calais, and then the ferry, it is very slow, and it gives you the mal de mer. No, monsieur, madame, I insist. I tell my pilot to fly you back to England. It is quick, no more than an hour, much more comfortable.'

'Thank you,' said Frieda, 'but we have quite gone off the idea of flying in light aircraft. Quite gone off it, you understand?'

For that moment Frieda thought that she heard her mother speaking through her.

'Ah, non, madame. My plane is not a little – tin can, is the word, I think? – non, that is Jacques. He hears I am buying the aeroplane, he buys one first, a little toy. Mine is much better. It has two motors.'

'And you're a better pilot, I presume?'

'Pilot? Mais non, I do not fly the plane. Why should I fly a plane? I have a pilot who flies the plane. I have a business, many businesses, do I write the accounts? Non, I have the accountant. Just so, I have the pilot.'

'We'll let you know, Monsieur Dubons,' Frieda said, moving on towards the hotel entrance, pulling Frank along by his hand.

'I insist,' Dubons said, trotting after them, tripping over his walking stick, falling down, jumping up to repeat the process. 'I must make the ammendations. And it will save you much time. You would have to get to Calais, sail to Dover, take the train to London, perhaps the Underground – ah! that Underground, I would not transport cattle in that – then another train. Too, too much travel on your journey home. The journey out, long, yes, but the journey home must always be short. My pilot says there is an airfield not far from Wellbury, and then the taxi to the stations, and just the short train journey.'

'Well, it would make the journey a little shorter,' said Frank, stopping.

'We could take a taxi straight home,' suggested Frieda. 'From the airfield.'

'Ah, non,' cried Xavier Dubons. 'To come home by train, this is most romantique. Your friends and family wait on the platform, the train comes chug-chug-chug slowly in, you lean out of the window, waving. Ah, such sadness we have no longer the steam engine. Casablanca, oh, how I weep for such days.'

'You know, monsieur Dubons, you have a point,' Frank said. 'About the shorter journey, I mean.'

'And I hear there is a strike at Calais,' added the Frenchman. 'The trawler sailors. They stop the boats. No one can sail in or out. Those sailors, ah! Barbarians!'

Frank and Frieda looked at each other. Finally Frieda nodded reluctantly.

'It's a nightmare when they do that,' she said. 'They have special contingency plans to stack up the traffic in Kent. I've studied it.'

'Bon!' exclaimed Monsieur Dubons. 'I make the arrangements.'

He bowed and walked away with the gait of a busy little man. A happy, busy little man managing not to trip over his own walking stick.

'You know, Free, if I had the choice between being shot at in a light aeroplane and travelling one stop on the Underground, I'd take the plane any day.'

'If you put it that way, yes, suddenly the plane sounds almost enticing.'

'And it does have two engines. Apparently.'

'Let's hope they both work. Or at least one of them.'

'And let's hope that our Monsieur Dubons is the harmless little fellow he's pretending to be.'

Normandy. Thursday. Evening.

Hair

Frank whistled in the bathroom as he combed his hair.

'You know, Free,' he said as she entered, 'there's something wrong with polo shirts.'

'Polo shirts?' She looked at the one he was wearing. It was one that she had chosen.

'And t-shirts. And jumpers.' He waved his comb at the mirror. 'You shower, shave, all the rest, comb your hair. Then you pull on a polo shirt or whatever, and you have to comb it all over again. It just seems a bit inefficient.'

'Perhaps you shouldn't comb it the first time. Wait until you've got your shirt on.'

'No, if you don't comb it straight after a shower it ends up sticking up everywhere. Mine does, anyway.'

He finished and put the comb down, arranging it and his toothbrush, razor and toothpaste precisely in line. Then he picked up his wash bag and dropped it on them.

'Damn!' he said as it fell off, onto the floor. Then he chuckled as the bottle of tablets fell out. He picked them up and showed them to Frieda.

'Elephant sedative,' he said. 'I got Doctor Neemes to prescribe them a couple of weeks before our wedding. I wasn't taking any chance of anything interfering. If they'd dropped a safe on my head I would have popped a couple of these and carried on.'

'Darling,' said Frieda, sitting on the edge of the bath and looking up at him, 'seriously, now. These headaches you've been getting – I am a bit worried, you know.'

He put the bottle back in the bag, replaced it on the shelf, turned to her, folded his arms and leaned against the basin.

'After I was shot,' he said, 'when I got out of hospital, I began to get these migraines almost every evening. Or that's what I called them. They were bad, really bad. I've never been so scared in my life. It was as if my brain was imploding. I knew when they were coming, my sight would start blurring and then I wouldn't be able to see. And then my brain would – well, implode. It's the most painful thing I've ever been through. Even worse was not been able to see anything, or even stand up, my muscles just seemed to stop working. I tried everything, paracetamol, paracodal, co-codamol, anything which was supposed to help, but nothing did. In the end I began to drink every night, half a bottle of whisky, that seemed to cure them.'

Frieda nodded. She remembered his gaunt look each morning at the station in those days. She hadn't realised that it came out of a bottle of whisky. Her ex-husband had drunk and lost control. Frank had been drinking to stay in control.

'Anyway, Neemes convinced me to give up the booze. He prescribed me those things, to take one as soon as I felt an attack coming on. The funny thing is, I never had another. Not since then. Touch wood.'

'So why did you get another prescription?'

'I don't know. I was terrified, I suppose. Terrified that one would come out of the blue. Firstly, I never want to have another attack like that again, you don't know how awful they are. And, secondly, I was determined nothing would get in the way of us getting married. Let's face it, we had enough other problems to sort out.'

Frieda smiled. Frank stood upright and held his hands out to her. She took his hands, stood up, and put her arms around his waist.

'You know something,' he said, kissing her, 'when I think about it, I haven't had even the suggestion of one of those since I decided to propose to you. I reckon my brain was just totally irritated with me for being obtuse. Once I decided to do the right thing it decided to leave me alone.'

'Silly.'

'Can't ignore the facts, my sweet. Now, shall we stroll out for dinner?'

They kissed again and walked back into the bedroom. Frank clicked his fingers.

'Of course!' he said. 'I should have realised. He wasn't calling for Emily. He was calling for Amelie. Simenon's officer.'

'He? Amelie? Frank, what are you talking about?'

'Jacques. In the aeroplane. When he was coming to. You said he was calling for Emily. I reckon it was Amelie he was calling for.'

'Frank, that's one hell of a leap. Amelie must be quite a common French name. Anyway, why would he call for her?'

'She's the only person who really means anything to him. And let's say she isn't as silly as she looks. What if they've got a nice little side line going on? She pretends to have turned up at the wrong hotel, hands over the heroin, and ...'

'Yes, precisely, Frank. And he hits her over the head?'

'Could have been an accident. Anyway, it's easy enough. Let's find out how many Amelies he knows. And then how many people named Emily.'

Frieda looked at him.

'Frank, would you like to go for a guaranteed dinner with your wife, or would you prefer sitting on your own with a telephone directory?'

Frank considered this.

'Sod it,' he said. 'This is Simenon's jurisdiction. He can check the phone directories.'

Wellbury. Thursday. Evening.

To honour and obey

Eric Johns looked at his reflection in his bedroom mirror. He looked good in a tuxedo, there was no doubt about that. But there was one little problem.

'I think you need to have a word with those dry-cleaners,' he called to his wife in the kitchen. 'They've shrunk these clothes.'

'Yes, dear,' came the reply.

'You just can't get the service these days.'

'No, dear.'

Eric Johns nodded to himself. It was the sign of a good marriage where spouses agreed unreservedly with each other. He had often made this point to young constables embarking on married life. He felt that his good advice had undoubtedly saved many a marriage. A thought struck him.

'You sure that you won't be coming on Saturday?' he called.

'Yes, dear.'

'Everyone else will be there.'

'Yes, dear.'

'It won't be for long. Just a couple of speeches.'

'Yes, dear.'

Eric Johns frowned. His wife hardly ever accompanied him to events where other police officers would be present.

'I'll go on first, then Pete Phillips will follow.'

'Yes, dear.'

His face assumed a cross between a frown and a pout. On the one hand his wife should be proud to see him speaking in public. On the other one of the reasons their marriage was so solid was that they never lived in each other's pockets.

'Dinner's ready, dear.'

Eric Johns patted the cummerbund he was wearing. A little tight. That dry-cleaner again.

Still, at least he would be able to tell his wife of what a great success his speech had been when he got home that Saturday evening. She often said that she preferred to hear his version of events rather than see them at first hand. Just as a loyal wife should do.

Normandy. Thursday. Evening.

What a lovely hat

'What do you fancy tonight?' Frank asked, scanning the drinks menu. 'Red wine? White?'

'I don't feel like drinking, Frank. A glass of water will be fine.'

'A glass of water? Free, we're on our honeymoon.'

He looked at her, puzzled, the skin on his forehead crinkling.

'Are you okay, Free? You aren't coming down with anything?'

'No, no, I'm fine,' she replied, looking down at the tablecloth, blushing slightly. 'I'll have a glass of red.'

'You sure you're okay, Free? You look a little – flushed, I think the word is.'

'I'm fine, Frank, I'm fine. Just a little too much sun, I think.'

'We can skip dinner, if you want, Free. In fact, it might be an idea to get you back to the hotel room and get you a doctor.'

'Stop fussing, Frank,' Frieda said with a slight hint to her tone which suggested that she wasn't entirely averse to the fuss.

'Okay, I tell you what, let's have a quiet dinner, and if you're still not feeling a hundred per cent afterwards, I shall fuss over you. After all, I am your husband. I think I have a right to fuss over my wife. I'm sure it's in the contract somewhere. Along with the "till death do us part" bit. I think it goes, "till death do us part, and the husband is given full and free right to fuss over his wife as much as he wants".'

She smiled, put out a hand and stroked his.

'Darling, I have a little present for you,' she said.

'A present?'

'Yes. You remember the onion demonstrators this afternoon?'

'Yes?'

'You remember those old-fashioned uniforms they were wearing?'

'Well ... Yes. Of course.'

'And you remember how the police were forced back? And

one fell over, almost on top of me?'

'Yes?'

Frieda looked around the restaurant, as if idly admiring the decor. At the same time she lifted her handbag into her lap and took something out. For the first time Frank realised that the handbag appeared far more bulky than previously.

'For you, darling,' Frieda said, handing over a slightly crushed French police officer's kepi.

'Oh, wow!' He looked at it, turning it in his hands. Then he grinned at her. 'You didn't?'

'I did.'

'Inspector Frieda Summers, you are a naughty inspector. Naughty Poppy!'

'It's in the contract. Just after the bit about the husband fussing over his wife. It says the wife is encouraged to obtain a kepi for her husband on their honeymoon if that's what he wants. More than that, it's her duty.'

They looked at each other and giggled.

'Better put it back in your handbag,' Frank said, handing it back. 'We don't want to flash it around too much. Simenon or someone might walk in and decide that it's French property. But it is nice. I love it. Not as much as I love you, but I do love it. You naughty woman!'

'It's the spoils of love. And everyone knows that all's fair in love and war.'

He smiled at her and shook his head.

'Frieda Summers! Tsk, tsk, tsk. Really, I think that you've lost all sense of propriety since getting married.' He chuckled. 'How did it feel when you half-inched it?'

She smiled back.

'Terrifying, for a second. After all, I am supposed to be a respectable police officer – if I had been caught my career could have been finished. And then it felt absolutely marvellous.'

'It's nice being naughty, isn't it?'

'You're a bad influence on your wife, Frank Summers. But you're right, it is nice to be naughty from time to time. I just hope the poor officer doesn't have to pay for it.'

'Not if they're like us. He'll get a bit of a bollocking and then it'll be lost in the paperwork.'

Frieda nodded. She was an expert at making objects appear and disappear on paper. You had to be if you wanted to run an operational police station while the bean counters were roaming the corridors counting pens and pencils. Funnily enough she had never even thought of doing otherwise. Fiddling the paperwork didn't even feel wrong. Certainly not as exciting as palming a French police officer's kepi. She had felt more light-headed afterwards than ever a gin and tonic had done to her.

While he wasn't looking she poured half the wine into a nearby pot plant. And later the second half. And then, after a lengthy and slow meal, they strolled back to their honeymoon suite, sans worries, sans Scotsmen, sans Simeon, sans Gaspode, and definitely sans any shadow of Madame Simenon.

As she lay in bed with her head on Frank's sleeping shoulder, Frieda remembered her teenage years, when she had once dreamed of falling asleep in bed in the arms of a strong young man.

The reality was better than she had ever dreamed.

Despite everything – or quite possibly because of everything – at that moment things were perfect. She had never been happier in her life.

There's a Chinese saying about that sort of thing. It was a good thing Frank was asleep. His view was that Chinese philosophers tended to look on the pessimistic side.

Admittedly, they were quite often right. Almost always right. But they were a gloomy bunch.

Normandy. Friday. Morning.

Is that a mobile phone in your pocket?

As soon as she had sent Frank on downstairs the following morning, Frieda dug her mobile phone out, sat on their bed and read Tricia's latest message. It wasn't good news. It appeared that both Eric Johns and Pete Phillips were intent on organising a welcome back party to convince them – Frank and Frieda – that no-one at the station had the slightest clue that their marriage had irretrievably broken down.

What had begun as a giggle over Eric Johns's ridiculous flights of imagination had now turned into both an extremely irritating interference and a serious worry. Irritation that Eric Johns was trying to interfere with her marriage – *her* marriage! – Eric Johns! – and a serious worry that Frank was going to find out what had been going on, and he wasn't going to be at all happy. One of the problems with Frank's easy going approach to life was that he made up for it on the rare occasions when he did get angry.

Such as when he had, more or less, beaten that mugger up.

It was difficult imagining anyone beating Eric Johns up any more than they might do so to a large marshmallow, but that wasn't to say that Frank might not relieve his anger by doing so.

Frieda dithered. It was not something she was used to doing. Her normal style was to take in a situation straight away and immediately begin giving orders. She tapped her fingernails on the casing of the mobile phone, desperately thinking of what she could say to Tricia. She began a message:

"Tell Eric Johns that when I get back"

She stopped. Firstly that was missing a comma somewhere. Secondly, what could Tricia tell Eric Johns? That she knew that he was entirely mistaken? How could she know? She quickly erased the message and began again.

"Suggest to Eric Johns that he is entirely mistaken and"

No, that wouldn't do either. Suggesting anything to Eric Johns was a waste of breath. You had to state it so simply and forcefully that he understood that, if he failed to take it aboard, he would never see another cream bun in his life. She erased that one.

"Eric Johns" she got as far as typing when she heard Frank's footsteps approaching. She checked her watch. It had been over half an hour since he had gone down, no wonder he was wondering what had happened to her. She switched the mobile phone off, rammed it into her handbag and stood up quickly, pretending to be fiddling with an earring.

'You okay, love?' asked Frank, entering the room.

'Yes, yes, I'm fine. Nearly ready.'

'You look a bit pale. Are you sure you're okay?'

'I'm fine, Frank, I'm fine,' she replied, regretting that she had stood up so fast. She really did feel a little dizzy. 'Stop being such a fusspot.'

'I'm allowed to be a fusspot.' He gave a smile which contained more than a hint of concern. 'To be honest, Free, after all that's happened so far, I do get a little bit worried when I'm away from you. You sure you're okay?'

'You are sweet, Frank,' she said, giving him a kiss. 'Now, let's get on to breakfast. I'm starving.'

'Me too.'

They left. Frieda had been in such a hurry she had done two things she hadn't meant to do. Firstly she had sent the message. Secondly, instead of switching the mobile phone off, she had turned its volume on to full.

'Eric Johns,' Tricia noted as she read the message on her mobile phone. She wrinkled her face and looked at Squishy curled up in Frank's leather jacket on her desk.

'Squish, I know Frieda doesn't like to waste words, but that is a bit brief, don't you think?'

Squishy yawned. She was hungry. She didn't feel like eating, but she knew she was hungry.

'See, Squish?' Tricia said, showing the kitten the message. '"Eric Johns". That's all it says. Maybe it's a new swearword.'

Squishy uncurled herself and stretched a little paw out to the mobile phone. She wondered whether she was supposed to eat it. It looked vaguely edible, it was bright pink, but even so she wasn't sure. She miawoed.

'Oh, Squish, you are so adorable, did you know that?'

'I think I shall have the full English,' Frank said to Cathy as she came out to take their orders. 'Seeing as this is our last breakfast here.'

'You're going back today?' asked Cathy. 'It seems so soon.'

'I know, I know. Actually, we aren't going back today, we're going back tomorrow. But we've been invited to a celebration breakfast tomorrow, and we can't really get out of that.'

'Oh, you'll love that. They don't do that sort of thing often, but it's almost like a day-long party.'

'Fortunately we'll have to leave before lunchtime. Though I wouldn't mind a day-long party if we didn't have to go back in the afternoon.' He looked at Frieda. 'What say, Free, we send the station a telegram – "Being held captive by the natives, will return a day later than expected, maybe two"?'

Frieda smiled.

'I wish we could. But I suppose it would be unfair on Percy and Pete Phillips.'

'Funnily enough I couldn't give a damn about Percy and Pete when I'm with you.'

'I'll get your orders going,' Cathy said, shaking her head and going back inside.

'You know, there's only one thing missing,' Frank said. 'Well, perhaps not missing. Just something I'd like.'

Frieda nodded.

'You want to know who attacked Amelie and stole the heroin?'

'Exactly.'

'Me too. It would round things up nicely.'

'Ah, well, can't have everything I suppose.'

There was a time when Frieda would have believed that Frank had given up on the case. Now she knew that he was just pretending to ignore it. Sooner or later his subconscious mind would get irritated by a lack of attention, and come up with a plan of sorts. Not necessarily a good plan, but a plan.

'There you go, Squishy, I'll bet Frieda will love that one,' Tricia Leigh said to the little kitten. Having miawoed at the camera in the mobile phone again while Tricia took a short video of her, Squishy had retired to the leather jacket. She had decided that the phone did not excite her appetite. She now looked back at Tricia with sad resignation in her little face. She closed her eyes and tried to curl up into a tighter ball, as if she were desperately cold.

'Oh, come on, Squish, my darling,' pleaded Tricia. 'They'll be back tomorrow. You'll see. Frank will be happy and smiling – smiling even more than ever. Please, please, Squishy, cheer up. Look, I'll send this right now, right away.'

Frank and Frieda had almost finished their breakfast when the peace and calm was suddenly interrupted by the sound of "It'll be just our little secret, just our little lonely lovely secret" being sung at a volume the original artist had never meant it to be.

And then, silence. Both had suddenly frozen, knives and forks hanging above their plates.

'Aren't you going to answer it?' asked Frank in what might have sounded like a strictly neutral voice.

'Answer it? Answer what, Frank?'

'Frieda, I'm not deaf. I do know what a mobile phone sounds like, whatever silly tune it happens to be playing.'

Frieda considered claiming that she had merely forgotten it was in her handbag.

'It will just be a message from Tricia,' she said. 'Nothing important. It can wait.'

'Frieda, you won't be happy until you've read it, and I won't be happy until you've got it out of your system.'

'Really, Frank, I'm really not bothered.'

'Frieda.'

'Yes, Frank.'

'Read the bloody thing, for Christ's sake. I'm trying to think.'

'Frank, you really are being silly now. It will just be another message from Tricia telling me that nothing has happened.'

That was a mistake, she realised. She had just more or less admitted that she had been using the thing the whole week.

He put his knife and fork down, pushed his plate away, and took a sip of coffee, turning away from her. Her feelings were torn. When Frank ignored food that meant that he was really angry or distressed, and she wanted to comfort him. The turning away was a signal that the silent treatment was about to commence, that he was withdrawing into himself.

On the other hand, who was he to give her the silent treatment just because she had brought a mobile phone with her and not told him? Did she have to seek his permission for every single thing she did? Did he expect her to be his good little wife, meek and submissive? Well, if that was what he thought, he was going to discover that he was wrong.

Maybe she should have told him about the phone, after all, it was such a petty thing.

But then, purely because it was such a petty issue made his over-reaction petty too.

If he wanted to sulk like a spoilt little brat, let him. She wasn't about to demean herself by saying anything to break the ice.

'Finished?' asked Cathy, coming out of the cafe.

'Yes, thank you, Cathy,' said Frieda.

'Thanks, Cath, good as always,' said Frank absentmindedly.

Cathy didn't need the half-full plates to tell her that something had gone wrong between these two. There was an arctic haze hanging over the table. Their turned-away bodies were physical representations of their unspoken thoughts.

'Come on, Free, let's get going,' Frank said, standing up. 'Cheers, Cath, see you later.'

Cathy watched them leave, Frank striding off, muttering, Frieda, a furious look on her face, grabbing her handbag and sweater, hurrying behind her husband while trying to give the impression that she was doing no such thing.

So much for true love, Cathy thought, picking up the plates and cups. That lasted all of five days into their marriage.

Frank rammed the gear stick into first and pulled out, just as Frieda sat down, and before she had a chance to close her door properly or put on her seat belt. She glared ahead, refusing to acknowledge his presence. She picked up her handbag and almost slammed it down on her lap. She grabbed the mobile phone and stabbed at the buttons, looking at the screen with a face proudly demonstrating its lack of interest.

Then her nose twitched slightly.

She looked up at Frank from underneath her eyelashes, surprising herself at her coquettishness.

'Pull over, Frank, there's something you should see.'

'What is it?' he asked, as if he weren't really listening.

'Pull over, Frank, you can't watch it while you're driving.'

Franked parked the car, irritation on his face. She showed him the message. It began, "Squishy wants to know when you'll be back", followed by a clip of the kitten miaowing at the camera.

'Ah, poor little Squish,' Frank said. He took the phone from Frieda. 'How do you play it again?'

Frieda put a hand on his shoulder and pointed out the button to press. Frank played it again, and then again.

'I feel guilty about leaving little Squish,' he said.

'Me too. I know Tricia will look after her, but I'm sure she'll misses us – you, especially.'

'Still, we'll be back tomorrow.'

Frieda hesitated.

'I'm sorry about the phone, Frank,' she said.

'Sorry? Why?'

'Well, I know you don't like the things very much.'

'That's one way of putting it. Personally I think that anyone who carries one of those things around is mad. But if you want one with you, well – there you go. What can I say?'

'You knew I'd have a mobile phone with me?'

'Of course I did. What I didn't want was being told that my mum was on the line and wanted to speak to me. To make sure that I was eating properly, dressing up warmly, and not trusting the French, even though they were really a lovely people, that sort of thing.'

Frieda looked at him. He was looking ahead, as if his mind were elsewhere. It was a bit much. She had spent so much time worrying about his reaction were he to find out, and had nearly died of a heart attack when the thing had gone off. He might show a little more emotion.

'Tricia's the only one who has the number,' she said defensively, irritated with herself and Frank.

He nodded.

'It's got to work. It's worth a shot, anyway. It's our only shot.' He stopped, and turned to her. 'Tricia's the only one who has this number?' he asked, surprised.

'The only one, darling.'

He smiled.

'Now that's a good idea,' he said. 'Tricia can be trusted. She won't give the number away, or get in touch unnecessarily. On those terms I might even carry one myself. But probably not.'

Frieda felt like pouting. It was bad enough that he wasn't showing the sort of explosion she had expected. But if there was anyone he should trust to have his mobile telephone number, it should be his wife, not her secretary.

'No, Free,' he said, reading her mind, 'my mother would just ask you for the number, and you wouldn't be able to lie like Tricia would. Not to my mum. She'd suss you out in seconds. She does with me.'

Now Frank was being unreasonably accurate.

'Anyway, time to get on with the plan,' he said, switching the engine back on. 'Everything's okay at the ranch, I presume. Nothing gone wrong?'

'No,' Frieda said, drawing out the "o" slowly.

He looked at her.

'You're going to tell me something else, aren't you, Free?'

'Well, you remember on Sunday evening, Simenon got one of his officers to telephone the station to confirm our identities?'

'Ye-es.'

'Well, it appears that the officer gave a little too much information. To Wellbury.'

'A-aand?'

'It appears that Eric got hold of the wrong end of the stick.'

He switched the engine off again.

'Oh, dear god, no. There is no such thing as the right end of the stick as far as he's concerned. What's he gone and done now?'

'He's got the station believing that I found you in the bath with a young woman on Sunday evening.'

'He what?' Frank chuckled. 'Well, I must admit that it's closer to the truth than some of his imaginings. I think I might wind him up a bit about that when we get back.'

'And, well, how can I put this? Tricia, Sam and Gertie have been encouraging his imagination.'

Frank put his chin in his hand and looked at her.

'Free, you put them up to that, didn't you?'

She studied her fingernails.

'And there's something else, isn't there? Something you were going to tell me, sometime?'

'Well,' Frieda said slowly, looking out of the window, 'apparently Eric Johns is convinced that we've broken up. That we're sleeping in separate rooms. But that we're keeping up a pretence of still being happily married.'

'I don't believe it. Even for Eric Johns that's ... probably a record.'

'And apparently Eric and Pete are thinking of having a surprise welcome back party at the Blue Bliss. So that we can all pretend that we had a very happy honeymoon with no baths filled with young women or anything like that. Or that I've taking a pot-shot at you with a hunting rifle.'

'A hunting rifle? How the hell did they manage to work that one in?'

'And the two of them are going to give little speeches, carefully avoiding any suggestion that they know that we're – well, estranged, I suppose.'

'Are they really? Interfering busybodies. Eric Johns should know better by now. I thought I had taught him to keep his nose out of my affairs.'

Frieda thought carefully before speaking. She dearly wanted to throttle Eric Johns and Pete Phillips – or at least see them spend the rest of their lives doing the graveyard shift and spending their beats patrolling whatever cesspits could be found – but she would do it slowly and clinically. Frank would explode.

'They mean well, Frank,' she said.

'They always mean bloody well. They're just very good at messing things up. And they have no right to interfere with our marriage. They are going to pay for that.'

He rubbed his jaw.

'Speeches, you said.'

'Yes, darling. Frank, I wouldn't worry about it too much.'

'I'm not going to worry about it at all. They're the ones who are going to do the worrying. Speeches carefully avoiding any mention of our being estranged, eh?'

'That's the idea, apparently. Frank, please, forget it.'

A slow smile spread across his face. He looked down at the mobile in his hand.

'How do you send a message on this thing, Free?'

'Who do you want to send a message to?'

'Trish. I have an idea.'

'Give it here. You tell me what the message is and I'll send it.'

Frank handed over the phone and explained his idea. When he had finished Frieda was giggling.

'Dear T,' she typed in. 'Lover Boy has come up with a brilliant idea. Read this carefully, I shall type this only once ...'

'Lover Boy?' asked Frank when she had pressed the send button.

'We've been using code words,' Frieda said, blushing slightly. 'I know it's a bit school-girlish, but ... Frank, I'm sorry about the mobile, I know I should have told you, it's just that I knew how much you hate the things. I'm sorry, Frank, I really am.'

'Nah, Free,' he said, putting his arm around her. She snuggled against his shoulder, as much as one can with a gear stick in the way. 'I should have realised that you'd want to keep one channel open. And that you'd make sure that only Tricia would know about it.'

'No more secrets,' Frieda said.

'Not too many, anyway. Not between us. Between us and Eric Johns and Pete Phillips ... well, that's another question.' He kissed her on the cheek. 'And thanks for the shot of little Squish. It'll be good to see her again, poor little thing.'

He switched on the engine again.

'Now, back to business. What do you think about the plan?'

'Plan? What plan?'

'That idea I was telling you about when we left the cafe.'

'What idea?'

'Didn't I tell you?' he asked, surprised. 'I thought I told you as we were walking to the car.'

Frieda looked at him. Gertie had occasionally complained that Frank sometimes thought you could read his mind. This was the first time he had done that to her. Right at that moment he reminded her of his father. The way his father might have given an entire lecture on the Ancient Romans without mentioning them once, as if it should be obvious, and then being puzzled when a student asked him where the Ancient Romans had come in.

'No, darling, you didn't.'

'Didn't I? I could have sworn I did. Oh, well, it's quite simple, really. We both want to know who done it, as it were.'

'Yes, darling.'

'Now, if this were Wellbury, we'd be thinking about evidence and such stuff. A conviction. But that doesn't matter here, it's not our jurisdiction. All we need is to be certain that we know who done it.'

'Yes, darling.'

'So, the plan is this: we get to Amelie before she gets out of hospital, as soon as possible, before any of her relatives arrive for the day, right?'

'Yes, darling.'

'And then we suddenly pretend that she's said something incredibly clever.'

Frieda's mouth opened. Then she closed it. Then she opened it again. Again closed it. Finally she found her voice.

'Amelie, Frank? Amelie says something clever? Darling, I think I see a slight flaw in your plan.'

'I did say "pretend", Free. It won't take much, she'll believe anything. We don't explain, we just talk a lot, tell her that she's made everything clear.'

'Clear?'

'Yes. We tell her that we've suddenly realised that there is some evidence in the room in which she was attacked which will tell us exactly who her attacker is. So we need to get in to retrieve it, and when we do, we'll have the answer. But we can't get into the room before midday. And she mustn't tell anyone, no-one at all.'

'Darling, can I just stop you there? I'm not sure that I understand. Firstly we're going to tell Amelie that there's some evidence that will conclusively reveal the identity of her attacker – evidence which, I presume does not exist – and then we're going to tell her not to tell anyone?'

'Yes! I reckon it could just work. We slip into that hotel room straight after and hide in the bathroom. The first person to come looking for the evidence is our man. Or woman.'

Frieda nodded, suddenly realising what Frank was getting at.

'Whoever it was will want to get to the evidence and destroy it before midday, when we're supposedly going to turn up. And telling Amelie not to tell anyone is a guarantee that she's going to tell some garbled story to everyone within half an hour.'

'Garbled enough for almost everyone to ignore it as just some silly nonsense the sweet little girl is always coming up with. Apart from our Mr X. Or Mrs X. Or even Miss X. They'll pretend to need to go somewhere on business or something, as soon as they're out of sight they'll race around to the hotel, where we'll be waiting.'

'And we step out and say, "So, it was you, Monsieur Jacques," or whoever.'

'And, if we play our cards right, we might even get a confession.'

'It will never stand up in court.'

'We don't need it to stand up in court, Free. That's Simenon's problem. I just want to know the who, why and how. Actually, I'll settle for the how on this one. And, funnily enough, our not being able to use it, if we do get   a confession, is a strong point. You know how people like to confess how clever they've been. We'll give them the chance to do it knowing it can't be used.'

Frieda liked the idea. She wanted to know the who, what and how just as much as Frank. And it could just work. A long shot, but it could just work.

Frank switched the ignition back on and gunned the engine. They drove away in a squeal of tyres.

Frieda wished that she was driving. She hadn't had nearly as many accidents as Frank.

Normandy. Friday. Morning.

Priming a songbird

When they arrived at the hospital entrance Amelie was just coming out, wearing a white frock, white shoes, and a white hat of the type normally only seen at Ascot on Ladies' Day. Behind her Jacques was struggling with three very large suitcases.

'Mademoiselle Amelie,' Frank called. 'Comment allez vouz?'

'Inspector Summers! And Mrs Inspector Summers! I am well. Very well. How are you?'

'Bien, très bien. Er, you're leaving the hospital, are you?'

'But yes. I am almost recovered, and I have no wish to lie in a hospital bed any longer. It is bad for my complexion. I have the look of an English rose, no?'

'Oh, absolutely. Very nice. But you sure you're okay?'

'She is not okay,' Jacques said in a bitter tone of defeat. 'She should stay at least another day. But will she listen?'

'You have not forgotten the celebration tomorrow,' Amelie said, ignoring him. 'You will come?'

'Mais, oui, but –'

'Oh! I shall be so happy!'

'Amelie,' began Jacques. She said something to him in French, patted his arm and kissed him on the cheek. He reluctantly turned and went back into the hospital.

'I have asked him to fetch my gloves,' she explained. 'I forgot them on the reception desk.' She sighed. 'He fusses so much, as if I were a little girl. "Amelie, you must relax", "Amelie you must not do that, let me do this for you." Oh, sometimes it is just too, too much! And if it isn't Uncle Jacques, it is Uncle Xavier. Uncle Xavier is looking after the rest of my luggage. Otherwise he would be fuss, fuss, fuss, too much.'

This might have made an impression on the others had she not said it with a childishly pleased pout on her face.

Frank started, and his eyes opened dramatically.

'That's it!' he exclaimed, snapping his fingers, surprising both Amelie, who had not been expecting such an outburst, and Frieda, who had.

'It is?' asked Amelie. 'It is what?'

'It's the evidence we've been looking for!' Frank continued, grasping Amelie's shoulders and looking into her eyes.

'Evidence?'

'Yes, evidence! Amelie, you are brilliant! What you said – just brilliant!'

'I am? I did?'

'Yes! Now I know – well, not who did it. But there's a piece of evidence in that hotel room which will tell us who did it. The one where we found you in the bath. And the credit is all yours.'

'But what was it that I said?'

'Don't worry about that right now. And shush, your uncle will be back shortly. Amelie, you mustn't tell anyone about this, not even your uncle, understand?'

'I –'

'Not even Inspector Simenon.'

'Inspector Simenon!' Amelie exclaimed. 'Hah! I will not tell him anything. He lied to me. He said he would give me my special handbag. Instead he gives me an old one. It looks the same, but it is not. He thinks I am so stupid I will not realise. Did I not put the heroin into my own handbag with my own hands? Did I not see it with my own eyes? Do I not know my own handbags?'

Frank's mouth tried to say something, but his brain failed to find the words.

'Good,' he said finally. 'I mean, er, yes. Now, let me see. About the evidence. We can't go back to the hotel directly, that would look suspicious.'

'The maids will be cleaning the rooms,' Frieda said. 'We'll have to wait until a quieter time.'

'Lunch,' said Frank. 'Lunchtime we'll slip into the room, and voila!'

'Voila?' asked Amelie.

'Precisement! Voila! We will have the answer!'

'Twelve o'clock,' Frieda said, just in case Amelie might be confused about what time lunch might be. 'That's the earliest we can go back.'

'Until then we'll wander around pretending to be tourists.'

'We are tourists, darling. Oh, Amelie, here's your uncle.'

'Remember, Amelie, not a word,' Frank whispered dramatically. 'Silence!' he added in his best French accent.

'Ah, my gloves,' Amelie said, taking the elbow-long white gloves from her uncle and delicately pulling them on one by one. 'It is the English style,' she said, giving Frank and Frieda an exaggerated wink. 'French men will never understand English style, not so?'

'Well, it's good to see you so well so soon, Amelie,' Frank said. 'You get on home and put your feet up. And we'll see you tomorrow at the celebration.'

'Thank you a thousand times,' Amelie said, giving him a goodbye kiss on each cheek, before repeating the process with Frieda. They parted with many "au revoirs" on each side, including a muted one from Jacques.

'Right,' murmured Frank as they walked away, 'let's drive around the corner and then straight back to the hotel.'

'Let's just hope that Amelie doesn't, for once in her life, decide to keep her mouth shut,' said Frieda.

'I know the gods can be perverse, but surely they could never be that perverse?'

Frieda almost laughed at the agonised look on Frank's face at the thought.

'So Simenon returned the wrong handbag,' she noted. 'Interesting.'

'So what was that charade about, yesterday, at the police station?' asked Frank. 'The one with the handbag? Simenon was teasing us, he knew that all we wanted to see was Amelie's handbag. And then, at the end, we get in a little revenge by pretending that we weren't interested, and were thinking of going. Next thing he's all too eager to show us, and to have you look at it closely. Yet according to Amelie it's not the right handbag.'

'Continuity of evidence,' Frieda said. Frank nodded.

'Seems to be the answer. Simenon doesn't touch the handbag at the scene of crime. It's given to a lowly constable to tag and bag. It goes into the evidence room, is logged, no arguments about its provenance. A few days later Simenon takes it out to return to Amelie. If there's an investigation they'll say, ah, foolish man, but understandable, she is an attractive young woman in distress. No-one will ask the obvious question, especially as Simenon has two British police officers to confirm that they saw him remove the handbag and log it out, two British police officers above suspicion. The obvious question being, is the handbag that went in the same handbag that came out? Not according to Amelie, and she should know.'

'And, if it isn't, why? Why would he want to swap handbags?'

'Perhaps because one has certain chemical traces to show that it contained the packet of heroin, and the other didn't.'

'That would explain a number of things. Why the heroin hasn't been found, for example. It never entered the room. Amelie was given a handbag with nothing in it.'

Frank shook his head.

'That doesn't work. Amelie said that she put the packet in the handbag herself.'

'Simenon could have swapped it at some stage.'

'Not while he was waiting in an unmarked car for her to turn up at the wrong hotel.'

They carried on in silence for a few moments as each tried to find an explanation for Simenon's behaviour, and failed.

'Whoever walks in first, that will be our man,' said Frank, deciding to ignore the question in favour of something more tangible.

'You're sure someone will turn up?'

'Oh, yes. I'm quite sure.'

'Gut instinct?'

'That, and the fact that, if no-one turns up, we are, to quote Georges Simenon, back to the first square.'

Wellbury/France. Friday. Noon.

Three bodies in the bath

Gertie, Sam, Susan and Tricia Leigh were gathered in Tricia's office.

'The latest communication from the other side,' announced Tricia, waving her mobile phone.

'What's Frank managed to do now?' asked Gertie. 'Start a small war? Kidnap the French president by mistake? Find himself in bed in the Louvre with Mrs French President? Or even the Portuguese ambassador's wife? Or the Russian ambassador's daughter-in-law?'

'No, but he has found out about Frieda's mobile phone.'

'Oh, dear,' said Susan. 'Not happy, is he?'

'Actually he seems more than happy.'

'He didn't throw a wobbly? Or throw the phone into the Channel?'

'Doesn't appear to have done. Frieda sent a message from him. He wants the surprise drinks party to go ahead.'

'He does?'

'Yes. Except he thinks it should be a surprise for the cream cake man and Pete Phillips.'

There was a short silence as the others considered this interesting reversal of the situation.

'That will be our Frank,' nodded Susan.

'Natural justice,' said Sam. 'I like it. Does he want us to do anything?'

'First of all we're to stress to Eric and Pete that there are certain words they must not use in their speeches.'

Each one nodded as the implications of this sank in.

'It's lunchtime,' noted Gertie. 'They're probably in the canteen now.'

'Shall we pop down for a cup of tea and a chat?' suggested Tricia with twinkling eyes.

In an alleyway not far away from the honeymoon hotel two figures were saying au revoir.

'Not long to go,' said the one in a whisper. 'Only a few hours. Tomorrow it shall be done forever. We shall be together forever more. For eterrrnittty,'

Then he sneezed.

'Monsieur Arneaux's polishing the glasses again,' Frank said as they watched the entrance to the hotel. 'He'll wear them out if he's not careful.'

'He'll see us going in,' said Frieda. 'We need a way of making him think that we've gone in and gone out again. We don't want him mentioning to anyone that we're upstairs.'

'Tell you what, why don't you go in, tell him you've just popped in to collect something and you'll be out again in a few minutes. Then I'll pop in five minutes later and tell him that you forgot something else, and I've just dropped in to collect it. That way he won't be sure if either of us is in or out. He'll probably presume we aren't. That he missed us leaving.'

'Sounds a bit weak, Frank. Wouldn't you be suspicious if a couple suddenly began to forget things every five minutes when for five days they hadn't forgotten a single thing?'

'I knew your efficiency would be a problem sooner or later.

It's not natural, you know, efficiency.'

'Frank! This is no time to be flippant.'

'Course it is. Go on, Free, just go in and make up a story. We've got to get in before Mr X turns up. Or Madame X, as the case may be.'

Frieda gave him a glare and walked over to the hotel as nonchalantly as she could. Much as she would have liked to believe that she was being casual, she had to admit to herself that the quick glances up and down the street before she entered the hotel were not those of a tourist, but the looks of a trained observer. And if she hadn't been honest with herself, the surprised look on Monsieur Arneaux's face as he watched her scan the small bar told her that she hadn't been successful with him.

'Ah, monsieur,' she said, smiling, 'I've just, er – I've just popped in to prepare a surprise for my husband.'

'Oui, madame?'

'So if you see him, and he asks, don't let him know I'm here. Or anyone else. Nobody must know that I'm here.'

'Oui, madame.'

'I'll be in and out in five minutes.'

Monsieur Arneaux watched her with both appreciation and relief as she walked up the stairs. Appreciation for the figure of a good-looking woman, and relief that her husband wasn't there to totally confuse him with whatever he thought the French language to be.

'Mind if we join you?' Tricia asked Eric Johns and Pete Phillips in the canteen. The two men looked up from their food and notes on their speeches to find themselves surrounded. Tricia, Gertie, Sam and Susan had sat down around them.

'Doctor Pleadle is concerned about your speeches,' Tricia continued. 'She thinks it important that you should avoid using certain words which might have an unfortunate psychological impact.'

Susan nodded, her face blankly serious. She didn't look at all like a person who regularly described most psychology as "navel gazing mumbo jumbo".

'And Sam here, of course, is an expert in the effect of words.'

Eric Johns and Pete Phillips were impressed. If the doctor and the witch agreed on something it was obviously serious. And Sam must know a lot about the power of words, after all she must use them in her spells, surely?

'Bon jour, Marie,' Frieda said as she passed the stocky girl vacuuming in the passage, 'if anyone asks I don't exist.'

'Bon jour, madame,' Marie sang back. She carried on vacuuming. The English lady, she thought, had said something about not existing. That was the problem with these foreigners and town folk. They thought too much. They thought until their thoughts made no sense at all.

Though perhaps, just perhaps, this vacuum cleaner machine was not too silly an idea after all.

'Of course,' said Sam, 'on the other hand there are certain words that you must use. For spiritual balance. Oh, and there's the way you walk. That is extremely important. It's important that you take three paces backwards before giving your speeches. For physical and mental harmony.'

Frank checked his watch. Once five minutes had elapsed he sauntered over to the hotel entrance. Unlike Frieda he was able to give a very good performance of an innocent stroller. He even managed to conceal his surprise at finding, not Monsieur Arneaux polishing glasses, but Madame Arneaux making notes in an accounts book. It gave him a sudden idea for an excuse for being there on his own.

'Ah, madame, ca va?' he asked.

'Very good, monsieur, and yourself?'

'Trèz bien, très bien. Ecouter, je suis on my way pour make la surprise pour ma femme, vouz comprehends?'

Madame Arneaux nodded to indicate that she had deciphered his meaning.

'So if ma femme turns up, could you tell her I'm not here? Tell her I'm waiting in the cafe dans le rue Eiffel? Or some other rue? Actually, if anyone turns up, could you tell them I'm not here?'

'Mais oui, monsieur.'

'"Bath", for example,' said Susan. 'You must definitely not use the word "bath". For obvious reasons.'

Eric Johns and Pete Phillips nodded and each wrote down the word "bath". It was obvious when you thought about it, but it took a scientific expert like Doctor Pleadle to point out the obvious. They probably would never have used the word "bath", but you never knew, it could have crept in somehow.

Imagine what effect that would have on the scarred mind? Eric Johns had a cousin who had honeymooned in Bath. That could have slipped in so very easily.

'The English couple, they are very romantic,' sighed Madame Arneaux in the kitchen. 'The husband has gone up to their room to prepare a surprise for his wife. Henri, you have given me many surprises over the years, but never a one you planned.'

Henri rubbed his cheek and considered this.

'I think there is a surprise he has not planned either,' he said. 'His wife went up not ten minutes ago to plan a surprise for him.'

'Henri! Why did you not say so? We must do something!'

'Do something?'

'Yes! They must not meet! It will ruin their surprises!'

'Do something such as what, my love?'

'Something! Anything!'

Being in the kitchen, they did not notice the shadow fall across the reception counter which moved silently and quickly to the staircase.

'Bon jour, Marie,' Frank said as he passed the girl in the corridor.

'Bon jour, monsieur.'

'Je suis pas ici, Marie, comprehends? Je suis un figment de votre imagination.'

'Oui, monsieur.'

Marie watched him hurry along. His wife did not exist, and he was not here. These English drank too much tea.

Acting on the thought, she looked around the passage, concluded that it was clean, and decided a break for coffee would be a good idea.

'"Body" is another one. And "wedding" and "marriage", of course.'

'That's going to be a bit difficult, isn't it?' suggested Pete Phillips. 'After all, we're supposed to be welcoming them back from their honeymoon.'

'Use a bit of imagination, Pete,' said Eric Johns. 'When you're trained in speech giving like I am it comes almost naturally. I presume "honeymoon" is another one, Doctor?'

Susan nodded. Seriously. Professionally. With her hands locked beneath the table, gripping them tightly to remind her not to laugh.

'Frank,' Frieda said as they stood inside the bathroom, the door closed, 'what if our Mr X is armed?'

'Good point, Free.' He thought for a few moments. 'I tell you what, they're bound to come in here. As soon as they do, we jump them. I'll hold them while you frisk them.'

'What if there's more than one?'

'Then we adopt the standard police approach.'

'Which is?'

'We blag it.'

'Ah, thank you darling, I always had wondered what the standard police approach was meant to be.'

'Sssh!' said Frank, holding up a hand. They listened. There was the soft sound of someone opening the outer room door very quietly.

The door closed and there was silence. Then the almost unnoticeable sound of squeaking leather as footsteps moved slowly across the carpet. Whoever it was stopped. They were looking around. Almost a minute passed before the feet moved again, this time towards the bathroom door. They stopped. And then moved back, probably toward the bed. A drawer was opened. And then slowly closed. And then silence.

Frank looked at Frieda with eyebrows raised. He held up a finger to indicate one. Then three, to indicate three. Then he made the gesture of opening a drawer, followed by a question mark.

There were three drawers. Why had the person only opened one?

Frieda shrugged and went back to listening. The footsteps were again approaching the bathroom door. The door opened slowly. Frank held up his fingers in sequence as if counting, one, two, three ... A man stepped into the bathroom and approached the cabinet.

'And "friends". That's a definite no-no.'

'What about "bullet"?' asked Gertie, struggling not to giggle.

'Yes, to be avoided at all costs. Anything to do with guns.'

'Breech,' said Sam.

'Barrel,' Susan put in. 'Stock. Anything that might trigger a reaction.'

'What about "cocking"?' asked Gertie.

'Oh, no, definitely no cocking. No, not even cocking a snook. Definitely not that.'

Eric Johns and Pete Phillips added "anything to do with guns" to their lists. At the rate they were going it would be easier to just decide which words they could use.

Madame Arneaux's eagerness to find a way to stop the honeymoon couple from meeting was interrupted by Marie's loud entrance into the kitchen.

'Ah, Marie. Inspector Simenon said that we can use that room again. It needs to be cleaned before lunchtime.'

'Oui, madame,' replied Marie, as Monsieur Arneaux tried to slip unnoticed back into the reception.

'Henri? Where are you going to? We must do something.'

'But what, cherie? What can we do?'

'You have no romance in you, Henri, '

The unromantic Henri failed to notice the shadow that flitted from the entrance to the staircase. It moved quickly upstairs.

'"Circumlocution",' said Susan.

'"Circumlocution", Doctor?'

'Oh, I just don't like the word.'

Eric Johns muttered a few words of thanks. He didn't know what the word meant. It sounded as if it involved mathematics, never one of his favourite subjects. Nothing ever added up properly in mathematics.

Frank stepped up behind the man in the bathroom, slipped his arms in-between the other man's, and brought his hands up behind the man's neck, trapping him, one foot between the other man's legs.

'Quick, Free, check for a firearm. Frieda frisked the man quickly and efficiently.

'He's clean, Frank,' she said, stepping back. Frank released the man and pushed him away against the opposite wall.

'Simenon!'

Georges Simenon looked back, more lugubrious than ever.

'Bonjour, Inspectors,' he said. 'Would you care to tell me what you are doing here?'

Frieda and Frank looked at each other.

'More to the point, Inspector Simenon,' Frank said, 'is the question of what you are doing here.'

Simenon shrugged.

'I heard that there was some marvellous new evidence here that would identify the crumpet,' he said.

'Really? And just who told you that?'

'Amelie told me.'

'Amelie told you? She told us she wasn't speaking to you.'

Simenon chuckled.

'She is not. She is unhappy with me for some reason. But she tells me that the great English detectives have found new evidence. What she is saying is that I am a stupid detective. So I look for the great English detectives so that I can sit at their feet and learn. But I cannot find them. So I come to the only place where this new evidence can be – here. So, what is this new evidence?'

'The new evidence,' said Frieda, 'is whoever comes to look for the new evidence and destroy it.'

'And that person, Inspector Simenon,' said Frank, 'appears to be you.'

Simenon looked from one to the other. And then he suddenly laughed in a low rumble.

'Ah, I understand,' he said. 'It is a trap.' He nodded as he digested the idea. 'Not a bad idea. In fact, an excellent idea, as there is nothing else we have. But, you see, you have caught the wrong bird in your trap.'

'Have we, Inspector Simenon?'

'Oh, yes, Inspector. Is it not my duty, having heard this strange story of new evidence, to come to find it?'

Frank and Frieda exchanged glances. Simenon was perfectly right. Frank smiled.

'Quite so, Inspector,' he said. 'It's the perfect alibi, really. Nothing we say would ever get to court, never mind stand up in court. But, just to satisfy our curiosity, why don't you tell us just how you did it?'

'How I did it?' echoed Simenon, shaking his head. 'You think –'

He stopped. They all froze. They had just heard the very soft sound of the outer room door being opened, very quietly.

'Perhaps your trap has not failed after all,' whispered Simenon as the three of them struggled to find space to hide next to the bathroom door.

'Is that it?' asked Pete Phillips, having used up all sides of every piece of paper he could find, including three paper napkins.

'Those are the obvious ones. I'll run through my reference books tonight to see if there are any I've missed.'

'It is too late, Henri,' said Madame Arneaux. 'By now they have discovered each other. So, no surprises. Henri, you should have done something.'

Henri scratched his head and looked at his wife in the kitchen. He didn't notice a third shadow fall across the reception counter, nor hear the tread of footsteps ascend the staircase. In fact, since the English couple had arrived, his hearing had deteriorated quite badly.

The door closed and there was silence. Then the almost unnoticeable sound of footsteps moving across the carpet, slowly. Whoever it was stopped. They were looking around. Almost a minute passed before the feet moved again, this time towards the bathroom door. They stopped. And then moved back, probably to the bed. A drawer was opened. And then slowly closed.

Simenon stared ahead of himself, concentrating. He held up a finger to indicate one. Then three, to indicate three. Then he made the gesture of opening a drawer, followed by a question mark.

There were three drawers. Why had the person only opened one?

Frank looked at Frieda and made a face as if to say, what's he on about, we heard that ages ago. She pushed a silent elbow into his side.

The footsteps were again approaching the bathroom door. The door opened slowly. Simenon held up his fingers as if counting, one, two, three ... A man stepped into the bathroom and approached the cabinet.

'Ah! We have you, my friend!' cried Simenon, grabbing the man in a bear hug. 'Inspector, check his pockets, please, he might have a gun on him.'

Frank frisked him quickly.

'Nope, no firearm,' he said.

'Bien! Now, monsieur, let us see what kind of bird we have caught in our little trap.'

'Well, I reckon we can live with that,' Pete Phillips said, putting his pen down.

'Now the words you must use for balance,' said Sam.

The two men reluctantly picked their pens up again, and sat as if two schoolboys ready to take down dictation.

'We've got to find a word that rhymes with hex,' Sam said. 'It cancels it out. So what's the opposite of hex?'

Eric Johns and Pete Phillips deliberately avoided each other's gaze. They could think of only one word which rhymed with hex, and they weren't about to say it.

Jacques Pointer looked back at the other three in the bathroom, indignant.

'I will sue you, Simenon!' he declared. 'Attacking an innocent man from behind like that, as if he were a common thief.'

'You would have preferred to be attacked a different way?' asked Frank. 'As an uncommon thief?'

Jacques tidied his shirt, nodding. Then he shook his head as he realised what Frank had said.

'Not attacked, of course. But a businessman of my station – if the flics wish to speak to me, they ask me correctly.'

'Enough!' cried Simenon. 'What are you doing here, Jacques?'

'It is simple. Amelie told me the English had discovered new evidence which would prove that she is innocent. Naturally I rushed here to find the evidence myself. I trust the English police, of course, but you would give the evidence to Simenon, and who knows what he would do with it.'

Simenon issued an oath which suggested that Jacques had better not repeat such an accusation.

'So where is this new evidence, Inspector?' Jacques asked Frank, ignoring Simenon.

'The new evidence,' said Frieda, 'is whoever comes to look for the new evidence and destroy it.'

'And that person, Monsieur Pointer,' said Frank, 'appears to be you.'

'Me? Absurd! I came here because I wished to protect the honest name of my niece, a girl who this fool still suspects.'

'You must think all of us stupid,' Simenon said. 'The only man who would come looking for this new evidence is a guilty one. Apart from myself, of course. No, Jacques, this one you will not get out from, no matter what fancy lawyer you buy. No jury will believe that you came here innocently. You come here on your own, without telling anyone, in secret? This is not believable! No, not believable at all!'

Jacques shrugged. He was about to reply when he stopped. They all froze. They had just heard the very soft sound of the outer room door being opened, very quietly.

'Perhaps your silly idea has not failed after all,' whispered Jacques as the four of them struggled to find space to hide next to the bathroom door.

'It was not my silly idea,' Simenon whispered back. 'It was Inspector Summers's silly idea.'

'In that case it sounds like a very good idea.'

'Shut up you two,' whispered Frieda. They shut up.

'"Pink",' said Sam. 'It's important that you get "pink" in. It's a very calming word. Very powerful, too.'

'"Pink"?' asked Eric Johns. 'How on earth are we supposed to get "pink" in?'

'It's easy when you're a trained speech writer,' commented Pete Phillips out of the side of his mouth.

The door closed and there was silence. Then the almost unnoticeable sound of footsteps moving across the carpet, slowly. Whoever it was stopped. They were looking around. Almost a minute passed before the footsteps moved again, this time towards the bathroom door. They stopped. And then moved back, probably to the bed. A drawer was opened. And then slowly closed.

Jacques stared ahead of himself, concentrating. He held up a finger to indicate one. Then three, to indicate three. Then he made the gesture of opening a drawer, followed by a question mark.

There were three drawers. Why had the person only opened one?

Simenon looked at Frank and Frieda and made a gesture with his finger to his head, indicating that the man was a fool. Frank nodded back, slowly, earnestly. Frieda shoved her elbow into him.

The footsteps were again approaching the bathroom door. The door opened slowly. Jacques held up his fingers as if counting, one, two, three ... Someone stepped into the bathroom and approached the cabinet.

'"Green" is also a powerful word,' Sam said.

'Green and pink?' asked Eric Johns.

'Oh, no, not both in the same speech, that would be very dangerous, mixing pink and green. Sergeant Johns, I think pink would be suitable for your aura, and Sergeant Phillips, you take green.'

Pete Phillips hid a smile. Getting "green" in would be easy. How Eric Johns was going to fit "pink" in, well, he was just glad he didn't have to do it.

Sam tried to keep a straight face as she watched them take notes. She was desperately searching for another ridiculous word for them to use. The only one that came to her mind was "pixies".

'Ah! We have you, my friend!' cried both Simenon and Jacques, each trying to grab hold of the man, falling over onto the floor with him.

'I will hold him!' Simenon shouted. 'You search for a gun.'

'Search him? No, I will hold him, you search him!'

'You do not know how to hold a suspect correctly.'

'Ah you saying I know how to search a man correctly? Do you think I am a flic like you?'

Frank shook his head at Frieda, sat down on the edge of the bath, took her hand and leaned against her, watching the scene with amused resignation.

'Get off me, you murderers!' cried the suspect. 'Pigs! Help! Police! Police!'

'Xavier?' asked Simenon.

'Xavier?' asked Jacques.

The small man threw them off with surprising ease and stood up, dusting himself off. The other two also stood up.

'Let me guess,' said Frank, 'Amelie told you the nice English poppies knew of some new evidence in here which would clear her name.'

'So you immediately came around to get the evidence before Inspector Simenon could,' said Frieda.

'Because you didn't trust him.'

'No,' said Xavier, sniffing contempt at both Jacques and Simenon, 'it was Jacques I did not trust. I knew he would rush around here to destroy the evidence as soon as he could. My plan was to make it safe and hand it over to the chef of Simenon.'

'Liar!' cried Jacques. Xavier shrugged and dusted some imaginary specks from his shoulder at the other man.

'So where is this new evidence?' he asked.

'The new evidence,' said Simenon, 'is whoever comes to look for the new evidence and destroy it. And that person, Xavier appears to be you.' He paused. 'Or it is you, Jacques?'

Both of them shrugged.

'If you wish to speak to me like that, I will have my lawyer with me,' Xavier said. 'And now, I leave.'

He took two steps towards the door. He was about to bow politely to Frank and Frieda when he stopped. They all froze. They had just heard the sound of the outer room door being opened, very loudly.

'"Trousers",' said Sam.

'We've got to use the word "trousers"?'

'No, that's one you have to avoid. Not so, Doctor Pleadle?'

Susan nodded.

'Well, thank god for that,' muttered Eric Johns.

'But "pants" would be a good one to get in, wouldn't it?' asked Gertie.

'Oh, yes, definitely. Pants. Very much so.'

Eric Johns and Pete Phillips solemnly wrote down "pants".

'Perhaps your silly idea has not failed after all,' whispered Xavier to Simenon as the five of them struggled to hide next to the bathroom door.

'It was not his silly idea,' Jacques whispered back. 'It was Inspector Summers's idea.'

'In that case it sounds like a very good idea.'

'Marmite,' said Sam.

'Marmite?' asked Pete Phillips.

'You peckish, love?' asked Eric Johns.

'No, no, you must avoid the word Marmite at all costs. It

might not be a problem, but it can divide people. People have strong feelings about Marmite.'

'I know what you mean, love,' replied Eric Johns. 'Personally I have no feelings either way, but some people do get a bit carried away.'

'Yes,' said Sam. 'I knew this woman who hated it. Her husband loved it. Whenever he got it out it led to incantations.'

'Incantations?'

'Oh, yes. Some of the worst incantations I've ever heard.'

'I've read of medical cases like that,' said Susan. 'Whenever the man got it out the woman went into incantations.'

Frieda did not need to tell them to keep quiet. Very soon it became apparent who the latest intruder was, and she wasn't an intruder at all. The sound of tuneless humming and loud noises announced that Marie had come to clean the room. A muffled thump suggested that she had dropped the vacuum cleaner on the carpet.

'Ah,' said Simenon softly. 'Well, I do not think there will be any more mysterious visitors today. In fact, I think we have all we need. I will take you two to the station and you can send for your lawyers and you can sit in a cell as long as you want, but you will tell me the truth sooner or later.'

'Inspector,' Xavier said, turning his nose up and stepping towards the mirror in front of the cabinet, 'you know that I have never committed a crime, unlike another present here.'

He ignored Jacques's muttered oath and took out what appeared to be a long wallet, but turned out to be a small toiletries bag, containing a comb, scissors and other instruments.

'And you know what my lawyer will say if you arrest me without reason or evidence,' he continued, carefully combing his moustache into place. Once satisfied he turned around and nodded.

'I will, therefore, leave,' he said, walking towards the door.

He paused as the tuneless humming approached the door. The door opened suddenly, a heavy arm and a heavier denim bag appeared; the bag swung around in an arc; the arm dropped the handles onto a hook behind the door, at the same time as the bag caught Xavier on the side of his head. The door closed and the humming continued. The other four watched as Xavier's eyeballs rolled slowly upwards. His hands stretched and he dropped the little black bag. And then he toppled, almost in slow motion, his knees crumpling as he slowly slid into the bath. The shower curtain made way for him, and then closed back over him as his head hit the far edge of the bath with a clunk. His body rolled back and forth softly a couple of times, and then there was silence, apart from Marie singing to herself above the sound of the vacuum cleaner.

'Well,' said Frank, 'that just goes to prove what I've always said – understanding the scene of crime is crucial. Now we know what happened.'

The others looked at the unconscious body in the bath and considered this idea for a few moments.

'There is just one little point, Monsieur Inspector,' Simenon said. 'At least one little point.'

'The heroin,' Frieda noted.

'Ah,' said Frank, 'yes, the heroin. Good point. We never did find the heroin, did we?'

Frank and Frieda looked at Simenon. Simenon looked at Jacques. Jacques looked at Xavier in the bath.

'So, Xavier,' Jacques said, nodding at the comatose body, 'perhaps it was not you who attacked Amelie. But it was you who stole the heroin. You who would make of Amelie the criminal.'

'But surely Marie would have seen her when she came in to get her bag?' asked Frieda.

'Not if she slipped a hand around the door to get her bag without looking,' said Frank. 'Just like she did when she put it there.'

'Wouldn't she check the bathroom to see if it were clean? She would at least pop her head in, surely?'

'Yes,' said Simenon, 'she would, er, as you say, pop her head in.' He looked around the small bathroom. 'Amelie is behind the shower curtain there, hidden. Marie looks around the door as she gets her bag, she gives the quick glance, and she sees ... that.'

He pointed at Xavier's black toiletry wallet on the floor.

'I am afraid, Inspector,' he continued, speaking to Frank, 'while it is a very good theory, it cannot work. Perhaps Marie only glances in, she does not see Amelie, Amelie is behind the curtain, but she would see that. She would see Amelie's handbag on the floor. And she would ask herself, what is this? And then she would find Amelie.'

'We could test that theory,' said Frank.

'Test the theory, inspector?' asked Simenon.

'Well, if we all get into the bath ...'

'We all get into the bath ...'

'And pull the shower curtain across so that Marie can't see us...'

They looked at the bath.

'We'll have to squeeze Monsieur Dubons up a bit,' noted Frank.

'We will stand behind the door,' Simenon decided quietly. 'And wait.'

'We can't all stand behind the door,' said Frieda. 'Marie will realise that we're there. That's what we don't want.'

'Inspector,' said Frank, 'you and Jacques stand in the bath, here, at either end. Frieda and I will hide behind the door.'

Simenon looked at him as if he were mad to think that a man such as himself, a police inspector, would do something as undignified as hiding by standing in a bath behind a shower curtain.

'Quick!' said Frieda, 'she's stopped vacuuming. She could be here any minute.'

Simenon pulled the shower curtain away and stepped reluctantly into the end of the bath. Jacques followed, stepping in at the front next to the taps, giving Xavier's head a kick to move it out of the way. Frank pulled the shower curtain back into place.

Marie's humming approached the door. She stopped, muttered something to herself, possibly because the music had reached the end and needed restarting. Then she opened the door and looked in.

'Eh?' she asked, immediately spotting Xavier's bag. She

stepped into the bathroom and picked it up. Then she slowly unbent herself as if she knew that she was being watched. She took another step forward towards the basin, reached the top end of the bath and pulled the shower curtain back.

'Morte!' she exclaimed as she spotted the unconscious Xavier lying in the bath. And then she spotted Jacques.

'Assassin!' she shouted. She reached over, grabbed him by the neck with both hands and banged his head repeatedly against the wall.

'Er, bon jour Marie, ca va?' asked Frank, giving her his most charming smile from behind the door.

'Monsieur! Bon jour,' replied Marie as she noticed Frank and Frieda, letting Jacques go. He slid down the wall, holding his neck and gasping, until he lay next to Xavier's legs.

'Vous etre bien?' continued Frank.

'Er, oui, monsieur, et vous? Bon jour, madame,' she added.

'Bon jour, Marie. You've met Inspector Simenon, haven't you?'

Simenon muttered something and stepped out of the bath. He immediately began throwing questions at Marie. She replied indignantly, hands waving all over the place. Finally Simenon nodded.

'Bon,' he said. 'Marie, you can go. Allez!'

This was met with further protestations and hand waving, mainly at Jacques and Xavier in the bath. Jacques had finally managed to stop gasping, and Xavier was sitting up, rubbing his head and asking querulous questions of nobody in particular. Simenon laughed.

'Come,' he said, 'let us go. Marie needs to clean the bathroom, and she refuses to do it with so many bodies lying around. Let us go down to the bar.'

They left a muttering Marie and went down to the bar, Jacques unwillingly supporting Xavier down the stairs. Once at the bar Jacques announced that he was taking Xavier to the doctor, and if Simenon objected he could … The final bit was in a French that only Simenon understood. He shrugged and let them go.

'Come, let us sit down,' he said. 'All this standing and hiding and attacking people. It is thirsty work.' He threw his coat down on an empty chair and gestured to a wide-eyed Madame Arneaux. 'Three brandies please, madame.'

'I'll have some tea,' said Frieda. 'Brandy doesn't agree with me.'

'Inspector?' Simenon asked Frank. Frank debated: tea or brandy? Tea sounded good, but sitting in a French hotel bar with a gruff French Inspector who always wore a rumpled old raincoat?

Frank was a great believer in savouring whatever little could be savoured from a disastrous case.

'Brandy, definitely,' he said.

'Ring,' said Sam, 'you have to use the word "ring". It's one of the most powerful words you can find.'

'Ring?' asked Eric Johns. 'But I thought we weren't to mention anything to do with marriage.'

'No. You'll have to use it in a different context.'

'Ring around a bath,' suggested Pete Phillips, whose wife had made just that complaint the previous evening.

They all looked at him.

'Ah! Sorry, of course not. No, no bath. No, er, what about, what about, um – ring around town? You know, as if you're calling around ...'

'Ring a ring o'rosies,' suggested Gertie.

'So, Inspector,' said Frank as Frieda sipped tea while he and Simenon sipped their brandies, 'what did Marie have to say?'

'I think you were right, Inspector,' Simenon replied. 'I think that that is how it happened. Amelie was in the bathroom doing her makeup. She hears Marie enter, she steps towards the door, Marie slings her bag onto the door hook without looking, the bag is heavy, the bag hits Marie on the neck, unfortunately just in the worst place. Marie falls into the bath, unconscious.'

'And Marie collects her bag afterwards without looking into the bathroom?'

'Oh, no, she did look into the bathroom.'

'But didn't see Amelie's handbag lying on the floor?'

'No. For two reasons. One, Amelie's handbag is white, the same colour as the tiles. And two, Marie cleaned the bathroom that morning. So for her it is clean. All she sees is a clean bathroom, no matter if it is full with a hundred white handbags. No guests have come or gone, no-one has been in the room, therefore for Marie it is clean. In fact she thinks Madame Arneaux is a little bit silly, asking her to make sure the room is ready. Yes, the clean sheets she puts on the bed, but the rest of the rooms are clean. Marie has already made sure of that, and when Marie has done something it stays done.'

'She spotted Xavier's little bag because it was black.'

'Precisely. And because she hadn't cleaned the bathroom. The flics had been there, and since then it had not been cleaned.'

'You seem to have changed your mind, Inspector,' Frieda noted. Simenon shrugged.

'Madame Inspector, as a police officer you know the need to think many different possibilities at the same time. Then, you choose the most likely one.'

'There is another possibility,' said Frank. Simenon sighed.

'Monsieur Inspector, other possibilities we do not need. Please, please, no other possibilities.'

'I was thinking about Marie's handbag. What if she held on to it as she fell into the bath?'

'That makes sense,' said Frieda. 'She's still clutching it, it goes into the bath with her, so it's not there for Marie to see. Until out Mr X comes along, takes out the heroin and drops the bag on the floor.'

Simenon sighed. Then he nodded.

'Yes, you are right. I do not say that my theory is wrong, but yours sounds equally possible.'

'Okay,' said Frank, 'let's say that that's what happened. Marie leaves the room. Amelie is in the bath, fast asleep. Someone enters, goes into the bathroom, takes the heroin out of her handbag, drops the handbag on the floor, leaves the room and disappears into the night.'

'Unless it was Marie who stole the heroin,' suggested Frieda. Simenon shook his head.

'No, Marie is too honest. I do not say it is impossible, but it is very doubtful.'

'So, who then?' asked Frank.

They sat and sipped their drinks in silence.

'Well, I think that covers almost everything,' said Tricia Leigh. 'And if you can let me have your final speeches by the end of the afternoon I'll type them up for you. Make them look a little more professional.'

'Thanks, Trish, you're a real love,' said Eric Johns.

'I'll take special care of them,' Tricia promised.

'It was a good idea, your plan,' Simenon said eventually. 'We could not have taken it to court, but at least, had it worked, we would have known who the guilty parting was.'

'You don't think you'll ever find out?'

'Oh, in a few years, maybe five, maybe ten, someone will say something, perhaps even write their memoirs, and we will discover the truth. We always find out. By then it will not matter, no doubt, but we will find out. It will become, as we say un secret de Polichinelle. A secret which is known to all. But, as the great Renard said, la vérité vaut bien qu'on passe quelques années sans la trouver – the truth which takes years to discover is all the more valuable.'

'You'll have to send us a postcard,' Frank said wistfully.

'Yes, Inspector, I commiserate. I know the feeling. But sometimes you just have to accept that you will not find out the truth. Not for a long time.'

'True. Ah, well, it's been interesting.'

Frieda looked from Frank to Simenon, recognising two men who were desperately trying to pretend to each other that they had, indeed, given up on any hope of discovering what had happened.

'It has indeed been interesting,' she said, finishing her tea. 'But now my husband and I are going to find somewhere for a late lunch, and then we are going shopping.'

'Shopping?' asked Simenon.

'Little presents for friends and family. My mother, Frank's parents, my secretary. And something for us, a little keepsake.'

'Ah, but of course,' Simenon said, standing up. 'Well, I wish you the peaceful time for the rest of your loonymoon. I am sure there will be no more exciting situations. Au revoir.'

He picked up his coat. Frank spotted something, leaned down and picked it up.

'You seem to have dropped something, Inspector Simenon,' he said. He held up a book. 'I don't quite understand the title, but it appears to be something about quotations. Translated into English.'

Simenon almost blushed as he grabbed the book and rammed it into his jacket pocket.

'For my niece,' he said. 'I must fetch Gaspode. Au revoir.'

'Bon chance to your niece,' Frank called as Simenon left as quickly as he could while holding on to the tatters of an image. 'I'm sure she looks just like you.'

Frieda watched him lean back with the air of a man who has just seen his football team scrape a draw against all the odds. He smiled ruefully.

'Simenon's holding the card we need,' he said. 'If only we had some more time we might find out why he swapped the handbags. It doesn't mean that he's guilty. It could just be a plan of his own to trap someone.'

'Quite possibly, Frank. And if we ignore him and go shopping he's quite likely to follow us and insist on telling us, even if only in a round-about way.'

'Good point, Free. And while we're doing some shopping, there's something I think we should get for Eric and Pete.'

'And what's that?'

'Boules.'

Normandy. Friday. Afternoon.

Two go shopping

'Interesting girl, that, Marie,' Frank noted as he pushed a trolley around the large supermarket on the outskirts of Caen later that day, finishing off their shopping duties after a trip to the market. Madame Arneaux, on hearing that they were going shopping, had been most insistent that they should race to Caen to get to the Saint Julien Friday morning market before the stallholders closed up.

'Yes, for the boules set the supermarket is good enough,' she had said, 'and no doubt you have friends who think that it is enough to have the word "France" on a packet of biscuits to make it exotic, but if you want the real camembert, the real andouille, you must go to the market. These supermarkets, if you can believe it, they use pasteurised milk in their cheese!'

Which, Frieda had thought, had been very diplomatic. She could think of very few people back in Wellbury who would not regard camembert as an exotic step too far, whether the milk had been pasteurised or had come from cows native to Devon since before the Norman conquest, and had been made in Bognor Regis, if EU rules permitted.

So, having spent an hour and a half trawling the market and purchasing such exotic foodstuffs for themselves and select others, they were now trawling the supermarket for a set of boules and other mementoes with "made in France" stamped on them for the less adventurous of their acquaintances. Frieda now gave Frank a sideways glance to make sure that he was not thinking of attempting his usual trick of amusing himself by trying to ride the supermarket trolley with his toes perched on the back wheels.

'In what way?' she asked.

'Well, you could say that she isn't very feminine, but that would be totally wrong. She's the type who will get married, have a dozen or fifteen kids, love them all to bits but know when to give a kiss and when to belt the living daylights out of them. As she grows older she'll become a grandmother and matriarch of a clan who will both venerate and fear her. She'll always know right from wrong, she'll never have any doubts, she'll never even understand the concept of grey areas. And she'll never change in a hundred years. She'll be as wrong as hell on occasions, but that won't stop them loving her.'

'And you find that interesting?'

'I almost envy her. Imagine going through life without once having to stop and wonder whether what you're doing is right or wrong?'

Frieda considered this.

'Can you imagine,' Frank said before she could reply, 'that you were given the option of an operation that would remove doubt from your brain forever? An irreversible operation. It would relieve you of all doubt, hesitation, self-reflection, everything. But once you had had it, you could never go back. So: do you choose the operation, or stick with doubt and uncertainty?'

'Frank, my darling?'

'Yes, my sweet?'

'Do you think that sort of question is really appropriate? Considering that we're on honeymoon?'

Personally Frank thought it perfectly appropriate, at any time, though perhaps accompanied by one or two pints of the beer on offer in the supermarket. But Frieda obviously did not.

'Okay, so what topic would be appropriate?'

'How about children?' she asked as they passed a display of prams.

'No, Free, definitely not. The ankle biters will turn up soon enough, and they'll take over our lives, no doubt. No, our honeymoon is just for us, you and me.' He smiled. 'You know, it's a pity we didn't get a picture of Amelie in the bath. I wonder if Simenon did and is willing to give us a copy.'

'What?'

'Of course it would have been better if she had been in the nude – with the naughty bits decorously hidden, of course.'

'What?'

'But we must get a shot of Simenon and Gaspode. And one of that crashed plane. And the street where that idiot tried to mug us.'

'Frank?'

'Yes, my darling?'

'What are you wittering on about?'

'Well, think about it, Free. Other couples get home, create a honeymoon album to show everyone. And all it is is boring pictures of the hotel they stayed at. "This is Jimmy lying next to the swimming pool." "This is Jimmy standing next to one of the orange taxis." "This is Jimmy in bed after he got food poisoning." "This is a shot of Jimmy's nettle rash." All that sort of thing. Now our album – well, we could start with pictures from the wedding, you looking radiant as you did in that beautiful dress, the earrings, all the rest, a few shots of all of us, then we go on to the bath where the body was found and so on. Much more interesting. People will actually want to see our album.'

All Frieda could see was the look on her mother's face should she ever show her such an album.

Thinking about it, that rather appealed.

She wasn't quite sure that it would appeal to Frances Summers, though. And in about twenty-four hours they would be back in Wellbury, being greeted on their return by her new parents-in-law. At least she would be able to claim that she'd brought their son back in one piece, despite his best efforts.

So long as the next twenty-four hours brought no surprises.

'Frank,' she said, just in case, 'stop doing that.'

Wellbury. Friday. Evening.

Romance in the ring cycle

'Nice place,' Tom said, looking around as he and Susan were shown to a table in Ginos. It was the most well-known restaurant in Wellbury, not only for the food, but because the proprietor had once started a long running argument in the letters column of the Wellbury Herald by posting an anonymous note decrying the lack of an apostrophe in the name.

'Best place in Wellbury for a really good meal,' Susan replied. 'They manage to get the match exactly right. Good food, good atmosphere, just the right kind of service. It's not actually a family business, but Gino makes it feel that way.'

'Quite, er, romantic, really, in a way,' Tom almost coughed. He had thought that he was going to be one of a foursome. At the last minute plans had changed somehow and now he was alone with Susan. Not that he minded, but he had a feeling that it had been carefully organised and he was powerless to do other than go along with everything that someone else was deciding.

'What do you fancy for starters?' asked Susan, hiding her red cheeks with a menu.

Great, thought Tom. Well done, old boy. Ten seconds into play and you've already fouled up.

He picked up the menu and tried to read it. It appeared to contain any number of Italian dishes he had never heard of, all of which sounded mouth-watering, but having obviously put one foot into it he had no urge to follow it with the second. He might find that he'd accidentally ordered dish water. Or, perhaps worse, a cheeseburger and chips.

At that moment a cheeseburger and chips sounded ideal. However he certainly wasn't about to mention that to Susan.

'Tom and Wilf are in Wellbury for the weekend,' Frieda said as they sat in their own restaurant in Normandy. 'Do you remember them?'

'Absolutely! I had a feeling that Tom really fancied Susan, and Wilf was trying to hide the fact that he had fallen in love with Gertie.'

'Oh, so your eyes weren't entirely on your new wife, then.'

Frank winked at her as he tried to detain an errant piece of pasta.

'I plead being in love. When a man is in love, he imagines – or wishes – all others to be in love too.'

Frieda looked at him, trying to control her own pasta from adventure. She giggled.

'I hope they do fall in love,' she said. 'I really do.'

'I'm sure they will, Mrs Summers. So long as they don't look to us wiser heads, being so long in the tooth as old married folks, to give advice and guide them upon the rocky roads ahead.'

He put his spare hand out and squeezed hers.

'You okay, Free? You looked pretty pale this morning.'

'I'm fine, Frank,' she said, squeezing back. 'It was just a little tummy upset. I'll be fine.'

'Ginos,' said Wilf, looking at the sign before they entered the restaurant, 'why does that speak to me of Shakespeare, of sonnets, of young lovers? Romeo, Romeo –'

'Because you're a prat,' said Gertie, taking his hand and dragging him into the restaurant.

'Er, Gerts, my sweet, my eternal love, Susan and Tom are over there. Do you think it's quite right that we should be sharing the same restaurant? They seem awfully – well, you know, awfully.'

'Give them a bloody wave every so often if you want, Wilf. God's sakes, I thought you knew how to treat a girl on a romantic night out.'

'Oh, I do, or at least I think I did, my sweet and voluptuous temptress, but –'

'Wilf?'

'Shut it.'

Tom waved weakly at the sight of Gertie and Wilf. For some reason he felt as if her were an embarrassed teenager on his first formal date, and Gertie and Wilf classmates. His feelings were interrupted by the sound of his mobile phone going off.

'Sorry,' he apologised to Susan, taking it out. 'Hello, Tom Gregson.'

He listened, a frown appearing on his face, to be replace with a glare of anger.

'You what?'

Silence while he listened further.

'Harrison, this number is for emergencies only. Do you understand what an emergency is? Let me give you an example. I am now, since you have decided to interrupt my evening, waste my time, and almost definitely ruin a personal relationship, going to switch this phone off. So, if you have any more questions about the water cooler or any other fascinating subject you can escalate it to Thompson. And you will also be able to explain to Thompson why I am no longer contactable. Understand? Moron!'

With that he switched the mobile phone off with as savage a motion as can be applied to a little button, looked around as if looking for somewhere to throw it, and then shoved it back into his jacket pocket with enough force to rip the lining.

Then he smiled weakly at Susan.

'Sorry about that. I made the mistake of agreeing that I could be contacted out of hours if there was an emergency. Unfortunately I didn't realise that it was a case of giving an inch and their taking fifteen foot. They seem to think that I can be called up at any time of the day or night for the most trivial questions. That was a chap called Harrison, he's doing some overnight support in the computer room. Apparently the water's run out in the water cooler, and he wanted to know if I knew where the bottles were to fill it. I'll fill him in on Monday morning. Sorry, I should have warned you it might go off. I totally forgot about it.'

'Yes, you should have warned me about it. We were discussing the other day how rude it is to leave your mobile on when going out for dinner.'

'Yes, I am sorry about that,' Tom blushed.

'There's no excuse for it, really. It's simple good manners.'

He looked distraught.

'I said I was sorry,' he said after a pause.

'It's okay, Tom, I'm just teasing,' Susan said, smiling. She had a number of things on her mind. Firstly a comparison between Tom and Frank. She could never have teased Frank, she had always been too busy trying to get Frank to be more serious. She felt much more at ease with Tom, a man who never acted like an eleven-year-old schoolboy – so long as Wilf wasn't around. Secondly, a feeling that she should let Tom in on the secret of the speeches planned for the following evening – to be honest and open if she hoped for a deeper relationship. But the girls had agreed that it would be better to keep that quiet for the time being. Not even the boys were to know.

Thirdly she was desperately trying to ignore the mobile phone vibrating in her own jacket pocket.

She couldn't see Gertie, but she had a deep suspicion that it was Constable Gregson calling her. Later she would murder her.

Normandy. Saturday .Morning.

The first breakfast celebration

Frank stepped out of the hotel, smiling broadly at the sunny day. And then stopped suddenly, mouth open, eyes wide.

'What's wrong, darling?' asked Frieda, coming out behind him. And then she stopped suddenly, mouth open, eyes wide.

Simenon's car was just down the street. Next to it Simenon appeared to be doing a jive of some form, hands bunched, arms thrusting back and forward, legs twisting. He looked delirious. Gaspode pranced around him, barking every few seconds.

'Ah!' he exclaimed, noticing them and throwing his arms open. 'My dear Inspector Frank. My beautiful, beautiful Mrs Inspector Frank!'

He rushed over and enthusiastically kissed Frank on both cheeks and then did the same even more enthusiastically to Frieda.

'Ah, but it is marvellous! It is wondrous! It is superb! It is magnifique! Please, read this. Read! Read!'

He pushed a note into Frank's hand. It was handwritten, in

French. Frank read it. As much as he could decipher. It made no sense.

'But, do you not see?' exclaimed Simenon. 'My wife has left – run off – with this Scottish boy.' He danced a jig. 'Free! I am free! Oh, monsieur, madame, Inspectors Summers, you do not know how much of the relief this is to me.'

'You certainly seem happy about it,' Frieda said with a touch of acerbity.

'Ah, mais non, my beautiful Mrs Inspector, I see you think perhaps you and your husband end up like me and my wiff. Non, this will not happen. You are both in love, I see that immediately. My wiff and I, we were never in love. Once she was very beautiful, very attractive, I say the sun is shining, she says how clever I am. We make love, she tells me I am a very good lover. Then she says she is pregnant and we must marry. What can I do? I know in my soul I do not love her, but what can I do? I think, yes, we get married, she is quite stupid, but she makes the good wiff, non? She cooks not too badly, she makes love well, how much more can a man require? Then, after we marry, she is not pregnant, she cannot cook, and she no more wants to make love. Arrgh!' The smile came back, almost demonic. 'And now I am free! Free!'

'Well, er, congratulations, Inspector,' said Frank.

'Merci, mon ami. Now I look forward to this breakfast celebration! Now I too can celebrate.'

Frank rubbed his jaw for a few seconds. Frieda recognised the sign at once. Frank was thinking. He was thinking of mischief.

'Just one little point, Inspector,' he said. 'I don't want to say anything that might disturb your ecstasy, but – suppose, just suppose that you're right about MacDavis. Suppose he is involved in the drugs trade. And suppose that it was your wife who somehow got hold of the heroin, to hand over to him. It would make sense of a sort.'

Simenon stared at him with the look of a man who has discovered that his winning lottery ticket has the wrong date on it.

'Non, c'est impossible!'

'Inspector,' said Frieda, 'I realise that you have probably never even thought of suspecting your wife, but what Frank says is possible. It has to be considered.'

'Are you mad? My wife?'

'Inspector, you know that people find it very difficult to suspect someone they have lived with for a long time.'

'Suspect my wife? Non! Is it a possibility? Oui! Perhaps she is involved! I understand that. I accept that. But do you not realise the consequences? If she and this MacDavis man are guilty they will be arrested and brought back here to France. No! I forbid it! Let them be as guilty as they can be, they must not come back here, especially not my wife! I beg of you!'

'Well,' mused Frank, tugging his earlobe, 'if they are in Scotland they fall under the jurisdiction of the British police. And as we happen to be British police ...'

Simenon stared at him, aghast.

'You would not do it. Please, please, tell me you would not do it. No-one could be so heartless, so cruel, not even an Anglais. Please, please, leave them be.'

Frank laughed.

'Just teasing, Inspector. There's absolutely no evidence against either of them. If we told the Scottish police that a French police officer suspected MacDavis of stealing some heroin, and, by the way, MacDavis and the police officer's wife have just run off together – I don't think they'd take us too seriously.'

Simenon waved a finger at him.

'You English! You like the joke, n'est ce pas? You are a cold and heartless people.'

'No, Inspector,' said Frieda, 'that's just my husband. He has a nasty streak in him which he calls a sense of humour.'

'Ah, madame, you are right. I apologise to the English people. In my excitement I condemn a whole race because of one enfant terrible.'

'Enfant terrible? I rather like that,' said Frank. 'I might have special cards made up. Frank Summers, Detective Inspector and Enfant Terrible.'

'Later, Frank. We'd better get a move on if we're to be on time for this breakfast celebration.'

'I will bring the car closer for your luggage,' Simenon said. 'Aargh, it is a beautiful morning! I feel I could start singing!'

'So,' Frieda noted as Simenon strode off to his car, Gaspode barking alongside, 'that's why she was so excited every time we bumped into each other. She must have been worried that we might work out what was going on and pass the word on to Simenon.'

'Yes,' said Frank. 'It's a good thing we're trained detectives, or she might have been in trouble.'

'It doesn't mean that she wasn't the one who stole the heroin, though. She might have taken it as a little nest egg.'

'Interesting thought. Remember what Simenon said about

MacDavis? Every time he turned up on holiday Simenon began getting vague information about possible drug deals. He ended up chasing his tail and never found anything. You don't think the information he was getting was coming from his wife, by any chance? While he's out staking out some hotel in the darkness she's cuddled up with MacDavis somewhere else?'

'Or even in the hotel MacDavis is staying in,' suggested Frieda. 'Now there's a thought.'

'Madame Simenon and MacDavis have slipped into his hotel. The same hotel we're about to book in to. She notices Amelie going down the corridor, follows her to find out what she's doing there, after all, Amelie's supposed to be somewhere else entirely.'

'But MacDavis had an alibi. He was nowhere near the hotel at the time.'

'Okay, he's not there, but she is, waiting for him in his room. Nobody has noticed her, she's not on the register, so officially she isn't there.'

'It's a possibility, I suppose.'

'She sees Marie coming out of the room Amelie has gone into,' Frank continued, 'she slips in quietly, finds Amelie unconscious, notices her handbag, finds the heroin, thinks, "Ah, well, seeing as I'm here I'll have that", and pops back to MacDavis's room.'

'Why would she take it?'

'She realises that something has gone wrong with Simenon's plan. She doesn't know what, but she knows that Simenon and others are going to turn up at any moment and start asking questions. She's been feeding false information to

Simenon for years every time MacDavis turns up, to blind him as to what's really going on between herself and MacDavis. She's now got a choice: she can leave the scene as it is and get out before anyone turns up, or she can use it to further lead Simenon up the garden path.'

'It makes sense,' said Frieda. 'She takes the heroin, not because she wants it, but because trying to find it will keep Simenon busy.'

'And remember how she turned up? The one and only time she voluntarily appears on the scene. I reckon that's because she didn't have a choice. She can't risk being discovered in MacDavis's room, can she?'

Frieda nodded.

'She walks down the staircase while Simenon's in the one room,' she said. 'He doesn't see her, but one or two of the constables do. None of them think it unusual. But she can't just disappear, in case one of the constables mentions that they'd seen her. So somehow or other she slips outside and comes back in to berate Simenon. The constables think she's been around all the time while Simenon thinks she's just got there.'

'If that's the case she does have a good sense of humour,' noted Frank.

'But then she has to decide what to do with it after she gets clear of the hotel. So what does she do, throw it in the nearest dustbin?'

'Unlikely. First there's too much chance of it being found, and that will give Simenon ideas – who would steal a packet of heroin just to dump it? Secondly, she is a police officer. Leaving heroin lying around would go against her training.'

'Yes, so she's going to put it somewhere where no-one will look, but if it is found it won't come to any harm. But where?'

'Somewhere such as the evidence room at the local nick,' suggested Frank. 'Slip it into a box containing evidence from some old crime and it won't be found for years, perhaps not for decades, until someone decides on a clean out.'

They mused on this as they brought out their luggage.

'I think I just might have a word with the Scottish police when we get back,' said Frank. 'A couple of quiet enquiries. Find out where MacDavis and Madame Simenon are, go have a few words. I'm pretty sure she won't mind telling me where the stuff is, especially if I promise not to tell Simenon how it got there, just where it is.'

Frieda smiled at him.

'I don't know why people think that you don't have any ambition, Frank,' she said. 'You're determined on finding the solution before Simenon does, aren't you?'

'Damn right I am. It's bad enough that he uses the same methods I do. Having him come out on top would be just too much.'

'But do you really think Madame Simenon did it? It sounds a bit too much of a coincidence.'

'It matches the facts. Everything falls into place. Like Simenon said, find the heroin and you find the – culprit.'

In Frank and Frieda's lounge in Wellbury Tricia Leigh was explaining to Professor and Frances Summers the plans for the following evening, including the possibility that the official speakers might have a little practical joke played on them.

'I'm not sure about that, my dear,' Frances Summers said. 'I do wonder whether Frank should be getting up to such things now that he's an inspector.'

'Oh, it's all right, Mrs Summers, Frieda knows all about it.'

'Ah, well, if Frieda approves, well, that's different. Such a sensible young woman.'

'That reminds me of when we were still students and Professor Graves was giving a lecture,' mused Professor Summers. 'We used to get up to all sorts of things.'

'I don't think they wish to know, Frank. Now, Tricia my dear, what about another cup of tea?'

As they were about to get into Simenon's car Frieda stopped and nodded towards another car parked a short distance away.

'Our friends in black,' she noted. 'Any idea who they are, Inspector Simenon? They've been popping up all over the place.'

Simenon looked at the car with its two occupants wearing black suits and dark glasses.

'I will make the enquiries,' he said. He walked over to the car and produced his badge. The other two appeared to show their own identification. There was an exchange which ended with Simenon laughing and pointing towards his head as if he thought the other two were mad. Then he said something accompanied by the movement of a thumb which didn't need translating as an invitation for the two men to leave. They drove past Frank and Frieda, looking directly ahead.

'What was all that about?' asked Frank when Simenon came up.

'Idiots!' said Simenon, a smile on his face. 'They are from a security service.'

'The security service?'

'A security service. It appears every organisation has one these days. It is as if your, what do you call it, the Potato Board? As if your Potato Board decided it needed a security service.' He laughed. 'Even us. Some fool of an administrator suggested that we too should have a security service. These bureaucrats have many meetings, and then they come to us and say, "You must have the security service." We ask, "Why?" And they say, "So that you can do such things as tap the telephones when you need." And much other nonsense. I was there with my chief when this was proposed. He looked at this man and said, "Monsieur, we are the police. Do you understand what that means? Or perhaps I should show you the printout of the last call you made to your mistress."' Simenon chuckled. 'Naturally there is no printout, we do not know if this man has a mistress, indeed we do not care, but his face becomes very white and he leaves very quickly.' Now Simenon sighed. 'But these new organisations, they are filled with idiots. They do not know what they are doing, and they end up with fools such as those two.'

'But why were they following us?'

'They claim they intercepted coded messages from your hotel room being sent by mobile phone. I ask them why two British police officers should send coded messages. They did not even know that you were British police officers, that is how bad they are. Idiots! Then I tell them that they are idiots, that if they stay they will make an international incident. With their silly faces in all the British newspapers. So they go.'

'Coded messages?'

'Precisely. Something about a cream cake man. Ridiculous!'

'Of course,' said Frieda, trying not to look at Frank. 'Absolutely ridiculous.'

'So,' said Simenon as he drove them towards the farm where the breakfast celebration was to be held, 'you look forward to returning home – to Wellbury?'

'I think I'd be looking forward to it a little more if we weren't flying back in a light aircraft,' said Frieda. 'Not after the last time.'

'Ah, no, you will be quite safe. Xavier Dubons does not take chances. It is Jacques who causes the problems. They have been that way since they were little boys. Dubons would buy himself a bicycle – a racing bicycle, very shiny and expensive, and Jacques would buy an old bicycle, falling to pieces, so that he could parade in the street pretending to be Dubons.'

'What about this plane Dubons says he has? And the pilot?'

'You can trust the plane and pilot. Dubons might dress like a fool, but he is very careful who he employs. That's where his money comes from, hiring the right people. Most of the time.'

'Aren't you a bit frustrated that we didn't catch whoever it was?' asked Frank. Simenon shrugged.

'Not now. Now I give up. Now I do not care. I can understand you feel you are leaving something unfinished. But I feel now, my life is beginning again. I have got rid of my wife, and I have a dog. I am a happy man.'

'But won't your superiors have something to say about your

wife disappearing like that?' asked Frieda.

'My chef will say nothing, Madame Summers. I think he will be almost as happy as I that she has gone.'

He laughed.

'I think perhaps I too invent the saying now: a man must never marry his wife. No, a man must never marry his wife.'

'It probably sounds better in French,' noted Frieda, looking at the passing countryside. 'That sort of thing normally does.'

Normandy. Saturday. Breakfast.

Le penny drops

The trestle tables were laid out in the apple orchard in a confusion of order, as if the phrase "straight lines" had never occurred to the organisers, or, if it had, they had shrugged it off as some simplistic notion probably emanating from the Germans. And the fact that the tables had no seeming relationship to each other allowed the occupants to converse loudly with several other tables at the same time. Frank, Frieda and Simenon – Simenon being treated reluctantly as an unfortunate but necessary adjunct to the wonderful English poppies – were led to the main table where a sparkling Amelie sat, protected by her black-clothed grandmothers on either side, and uncles Jacques and Xavier next to them. Frank and Frieda were seated directly opposite Amelie, while Simenon was given a place next to Jacques. Whether this was to irritate Simenon or Jacques, or both, was not quite clear, but it seemed to have the approval of the others, judging by the cackles of amusement it created.

Jacques and Simenon nodded curtly to each other. Jacques offered Simenon some red wine with the air of a man who hopes it might poison the other. Simenon declined with a curt shake of the head and poured himself a glass of water with the air of a man who would no more drink with his companion than he would push hot needles through his head.

'Gaspode!' cried Amelie. 'Oh! How you have grown! Give your Amelie a kiss!'

Gaspode took one look at his former mistress and disappeared under the table, seeking Simenon's leg for protection.

'Ah, such a cute little puppee,' said Amelie. 'He teases me all the time,' she announced to Frieda and Frank.

Frank was tempted to show Amelie the footage of his own precious little Squishy, but quickly thought better of that. Amelie would gush for at least five seconds before forgetting all about the kitten. And Squishy would not approve.

'Let the feast commence!' cried Xavier. He was not a natural crier, but the food appeared rapidly, possibly because the cooks and chefs he had hired had their own idea of timing, and the timing was now right. The first thing that appeared in front of Frank and Frieda was a bowl of steaming roast drumsticks. It was rapidly followed by others of potatoes, beans, beef, goat – everything that could ever be called food. If ever there was an order of courses at such an event it seemed to have been disposed of for the morning.

Frank rubbed his hands. Frieda grimaced and drew back.

'You okay, Free?' he asked.

'I'm fine, Frank. It just looks a little greasy.'

'You sure, Free? You're looking a little pale.'

'I'm fine, Frank, really I am.'

Frank, alarmed by Frieda's white face, was about to suggest that they leave the breakfast and seek a doctor when one of the old crones in black stood up and offered Frieda a basket of the fruit on the table. She seemed to be suggesting that the fruit would be better for Frieda. She also seemed to be suggesting that Frank, brave hero as he was, and the angel who saved poor Amelie, was but a man, and who knew what such creatures were good for?

Frieda gratefully took a plum and sat sucking on that. The old crone turned to a passing waiter and gave some orders. Within a few minutes a teapot arrived in front of Frieda, with a proper tea cup and saucer. The old crone sat down, immensely pleased at the look of thanks Frieda had given her.

'Ah! I have an announcement,' cried Amelie, clapping her hands. There was a slight pause in the hubbub at the tables close by as she took a white handbag from beside her and beamed at Frank and Frieda. 'You see,' she said, 'I have found my handbag all by my own. Without anyone's help.'

This was translated to the others by one of the uncles, and all the relatives showered her with proud smiles while haughtily excluding the bumbling Detective Inspector Simenon. They all knew about how Simenon had tried to pretend that the cheap little handbag he had given their little Amelie was hers, but of course she was too smart for him, she was a girl who knew her handbags. Simenon himself was staring at the handbag she had produced. His eyebrows were approaching his hairline.

'It looks like the other one,' Amelie continued, 'but it has this pretty little red letter A here. A red little A for little Amelie.'

Frank glanced sideways at Frieda.

'We'll have to call this the clue of the scarlet letter,' he whispered.

'I don't think Amelie would understand that, Frank. Not even if you explained it to her. Just as well, probably.'

'And I bought a little something for the wedding couple,' Amelie announced, opening the handbag. 'It's just a little thing. Mmm! Now, where has that naughty little thing gone?'

'No, really, you shouldn't have done,' Frieda began the standard protest as Amelie hunted around in what appeared to be a handbag too small to lose anything in, but obviously one that had conquered Amelie's minimal organisational skills.

'And what is this?' she asked, taking out a small parcel wrapped in red paper, looking at it in surprise. 'What are you? Where did you come from?'

Her pretty forehead crinkled in concentration. Then she burst into a happy laugh.

'I remember!' she cried. 'I remember! My memory has come back! Ooh, la la, I can remember!'

All the others began chattering in expectation as this latest revelation was translated. Simenon, Frank and Frieda noticed, had put a hand over his eyes. They looked at each other as the meaning of Amelie's words sank in. Frieda closed her eyes and put two fingers to her temple. Frank closed his eyes and pinched the bridge of his nose. The relatives had to wait for Amelie to continue before they realised what was happening.

'Yes, I put the heroin in this handbag,' she said. 'It is my lucky handbag. And then I thought, well, I do not want to risk losing my lucky handbag while on a dangerous undercover mission, so I took an old handbag instead.' She giggled. 'And

I left the heroin in my lucky handbag. So it was lucky after all!'

The chattering of the relatives slowly died as the translation of this rippled through them. Amelie looked around, her happy smile only very slowly fading as she realised that perhaps the others did not feel as happy.

'Ah, perhaps ... well, was I a little bit silly?' she asked in a pleading, little-girl voice. Simenon coughed, took his hand from his head, reached over for a bottle of red wine and poured himself a full glass. He took a deep draught before sighing.

'Just a little, ma petite,' he said. 'Well, not to worry, you are safe, that is the important thing. And here's to our guests, the happy English poppies, Madame et Monsieur Summers.'

The others cheered up. Perhaps Amelie was a silly little girl, but here were the newly-wed couple, it was still a celebration. And they intended to celebrate.

Normandy. Saturday. Midday.

Going home

'So, Inspector Frank and Madame Inspector Summers, it appears we managed to solve the case in the end,' Simenon said as they drove towards the airfield, having made their excuses before they became bloated with food and sated with wine, leaving behind a party which was developing into an all-day event destined to run the gamut of family arguments and end up with loud and tuneless singing and declarations of familial devotion. 'An unusual case, in my experience.'

'Oh, no, Inspector Simenon,' replied Frank, 'we get that sort of thing in Wellbury all the time.'

'Yes? In which case I look forward to a visit.'

'Inspector Simenon,' said Frieda, 'I must warn you that Wellbury is really a boring little town in terms of police work. Unless, and until, my husband gets involved.'

Simenon laughed.

'That I can believe, madame.'

'So, Inspector Simenon,' asked Frank, 'when did you decide to take us off the list of suspects?'

'When I saw Amelie take out her handbag.'

'You suspected us to the end?'

'I had you on the list to the end. It is a problem between the thinking of the head and the feeling of the heart – what you call gut-feeling in English. You see, you choose for your honeymoon the hotel which is being renovated. The cost is less, this is the action pragmatic. But you bring your personal wedding gifts with you, the clarinet and saxophone neither can play. This is the action romantic. '

'Damn, I never did get a chance to try the sax,' said Frank.

'Probably a good thing, Frank,' replied Frieda.

'And then there were the possibilities. You were part of the gang and somehow knew about the heroin. Unlikely. You were there purely by accident, but decided to take advantage when you discovered Amelie. Yes, this could be. In fact, with the facts I had, it seemed that it was either this or the girl Marie had been responsible – yet she seemed to be just a simple peasant girl. Now, if you were responsible, the next question. Were both of you involved, or just one? Was it possible that one had somehow managed to fool the other and me?'

'In which case it would have to be me,' said Frieda, 'since I discovered Amelie.'

'Ah, but you never looked inside the handbag,' pointed out Frank. 'I could have had a sneaky-peek and lifted it while you weren't looking.'

'That is precisely the problem,' Simenon said, 'too many possibilities, too little evidence.'

'Good old Occam's Razor,' noted Frank.

'You considered the possibility that the heroin had never been in the room?' asked Frieda.

'Yes,' sighed Simenon, 'and that is where I failed entirely. It is unforgivable, since I had all the facts, so my logic should have been good. Yet my logic told me, if the heroin had never been in the room – if Amelie had not brought it with her – then she was part of a conspiracy, one which had gone wrong. And, I thought, no, I know Amelie too well. She is not clever enough for this. She is too good. I let my heart become indignant at the thought and reject it. For Amelie I have too much the softness. Instead I should have asked, could she have lost it somehow?

'You never checked the handbag in the bathroom for traces of the packet of heroin?'

'No. That was unfortunate. Perhaps it was unconscious. Perhaps I suspected that Amelie was involved, and did not want proof of that. Ah,' he sighed again, 'perhaps I am getting too old. I make the simple mistake of not asking the silly questions. Always I approach a case asking the silly questions. A robbery is committed. But is it a robbery? A man says he was attacked. But was he attacked? A jewel is stolen. But was it stolen? Indeed, was it a jewel? Always I ask, is what I see the truth? This time I did not ask that silly question.'

'We all make that mistake from time to time,' Frank said. 'It's a bit like knocking your shin against the coffee table every so often. It reminds us not to take things for granted.'

Simenon grimaced at the analogy as if he weren't convinced, and still blamed himself.

'And when did I come off your list of suspects, Inspectors?' he asked.

'About the same time as we came off of yours, inspector,' Frank laughed. 'We made a similar mistake. Amelie told us that you had given her the wrong handbag. Now we knew that Amelie wouldn't lie, so that meant that you had switched the handbags for a reason. It didn't make sense, because we couldn't believe that you were involved. Yet all the facts pointed that way. We made the classic mistake of confusing honesty with accuracy. After all, Amelie would not make a mistake about her own, special handbag she had had since she was a teenager.'

'I suppose she was still suffering from concussion,' Frieda said. 'Otherwise she would have remembered as soon as you gave her back the old handbag.'

Simenon uttered a grunt which might have been a laugh.

'I do not think Amelie had concussion. Or perhaps you could not tell the difference. Amelie cannot remember what she has done an hour before. She is very enthusiastic, and she tries hard, but you give her a green file to look after, five minutes later she has a pink file and believes honestly that is the file you gave her. You do not know where the green file is, you do not know where the pink file has come from, but there you are.'

'Tell me something,' said Frank, 'Amelie's family are all crooks to one extent or another, or they all try to be. Yet they seem very proud that she is a police officer. Don't you find that strange?'

Simenon nodded.

'There was the time that I did. When I heard that she had joined the police I had her transferred to my section. I thought it a triumph, I had the niece of Jacques and Xavier working for me. I did wonder whether she would be loyal to her family before the police, but one look in her eyes told me that she was honest. I did not realise that the family were happy she was working for me because she was so stupid she could never have got a job anywhere else.'

'What will happen to her?'

Simenon shrugged.

'She will go on working for me. I will shout at her every day, and then regret it when she starts with the tears. Each evening I will take Gaspode for a walk on the beach and enjoy the sea air. Each day I will wonder why I do not fire her. Then, in a year or two, she will meet some man who will not realise just how stupid she is, he will fall in love, they will marry, she will leave me, and I will walk Gaspode every day and miss her. That is how life works, monsieur.'

He smiled as he turned the car into the road leading to the airfield.

'You shall have to visit again,' he said. 'With les enfants. I look forward each year or so to seeing you en famille.'

'We'll do that,' promised Frieda. 'First of all we have to survive crossing the Channel in a flying tin can. And, Frank, if anything goes wrong, I'll be blaming you.'

What awaited them was not quite a flying tin can.

'Oh, wow!' breathed Frank as they stepped from the car. 'Now that's a beauty!'

A twin-engined aircraft stood outside the hangar, gleaming, almost aware of its own appearance, a thoroughbred of the skies.

'Well, at least it's got two engines,' noted Frieda. 'Just in case one fails.'

Simenon called out and a man in his late thirties to mid-forties appeared under the wing of the plane. He came towards them.

'Mr and Mrs Summers? I'm your pilot, name's Danny Carter,' he said with an Australian twang.

'How do you do?' said Frank, shaking hands. 'I'm Frank, and this is my wife, Frieda.'

'It does fly properly, doesn't it?' Frieda asked, still looking at the plane. Danny laughed.

'One of the best aircraft I've ever flown,' he said. 'Don't worry, I've been flying almost every day since I was fifteen, and I've never had a serious accident.'

'What about the not-so-serious ones?'

'Oh, I ripped the wheels off a Cessna once while trying to land in a thunderstorm. All in all I was lucky, that time, visibility was zero, petrol was zero, I had to put her down somewhere or other.'

'Are we, er, expecting any thunderstorms on the way?'

Danny laughed again.

'No, Mrs Summers, ever since then I've been extra careful to check the forecast and add a little leeway. The forecast is for clear skies all the way. Let me get your bags.'

Once the bags were stowed Frank turned to Simenon.

'Going back to gut feeling, Inspector,' he said, 'you do know that there's another term for it in English?'

'So? And what is that, Inspector Summers?'

'We call it the offal theory.'

Frieda sighed.

'A bit like your jokes,' she said. 'They pretty offal too.'

Simenon laughed.

'A little gift for you Inspectors Summers,' he said, taking a book from his pocket. 'A memento for your bookshelves.'

Frank took it. It was the copy of famous French quotations translated into English. Frank smiled.

'We'll treasure it, Inspector. Bon chance et merci for everything.' They shook hands.

'The good luck, Inspector. And Madame Inspector.' He kissed Frieda on both cheeks and she and Frank boarded the plane. They waved to him as the aircraft took off, and watched until he and Gaspode were two small specks.

'Lovely,' said Frank, looking down.

'Just one thing, Frank. You are not going to try to fly this aeroplane. Danny,' she called to the cockpit, 'you will not allow my husband to play with the controls, understand?'

'No chance, Mrs Summers,' Danny called back. 'There are very few experienced pilots I feel comfortable flying a plane I'm in, there's no way I'd let a non-pilot try his luck. I'm rather fond of my own life.'

'Good,' said Frieda as Frank made a face at her.

'I'll take her along the coast so you can see the beaches,' Danny said. 'Then across the Channel to the white cliffs, and up the east coast. Have you ever seen Wellbury from the air?'

'No, come to think about it, we haven't.'

'Then it'll be a new experience for all of us. I've never landed at that airfield before.'

Frieda's mouth twitched. But the comment was forgotten as they enjoyed the view. The flight was smoother than they had expected, and like all enjoyable things, seemed to be over too soon. It was as if only minutes had passed before Danny was circling Wellbury before contacting the nearby airfield and requesting permission to land. And then they had landed. And were in a taxi. And at the station. And the train pulled in. And they were aboard the slow-moving train, heading home.

'What would you have done if you'd discovered that I had nicked the heroin?' asked Frank.

'Don't be silly, Frank. Why on earth would you have taken it?'

'I could have been starting a new career as a master criminal. I think I could be quite good as a master criminal.'

'And when were you planning on this career change?'

Frank grinned.

'It was only a thought. I can't seriously imagine being anything but a copper.'

'Well, you can stop thinking about it now, you've got a wife to support. You're going to have to pretend you're all grown up now.'

'I do?'

'Yes. No more acting like an eleven-year-old.'

'No, I meant the bit about having a wife to support. I was rather hoping you would be supporting me.'

'Idiot.'

They looked at each other and smiled. They leaned forward and kissed, softly and gently. The kiss of two people who find themselves comfortable together, and look forward to a long life together, whatever happens.

Wellbury. Saturday. Afternoon.

Home

'Home,' said Frank as the train pulled into the station. 'It's a nice word that, home.'

'A lovely word.'

The doors opened and they lifted their suitcases onto the platform. A small knot of people at the end of the platform waved, called out and began coming their way.

'Ah, the welcoming party,' noted Frank. 'There's mum. Dad. Susan. Gertie. Tricia. And the Chief Inspector. And Tom and Wilf. Uncle Tom Cobley and –'

'Darling, stop chattering and give your mother a kiss.'

'So, my boy, how was it? Did you get to see the landing fields? And Pont Hoc? And the remains of Mulberry?'

'Frieda! You're looking – blooming!'

Tricia had stood slightly back while the others claimed their share of the kisses and hugs. At the sound of Frank's voice something began to stir in the leather jacket over her shoulder.

'Frank!' she called. 'Someone's been missing you more than all of us.'

Squishy's head popped out of the pocket. She saw Frank and uttered a wide-eyed cry, trying to scramble out of the pocket.

'Now, Squish,' said Tricia, lowering the jacket to the platform so that Squishy could get out, 'be careful, and don't go near the tracks.'

Squishy paid no attention. She wasn't interested in any silly tracks. She made it out of the pocket and raced up to Frank through the forest of legs, scrambling up his leg with her claws.

'Ah! Squish, careful now, that hurts,' he cried, bending down and lifting her gently. 'You've missed us, haven't you, you poor little thing? It's okay, we're back now.'

Squishy miaowed and licked his chin. She was determined to get as close to him as possible, just in case he disappeared again, in which case she would go with him.

'You are a silly sod, aren't you,' Frank said, holding Squishy so that the kitten could nuzzle into his neck. 'You're supposed to be a cat, not a doggy.'

'I think we could all do with a cup of tea,' announced his mother. 'I'm sure Frank and Frieda could.'

'Good idea, Mrs Summers,' said Susan. 'Tom, Wilf, you get the suitcases.'

Tom and Wilf looked at each other as the others moved off. They each shrugged and began picking up various items of luggage.

'The way I see it,' said Wilf, 'is that, in about five years' time, everyone will be used to Frank and Frieda being married. And

Squishy will be a grown up cat, independent, and no longer an adorable kitten.' He sneezed. 'And then Gertie and Susan might just be able to think of us as individuals from time to time. As opposed to being handy baggage carriers.'

'You mean that, when they suggest going out for drinks, they'll be thinking of a romantic evening for two, as opposed to a get-together of a large bunch of mainly policemen in a night club?'

Wilf considered that as they walked.

'Pandora,' he said.

Wellbury. Saturday. Evening.

Surprise!

Eric Johns and Pete Phillips stood at the back of Wellbury police station, an incongruous sight, two men in evening dress waiting in a car park.

'This is daft,' said Pete, 'we could have parked down the road from the Blue Bliss and walked if they were worried about Frank and the Inspector seeing our cars.'

What really worried him was the way that all the constables who had passed them had sniggered as if they knew something that Pete and Eric didn't. Eric had dismissed it as mere jealously at the sight of how smartly dressed they were. Pete could not help but wonder. Something just did not feel right.

'Attention to detail, Pete. Frank and the Inspector are supposed to be there for a couple of quiet drinks with his parents and one or two others. They'd start to wonder if they saw our cars parked anywhere close. And if they thought the place was full of coppers they'd go somewhere else, like the Hangmans.'

Pete tried to think of a reply, but the only one that came to mind was a repetition of "This is daft." He knew it was daft. It was downright silly. But whatever objection he had come up with Eric Johns had had an answer for. Not very good answers, but answers all the same. All in all he was dying for a pint and hoping to get this silly speech out of the way. He had explained the situation to his wife, and she had been extremely critical. If Frieda and Frank were having problems, she had said, then it was not up to him or Eric Johns to interfere. He had tried to point out that interfering was exactly what they weren't doing, since the whole plan was to pretend that no-one knew that Frank and Frieda were having problems, but his wife had got the idea in her head that they were interfering, and that it was none of their business and they should under no circumstances do so. She had repeated this so often that he had ended up wishing that he hadn't told her anything.

Despite her criticisms she had insisted on going to the Blue Bliss that evening. She was not going to interfere, but she did not see why she couldn't have a few drinks with her husband every so often, after all how often did they get a chance to do so these days? It was another point that was bugging Pete Phillips. Frank and Frieda would turn up at the Blue Bliss, his wife would be there but he wouldn't. Surely it wouldn't take them longer than two seconds to wonder why. Before he could follow this thought up Susan's MG pulled up with a squeal of brakes.

'Get in the back, quickly,' she called, opening the passenger door and pushing forward the back of the front passenger seat, 'before anyone sees us. Come on, quickly, quickly!'

The two men looked at each other in surprise before hurriedly obeying her order. The back of the MG could probably have accommodated a small child in reasonable comfort. Eric and Pete only just managed to squash themselves in, Pete's elbow in Eric's side, his head held down by the roof.

'What's the rush?' asked Eric Johns, following this by an 'Aaaarggh!' as Susan put her foot down on the accelerator and the car shot off.

'No rush,' she replied, in total contradiction to her speed as she took a corner, only the added weight of the two men stopping the car from lifting onto two wheels. 'I just like driving fast.'

Eric John's face was up against the window. He looked at the tarmac a foot or so below in horror. He was about to suggest that they take it more slowly when his face was pushed along the window by the sudden deceleration of the MG.

'Damn!' said Susan, 'they must have changed the synchronisation of the lights. I can normally get this one on green if I hit forty from the corner shop.'

'Forty?' squeaked Eric Johns.

'Er, Doctor Pleadle,' began Pete Phillips.

'Now, you've got your speeches,' Susan said, dropping the clutch and racing off as the lights turned green. Two muffled grunts from the back where the men were trying to fall backwards and finding no space to do so suggested the affirmative.

'The latest intelligence is that Frank and Frieda got back at around four,' Susan continued in the vein of someone who hadn't been on the railway platform to meet them earlier that day. 'We don't expect them to leave until about quarter to six, but we've got a patrol car watching the house from a discreet distance, just in case they leave early.'

Pete Phillips would have liked to have been able to look at Eric Johns with raised eyebrows, to see if he shared his own stupefaction at the idea of Doctor Susan Pleadle apparently running Wellbury police force. Unfortunately all he could see, out of the corner of his eye, was the top of Eric Johns's head.

'The patrol officers reported – bloody truck driver! What a stupid place to try to reverse – the patrol officers reported that the targets appeared to be somewhat distant, as if they'd had an argument. Which means that Frieda's probably not in a good mood.'

Susan's apparent decision to speak as if she were out of some B-grade American cop movie was overshadowed by the news that Frieda was not in a "good" mood. You might as well describe a force ten storm as a slight breeze.

'So we're going to have to make sure that everything goes off perfectly. No mistakes, absolutely none. Blasted cyclists! The slightest foot put wrong and we'll have a situation on our hands.'

The two men were thrown – as far as two squashed men could be thrown – to one side as Susan raced around a roundabout. They could have sworn that she actually went around twice before shooting back out onto the straight road as if being shot by a sling. They were wrong. It was three times.

'When you come out to make your speeches, have a look at their table,' Susan continued. 'If Frank hasn't got a pint in front of him then it's bad news.'

The MG decelerated abruptly before immediately speeding up again.

'Phil Walters has set up a podium in the Members Only bar,' Susan informed them. 'It's got a microphone, so you don't need to worry about having to raise your voices above the noise.'

Eric Johns, had he not being concentrating on trying to reduce the number of times he was being bounced around in a very small space, might have pointed out the benefits of learning to project your voice. If you were a trained speech-maker, of course.

'That's if it works, of course,' added Susan. 'When I left it was squeaking a lot, the way they do sometimes. I hope they've fixed it by now. Okay, we're here, I'll take you around the back.'

The two men weren't too sure how they had managed to arrive at the Blue Bliss so quickly without the aid of a siren, but they were greatly relieved when the MG came to a stop at the back of the night club, especially after the way Susan brought the car to a stop. It appeared to involve doing a three-sixty-degree turn and going from fourth gear into reverse at the same time.

'Come on, quickly, quickly,' Susan said, opening her door. 'Hurry up, hurry up,' she added as Eric Johns and Pete Phillips tried to unsqueeze themselves. They managed to do so and hobbled after her to the back door.

'Right, follow me. Phil Walthers has put a closed sign on the snooker room door. You're going to wait there until Frank and Frieda arrive. Wait! Stop!' She peered around a corner.

'All clear, come on, hurry, hurry, surely you two can move faster? Aren't police officers supposed to be physically fit?'

There were two police officers who did not feel at all fit, especially not with all this stop-start-stop malarkey.

'Right, here we are, inside, inside.'

Eric Johns and Pete Phillips gratefully stumbled into the semi-darkened snooker room as Susan closed the door behind the three of them.

'Half an hour,' she said, checking her watch. 'Now, no noise, we don't want anyone passing and hearing anything. You know how curious Frank can get.'

'It's a bit warm in here,' observed Eric Johns, running his finger around his collar.

'Yes, apparently there's a problem with the air conditioning, Mrs Blower is trying to fix it.'

'God help us,' muttered Pete Phillips. 'With Mrs Blower on the job – we'll either be fried or frozen before the night's out.'

'It's only for half an hour, you can handle that, surely,' Susan said, her tone suggesting that they should stop acting like whining little boys. 'Now, I'll get you something to drink. A couple of glasses of iced water. I'll be back in a second.'

'Er, any chance of a pint, er, Doctor?' asked Pete Phillips.

'A pint?' asked Susan as if it were something really not good for his health. 'Very well, but just one. Back soon.'

'Iced water?' muttered Pete Phillips as the door closed. 'The woman's mad.'

'She is a doctor,' Eric Johns pointed out, unbuttoning his jacket and taking it off. 'Very anti-alcohol, doctors are, these days.'

'Yeah? And what about the bit about Frank not having a pint in front of him being bad news? She didn't seem to think Frank should be drinking iced water.'

'She's probably still got a soft spot for him. You know what these women are like.' He looked at his jacket, turning it around and stroking any creases out of it, before draping it tenderly around the top of a bar stool. 'The price of dry-cleaning these days! It's a wonder any of them are still in business.'

'I hope we don't have to stay here too long,' Pete Phillips said, shrugging off his own jacket and hanging it on a stool next to Eric's, 'this place is like a bloody sauna.'

'Fortitude, Pete, fortitude. We are here, not for ourselves, but as friends and colleagues of the married couple. To provide what little aid and assistance we might be able to in their hour of need. Tell you what, while we're waiting, I'll give you a chance to revenge yourself for the last time I beat you at snooker.'

'Last time? I won our last game. I –'

'Now, now, Pete, did I say the last time we played? I said the last time I beat you. Not quite the same. You aren't nervous, are you?'

'Course I'm not nervous. What's there to be nervous about?'

'It's nothing to be nervous about, Pete, public speaking. Even if you aren't trained in it like I am.'

Wilf and Tom stood just inside the entrance in the Members Only bar, each with a pint in hand, leaning against the bar top. They stood in the attitude of two men who know they have the right to be there, but feel separated from the main group.

'I'm to behave myself, apparently,' said Wilf, sipping at his pint. 'I have to admit that behaving myself is not my usual philosophy of life.'

Tom considered this. Wilf had an artistic disregard for rules, whereas he, Tom, was much more of a conservative type. He had a firm belief in politeness, manners and opening doors for ladies. Wilf also believed in opening doors for ladies, but he did it with a flourish that made a joke of it, whereas Tom found that his manner either caused the lady in question to nod approvingly at such a good old-fashioned gesture, or he was accused of being sexist – and some other words he preferred to forget. He envied Wilf his almost piratical approach.

'I've also been told to be on my best behaviour,' he said. 'I think it's the first time I've been told that since I was ten years old.'

Wilf nodded.

'Susan's always been like that,' he said. 'Comes of being a bossy older sister.'

'She's not that bad,' Tom demurred. 'Is she?'

Just then Tricia Leigh appeared in front of them, carrying a stack of papers in her arm and wearing an "I'm organising things so just do as you're told and we'll all get along fine" look.

'One for you,' she said, giving Wilf a sheet. 'And the second sheet for you. And one for you,' she gave Tom a page, 'and the second sheet for you. Put them away and don't show them until the speeches start. You can read them then.'

'Yes, Miss,' Wilf said automatically, but Miss had already swept away. The two men glanced at their papers.

'These look remarkably like speeches,' Wilf said.

'I would say that these are the speeches,' Tom agreed. 'What exactly is going on?'

'I don't know. Didn't Sue tell you?'

'Only to be on my best behaviour.'

Wilf nodded.

'When I find myself in a situation where I don't know what's going on, I find the best approach is to have another drink,' he said. Tom nodded. He wasn't sure that Susan would approve, but he was quite sure of one thing, and that was that he needed another pint.

Pete Phillips was saved from telling Eric Johns exactly what his opinion regarding public speaking was coming to by the entrance of Gertie carrying a tray with two pints on it.

'One pint of Bass for Sergeant Phillips, and one pint of lager for Sergeant Johns,' she announced.

'Love, you're an angel,' Pete Phillips said, taking his Bass and sinking a good quarter of it. 'Aaah, that's better. It's like a hot-house in here.'

'Calm yourself, Pete,' Eric Johns said, studying his lager as if it were a work of art to be enjoyed. 'You mustn't gulp it down. But, you're right, it is a little warm,' he concluded, gulping down almost half.

'I'll get another couple,' offered Gertie.

'Cheers, love, another pint would set me up just right.'

'You aren't thinking of playing snooker, are you?' Gertie asked, noticing the cue in Eric's hand.

'Well, just a quick game to while the short time away. Why, is there a problem?'

'The snooker room is supposed to be closed. People might wonder if they heard the sound of snooker balls. If you're going to play, it might be better to use the table right at the back of the room. And keep it as quiet as possible.'

'That's okay, love, we'll have a game some other time,' said Pete.

'Any excuse,' murmured Eric.

'Excuse?'

'I'll get the next round,' Gertie said, slipping out the room.

'Look, Eric, I can beat you with one arm tied behind my back, I don't need any excuses.'

'Strange that I always beat Harry Wheatley, and you never.'

Pete Phillips gritted his teeth. Eric Johns regularly beat any constable he challenged. The fact that he had a bad habit of saying "You know, son, that reminds me," or "You know, son, the way you're gripping the cue," just as his opponent hit the ball was no doubt pure co-incidence. The general agreement amongst the constables was that the best thing to do with Eric Johns was to lose quickly against him and get away as fast as possible.

'Okay, we take the table right at the back,' Pete said. 'Ten quid, okay?'

'A gentleman never plays for money,' Eric Johns replied as he moved towards the darkened back of the room, Pete Phillips following with a cue which appeared to want to hit the back of Eric's head.

'Just keep it down,' Pete muttered as they put their pints down on a ledge next to the snooker table.

'I never –' Eric began. 'Quiet, someone's coming! Quick, down, behind the table.'

The door opened and someone entered. The two men crouched behind the table and looked at each other.

'Probably Gertie,' Pete mouthed at Eric.

'What's that?' Eric mouthed back. 'It's probably only Gertie.'

They raised their heads slowly, risking a peek over the top of the table. There was no-one to be seen.

'Are you okay, Sergeants?' asked a black-dressed Sam Nightingale next to them, holding a full pint glass in each hand.

The two men shot up, choking away screams, bouncing off each other.

'Good god, love, where did you come from?' Eric managed to gasp.

'Gertie asked me to bring these drinks through. Are you sure you're okay?'

'Aye, love, we were just worried you might be Frank coming in,' Pete said, taking his pint.

'Just taking no risks, Sam,' Eric said, taking his. 'Security, it's automatic when you've been in the force as long as I have.'

'I'm sure,' Sam replied. 'It's probably best to be cautious. Mrs Blower is wandering around with a screwdriver, looking for the central heating unit.'

'Oh, god, anything but Mrs Blower,' muttered Pete.

'Yes, well, it shouldn't be long now. The Inspectors arrived a few minutes ago. Doctor Pleadle will come to call you when we're ready.'

They watched her black-clad form glide out of the room.

'Bloody hell fire,' whispered Pete, 'how did she know where we were? It's almost pitch black here.'

'Second sight,' said Eric. 'She doesn't need light to see. Well known fact.'

Pete Phillips grimaced, not noticing the small CCTV camera almost tucked into the ceiling. It was pointing at them.

'Tell you what, Eric, I'll be glad when this is over.'

'Won't be long now, Pete, only a few more – oh, Christ no!'

This last whispered ejaculation was a response to the unmistakeable sound of Mrs Blower approaching. The two men dropped to the floor.

'Now this is the laundry room,' Mrs Blower boomed, opening the door and coming into the room. 'My goodness, no, it's the snooker room. They must have moved it again. You've never seen the snooker room, have you, Inspector?'

'No, I haven't. I'm not ungrateful for what you've done for my officers, but personally I feel it doesn't give a good image for police officers to be seen in public playing snooker.'

Eric Johns and Pete Phillips stared at each other with wide open eyes. There was no mistaking the sound of Frigid's voice in a bad mood. And when she was in a bad mood someone was about to cop it. Eric Johns looked at Pete Phillips, mouthed the word "Frank", and pulled his finger along his neck.

'You know, I've never thought of it that way,' Mrs Blower said. 'Nelson loves the room. He loves chasing the balls when they come off the tables. He always come in here when he knows that Sergeant Johns is playing.'

Eric Johns sensed something breathing at his neck. He turned slowly to find the young dog Nelson panting at him, face to face, bright eyed.

'Now Frank is really good at snooker,' Mrs Blower continued. 'But then I imagine he's good at most sports. Nelson? Where has he gone to? I wonder if it's time for his walkies.'

'It's time that Inspector Summers began showing a good example to the others,' Frieda said. 'He will have to learn to curtail several of his former habits.'

'Look at this!' exclaimed Mrs Blower. 'You just can't get the staff these days. Waiters leaving their jackets lying around in the laundry room. And they'll have left receipts in their pockets like they usually do. Yes, look at this, bar receipts. Or something. Honestly, as if the paperwork wasn't difficult enough as it is. I'll take these with me to the office. Now, shall I show you the snooker room? It's around here somewhere.'

Pete Phillips's face dropped as the door closed. He turned to Eric Johns who was trying a feeble smile on Nelson.

'Eric! She's taken our jackets!'

'Nice doggie. Nice doggie, Nelson. Lie down and I'll find you a biscuit or something. Sit?'

'Eric! Did you hear me? Mrs Blower's taken our jackets.'

'She's what?' Eric asked, standing up slowly.

'Come on! We've got to get them back. My speech is in the pocket.'

'Hold these,' Susan ordered Tom. He obediently took the two jackets.

'Right,' said Gertie, checking the pockets, 'all traces of speech removed. Give me the larger jacket.'

'Come on,' said Susan, 'let's get the first entertainer on stage. You keep hold of that jacket, Tom, we'll be back for it shortly.'

The two men watched Susan and Gertie hurry back to the snooker room, Pete Phillips's jacket in Gertie's hands.

Silently they both took deep pulls on their pints.

'Memorised,' Eric muttered as they hurried to the front of the snooker room, Nelson gambolling after them, enjoying this strange new game.

'Yeah, I know, I know, you've memorised yours. Well I haven't.'

'Most of it. Most of it.'

They skidded to a halt as the door opened.

'There you are,' said Susan. 'Come on, Sergeant Johns, you're on.'

'Doctor, Mrs Blower's taken our jackets,' said Pete.

'Your jackets?'

'With my speech in the top pocket.'

'I've memorised mine. Most of it.'

'You can't go out there without your jackets.'

'Wouldn't look professional. I've never done a speech without my jacket.'

'Wait here. I'll see what I can do. She can't have gone far.'

The two men stood staring at the closed door in silence. Nelson sat and looked up at them, panting. Three seconds later the door opened again.

'I've managed to get one jacket back,' said Gertie. 'Come on,

Sergeant Johns, put it on. Hurry. Before Frieda decides to leave.'

'It's not my jacket,' Eric protested as Gertie forced it on. 'It's Pete's.'

'It will have to do, you're already five minutes late. Come on, it's a tuxedo, that's good enough.'

'But, but,' Eric tried to protest as he was hustled out. The jacket was too short in the stomach and too long in the arms. Sam appeared in the doorway as Gertie and Eric Johns went out.

'You stay there,' she said to Pete Phillips. She closed the door on him and turned to Eric Johns in the corridor. 'Now, we couldn't get the speech off Mrs Blower, but Gertie's got an early draft, you can use it as a prompt.'

'Almost memorised,' Eric muttered as they hurried him along the corridor.

'Just remember not to say the forbidden words,' Gertie said. 'Now, ready?'

'And don't forget, walk backwards for three paces,' Sam added.

Eric paused at the doors to the Members Only bar. He nodded and squared his shoulders.

'Let the show commence,' Gertie said, giving him a helpful shove through the doors. He stumbled in, just managing to walk backwards for three paces by turning in a circle three times. Then he found himself the sudden centre of attention, Frank and Frieda sitting next to each other at a table with their parents, Percy Hanson and the Chief Inspector, other tables full with what appeared to be the entire contingent of Wellbury police force. They gave a loud cheer as he collected himself and walked up to the microphone. There were spotlights directly overhead, about a foot above him. If anything it felt hotter than the snooker room. He coughed and put the piece of paper Gertie had given him on the podium. He looked up and glanced apparently idly at Frank and Frieda's table. Instead of a pint there was a cup of tea in front of Frank.

A delicate, patterned, porcelain cup of tea.

'Ladies and gentleman,' Eric Johns began, trying to quell the thousands of suggestions his imagination was offering him, most of which had something to do with the fact that Frank only ever, ever drank tea out of a mug, and he certainly would not sit sipping tea in a pub if he had any choice in the matter. 'Friends, colleagues and all here tonight. Unused to public speaking as I am, I was most honoured when asked to give a little speech at this surprise –'

He was interrupted by calls of "Speech! Speech!" and "Surprise! Surprise!"

' – when asked to, when asked to, er, yes, yes, quite so.' He looked down at the paper. 'May I say, to begin, to begin –' He paused slightly at the difference between his original speech and this one, before soldiering on. 'To begin, what a fine bah-bah-bah-'

'Bar-bar-Barbaran?' called a wit as Eric Johns looked in terror at the word "body" on the page. Someone had helpfully underlined it, just in case he should miss it.

'Group!' he almost shouted. 'Group of men, fine group of men, fine group of men, yes, and women, of course, yes, and women, fine group of men and women assembled here tonight to welcome back our friends and colleagues from their ordeal. Ordeal? I mean, er, not ordeal, no, er, slight, slight misprint. To continue. A bah-bah-group of fine men and women whe-whe-whe-wher –'

'He wants a where-where,' called someone else as Eric Johns struggled with the highlighted word "wedded".

'Where all put their shoulders to the wheel, yes, united as wha-wha-wha, as a group, a group.'

He put out a shaking hand and took a sip from a glass of water before returning to the paper. He failed to notice that almost everyone in the audience also returned their attention to pieces of paper carefully hidden in front of them.

'Indeed, these are the very ma-ma-ma' he stuttered, now totally thrown, both by the underlined word "Marmite" and the meaningless sentence "Indeed, these are the very Marmite days of our lives."

'Ma-ma-ma?' came a call from the audience.

'Mama-mia!' someone else replied.

'Here we go again!'

'My, my!'

'How can we resist you?'

'Of course,' Eric Johns said, as loudly as he could with a drying mouth, trying to out-shout the others as sweat poured down his cheeks, 'of course, that is not to say, bearing in mind, and remembering the specific, ah, specific, things – things, things which we all know, know to be, which is quite important when you come to think about them.'

The audience quietened down, fascinated by where Eric Johns was trying to go and how he might get there.

'So in conclusion,' he said, seeing an escape gap and mentally sprinting towards it, 'in conclusion I would like to say, welcome back to the, er, welcome back to our colleagues, and may you have many, um, yes, welcome back.'

With that he stumbled from the podium. Tricia Leigh guided him to a table alongside the main table, where a pint of iced water awaited. There was desultory clapping from an audience who felt that he had escaped too easily.

'Who's on next?' asked one.

'Jumbo the clown,' came a reply from the other side.

Tom and Wilf looked at each other.

'I think we're seeing the ritual punishment meted out to one of the tribe who has transgressed tribal norms,' noted Wilf.

'A bit barbaric,' replied Tom. 'At least in the rugger club we'd just have stripped his clothes off and thrown him in the mud.'

Wilf thought about this.

'I think I'd rather stick with the speech option,' he said.

Inside the snooker room Pete Phillips licked his lips and looked at the half pint of lager Eric Johns had left behind. He was hot, nervous and thirsty. The room was boiling. He could also hear what sounded like jeers and cat-calls coming from the Members Only bar, which tended to suggest that Eric Johns was having a tough time of things. He did not enjoy lager, and he was loath to mix that and the Bass, but he was definitely thirsty.

Just as he was about to convince himself that a sip couldn't cause any harm the door opened. He flattened himself against the wall. Sam Nightingale entered, appearing surprised at the sight of him squashed up against the wall.

'Sergeant Johns has made a right hash of things,' she said,

handing over a jacket. 'Fluffed his lines, kept losing the thread, stuttering and stammering. And it's a cruel audience out there. You're going to have to rescue things.'

'Rescue things?' he asked, struggling to fit the jacket on. It was Eric Johns's jacket. It had plenty of space where the stomach would be: apart from that the rest of it was too small, and the material under the armpits was digging into his flesh.

'I don't think the Inspector likes her people making fools of themselves. Oh, by the way, Tricia found an early draft of your speech in case you needed it.'

'Thanks, love,' Pete said, grabbing the folded papers.

'Now come on, let's see what you can do to save us from a disaster.'

He followed her to the entrance to the bar.

'I'm going to my table,' she said. 'Wait five seconds and then come in. And don't forget, three paces backwards.'

He watched her enter the bar, determined that he wasn't going to make himself look a right idiot by entering the room walking backwards.

So he stepped back three paces in the corridor and executed the backward steps there. Then he set his shoulders and entered. It was a long walk to the podium, and he seemed to be under a barrage of witty repartee concerning his jacket. He had hoped to use the walk to quickly scan the notes, but his eyes were covertly drawn to the main table, the tea cup in front of Frank, and what resembled a court-marshal consisting of Frieda, Frank, Frank's parents, Percy Hanson and the Chief Inspector.

And then his eyes were drawn to the unlikely sight of Eric

Johns greedily draining a pint of iced water. If the man was that bad things had undoubtedly been rough. He decided that there was only one way to play this: keep his eyes on the page, read exactly what was there, get through it and sit down as quickly as possible.

He was quite a bit taller than Eric Johns. Almost hitting his head on the lights above the podium was not a good start. He could feel their heat immediately begin to burn into the top of his head.

He coughed, took a breath, and ploughed in.

'First of all I thought I'd kick off with a joke about maaa!'

'Maah? It's the sheep joke!' cried someone.

Pete didn't notice. All he could see was the underlined "Mothers-in-law". His wife was watching him. The first and only time he had made a mother-in-law joke in her presence she had responded with a frosty "That's my mother you're talking about." And here was Frank's mother sitting in front of him, who was now Frigid's mother-in-law. Wherever he looked he could see disapproval ready to break out if he read that one out. He recognised it. It was the one with a lemon. And the punch-line was missing.

'Ah, sorry about that,' he said, 'wrong page.'

He quickly turned the sheet over and began again.

He looked at the new page. It was headed "The Cricket Joke". He breathed deeply. That had to be innocuous. He counted to three.

'Right, here we are, the cricket joke. This bloke books himself into a hotel for the afternoon for a bit of ...'

He stopped as he read the next bit: "nooky with his girlfriend when he finds his wife in the bath."

'A bit of what?' called the audience.

'A bit on the side?'

'A bit of relaxation?'

'Ah, yes,' Pete Phillips said quickly. 'Sorry about that, some water got onto the page. Anyway,' he continued, realising that, for some reason, the notes in front of him were useless. It would be better to ad lib.

'Jokes aside,' he continued, 'we're all here to, to, er, welcome back two of our colleagues, from, er, from France! And what a terrible, I mean, obviously it must have been wonderful, but we all know what France is like, don't we?'

He almost got away with it. His audience could sympathise about the Frogs. And then someone shouted:

'Oi! Keep to the script!'

'That's cheating, that is. Keep to the script. Let's hear the cricket joke.'

'I want to know how the lemon joke ends!'

He looked up at the noise. He noticed that everyone appeared to be waving pieces of paper. Eric Johns was looking around, understanding slowly seeping into his wide-eyed face. The audience was comprised of people who had not been happy with the semi-order Eric Johns had issued for them all to be there. Now they were exacting revenge.

Frank and Frieda were holding hands underneath their table. And Frank had a pint in front of him. The tea cup was in front of Frieda.

'This is a wind-up, isn't it?' Pete asked.

'Surprise!' the audience shouted in unison. Frank grinned,

stood up, and took the kepi Frieda handed him. He put it on and walked to the podium amidst cheers and wolf-whistles.

'Well done, Pete, you got there in the end. You go sit down and have a pint.' He stood next to the podium and turned to the assembly. 'And now, mes amis, allow me to tell you the true story of the young woman in the bath. Quiet, please, quiet now, or you'll miss the salacious bits.'

'I'll bet there aren't any salacious bits,' Percy Hanson called out.

'Ah, mais oui, mon Inspector, c'est tres, tres salacious bits. the only problem is that they're in French.'

'Spoilsport!' cried Tom.

'It pays to improve your education.'

'That's okay, I can speak French,' Wilf said. 'I'll translate.'

'Not the sort Frank speaks,' Frieda murmured.

'Actually, it was quite an interesting case from the deductive point of view,' Frank said, causing Frieda to raise her eyes to the ceiling.

'Excellent,' puffed the Chief Inspector. 'I'm always ready to listen to a good old story of deduction. Carry on, Frank, carry on.'

'Mes amis, Wellburians, colleagues et countrymen, donnez moi votre ears. C'est le samedi nuit, et Frieda et moi sont ici l'hotel sur l'honeymoon ... '

When Frank had finished and stepped down to applause the Chief Inspector stood up and went to the podium carrying his glass.

'Ladies and gentlemen,' he said, the audience hushing

435

themselves, 'I won't keep you long, and I promise not to tell any jokes, though if someone has time later I would love to hear the end of the lemon joke. However, the first thing I would like to say is simply this: welcome back to the happy couple. Ladies and gentlemen, I give you the happy couple.'

He raised his glass and there were calls of "the happy couple!"

'I'm sure we're all happy to have Frank and Frieda back,' he continued, 'and by the sounds of things the French probably happy that they're back here too. I think my only concern is in wondering what Wellbury will have to face now that Frank has brought back his inimitable manner of finding himself in the strangest of circumstances. We wait with bated breath. It might not be enjoyable, but it will be interesting.'

This was met with cheers and whistles.

'Finally, I popped into the station on my way here and found a message waiting for me.' He took a piece of paper from his pocket. 'It's from an Inspector Georges Simenon of the French police. He says, "I would like to commend Inspector Summers for the professional help given to myself and my fellow officers over the past week. Such an officer, indeed such a detective, is a rare pleasure to meet. Should Inspector Summers ever wish to make a return visit we would be most welcoming. And we would not object too much if she brought her husband along. Signed Georges Simenon. And he adds a P.S.: Please tell monsieur Inspector Summers that we French also have the sense of humour.'

The others in the bar burst out laughing at an almost chagrined Frank Summers. The Chief Inspector stood down from the podium and rejoined the group at the main table.

'Cheeky sod,' Frank said. 'He's just getting a little revenge in because I thought he might be the one who had nicked the heroin.'

'You mean you might have made a mistake? You, Frank?'

'I'm always making mistakes, everybody knows that. But there's one mistake I know I didn't make,' he said, giving Frieda a kiss, accompanied by "Ooohs" and sighs from the other women present. Frieda blushed.

Frank met Pete Phillips in the gents a while later.

'You got me there good and proper, you bugger,' Pete said with an amused grin. 'No hard feelings, though. I knew I should never have listened to Eric Johns.'

'How is old Eric? He seems to have disappeared.'

'He's in the snooker room teaching the others how to play. He's already convinced himself that he gave a great welcome back speech, and never believed there was anything wrong between you and Fabulous.'

'Already? Blimey, I knew his imagination worked fast, I didn't think it was that fast.'

'Fastest thing on no wheels,' commented Pete. 'Still, good honeymoon? Apart from being shot at, mugged, finding bodies in the bath, that sort of thing?'

'Brilliant honeymoon, Pete. Best I could think of. My biggest worry was that we'd get bored – bored doing nothing and bored with each other.'

'Really?' queried Pete as they walked out.

'Yup. I think that's where marriages go wrong, when nothing happens. And the worst thing is to start off with a boring honeymoon. A honeymoon should be the foundation of your married life. Afterwards you know there'll be times you have to work to keep things going, it won't all be flowers and sunshine, but if you've had a strong start you've got a better chance.'

Pete nodded. His own honeymoon had been, from that point of view, rather boring. Frank, as always, had proved himself a jammy dodger.

Though he hated to think what might have happened had his own wife found a woman in their honeymoon bath.

As they walked back towards the bar Eric Johns came around the corner.

'How's the snooker going, Eric?' asked Frank.

'Ah, good, good, Frank,' Eric replied, a slight concern in his eyes suggesting that, faced with Frank, he had not entirely convinced himself of his own recollection of the evening.

'Oh, by the way,' Frank continued, 'there is one subject which came up while we were on honeymoon which I think you could answer, Eric.'

'Me?' asked a startled and worried Eric Johns.

'Yes. It's an interesting question. Tell me, do you prefer your peas on the right side of the plate or the left?'

'My peas?'

'Or carrots. Or maybe you think they should go at the top or the bottom.'

'Top or bottom?'

'Personally I think top or bottom is a non-starter, so that leaves left or right. Which do you think?'

'Frank, let me get this right, you're asking whether I prefer having my peas on the left or the right side of the plate.'

'That's it. That's precisely it. Which do you feel more comfortable with?'

Eric Johns thought carefully about the question. Frank was quite right. In matters of culinary correctness and good taste Eric Johns was a master. The little details were the most important. Finally he decided.

'The left,' he said. 'it has to be the left. No doubt about it.'

Frank rubbed his jaw, a slight suggestion of uncertainty on his face.

'If you say so, Eric. Ah, well, better get back.'

'So what was that all about?' asked Pete Phillips as they walked on. 'Peas and carrots and what side of the plate they should be on?'

'I don't know, Pete. I just have this feeling that it might be crucial to our marriage.' He stopped and turned to the other man. 'You know, I sometimes have this image of myself and Frieda sitting at home many years from now, retired. And I ask her, "So, what side do the peas go on?" And she hasn't a clue what I'm talking about. Except that I've spent my entire marriage trying to work out which side of the plate the peas go on.'

He carried on walking.

'Perhaps that's the trick to a successful marriage,' he muttered, partly to himself. 'Perhaps with some things it's better never to find out which side the peas go on.'

Pete Phillips shook his head. He had a horrible feeling that what Frank had said was both deep and accurate. The clue that would reveal the Holy Grail of a good marriage. The trouble was that he hadn't the first idea what it meant. Neither, apparently, did Frank.

Gertie and Susan sat at a table with Wilf, Tom, and Sam. Having accomplished Operation Cream Cracker they were now intent on returning to their own interests, namely the two young men. The two young men, however, seemed to be fascinated by Sam. Sam, with her red hair, green eyes and freckles would have been an object of fascination for most young men, even when she wasn't wearing a black motorcycle jacket, a tight black top and tight black trousers. Realising this both Gertie and Susan had told their respective suitors that Sam was gay. Instead of cooling their interest this fact appeared to stimulate it. Then the girls had made the mistake of pointing out that Sam was a witch. Entirely predictably this made them only more fascinated. And Sam, after a couple of gins and tonic, was losing some of the reserve she adopted at work. Tom and Wilf were hanging on her words and her sparkling, mischievous eyes.

'I have to admit that I'm really enjoying being in Wellbury,' she said, tossing back her hair and almost taking Wilf's eye out with it. 'I thought I was going to hate it, but so far it's been great fun.' She took a sip of her drink, smiling at Tom. 'You know, I rather suspect that it might be at the centre of some powerful ley lines.'

'Ley lines?' asked Tom. 'Do you really believe in ley lines?'

Sam chuckled, almost a giggle.

'That's a bit like asking whether you believe in the power of music,' she said. 'Do you believe in the power of music?'

'Well, yes, but –'

'Some people don't. Some people can't feel music. All they hear is a lot of noise, which they probably find irritating more than anything else. It's the same with ley lines. And with witches. Ask two witches to define what it means to be a witch and you'll be lucky if they even vaguely agree. Ask someone to define the power of music and most people can't do it – those that try won't agree. Ask someone what a ley line is and you'll all sorts of replies, most of which will be total rubbish, because you can't really define ley lines to start off with.'

Someone passing was very good at defining things. Phil Walthers, co-owner of the Blue Bliss, but chiefly the editor and entire staff of the Wellbury Herald, was not a man to eavesdrop, but as a journalist he had incredibly good hearing and the ability to sort out different strands of vague conversation without thinking about it. The last week had been extremely quiet, and he had been forced to resort to coming up with fillers on the "Where are they now" type. He didn't believe in nonsense such as ley lines, but Wellburians were particularly susceptible to that kind of hocus pocus.

It went against the grain. But he did have a newspaper to get out. And a harmless little filler could cause no damage. It would give some types of people something to natter over: "Wellbury: Ley Line Centre?". A good title. And, after all, everyone knew that when a newspaper headline ended in a question mark, the answer was invariably "No". Didn't they?

'And now,' said Frank, 'I think it's time for a quiet night in. It's been a long day.'

'Amen to that,' said Frieda. 'A quiet night in would suit me down to the ground. And just for once, Frank, no bodies in baths, no ghosts, no aliens, nothing of that ilk for one night, okay?'

441

'For you, my sweet, anything. Anyway, we're back in Wellbury. At least Wellburians are generally civilised enough to take the weekend off. They only create mayhem during their working hours.'

'It's been a particularly quiet week on this side of the Channel,' noted the Chief Inspector.

'Now where's Squishy gone?' asked Frank, looking around. 'Squishy? Don't say she's gone walkabout. Where are you, Squish?'

'Must be around here somewhere,' the others murmured, looking around the floor about them.

'Squishy!' called Tricia. 'Where are you, Squish? Has anyone seen little Squish?' She stopped as Frank uttered a chuckle.

'She's joined the Foreign Legion,' he said. They turned around to find a bleary-eyed little Squishy sitting up in the upturned kepi, looking at him in puzzlement.

'Ah, poor little Squish, you've had a tiring day, haven't you?' asked Tricia.

'Yes,' said Frank, standing up and picking up Squishy in the kepi, 'time for your din dins, Squish, and then you can snooze on Frieda's lap while we fall asleep watching television, what do you say to that?'

That sounded an excellent plan to Squishy. She insisted on having Frank near, but she preferred sitting on Frieda's lap. That could have had something to do with mealtimes, when Frieda, unbidden, continually fed the kitten with tiny morsels from her plate. Frank always had to be reminded that he had a starving kitten on his lap, and then he would pass her such a large piece of sausage or something Squishy had to resort to most un-ladylike attempts to make the gift manageable.

The gods of coincidence and confusion have a strong sense of humour. That evening Eric Johns went home to find that his wife had prepared one of his favourite meals, chips, eggs and peas. With thickly buttered bread and a bottle of HP sauce to hand.

The peas were on the right.

He sat looking at the plate for so long his wife began to wonder if she had unknowingly burnt something.

Finally he slowly and carefully moved the eggs and peas around until the peas were on the left.

'That's better,' he said, and began tucking in.

His wife stared at him. Even after so many years being married, she decided, you still never really knew how your husband's mind worked. She wondered whether it was true of all men, or just her own husband. For a moment she regretted not having gone to the Blue Bliss. She might have had a chance to find out whether Frieda Summers was likely to encounter similar problems with her new husband. Or perhaps she already had.

If not, she probably would soon, Mrs Johns decided. Men were a strange breed.

Wellbury. Sunday. Breakfast.

Summerstimes

Frank and Frieda woke up to find the sun attempting to stream past the curtains, announcing a glorious beginning to a late summer's Sunday. Outside was so silent and peaceful the calm could almost be felt seeping through the window. When Frieda awoke she did not move, thinking Frank to be still asleep. After a few moments she lifted her head slowly and looked at him. He smiled back and caressed her hair.

'I was wondering whether to take up golf or not,' he said.

'Golf?'

'I've never understood why anyone would – as I seem to recall someone saying – want to ruin a perfectly good walk that way. I've been thinking about it. Take today. Today's a good day for doing as little as possible. Lounging around. But we'd both be bored with lounging around doing nothing within half an hour. I suddenly realised what golf is. It's a way of lounging around doing nothing while pretending that you're doing something.'

'And so you've decided to take up golf,' she said, closing her eyes and resting her head on his chest.

'God, no, I tried it a couple of times before, it bored me to tears. No, nice as the thought is, I think the chances of us having peaceful Sundays doing very little will be rare, so I intend to make the most of today. Read the newspapers. See if there's a film on telly this afternoon worth watching. Maybe sit out in the garden in the sun.'

'Watching telly?'

Frank was about to reply in the negative when he chuckled.

'And why not? We could have an umbrella over the telly to shade it.'

'No, Frank, you are not taking – the television outside.' Frieda caught herself just in time. She had about to say "my television".

'No, I suppose not. Well, I'm going to get up and have a shower. The garden and the sun are waiting.'

'Frank, there is something I need to talk to you about.'

'Hey! If it stays sunny we could have a barbecue. Mum and dad love barbecues. Mum reckons it means that she doesn't have to cook, which isn't entirely logical, since she really puts more effort into making salads and marinating the meat than a usual meal, but there you go. Dad just likes barbecues. He seems to think of them as a rather enjoyable foreign invention for some reason.'

'Well, I don't see why not,' Frieda replied, the something she needed to talk to Frank about forgotten as she contemplated the solving of two problems in one go. Firstly the question of lunch, and secondly the question of who would make lunch. Frances Summers would automatically feel that she should be doing the cooking for her two men, whereas it was Frieda's – her and Frank's – house, so it was really up to her – to her and Frank – to look after that side of things. After all, Frank's parents were their guests.

She would be more than willing to share the kitchen with Frank's mother, but the first thing Frances Summers would do was to shoo her son out. Frank had proved himself quite comfortable in the kitchen, and Frieda didn't want him getting the idea that the kitchen was her space and he wasn't welcome. That was the way Frances Summers had been brought up, and a way she was happy with. It wasn't going to be Frieda's – and Frank's – way.

She smiled at the idea of Frank playing golf. He would never have the patience. Even now she could hear him humming away in the shower, badly as usual.

Once he had finished showering and dressing Frank clattered down to the kitchen, before clattering back up with a cup of tea.

'Mum's put out stuff for breakfast,' he said. 'She said she doesn't want to get in your way, but she thought just putting out the eggs and bacon wouldn't be a problem. I think she's having a problem stopping herself from doing anything else, like cooking.'

Frieda sipped her tea.

'What do you fancy for breakfast, Free? Egg and bacon? Mushrooms? Sausage, tomatoes, the full set?'

'I think a couple of slices of toast will do for me. You go ahead, Frank. I'll be down in a second.'

Frank clattered off back downstairs, humming loudly. Frieda continued to sip her tea, enjoying the sun streaming through the open curtains. Her mother had told her that a wife's happiness consisted of her husband's happiness. It was one of those half-truths. She did feel incredibly happy with Frank bouncing around, singing softly, however badly. The missing half was that a husband's happiness must also consist of his wife's happiness. And the great thing was that she was now sure that Frank understood that. Or perhaps, more correctly and more importantly, he felt that. Time, she decided, to have a leisurely shower before joining her happy husband. Other things could wait. At least for a day or two.

After her shower she wafted – it felt like wafting – downstairs to find a worried Frances Summers sitting on her own at the kitchen table.

'I'm terribly afraid I've made Frank angry,' she said.

'Frank?'

'Yes. It's never happened before. Such a silly thing, too. You see, when he said that you were just going to have some toast, and he was going to make himself some eggs and bacon – well, I suppose I'm just too used to cooking for him. I told him to sit down while I did it. Normally he would have said, yes, mum, and let me do it. But he said that he was quite capable of cooking his own breakfast. I told him not to be silly, to sit down and be a good boy. He insisted, and so did I, I'm afraid.'

She twisted a little handkerchief in her fingers.

'Before I knew what had happened he had decided that a cup of tea would be enough, he wasn't really hungry, and then he went off with his father to buy a Sunday newspaper.' She sighed. 'It's silly, really, so silly. I promised his father I wouldn't interfere or get in the way. But just for a moment it was as if he was my little Frank again. You know, I've never felt that he recovered fully from being shot. And then, this morning, he was just like a happy schoolboy again. And then I had to spoil it.

She looked at Frieda.

'I can't imagine you would have been very happy if you'd come down to find his mother cooking his breakfast for him, not in your kitchen.'

Frieda sat down. Was she bothered if Frank's mother cooked

447

him breakfast in her kitchen?

She wasn't sure. On the one hand she was prepared to fight tooth and nail, quite literally, against anyone who interfered in her marriage.

Well, perhaps not quite literally. Something big and heavy would be her first choice of weapon.

On the other hand she really couldn't feel that Frances Summers cooking her son his breakfast constituted any kind of interference. She knew people who would do that sort of thing as a calculated insult, as if to show her how lacking she was in her wifely duties – and that would really rile her – but Frank's mum?

'Frieda? You're very quiet. I am really sorry, I know I shouldn't have done it.'

'Oh, sorry, Mrs Summers, no, I was just lost in thought there for a moment. I was just thinking that I really don't mind you cooking Frank his breakfast.'

In fact she felt sorry for Frances Summers. Her mother-in-law had forgotten for a few seconds that she was not in her own home, and had managed to alienate her son and looked as if she were worried that she had also upset her daughter-in-law. For Frances Summers the kitchen was a woman's sphere, and for anyone to trespass into that sphere uninvited was probably the worst social crime, a crime she had now committed.

Which was ironic. Frieda's whole intention was to avoid becoming the sole owner of the kitchen.

'I didn't think you would mind too much,' Frances Summers said. 'If I thought at all, that is. The problem was that I should have realised that Frank might not like it. I suppose that he was worried that it might upset you.'

Frieda nodded. She could easily imagine Frank seeing such a simple thing as a potential source of division between his mother and his wife. Presumably it was the main reason he had chosen the only way out and decided not to have any breakfast whatsoever. It would be easier going hungry than having to deal with any disagreement between the two most important women in his life.

Or perhaps he was just escaping his mother's fussing over her little boy. Or even a combination of all three. Or four. Or however many it was.

'If only he had just said something instead of walking off like that,' Frances Summers sighed.

'He has changed a bit,' Frieda replied. 'I'm not sure whether that's because of his accident, or whether he's feeling more responsibility since he decided to get married. He goes into himself at times.'

'I've noticed that. It's almost as if other people cease to exist. Or as if he's day-dreaming, or gone into a trance.' She paused. 'Maybe you could cook him breakfast when he gets back?'

'That would probably make things worse. I think it's best just to leave him to get over it.'

'I suppose you're right, my dear. I am really sorry, Frieda. I promise it won't happen again.' She sighed. 'Frank – my husband, Frank – said that we should leave both of you yesterday, leave you on your own. I think he was right.'

'No,' said Frieda, standing up and switching the kettle on. 'No, it would just have been something else sooner or later. Better that we get things sorted out now. Another cup of tea?'

'Yes, that would be lovely, Frieda.'

'The thing is,' Frieda said, emptying the teapot and refilling it, 'we have a conflict of interest in Frank.'

'Oh, no, my dear, I'm sure we don't.'

'Yes we do. You want to look after your little boy, I want him to act like a grown man, and to do his share of things. I have no intention of allowing him to think that he can come home expecting that little wifey will have his meal on the table.'

Frances Summers made a sad face.

'It is difficult,' she said. 'When they come home from football practice, mud all over, and run into the kitchen to ask, "What's for supper, mum?" And he's just so full of smiles and energy, you just can't help but feel a tug at your heart. It makes you feel wanted, needed. It's a lovely feeling.'

Frieda poured the tea. She could imagine the feeling. She could even imagine the grown up Frank, her husband, coming home, putting an arm around her waist as she prepared dinner, and saying "What's for supper, my sweet?" She could imagine the warm glow of being appreciated.

Without, hopefully, the mud. Though with Frank that was entirely possible.

But becoming a kitchen drudge was not part of the plan. She had her career. It was a question of balance. It was a question which she decided could be put off for that day.

'Did he tell you that we were thinking of having a barbecue for lunch?' she asked.

'A barbecue? That's an excellent idea. His father will love that.'

'It was Frank's idea.'

'He must be growing up. I mean, he's always been a

thoughtful boy – to some extent – but his normal approach to meals is to order a take-away pizza. Which has always worked, because his father loves take-away pizza.'

'Well, why don't we make a start on some salads? The menfolk can sit in the lounge or outside while we're busy.'

Frieda didn't mind Frank not lending a hand if he had to keep his father entertained. After all, Professor Summers could hardly be expected to know anything about kitchens. Modern kitchens, anyway.

However, if they were entertaining colleagues from work, for example, Frank would not be out in the garden drinking beer with his buddies and discussing football. Frieda was quite capable of enjoying doing that herself. And she understood the off-side rule which was more than could be said for most of them.

Frank and his father returned after a long walk. Nothing was said about breakfast. Frank acted as if he had forgotten all about wanting breakfast. Though he did look a little surprised to return to find Frieda and his mother apparently happily chatting as they prepared salads in the kitchen.

'Right,' he said, after he deposited his surprise and the Sunday newspapers on the table, 'what can I do?'

'You can go down to the supermarket and get some sausages,' Frieda said. 'The Greek supermarket down the road. They have a little butcher's section. Get some spiced sausages, and some plain ones.'

'Okay. Anything else? Onions, green peppers, herbs and spices?'

'No, we're okay on those.'

Frank and his father trundled off on this domestic errand.

Frank's mother was quite impressed.

'I never suspected that Frank knew what a green pepper was,' she commented.

'If it's a topping on a pizza, Frank knows all about it,' Frieda replied.

The men, on their return, were sent out into the garden to drink beers quietly and not disturb the working women. Professor Summers greeted this unexpected liberality with a happy smile. It wasn't often he was allowed a quiet pint. His wife had ruled that wine and sherry were the only acceptable alcoholic drinks he was permitted to indulge in, and then only to a limited extent. Frieda had over-ruled her by pre-empting her.

And he had two new books on Ancient Greece for review, one by a man he liked but disagreed with, and another by a colleague he couldn't stand, but whose conclusions were generally in line with his. He was going to have quite a bit of fun reconciling that dilemma. Could life be better?

'I have to admit, Frank,' he said, having debated which book he would begin with by deciding to browse both simultaneously, 'that I was somewhat uncertain when you told us you were going to be married. Marriage is a very difficult enterprise. Your mother and I were lucky, of course, but even we had our ups and downs. My goodness! That is an excellent photograph. You know, Simpson talks a lot of nonsense, but he does do excellent photography.'

'You had ups and downs?' asked Frank, not surprised by the fact so much as the admission.

'A very difficult enterprise. And of course the most important thing is that you are happy. Frieda strikes me as a most charming young lady. I'm quite sure that you've made absolutely the right decision. Ah! I thought so. Here it is, in the small print. It's not an original at all. It's a modern vase based on an original. Of course he doesn't show the original. No, that would make it too obvious how he's changed it to suit his own ridiculous assumptions.'

'She seems to be in a strange mood this morning.'

'Your mother?'

'No, Frieda.'

'I wouldn't worry about it. You'll get used to it. Personally I think that he's quite possibly what they call a closet gay, I think the term is. He seems fixated by the idea of the Greeks' approach to sex.'

'She seems quiet this morning, almost withdrawn. You might not think so, but I'm sure of it.'

'Frieda's not the type to natter on about anything and everything like some women, Frank. I think you're very lucky in that respect. Mugs and vases! If you only read Simpson you'd end up believing that the only things the Greeks ever created were mugs and vases. Let's see if he's actually managed a picture of a stele this time.'

Inside the kitchen the work had been completed, the salads and meat were either on the worktops or in the fridge, everything had been cleaned up, and the two women were relaxing for a few minutes. Frances Summers sat at the table, Frieda held a cup of tea and looked out of the window. Frank was tending to the barbecue while his father leafed through his books, combining that with an ongoing chat of some kind with his son.

'Mrs Summers,' she said suddenly, 'can I tell you something in confidence?'

'Now, my dear, I've told you to call me Frances. Now, what's wrong? I've noticed that you seem worried about something. If it's that business this morning, well, we have sorted that out, haven't we? And if it's something to do with Frank I'm sure it's just a misunderstanding. And if it isn't, I'll make sure he does the right thing. What is it, Frieda? Nothing physical, is it?'

'You could say that – Frances.' She rubbed her left hand with her right, looking at the engagement and wedding rings. 'It's difficult to explain.'

'Frieda, between Frank – my husband – and Frank – my son – everything is difficult to explain. So just tell me all about it.'

'I think I'm pregnant,' Frieda blurted out. Mrs Summers looked at her.

'But, Frieda, it's only been ...' She tailed off, realising that simple arithmetic might lead into the rather dangerous area in which questions could arise as to how intimate the bride and groom had been prior to the honeymoon rather than during it.

She smiled, stood up and took her in her arms.

'I don't know why,' Frieda said, tears in her eyes, 'I'm late, I was worried it would spoil the honeymoon, but I could be late for all sorts of reasons, I mean the wedding was such a worry, and –'

'Yes, yes, my dear,' Frances Summers said, patting her on the back. 'Maybe you are, and maybe you aren't, but in my experience if you think you are you normally are.'

'The honeymoon was absolutely perfect. And now this has to happen.'

Frances Summers blinked.

'Frieda, you started off with a body in the bath, you were almost killed in a plane, someone tried to mug you, the local police kept hounding you, and the security services thought that you were sending secret messages around the world. If that's a perfect honeymoon, I would have thought being pregnant somewhat of an anti-climax.'

'But what will Frank say? I know he says he wants lots of children, but so soon? And I don't want to tell him in case it's a false alarm. What if he's happy, but I'm not pregnant after all? What if he's not ready and I am? We really need more time!'

'Now, now, Frieda, come, sit down. Let's have a nice cup of tea and I'll tell you a story.' She sat a tearful Frieda down and poured hot water into the teapot.

'Now I know I'm an old-fashioned type, my dear, I always was. I've only ever wanted to be a housewife and mother. When I married Frank's father I couldn't wait to start a family. I had dreams of six children at least. But nothing happened. To make a long story short, in the end the doctor told us that we couldn't have any children. I was devastated. I didn't have any career or anything else to fall back on. Instead I was faced with sitting in a lonely house all day for the rest of my life – going quietly mad, I would imagine. I took a job as a teacher, a primary school teacher, which was very nice as far as it went, but at the same time ... seeing all those lovely children every day, knowing that I would never have one – I often cried myself to sleep. In the end I gave it up to teach English Literature at university. At least the children there were older.'

She began pouring the tea.

'I imagine I was being very selfish. I didn't even think how Frank – my husband, Frank – was taking it. In fact I rather blamed him for losing himself in his work. Now I'm not sure that he didn't do that because I refused to discuss the issue. I was so upset I wouldn't even discuss adoption. Anyway. Anyway, we'd got to a state of resignation, I suppose you could call it. There were times life didn't seem worth living. And then, after all those years, I discovered that I was pregnant.'

She wiped her eyes with her little handkerchief. Frieda found her own eyes running again.

'Well, it's probably a very boring story for everyone else, but to us Frank was a miracle baby. That's why he means so much to us. His father might not show it, but he's doted on little Frank ever since – or probably before – he was born.'

'What are you doing in here while the sun's shining outside?' asked the miracle boy, entering the kitchen at the worst possible time. 'Summertime, a few beers and the living's easy.' He paused at the sight of Frieda's red eyes. 'Free, what's wrong? Free, come on, tell me what's wrong. I'm your hubby, darling, what's wrong?'

'Frank, get your beers and go outside,' ordered his mother.

'But, mum –'

'Out, now.'

'But –'

'Frank.'

'Yes, mum.'

'And don't forget your father's beer.'

'Yes, mum.'

Frank opened the fridge, took out two bottles of beer, and slunk out of the kitchen with a backwards glance. Squishy took one look at Frieda and Frances and followed him. There would definitely be no tuna for her there.

'Dad,' Frank said, sitting down on the patio outside, putting a bottle of beer next to his father's glass and opening a bottle himself before taking a sip, 'did you ever come into the kitchen to find mum crying on grandma's shoulder?'

'Not that I remember, Frank,' his father replied, attention on his books.

'Must be just me, then.'

'Oh, I wouldn't worry about it, Frank, women cry for absolutely no reason, or possibly any reason. But it is interesting.'

'What is, dad?'

'Your drinking from the bottle rather than pouring it into the glass. I would imagine a similar thing happened with the Greeks. The problem is evidence. Everybody goes on about drinking jugs which show older men seducing younger men, it gives the wrong impression.'

Frank took a pull on his beer. He was used to his father's rambling way of talking around a subject. What he was much more concerned with was why Frieda was sitting in the kitchen crying. Crying to his mum. After all, he was her husband, shouldn't she be able to share her worries with him?

Didn't she trust him? Was she scared of showing any sign of weakness to him? After all, she prided herself on her strength and efficiency.

Had he already failed as a husband to the woman he had married?

'Load of bollocks,' he muttered to himself, as if he weren't quite sure.

'Not quite the academic description one might expect,' his father replied. 'Though as far as Simpson goes it's very accurate. Anyway, it's more a question of lack of evidence.'

Frank nodded.

'Right as always, dad. Evidence. I'm a trained police detective, and not a bad one, I reckon. So I should be able to evaluate the evidence, come to a conclusion, and act upon that conclusion.'

His father paused, struck by this thought.

'You know, Frank, I've often wondered why you chose the police force. Now it makes sense. Incredibly obvious, once you come to think of it. Exactly the same disciplines required in the academic world. Objectivity. Curiosity. An ability to sift evidence and make sense of the scraps.' He sighed. 'But that's what we're missing here, evidence. Hardly a scrap.'

'Tears. That's evidence.'

'Tears, my boy? You aren't thinking of amber, are you? It would be nice to think that some tears would leave traces thousands of years later, a bit like dinosaur tracks, but I haven't heard of any being found.'

'Thousands of years? Dad, what are you on about?'

'The ancient Greeks, of course. I told you, the ordinary people, not the aristocracy. I'm convinced that the average person lived much the same as we do today – within context of the different technologies, naturally, but all this nonsense about boy lovers, it's ridiculous. Imagine if someone described the life of a middle class family today only with reference to Lady Diana. They'd be laughed out of the lecture room.'

'Dad, could you forget the ancient Greeks just for one minute? I'm trying to work out why Frieda is sitting in the kitchen crying her eyes out.'

'Oh, I wouldn't worry about that, my boy. I told you, women cry for absolutely no reason, it's a well-established fact. Believe me, Frank, it's probably something utterly trivial which she'll have forgotten about by this evening. Having lived with your mother so long nothing would surprise me.' He looked up at Frank. 'Don't get me wrong, Frank, you know that your mother and I love each other dearly, we've probably enjoyed a marriage others would envy. But, as I say,' he continued, returning to his book, 'don't worry about it. You'll get used to it. One day you'll find that, as far as women go, nothing will surprise you either.'

Frank pinched his nose, between his eyes.

'I think I need a little headache tablet,' he said. His father looked up.

'Headache tablet? I've got some aspirin here somewhere. Apparently half an aspirin each day is good for you. I take half of one every second day, waiting for the next report which says it's bad for you. Then I'll stop.'

He handed Frank a strip of tablets. Frank popped one out and threw it down his throat, followed by a sip of beer. He went back to the barbecue.

'Why do those things always taste so bloody awful?' he asked.

Squishy looked up at him. She miaowed and tugged at his leg. Inside the kitchen Frances Summers was shaking her head sadly at recollections of Frank's childhood.

'I remember when he was about six,' she said, 'he asked why

he didn't have any brothers or sisters. He really wanted a brother or sister, you see. And I tried to explain – it's so difficult with children. I tried to explain that sometimes people just couldn't have brothers or sisters. And then he looked at me with such a pleading little face and said, "Can't we have just a little one? A little sister?" '

She wiped her eyes and chuckled softly.

'Dear little thing. Anyway, the point I was going to make is that, when he accepted that he couldn't have a brother or sister, he said, as children do, that when he was grown up he was going to have lots of children. Of course, children do say these things without meaning them, or understanding them, but Frank never forgot. Years later he would tease me, whenever I grew soppy-eyed at the sight of a baby in a pram. "Don't worry, mum," he'd say, "when I get married and settle down you'll have lots of little grandchildren to look after. You can have plenty of fun wiping their noses and changing their nappies. It will save me the job."'

She sniffed, wiped her nose, and put her handkerchief away.

'So, you see, Frieda, you don't need to fret about Frank. I'm not saying it won't be a shock to him, but it will be a very pleasant shock. He probably won't be able to speak for a while – I know, unusual for Frank – and then he'll be all over you, insisting that you sit down and take care of yourself. His father was just the same.'

Inside the hall the telephone began to ring.

'I'd better answer that,' said Frieda. 'Thanks, Frances. I do feel better now. I was just being a little silly.'

'It's good to be a little silly from time to time.'

'Pregnant,' said Frank's father.

'Sorry?'

Professor Summers looked up.

'Are you okay, Frank? You don't look too well.'

'I'm fine, dad,' Frank replied, rubbing his temples. 'What did you say?'

'Well, my boy, once you've eliminated all the impossible, whatever remains, however improbable, must be the truth.'

'Dad, you're quoting Sherlock Holmes to me? Squishy, what's up?'

'Frieda's pregnant. Ask yourself, what could she possibly cry over?' asked his father, looking back down at his books and completely reversing his former argument. 'Go through all the permutations, I can find only two. Either you've upset her or she's pregnant. And since I have no evidence of your upsetting her, I conclude the latter.'

He looked up, a broad smile on his face. It disappeared as he saw his son on his knees, holding his head.

'Frank? Frank! What's wrong?'

'Migraine ... tablets ... in –'

His father jumped from his chair and crawled to his son's side.

'Frances!' he shouted. 'Frances! Get an ambulance! Now!'

Frances Summers vaguely heard the cry. She was thinking of Frank and Frieda having the family she had always dreamed of. Both would be busy. They would welcome old Nan to look after her grandchildren. She wandered out to find out what this ridiculous shouting was about.

'Oh, my God!' she whispered as the sight of her husband cradling her little Frank met her eyes.

'Get a bloody ambulance!' her husband shouted. 'Now!'

'It's Aggie,' Frieda said, re-entering the kitchen. 'She's been attacked –'

She paused as she realised that there was no-one there. Frances Summers staggered back into the kitchen.

'Ambulance!' she cried. 'Frank's having an attack.'

Frieda did not hesitate. She ran for her police radio. She called as she ran back.

'Control. Control, come in. Now!'

'Control here, over.'

'Get an ambulance over here right now, Control. Understand?'

'Repeat, please, Inspector. Where is "here"?'

'My bloody house, Control. Inspector Summers needs an ambulance right now, got it?'

'Understood, ma'am.'

The radio went flying as she came out the kitchen door. Frank was being supported by his mother and father. He was trying to stand up, but his feet kept sliding.

'Darling! Frank! Frank, speak to me! Frank, speak to me!'

He looked up at her, his face twisted, his arms bent, as if he were desperately trying to hold on to something.

'Free,' he whispered, 'Free?'

'I'm here, darling. Frank, I'm here. Frank, hold on.'

'Free –'

'Yes, my darling, I'm here. Don't try to talk too much. I'm here. Darling, we're all here. Try to relax.'

'Free –' He looked her in the eyes and tried to grasp her hand with his claw. 'Free ... I want ... a ... a girl baby.'

And then he shuddered, appeared to grasp one last time at life, and his eyes closed.

Somewhere a siren cried.

Wellbury. Sunday. Afternoon.

This is the end

Frieda and Frances sat on a bench in the corridor of the hospital. Professor Summers stood a while away, looking out of a window. The Chief Inspector and Percy Hanson were silent a few yards from the bench. A doctor came down the corridor.

'Mrs Summers?' he asked.

'Yes,' said Frieda, standing up.

'Yes,' said Frances Summers, standing up. They looked at each other.

'I'm Frieda Summers,' Frieda said to the bemused doctor. 'Frank's wife. This is Frances Summers, his mother.'

'Ah,' said the doctor. 'Well, the good news is that he's sleeping peacefully now. I think the danger's passed.'

'What was it?' asked Frieda. 'What happened?' The doctor scratched his cheek with a pen.

'It's too early to say,' he said. 'The only thing I can tell you with any possibility of certainty is that he appears to have suffered some form of anaphylactic shock. An extreme reaction to something. He wasn't stung by a bee or something, was he? We haven't been able to identify anything.'

They turned to Frank's father who had joined them. He shook his head.

'I don't think so. Frank would have mentioned it, I'm sure.'

Frieda wasn't so sure. Frank's father had explained his guess that she was pregnant just before Frank had begun having a seizure. Frank probably wouldn't have even noticed a bee sting compared to that shock.

'The problem is,' the doctor continued, 'it isn't just the question of an anaphylactic reaction. From what I gather he suffered severe headaches – migraines – after his accident. It's a combination of a number of things. I'm afraid we're going to have to keep him in for a while, for observation. I'm afraid there might be an epileptic element.'

'But he's okay? He isn't – I mean, there isn't – he won't -'

'I can't promise anything, Mrs Summers. But he's in good hands, the likelihood of a recurrence so soon is minimal, and if that remote possibility does occur, he couldn't be in a better place. The best you can do is go home and relax. He'll be out in a few days. A week at most.'

'But, if you don't know what caused it – it could happen again? Without warning?'

The doctor looked uncomfortable.

'I'm afraid so. We do have some stuff to handle the immediate effects, if it does re-occur, but ... I'm sorry, hopefully the tests we do over the next few days will tell us more. Now, if you'll excuse me, I must get on.'

Frieda and Frances sat down again as the doctor left.

'You'll take it over, then?' Frieda heard the Chief Inspector say to Percy Hanson.

'Of course. Under the circumstances.'

'What?' asked Frieda. 'Take over? Under what circumstances?'

'Just a little case, Frieda,' said the Chief Inspector. 'Nothing to worry about.'

'What little case?'

'A few reports about elderly ladies being attacked. Coincidence, I rather suspect. I was rather hoping Frank could take it on, but obviously that's out of the question.'

'Nonsense! He's had a slight attack. He'll be fine before the end of the week. Anyway, I can handle it.'

'Frieda,' the Chief Inspector said as gently as he could, 'we don't know what the problem Frank has is exactly. I don't want to – Frieda, let's not worry about it now, shall we? Let's just concentrate on his getting better.'

Frieda looked at him. She remembered the officer she had once known who had had to retire because of ill health. The one who had been prescribed the same tablets in Frank's wash bag.

'Frank's career isn't over,' she said. 'You will not put him out to grass. He will be fine.'

The Last Waltz?

Follow Frank and Frieda's haps and mishaps in the coming *Hordes*. The Detective Inspectors Summers have one or two problems. She is pregnant. He is under threat of forced early retirement for health reasons. She has banned him from work until the results of his medical tests come back. He is determined to investigate the causes behind what appears to be a sudden spate of attacks on little old ladies all over Wellbury. He has also been challenged to a duel of double chess from "a mason", with apparently serious threats about what will happen if he loses. The Cult of the Clueless are causing the wrathful Know-alls to take to the streets. Possibly worst of all, the little old ladies have banded together to form The Old Birds' Army to defend themselves, and they believe in pre-emptive assault. All in all, for the Summers, the approach to their first Christmas together could be looking a lot better.

Other novels by Bill Dughaille:

The FFSG series (aka the Wellbury Chronics)

Summers

The first in the FFSG series.

Detective Sergeant Frank Summers is a man on a mission: to keep his head down, stay out of trouble and enjoy the relaxed atmosphere of the easy-going, genteel town of Wellbury, his new posting. It's a town just made for him, where, he believes, even the criminals take bank holidays off. But, while perceptive in his professional life, he tends to miss the subtleties in his private life. In this case he fails to realise that his own tranquillity is being threatened by three women and a philanderer. The fact that the women in question are his boss, his constable and the local pathologist adds just the touch of danger to his life that he had hoped to avoid. The philanderer has been dead several decades. The women are very much alive.

The Eighty-five-percenters

The second in the FFSG series.

Detective Sergeant Frank Summers is faced with an unexpected crisis as the staid citizens of the genteel town of Wellbury rapidly descend into disorganised anarchy after a sociology professor announces on radio that eighty-five percent of the population will die in a coming cull. The prediction appears to be coming true as apparently total strangers are felled one by one according to a list of the ten-most-disliked Wellburians, from nagging neighbours to estate agents ... and the police, at a poorly performing number ten. But Frank fails to realise that there is a graver danger closer to home. Three women have decided that he is their responsibility: his boss, his constable and the local pathologist have agreed to become best of enemies. Now they intend to re-arrange his fate the way it should be. And they aren't asking anyone's permission.

Fakes, Fraud and Deception

The third in the FFSG series.

Detective Sergeant Frank Summers is in the doghouse, despite having recently arrested an internationally sought con-artist. And since he is in the doghouse he has no intention of pointing out that there is something very strange about the attractive French police woman who has come to interview the arrested man, not to mention the two detectives claiming to be from Scotland Yard. Oh, no, he is going to stay well out of the way this time. Definitely.

Jokers

The fourth in the FFSG series.

The doctors have pronounced Detective Sergeant Frank Summers physically fit following recovery after his shooting, but his colleagues fear that his sense of humour was extracted along with the bullet. They are, as always, more than willing to interfere in his life in the pursuit of a good cause. If that wasn't enough, a bunch of criminals calling themselves the Joker Gang are laughing at him, the university students are creating mayhem during their rag week, and someone called The Shocker is trying to kill him. The only advantage is that it take his mind off of the ultimatum the three women in his life have given him, one that he has only until the Sunday to resolve. Or leave town.

Prophecies

The fifth in the FFSG series.

Detective Sergeant Summers is under a hex, otherwise known as his colleagues. First they don't want him to get married, then it is imperative it must happen. Then they decide that a prophecy has been made which threatens the wedding. They don't believe in prophecies, but aren't sure that prophecies understand that. So they'll have to Do Something About It. And if their bumbling efforts aren't enough to ensure he never makes it to the altar, he has to cope with visiting aliens and resident ghosts. He does have tiny Squishy to protect him, but what match can even this plucky little kitten be against a prospective mother-in-law?

Others:

The Window

Jim Allbright, ex-bobby and now easy-going window washer, innocently responds to an advert for window washing placed in the newspaper by the local council. The response is a torrent of paperwork, political correctness and a computer system doing exactly what it was told to do, but not quite what was intended. But if the system cannot be beaten, the interchange of letters can be used to have a little fun and get to know some of the people struggling behind it. There's Sandi, who signs herself as "(pp the Administrator)"; her four-year old little angel Helen; Graham, a shadowy computer programmer who definitely has too much time on his hands, and a slew of Project Managers and Senior Administrators eager to ensure standards are upheld no matter how many problems they create. Against a run of bad luck and circumstances Jim and Sandi aim to meet up one day, eventually. Hopefully. The window might even get washed. Maybe.

Diary of a Sane Man

In a cross between 'Last Of The Summer Wine' and 'One Flew Over The Cuckoo's Nest', set against a backdrop of the brave new world of New Labour's end of honeymoon, Fred is the Last Cynical Optimistic Realist.

Believing that he's found the perfect niche – three square meals a day plus all the newspapers he can read just for occasionally pretending to be mad – he's not going to be the one to rock the apple cart. Oh, no.

Safe from the wiles of women and the woes of the world, he's not going to rock the boat. Oh, no.

No, he's just going to sit and observe, and comment quietly on the insanity of life outside.

Well, maybe just little one tug of the loose strand of wool on life's jersey ...

Did you know they elected a monkey as mayor in Hartlepool?

The Weekend At Longwood

A whodunnit in the classic sense, set against the backdrop of World War II and the trials, tribulations and romances of nine suspects.

A group of friends get together during the last weekend of August 1939 at the rural retreat named Longwood, just a few miles from Portsmouth. They are there to celebrate the last time they will see Georgina Riley, famed American novelist and socialite, for some time, as she is scheduled to leave for her native New York in order to marry her childhood sweetheart. During the afternoon they good-humouredly assign to each other the most suitable names of the nine muses, the daughters of Zeus and Mnemosyne:

Calliope: the muse of epic poetry and rhetoric

Clio: history

Erato: love poems and mimicry

Euterpe: lyric poetry

Melpomene: tragedy

Polymnia: hymns to the gods and heroes

Terpsichore: dance

Thalia: comedy

Urania: astronomy, astrology and prophecy

The following morning Georgina is discovered in her bedroom covered in blood, her throat slit, barely alive. Her American maid is dead. A tiara Georgina had been flaunting the day before has disappeared.

Detective Inspector Rudman arrives to investigate. But with Georgina in a coma and no solid evidence there is little he can do apart from haunt their lives. With Germany's invasion of Poland a week later they disperse across the land, some to the air-force, some to the army, others to reserved civilian jobs. But Rudman does not give up. Wherever they are he can be found. Whatever other duties he is tasked to, he will find time to keep tabs on them. Whatever the defeats and victories of the Allied cause, he has only one aim: to find the person responsible for the murder done that weekend in Longwood. The war ends; some of the Muses have survived, some not. Some have prospered, some married, some matured, others have found despair. And then comes invitation to spend another weekend at Longwood. The message is that Rudman has found the evidence he has been looking for.

And so one of the surviving couples motor slowly down to Portsmouth, remembering the original weekend, the trials and the tribulations of the past years, and wonder: what will be revealed during the coming weekend at Longwood?

Firelight

A modern-day tale of an ordinary family gathering at Christmas; the good, the bad, the dysfunctional and the forgotten.

George Browne and his wife Winifred have retired to a large, run-down pile in the country. Rumour has it that it was once the abode of a mad aristocratic family with a penchant for Satanism, and that both they and their victims still haunt the corridors. Other rumours are that it was a lunatic asylum for much of the nineteenth and twentieth century, and bodies of the inhabitants are buried around the large gardens in unmarked graves.

The Brownes are an unremarkable retired couple who, depending on who you might ask, have bought it as an investment, or alternatively as somewhere with enough bedrooms to accommodate their children, grand-children, and the little baby great-grandchildren. Too often in the past excuses have been made at special times, the most common of which has been of the "I don't want to put you to any trouble" variety. That excuse can no longer hold water.

Now it is approaching Christmas. Winter has set in, but the house is snug with oil heaters and real fires. As the various relations arrive, or don't arrive, it becomes clearer why invitations might have been refused in the past. The men of the family believe in having their way. The women of the family are strong-willed in their own different ways, and have various means of getting what they want.

The guests of the family - friends, boyfriends, girlfriends, wives and husbands - discover that their partners have a totally different side to them as the explosive hatreds of long-nurtured fights and feuds simmer to the surface before quickly boiling over.

One evening Winifred Browne encourages them to each tell a story as they sit in the lounge with the large fire warming them, the television off, no access to broadband, computers or mobile connections. Reluctantly at first they begin. As each evening passes: with different members taking turns, they announce in stories the feelings and hopes they cannot voice in public.

Finally it's the turn of Winifred Browne. Her story will be the one that tells them who they are, where they come from, and maybe why they have turned out the way they have.

For further details on these visit:

www.dughaille.info